VENDETTA

Additional fiction by the Author

BLOOD BROTHERS, pseudonym David E Scott, pub. 1997

ISBN 1 86106 097 1

The BULLDOG, the WHIPPET, the BAT and the FALCON, David E Scott, pub. 2000

ISBN 0 75410 924 0

OPERATION GAN, D Eric Sturdy, self-publication 2003

ISBN 0 9544449 0 6

VENDETTA

D Eric Sturdy

First Impression - 2006

Self - publication by D Eric Sturdy, Newport, South Wales

Facilitated and printed in Great Britain through **e/booster limited** 502, 14 Tottenham Court Road, London WIT 1JY
Email: **office@ebooster.co.uk**

Authors E mail Enquiries: **sturdyp@aol.com**

ISBN 0 9544449 1 4

Dedicated to my son, Huw

Acknowledgements

VENDETTA would never have been completed without the contribution of John and Pat Cox who undertook the typing and type setting and their son David Cox who was instrumental in arranging the final lay out in its publication format. For *Vendetta's* cover I am indebted to the combined expertise of my granddaughters, Claire and Sarah Whitefield. Facts about the Mafia were culled form voluminous writings on the subject by a variety authors; fictional characters in the book are entirely a figment of my imagination and I take full responsibility for introducing them into the Mafia killing mayhem prevalent in America, Italy and Sicily in the 50's and 60's.

VENDETTA

"A hereditary blood feud between two families perpetuating retaliatory acts of revenge."
(Readers Digest: Universal Dictionary)

A traditional Sicilian trait, adopted by the Mafia worldwide, in which long memories of transgressions committed, often many years previously, resurface and usually culminate in revenge and murder of the miscreant, or his Family and immediate associates.

The Author recognises that the use of the F – word is commonplace among America's Mafia fraternity and has been so throughout the 20th Century. The Sicilian Mafia and Italian Camorra inherited the trait from their American cousins in exile in the 50's and 60's. The Author feels uncomfortable to see the word in print in his own writings and, where appropriate, has compromised by using the word 'friggin' in the belief that readers will use their own discretion.

Preface

THE BIRTHPLACE OF THE MAFIA, Sicily is an island separated from the toe of the Italian mainland by the Straits of Messina, three miles wide at their narrowest point. Frequently described by cartographers as a football impaled on the end of the Italian toecap no other country has been kicked at out, or passed from hand to hand, as much as this oft-maligned island. Like a sequestrated bunion it has throbbed painfully through the ages, a constant reminder that the islanders are Sicilian and only tenuously part of the Italian nation. Sicilians have never achieved independence and have suffered occupation and domination by a succession of foreign powers each with its own language, culture, cuisine and religious beliefs.

The original tribal settlers in the western half of the island between the 12th and 5th centuries BC were Siculi, Sicani and Elymni, mainly fishermen and hunters. For four centuries BC the eastern half of the island, around Syracuse, became the most westerly territory of the Grecian Trojan Empire. The Greeks employed the indigenous Sicilians as shepherds, farmers and vintners and some were either enslaved or press ganged into the Trojan Army. In 254 BC the Romans established a base at Palermo and by 212 BC ousted the Trojans from Syracuse and Roman domination continued for six centuries. Sicilians were again enslaved and thousands met their fate in the arenas and amphitheatres of the Roman Empire. Sicily's fertile lands became 'the granary at whose breast the Roman people fed.' The next invasion came from the south, from across the Mediterranean, by Arabs, Moors and Saracens who brought their own benign culture, religion, cuisine and architecture and, with collapse of the Roman Empire, ruled the roost in Sicily until the arrival in Palermo of

Count Roger de Hauteville in 1071. A knight in the Crusaders he claimed the island for France and Christiandom and one of his descendants, Charles of Anjou, proclaimed himself King of Sicily in 1266. The French were supplanted by the Spanish House of Aragon and, in 1442, Alfonzo V was crowned 'King of the Two Sicily's' encompassing Naples on the mainland which, at that time, was also called Sicily. For three centuries Sicilians were cruelly dominated by a succession of Spanish royals who controlled them with an iron fist and matters only marginally improved with the reappearance in 1734 of the descendants of the French House of Bourbon. Apart from a nine year period between 1806 and 1815, when Britain was awarded sovereignty over the island in return for Lord Nelson's defeat at sea of an invading Spanish fleet, Sicily was under French rule. Garibaldi's invasion in 1860 ejected the French despots and brought unification with the Italian mainland and, to the present day, Sicily has been an integral part of Italy though the island's inhabitants insist they are, first and foremost, Sicilian.

It is difficult to explain how the Sicilian, occupied by the Greeks, enslaved by the Romans, plundered by the Moors and Saracens, sub·igated and denied self-determination successively by Spain and France and finally assimilated by Italy, has managed to survive and protect his identity. That his bloodline is irreparably flawed is incontrovertible and, through centuries of oppression and exploitation by alien powers, the tough little Sicilian has proved durable. Proud, stoic, withdrawn and suspicious by nature he is an unfathomable man, religious and utterly devoted to his own family and his immediate friends and aggressive in defence of his clan. If a member of his family steps out of line and transgresses the undefined code of honour that exists in his society he is prepared to deal with the miscreant without recourse to the Law and to accept the consequences of his actions without flinching. Questioned about his deeds he will remain silent at all times. He is born with the inherent virtues of honour towards his fellow-men, devotion to his maker and clan and silence about all matters related to his 'family.' It is only a minor readjustment for such a person to graduate into the ranks of the Mafia where onore, fratellanza and omerta are binding membership pre-requisites. Thus a section of Sicilian males progressed imperceptibly into the ranks of a secret brotherhood whose present-day interests have extended beyond family and clan and whose activities include protection, bribery, extortion, gambling, prostitution, drug-trafficking and outright mayhem and murder.

The appellation 'Mafia' is compiled of two Arabic words for boldness and protection but its usage amongst indigenous Sicilian families is shrouded in mystery. The original mafiosi were descended from the ranks of the gabelotti who were first appointed by absentee landlords to levy taxes and manage their estates. Most of the larger estates were parcelled-off into quilt-patches of peasant-owned messadria, or smallholdings. The gabelotti paid the landlord an annual lump sum and were given a free hand to extort the maximum rental from peasant farmers. In addition the poor peasants were made to pay protection money to ensure survival of their messadria. Originally simple villagers, the bailiffs distanced themselves from the peasants and built fortified houses remote from their sources of income. And to impress their authority on the hapless population, and to reinforce their protectional function, they were always armed with loaded shotguns. After Napoleon's defeat at Waterloo in 1815 there was a mass exodus of Bourbon nobility from Sicily and the gabelotti found themselves in charge of vast estates and, for their own protection as much as for anything else, they formed themselves into an armed regional cadres. When Garibaldi and his one thousand red shirts invaded Sicily in 1860, with few exceptions, the bailiffs were placed in command of their rural fiefdoms. As a consequence of the unification of Italy and Sicily, grace and favour estates were granted to Italian noblemen who had supported Garibaldi and most of these were content to remain absentee landlords which played into the hands of the Sicilian padrones.

In the late 1800's Mafia wealth came from the land and its providers were called the Mafia del Giardini. The accumulated wealth was used to appoint and purchase favours from politicians and to secure government contracts, thereby acquiring power for the Cosa Nostra. Around 1880 a secret initiation ceremony was introduced and prospective mafiosi had to swear fealty to the virtues of honour, silence, family loyalty and subservience to the Padrone. Each district had its own Don, a leader voted into power by his peers, and, in 1890, Don Vito Cascio Ferro, based in Catania, emerged as Capo di Tutti Capi for the whole of Sicily, the first Boss of Bosses in any Mafia organization and the first godfather in the true sense of the word. Clans of the Societa Onorata were referred to as 'cosche,' a fanciful reference to the intricate interweaving of artichoke leaves. In Don Cascio's time Men of Honour obeyed the strict rules imposed on them by their Societa and swore not to profit from prostitution, kidnapping or to make improper advances towards womenfolk of another Man of Honour. Premarital virginity was prized in females and Men of Honour who raped, or dishonoured, a female member of another family was regarded as dead. Womenfolk, not members of a Cosa Nostra family, were however fair game for Men of Honour. Sicilian mafosi were ardent churchgoers and swore not to murder women, children, the police or the judiciary. Should a Man of Honour transgress any of these rules, he was as good as dead – 'morto del cuare delgi amici' – and dealt with from within the family. These restrictions gave the Societa Onorata an unwarranted air of respectability which persisted in Sicily until the end of World War ll. Mussolini's accession to power in the 20's curbed the Mafia's activities to some extent. The Fascist dictator's purges in the 30's were largely ineffectual, especially in the rural districts, and only served to drive members of the Honourable Society underground and to tighten their secrecy and security. When Allied forces invaded Sicily in July 1943 the Americans were made welcome by the Sicilian Mafia. Vito Genovese, a New York mobster who had been deported to Italy, was appointed liaison officer to the American Task Force and he ensured most post-war political appointments in Sicily and Southern Italy were filled by Mafia members. The American invaders played a significant role in resurgence in power to the Sici..an Mafia and accelerated by twenty five years the introduction of American ideals and New World gangsterism with consequent loss of the Mafia's traditional values of honour, faith and family.

During the same lifespan a similar organisation emerged in Southern Italy where Calabria was the birthplace of a secret society known as the Camorra. They operated on the same principles as the Mafia and, if anything, were more vicious and bloodthirsty than their Scilian counterparts. In particular, Camorra hit men, the n'drangetta, were renowned for their ruthlessness and killing efficiency. Mainly based in Naples and Calabria, by the early 50's they were infiltrating Mafia families in Catania, Messina and Palermo and soon took over control of these cities. By their ruthless muscle and fire power, the n'drangetta antagonized the traditional rural Sicilian Mafia and inevitably resulted in open conflict between town and country mafiosi which lasted for four decades.

The Mafia cult in the major cities of the United States owes its origin to a Sicilian Capo di Tutti Capi, one Don Vito Cascio Ferro, who turned up in New York in 1901 and brought his ideals of a Societa Onorata with him. Irish, Jewish and Polish ethnic groups had already established underworld gangs in the larger cities on the eastern seaboard and the Mafia took about ten years to become operational in New York where, by the outbreak of the First World War, Joe the Boss Masseria emerged as a figurehead.

A native of Castellammare del Golfo in Sicily, Masseria was a 'Mustache Petes,' an old style traditional mafioso with grandiose ambitions of becoming Capo di Tutti Capi in North America. Back in Sicily once more Don Cascio Ferro had his own ambitions in this direction and, in 1927, sent Salvatore Maranzano, another native of Castellammore del Golfo, to pave the way for his triumphant return to unite New York's Sicilian crime families. Two years later the plans backfired when Don Vito Cascio was gaoled for life by the Fascists on trumped-up charges of smuggling. Meanwhile Maranzano recruited gunmen from his hometown and posed a threat to Masseria's supremacy in New York. By 1928 Joe the Boss's lieutenant was an up-and-coming hoodlum of Sicilian extraction and reared in the slums of Brooklyn. Charles 'Lucky' Luciano seized his chance to play one Mustache Petes against the other resulting in the Castellammarese War which raged between 1928 and 1931 and countless Sicilian immigrant mobsters met their fate on the streets of New York. The war played havoc with the Mafia's income from bootlegging and, disaffected by the long, drawn-out conflict, Lucky Luciano ended hostilities by assassinating Joe Masseria at a Coney Island restaurant on . .pril 15th 1931. He then switched his allegiance to the Maranzano family. The uneasy alliance between Luciano and Maranzano came to an abrupt end five months later in a double-cross when the latter's plan to rubout Luciano backfired and he himself was stabbed to death in his office by a Jewish hitsquad contracted to carry out the killing by Luciano.

Lucky Luciano brought a new ethos into the affairs of American underworld mobsters. He had a broader vision than the narrow-minded Sicilian - sourced 'Mafia di Vecchio Stampo,' or Mustache Petes. He found a place for Jewish and Polish mobsters in his organization and, in 1932, having disposed of the remaining Mustache Petes, he created a National Crime Syndicate composed of two Jewish, one Polish and four Italian crime bosses from

Chicago and the American eastern seaboard. The Syndicate was responsible for planning organized crime in North America and had its own enforcement arm called Murder Inc. which carried out executions on its behalf. Luciano's emergence spelled an end to Sicilian dominance over the New World mobsters and the new hoodlums had no reservations about profiting from prostitution, bootlegging, kidnapping and drug-trafficking.

Italian gangsters in Chicago were not held back by the Mustache Petes. Throughout the 20's and 30's they had a free hand and the likes of Al Capone, Jonny Torrio and Tony Accardo, all Brooklyn-born hoodlums, became legends in the American underworld. Heavily populated by Irish immigrants with their own crime organizations, Boston's Mafia had only a precarious foothold. Propagation of Mafia families into California, Nevada, Miami, Tampa, Las Vegas and New Orleans occurred in the mid-thirties and a generous percentage of their income was channelled into the coffers of the National Crime Syndicate. The Mob's total control over Cuban drug-trafficking and gambling extended from 1936 to 1958 when the corrupt president, Fulgenio Batista, was deposed by Fidel Castro and Mafia mobsters were evicted from the country.

In the late 30's, and after World War II, many American crime bosses, having made their fortune in the New World, returned to Sicily and Southern Italy where they put their American-acquired ideals into practice. Though himself gaoled in 1936 Luciano, via the National Crime Syndicate, exercised some control over these 'retired' mobsters and his influence became absolute when he himself was paroled and deported to Naples in 1946. From this period onwards, until his death in 1962, the Big Boss received regular financial support from his 'Family' in New York and from the Syndicate. In his position in Naples he exercised control over the Camorra in southern Italy but, despite the proximity of the most powerful Mafia figure in the world, Sicily's agrarian dons kept Luciano at arms length. They reasoned that Mafia crime families worldwide originated in the messadria in Sicily and the Sicilian Cosa Nostra had every right to demand sovereignty over the deposed American mobsters. In particular, they still bore a vendetta against Luciano who had engineered the Castellammarese Wars in the 30's and he, and his likes, should pay homage to the Sicilian bosses who had remained in Sicily and, to a certain extent, maintained the traditional values and virtues of true Men of Honour.

CHAPTER 1

Turn of a card

July 1936, Cannes.

DUCA del LOMBARDI SAT SWELTERING at a gaming table in a salon prive of Palm Beach Casino, his troubled blue eyes rigidly fixed on the card in the croupier's right hand. Strikingly resembling the American actor George Raft, the croupier was getting impatient as he awaited the Duke's call. This was not an ordinary game of baccarat and the stakes on the table were astronomical by any standards. A million francs hinged on the card the croupier was about to release from the banco and the Duke's choice was simple. He could either pull out and lose 100,000 francs or, if he matched the other player's million franc injection into the pool, and if the card in the shute was in his favour, he would be wealthier by three million francs—simple mathematics and he could do with that sort of money. His liquid assets were evaporating rapidly. Benito Mussolini and the Fascists were seeing to that. In fact he was seriously in debt and his trip to the Cote d'Azure was in an attempt to recoup some of the money he had lost to the State. He took a long draw from his ivory cigarette holder and looked across the table into the dark-brown, mocking eyes of his Neapolitan adversary. There was no sympathy or understanding on the inscrutable, gloating face of his fellow jouer. He was now in a quandary. In the past he had dealt with similar situations with aplomb and authority, secure in the knowledge that his financial resources were more than adequate to honour his bets. But this was different and he knew there was no money in the bank to cover his gambling. The cigarette holder trembled slightly and rivulets of sweat coursed downwards inside his stiffly-laundered, pristine-white shirt as he pondered his decision. Doing his duty the croupier gave the duke a further minute to consider his next move whilst the audience held its breath.

"Monsieur le Duca. Your call sil vous plait."

The Duke of Lombardy was a direct descendant of the French House of Bourbon and his forebears had served with distinction in the French army. In 1797, when Napoleon was Emperor of France and King of Italy, the family were granted a large estate and castle at Fabrica Curona in Lombardy, a town house in Genoa, a summer villa in Rapallo and a permanent berth for the family yacht at Portofino. Two smaller estates belonged to the Duchy, a mountain farm at San Sosti in Calabria and Masseria Rosella Dara, a large area of scrubland and citrus groves with a fortified hilltop house at Portella Sant Agata in Sicily. The duke's forbears had deserted the Piedmontese cause and supported Garibaldi's campaign in 1860 and, as a consequence, were allowed to keep their inherited houses and estates intact after unification of Italy and Sicily.

The fifty-five year old duke was an aristocrat to his fingertips. He had blazing blue eyes, an aquiline nose, a full head of dark hair, greying at the temples, and a neatly-trimmed grey, military moustache. He was always elegantly dressed and chain-smoked Balkan Sobrani cigarettes held in an ivory holder. His habits were temperate but he was a compulsive gambler and to satisfy his craving his yacht, the Cantora, had taken him from Portofino on a casino-crawl of the Cote d'Azure berthing each night in Nice, Cannes or Monte Carlo. The Palm Beach Casino at Cannes was his favourite and La Cantora had a reserved mooring at the Port du Palm Beach yacht club. His compulsion did not drive him into a casino every night. The duke was a superstitious man and believed in omens and astrology and only ventured forth to gamble when all signs were propitious and in his favour. But when the green light flashed his obsession took control and, loaded with francs and dollars, he made a beeline for a game of chance. The ritual of his gambling night-out was strictly observed. He dressed in a gleaming white shirt and black necktie, grey flannels and a tailor-made dark-blue blazer with shiny gold, naval buttons. On board La Cantora he drank two glasses of pernod and carefully placed three Davidoff cigars in his breast pocket while, in his blazer pocket, he had two unopened packets of Balkan Sobranis. He dined on a lobster thermidor and a bottle of dry Alsace wine at Piero Premier Restaurant in Rue Felix Fauvre on the north side of La Croisette and, at exactly 9.00 pm, took a cab ⋅ Palm Beach Casino to arrive at precisely 9.30 pm.   To the duke gambling was a serious occupation and never had it been more serious than on this occasion. He had settled down at a baccarat table in the ornamentally-chandeliered salon privé. At first there were five players and the stakes moderate but by midnight the only remaining punter in the game was a podgy, round-faced, balding man with dark-brown, protruding eyes and a mouthful of rotten teeth. Introduced to the duke as a business man from Naples, Signore Barutti was having an exceptional run of luck and rapidly eating into the duke's capital. As his losses mounted, so did the duke's determination to beat 'the fat little Neapolitan'. Off-duty croupiers, players and the casino manager gathered around the baccarat table in the smoke-filled salon as the tension mounted. The duke's credit with the casino had already exceeded his limit. After a sidelong glance at, and an imperceptible nod from, the casino manager the duke prepared to match the Italian's million franc talisman. The onlookers gasped and held their breath and all eyes turned towards the Duke of Lombardy. His facial expression remained unchanged but inwardly his brain was in a seething turmoil and, from deep inside his subconscious, a little voice urged him to match the Italian's stake –'Its your lucky night and your luck is bound to change'. He needed a ten or a knave to beat the banco and take the pot. The George Raft look-alike's voice again broke the silence in the salon "Sils vous plait, Monsieur Le Duca.

Your call please."

The duke took a deep breath and with a rapid pronation of his right hand indicated he wanted the final card exposed. Amid gasps of incredibility the croupier flipped a queen of spades face upwards. As the ivory chips were being shovelled across to Signore Barutti, whose flat, sweat-sodden face was wreathed in smiles, the duke rose to his feet and addressed the manager "El Padrone. I wish to see you and the Signore in your office".

The Manager bowed politely and led the two players to his study.

"El Padrone. I am two million francs in debt to Signore Barutti. I have exceeded my limit with your casino and I have no readily availably cash with me. Will Signore Barutti accept the deeds of my estate in Sicily in settlement? I assure you, gentlemen, Portella Sant Agata estate is worth eight times my debt to the Signore".

The manager cocked a quizzical eye at the duke and then turned to face the Italian.

"What do you say Signore Barutti?"

The Neapolitan had no hesitation in accepting the duke's settlement.

"In that case," the duke added, "I will return to La Cantora and you have my vord you will receive the signed deeds within the hour. All I need is the name of the benefactor from Signore Barutti. And now gentlemen I shall leave you. Bonsoir" and he slowly rose to his feet and strolled out of the salon privé. As he walked briskly back to La Cantora he reflected that, thanks to Mussolini's fiscal policies, neither the Calabrian nor the Sicilian estates had provided any worthwhile revenue for many years. He had inherited his title and estates from his uncle but had never visited either of them and now there was no reason to undertake a tiresome journey to Sicily!

Having signed the transfer deeds in favour of one Signore Fabio Caruso of Naples he dispatched La Cantora's captain with them to the casino. Smoking a Davidoff and clutching a brandy the duke took a turn on deck and reflected on an enjoyable, though unprofitable, evening at the Palm Beach Casino. Like all professional gamblers he shut the loss out of his mind. There was no use crying over spilt milk and he still had his yacht, a farm in Calabria, a town house in Genoa and a summer house in Rapallo and, of course, his messadria granda in Lombardy. Plenty of available assets for future gambling excursions to the French Riviera. He flicked the stub of his Davidoff over the side and, with a clear conscience and untroubled mind, retir d to his bunk. Within a minute he was soundly asleep.

July 1936, Naples
Salvatore Barutti was sweating profusely as he climbed the stairs to the top floor of an unpretentious apartment building overlooking Naple's dockland. The heat of midday and apprehension about his visit to Naple's Capo di Tutti Capi were the reasons for his discomfiture. He was always nervous and in a lather when he had to meet Don Fabio Caruso. He wore a baggy black suit and a crumpled, sweat-sodden white shirt and constantly dabbed his forehead with a dirty white handkerchief. With trepidation he timidly pushed the doorbell, almost jumping out of his skin when he heard the faint peal of bells in the dark interior of the penthouse apartment. Salvatore kept wondering why he was always nervous and on edge during his meetings with Don Fabio Caruso? After what seemed an eternity the door was unlocked by a swarthy Neapolitan in shirtsleeves carrying a revolver in a shoulder holster underneath his left armpit.

"Avante Signore Barutti" the powerfully-muscled bodyguard barked curtly and led Salvatore down a dark corridor, across a spacious, sun-drenched lounge and on to a secluded balcony where Don Fabio sat under a sun-umbrella nursing a glass of Frascati. Salvatore knew the drill and reverently bent forwards to kiss the back of Don Fabio's be-jewelled right hand. Don Fabio was Salvatore's age, in his mid-fifties, and had a stocky body tending towards middle-age corpulence. His broad, pock-marked, weatherbeaten face was surmounted by a crop of gristly, grey hair and his deep-set brown eyes shone like beacons from beneath lush, black eyebrows. He wore an open-necked white shirt, black trousers and waistcoat and expensive sharply-pointed, grey leather shoes. Pushing the Frascati bottle across the table he invited Salvatore to sit down and have a drink.

"Well Salvatore, how was your trip?"

The accountant sipped his dry wine and nervously licked his lips.

"I think you will be pleased with my visit to the Cote d'Azure. Here I have deposit slips and numbers of two accounts in a Swiss bank in Locarno. As you ordered, Don Fabio, I converted our lire into Swiss francs."

He mopped his perspiring forehead and continued "I had a look at two casinos, one in Cannes and the other in Monte Carlo, with a view to our involvement in their business. There's little hope in the South of France as they're controlled by the Municipality who will not allow foreign nationals to invest and, in Monte Carlo, the Prince of Monaco owns the casino. But I had some luck in Cannes. Using the money you allowed me I had a run of good fortune at the baccarat table. The principal player was Duca del Lombardi and he had no ready cash to cover his debt. So I got him to transfer the deeds of an estate in Sicily in your name" and, with trembling fingers, Salvatore fished out the deeds from a sweat-stained manilla envelope and laid them out on the table for Don Fabio to inspect.

For three years Salvatore Barutti had acted as a courier for the 'organisation', transporting money into numbered accounts in Switzerland and France. The day after his casino coup he had deposited half a million francs in his own name in Banco Municipale Monaco in Monte Carlo and was petrified Don Fabio might discover his nest-egg. He regretted his actions and had suffered pangs of remorse and fear as he travelled southwards on the Ligurian express to Naples. And now, in close proximity to the most ruthless n'drangetta in Italy, his nerve was on the point of cracking. Salvatore Barutti knew full-well the consequences of exposure and revenge from the Cosa Nostra was always swift and frequently terminal. He had decided beforehand to practice the Mafia's main credo of 'omerta', or silence, but the tension within him was rapidly mounting and he was about to jump to his feet and confess when Don Fabio looked up from the tabl, with a broad smile on his face "You have done well Salvatore. My Family now has a messadria in Sicily. My friend Don Triddu in Palermo will know all about Portella Sant Agata."

Salvatore was offered another glass of wine but declined and got to his feet, anxious to be away from the Capo's apartment. Don Fabio kissed him on both cheeks and with a friendly arm draped around his shoulder, escorted Salvatore to the door. Barutti had barely negotiated the second flight of stairs when Don Fabio summoned his lieutenant.

"Barutti has been lying to me. He won more money at the casino than he declared. Find out if he has money in his apartment or a secret bank account. If he is cheating he has to be removed. We can easily find another laundryman."

Don Fabio Caruso had graduated from the ranks of the n'drangetta and believed in immediate execution if a clan member committed an atrocity against his Familia. Naples and Calabria were riddled with these ruthless mafiosi. Don Fabio's lieutenant was thorough and expeditious and, on searching Salvatore's tenement flat, he found a Monaco Municipale Banco's credit slip for 500,000 francs in the inside pocket of a black suit. An execution was carried out on the same night. Barutti was forcibly taken to the dockside and refused to confess, knowing full-well if he did so the outcome would be the same. He was allowed to smoke one cigarette and then shot through the back of his head and his body dumped in the harbour. From the balcony of his penthouse apartment Don Fabio witnessed recovery of the body by the Carabinieri on the following day. He had no regrets for ordering the execution of his best laundryman. Salvatore had broken the Mafia code for which the punishment was death. So be it! The Carabinieri's half-hearted investigations into the shooting, and the subsequent inquest, came to the standard conclusion in cases of gangland assassination – 'death by misadventure or murder by a person, or persons, unknown.' It was indeed a lethal misadventure for the unfortunate Signore Salvatore Barutti

October 1936, Palermo Province.
Accompanied by two armed lieutenants, Don Fabio Caruso crossed on an overnight ferry from Naples to Palermo in mid-October and was met at the dockside by Don Triddu Caminiti, Palermo's mayor and senior Capo of Palermo Province. They were driven to Don Triddu's residence on the northern outskirts of the city, a palazzo of Moorish design enclosed by a twelve foot stone wall with an imposing gilded Arabic entrance gate and an ornate mosaic hallway. As befitted the importance of his visitor Don Triddu observed all the proprieties and business was not discussed until the visiting entourage had wined and dined and welcoming speeches had been exchanged. Armed with a bottle of Cognac and a supply of Cuban cigars the Dons retired to an inner sanctum for a face-to-face discussion.

"I am honoured by your visit to Palazzo Sclafani, Don Fabio. I will make sure you receive true Palermian hospitality while you're here."

Don Fabio inclined his head and took a long contented puff on his cigar sending billows of smoke in ascending spirals towards the loggia's Byzantine ceiling. There was a long pause for effect.

"I hear you are having difficulties with some gabelotti and Dons in your province. I have similar problems in the very south of Calabria. I thought we might discuss our inconveniences and work out a solution in dealing with the troublesome Dons."

Heartened by his visitor's opening remarks Don Triddu relaxed and launched into a detailed description of his provincial fiefdoms.

"My province consists of all the land west of the road running from Termini in the north to Agrigento on the south coast. It includes the large towns of Sciacca, Mazara, Marsa a and Trapani. Each town and region has its own Don and there are sixteen Capos in my province and I have to employ a large number of gabelotti to maintain order and collect taxes. My interests are here in Palermo where I control the docks, the building trade and the food markets and therein lies my difficulty. Traditionally provincial dons control the markets but, since I took over I have had trouble with the Mafia dei Giardini. There are daily fights and sometimes killings in Vucciria market. I am a true old-fashioned Mafia di Vecchio Stampo and these squabbles sadden me. Many padrones in the rural fiefdoms refuse to pay taxes and my gabelotti run a constant war against them. And, of course, we have to contend with Il Duce's secret police and armed militia."

Don Fabio polished off his brandy and refilled his glass before replying "To deal with rebellious Camorra in the remoter parts of Calabria I have recruited renegade bands of n'drangetta to patrol my province and extract taxes. You have to meet force with force."

Don Fabio paused to relight his cigar and produced a tattered envelope from his jacket pocket and placed it on the table before Don Triddu.

"This is the main reason for my visit. As you will see it is the title deeds for an estate in your province. I acquired it from the Duca del Lombardi who has signed the deed of transfer. I need to know from you how best to manage this estate to the advantage of both our Families."

Don Triddu leapt to his feet and turned towards a wall map. "Masseria Rosella Dara is a rugged hilly estate to the west of the road linking Corleone with Piana and Palermo. The estate house is on a hill top at Portella Sant Agata. With little cultivated land it mainly produces olives, citrus fruits and wine and the Padrone has large herds of sheep and goats roaming the hillsides. Angelo Muzzi runs the estate which cannot compare with the one to the east side of the same road. Don Carlo Cecci's fiefdom at Godrano has acres of arable land and is the chief supplier of oil, fruit, cereals and wine for the markets here in Palermo. Portella Sant Agata has one important asset, Lago delio Scanzano, the only supply of fresh water in the region in the dry season."

Don Triddu paused for breath and continued "Anglo Muzzi has been a thorn in my flesh for quite a while. He has linked himself with the Corleonese and is an active trouble- maker in Vucciria market. I would pleased to see the back of him."

The Neapolitan don responded quickly "Since I acquired these deeds in July I have given the matter much thought and suggest we put a new Family on the estate. The man I have in mind is my nephew, Giovanni Cucinotta, who will make an excellent Padrone and I will ens ire he is cooperative with your Mafia dei Cantieri here in Palermo. Do you agree Don Triddu?"

The Palermian Don accepted without reservation. The men stood and shook hands and a binding deal was struck between the two men of honour. It was thus ordained that Giovanni Cucinotta would become the next Padrone at Portella Sant Agata. Later Don Triddu looked a little perplexed "Who's going to tell Angelo Muzzi he's no longer wanted? He's a fiery customer and a handful at the best of times."

Don Fabio replied with a wry smile "That's a problem you must face Don Triddu. If you need a hitsquad I will send my n'drangetta across from Naples."

"No! It will not come to that. I will manage Muzzi's dismissal myself. Tomorrow we'll take a trip to Santa Agata to see Muzzi and look over his estate."

Protected by two gabelotti the Dons motored the 40 kilometres southwards from Palazzo Sclafani to Portella Sant Agata on the following day. Progress along the narrow road was slow, mainly due to tortuosity of the byroad but also to frequent hold-ups by mule trains returning from Palermo's market and guarded by armed gabelotti astride mules. Don Triddu Caminiti explained that the muleteers were disarmed by his men on the outskirts of Palermo but many carried knives and coshes into the market place where they sold their wares to unauthorised traders and scuffles were a frequent occurrence.

The cars wound their way laboriously through Punta delia Moarda and Piana and then ascended sharply to pass through Portella Sant Agata, a clustered hamlet of a dozen peasant dwellings on each side of a rickety wooden bridge straddling a ravine. About ten minutes drive beyond the hamlet the road track climbed sharply and, at the top of the rise, Angelo Muzzi's fortified house stood in splendid isolation surrounded by an eight-foot stone wall with two armed gabelotti protecting its entrance. One of the guards approached the car and recognised the Palermian don.

"Signore. I have come to visit Angelo Muzzi. Please tell him I'm here."

The second guard intervened.

"Don Angelo is away in Corleone visiting a sick relative."

The visiting party disembarked to stretch their legs and take in the view from their vantage point. The town of Marineo was visible in the distance to the east across an oval shaped valley divided into a patchwork of green fields and its sloping sides covered with vineyards, olive groves and citrus orchards. To the south the cigar-shaped Scanzano lake stood out clearly. There was evidently no invitation for the visitors to enter the house and no prospect of seeing Muzzi. Don Triddu addressed the senior guard in an authoritative voice "Immediately your Boss returns tell him I must see him at Palazzo Sclafani. The matter is of utmost importance."

The gabelotti simply shrugged his shoulders and walked away. As soon as the party were again on the move Don Triddu exploded "I've a good mind to press on to Corleone and look up Muzzi's sick relative. The cunning old fox is hiding somewhere and avoiding us and his behaviour is insulting to you Don Fabio. I'll have great pleasure in throwing him off his estate."

Three miles south of Muzzi's fortified house the road ran along the west bank of Lago delio Scanzano and formed a Y junction with the Corleone/Bolognetta road. At Bivio Lupo, on the eastern bank of the lake, the cars swung eastwards for eight kilometres across the fertile and cultivated basin of the vast Godrano valley, acre upon acre of arable fields and miles of citrus and olive groves and vineyards on the hillsides, originally planted by the vintners of Provence during Bourbon occupation. It was easy to see why the lion's share of produce sold in Vucciria market came from Don Carlo Cecci's eatate. A mile north of Godrano village, and a similar distan e short of Cefala, they came to a flat plateau where the road ran through a farmyard with a walled mansion on the left hand side and a group of outhouses and red-roofed barns on the other side. Don Triddu ordered the cars to pull up in the farmyard and he strode across the road to the estate house. There were no guards protecting Don Cecci's property and the Padrone himself met the visitors on the doorstep and escorted them into a cool parlour in the interior of the house where they lunched on rye bread, goats cheese and pickled olives washed down with a glass of cool dry wine poured from an earthenware pitcher. Don Carlo Cecci explained how his father absorbed all Godrano's messadria into a self-sufficient commune which enjoyed the major share of trade in Palermo's markets. He admitted his neighbour on the other side of the Eleutero River made trouble from time to time. There were minor clashes about levying taxes from the peasant-force at Marineo and, in the hot summer months, for supplying fresh water from Lake Scanzano. Don Carlo made the point of stressing he was an agrarian Mafia dei Giardini but enjoyed a good relationship with most of his neighbours and, in particular, with Don Triddu Caminiti, his Capo in Palermo.

Angelo Muzzi was in no hurry to pay a call on Don Triddu and by November he had a valid excuse for no travelling to Palermo. Torrential rains struck northern Sicily and dry river beds became raging torrents and the low-lying valleys and surrounding citrus groves were converted into turbid, brown lakes. The deluge and flash-floods washed away sections of the mountain roads and many grazing animals fell victim to the flood waters. When the floods receded the fields were covered with a thick layer of gluey mud. Muzzi delayed going to Palermo as long as possible and it was Christmas week before he turned-up in Vucciria's morning market with two of his senior gabelotti who were formally disarmed by the Carabinieri. Muzzi was escorted across the market square, up via Vittorio Emmanuele and through a labyrinth of side-streets in the Albergheria, to Don Triddu's Moorish palazzo.

"I've been expecting you for weeks, Muzzi."

Don Triddu's voice was cold and dispassionate and the traditional embrace and customary offer of wine was not forthcoming. An air of gloomy foreboding pervaded the darkened room. Muzzi stood arrogantly in front of his Capo and realised he was in for a roasting.

"We have been isolated at Sant Agata for five weeks and the rains washed away large sections of the road between here and my estate. I could not have come sooner."

Don Triddu scratched his scalp and brushed back a strand of greying hair with his fingertip. He looked up sharply at the dishevelled and shabbily-dressed braggart before him.

"Be that as it may, I will come to the point immediately. I have known since July that your landlord, the Duca del Lombardi, has sold your estate to a don from Naples who'll take over Sant Agata in April and bring his own gabelotti across with him. This means you must be out of Sant Agata by Easter."

Muzzi was dumbstruck. His pock-marked face was suffused and he spluttered and eventually exploded "I don't believe it after all these years! They can't do this to me. What about the Cosa Nostra and honour? Damn it! I deserve better treatment than this and what if I refuse to move? What will you do to me if I refuse to go?"

Don Triddu expected an outburst from the old renegade but not a direct threat to disobey his orders. He replied with finality and authority "You will do as ordered and, I repeat, you will vacate Masseria Rosella Dara by Easter time. The decision is final and this interview is over. You may now leave."

But Muzzi stood his ground and turned on the seated don.

"This will be a sorry day for you, Don Triddu, and you will live to regret your actions. I have done nothing to discredit the Cosa Nostra and loˢ k at the thanks I get! It seems the rules are different for town Mafiosi and my Giardini friends. Together we'll become strong enough to overthrow your Palermo puppets. Then you'll see what happens! No more silly orders like this one and, mark my words, you'll see who comes out on top at the end of the day."

His face contorted with rage, Angelo Muzzi stormed out of Don Triddu's study. Experiencing both sympathy and resentment the Don watched him depart and thought 'There goes a dangerous man who might turn pertito. He certainly is vengeful and I shall have to watch my back at all times.' By his vicious outburst Muzzi had flagrantly transgressed the Mafia code of honour and Don Triddu had every right to demand just punishment. But he felt some compassion for the fiery mafioso and let matters slide. He would have been better advised to take positive action on that dank December day and Muzzi, true to his word, was a thorn in Don Triddu's flesh for six years. But this was Christmastime and the season of goodwill to all men and Don Triddu Camaniti's christian conscience overrode his inborn Mafia instincts to punish the miscreant there and then.

CHAPTER 2

A meeting of Men of Honour

THE CECCI FAMILY HAD MANAGED GODRANO ESTATE for four generations. In 1848 one of Don Carlo's forebears, also named Carlo, emerged as undisputed leader of an unsuccessful peasant uprising against the rule of King Ferdinand VI. Twelve years later he joined forces with Tancredi, a soldier-of-fortune and Prince of Falconeri, who deserted the Royalist cause and became one of Garibaldi's lieutenants. Within a year Garibaldi and his one thousand red shirts had 'liberated' Sicily from the restrictive French Bourbon regime. After the battle of Aspromonte on the mainland, Tancredi returned to his uncle's estate at Salinas, near Palermo, where he settled down and married the daughter of Calagero Sedara, one of Palermo's self-made and devious leading citizens. During persecution of French landlords after 'liberation' in 1860 Sedara cunningly, and cheaply, bought vacated estates for a song. Celebrated as a hero, Carlo Cecci returned from the Italian mainland in 1864 and, in recognition of his service to Garibaldi, Tancredi insis ed his father-in-law handed over Godrano estate to the Cecci family. Meanwhile Sedara had appointed his own loyal servants to control Palermo's markets and adopted them into his 'Familia' forming a brotherhood of men. Thus Sedara's and Tancredi's 'Family' became the forerunner of the Cosa Nostra in Sicily and Carlo Cecci became one of his first-appointed Padrones. From 1864 until 1943 a succession of Cecci males ruled the roost at Godrano but, with no heir-apparent this was about to end.

Known as a messadria granda, Godrano is a ten kilometeres square estate encompassing the villages of Godrano itself, Bolognetta, Cefala and Messojuso and bounded on its west side by the Corleone/Bolognetta road and on its east side by a wider highway forming the boundry of Palermo Province and running northwards from Agrigento, through Lercara, and on to Palermo. To the south the 1,200 ft. Rocca Buscambra range separates Godrano from the territory of the Corleone family. More than three-quarters of the estate is crop- producing and the hills are covered with olive and citrus groves and productive vineyards. Herds of sheep and goat graze the undulating, scrub-covered foothills and the rock-strewn mountains surrounding a fertile valley basin.

At the age off 37 Carlo Cecci had inherited Godrano estate on the death of his father in 1920. He married in 1910 and his wife bore him three girls, Anna in 1912, Gina in 1916 and Carla 10 years later and undoubtedly the apple of her father's eye. His wife tragically died giving birth to Carla and, to his regret, Carlo Cecci had no son and heir. Don Carlo was a kind and benevolent Padrone. Morally and religiously, just like his father, he was strict and unbending but, unlike his father, he was not a hardline mafioso. He was tolerant of smallholding peasant farmers who could not pay their taxes and frequently turned a blind eye to their common practice of bartering amongst themselves. He was particularly kind and generous to the widows and children of his employees but there were two virtues Don Carlo held sacrosanct – he showed no mercy to murderers and rapists and upheld the principle of chastity before marriage, which was strictly observed in the Cecci household. Over the years Don Carlo had absorbed most of the smallholdings in his territory into one commune and peasant-farmers received weekly payment for the fruits of their labour. His leniency and lack of aggression towards his workforce was tolerated by the Boss in Palermo for, after all was said and done, Godrano was the breadbasket that kept their bellies full and there was no desire to antagonise the provider.

Mussolini's anti-Mafia campaigns were at their height in the early thirties and Italy's Calabria and Sicily became elective targets for his purges. Carabinieri Inspector Mori and a team of secret agents spent months in Palermo where they drove the local mafiosi underground. In the small hilltown of Ganci, one hundred alleged mafiosi were arrested and, according to Mussolini, Mori had wiped out all the Mafia in Sicily in one fell swoop. But nothing could be further from the truth. The Cosa Nostra was alive, kicking and surviving, aided and abetted by an oath of 'omerta' and the fact that Mori's Carabinieri and Mussolini's Blackshirts were bribeable. Il Duce delivered a rousing speech in Palazzo Majore in Palermo in 1937 claiming Sicily was on the verge of one of the happiest epochs of its 4,000 year history – a prediction greeted with disbelief and derision by the Mafia fraternity.

Don Carlo Cecci's troubles started in the same month as Mussolini's 'memorable' speech to the Sicilian people at Eastertime 1937. A new Don from Naples and his n'drangetta Family moved into the neighbouring estate at Portella Sant Agata. Wedged into a triangle between the Corleone/Bolognetta road and the main road from Corleone to Piana and thence to Palermo, the hilly Messadria Rosella Dara had a productive capacity of only a tenth of Godr 'no's. The previous occupant, Angelo Muzzi, had been a nuisance and a troublemaker but, with the advent of Giovanni Cucinotta, the whole scenario changed radically. One of Don Fabio Caruso's lieutenants in Naples, Giovanni Cucinotta, had been rewarded for loyal services and for supervising the execution of Salvatore Barutti. He was granted the fiefdom of Sant Agata by his uncle with instructions to use all means in his power, short of brute force, to acquire the lucrative Godrano estate for his Familia. The Palermian don and Don Fabio Caruso had agreed in secret that such a move would benefit all parties. Don Triddu Caminiti in Palermo was aware that control of his province was slipping through his hands, partly due to pressure from Mussolini's secret police, but mainly due to the emergence of a group of Mafia dei Giardini led by the powerful dons of Corleone. Godrano acted as a buffer state between the militant Corleonese and his own town Mafia dei Cantieri in Palermo. Don Carlo Cecci sat on the fence for two years but Cucinotta's actions pushed him into bed with the untrustworthy Corleonese who were undoubtedly predators and would seize his estate at the drop of a hat. By 1939 Cecci had opted to join forces with the Corleonese though he still pledged allegiance to Don Triddu Caminiti.

Don Giovanni's knowledge of farming and rui.,l ecology was negligible. He brought a ruthless Neapolitan n'drangetta regimen to Sant Agata and, in this, he was aided by his adult sons, Andreo aged 28 and Santo aged 25 years. In 1937 his third son, Giudo, was only thirteen years old but already showing signs of ruthless aggression. The Sant Agata mafiosi levied higher taxes and extorted protection money from peasantry, and failure to pay led to confiscation of their messadria, contamination of food supplies, arson and physical beatings which prevented the victims from labouring. Giovanni's sons were the enforcers and, occasionally, the beatings were overzealous and led to a victim's death. These incidents were never reported to the Carabinieri which only brought further, and more severe, reprisals from the n'drangetta. In any event Don Giovanni Cucinotta was judge and jury at Messadria Rosella Dara.

During 1938 Don Carlo Cecci was cautiously drifting towards union with the Corleonese who wanted open confrontation with the n'drangetta in Palermo and the Padrone at Sant Agata. His position was precarious and he was restrained by the thought he might lose the one and only outlet for his produce in Palermo's Mafia-controlled markets. He had three ageing gabelotti to run Godrano and, for muscle power, he relied on the militant Corleonese. By June the citrus groves and vineyards were laden with fruit ready to harvest when the feeding streams from Lake Scanzano suddenly ran dry. Ripening crops wilted and overripe fruit began to desiccate in the scorching sun. Almost on cue two armed men on mules appeared on Don Carlo's doorstep. Andreo Cucinotta was the spokesman.

"Don Giovanni wishes to inform you we have cut-off your supply from Lago Scanzano. The level is low and we need to preserve water for Sant Agata."

Don Carlo knew this to be untrue but Andreo persisted "We will now levy a charge for use of water from our lake and I will collect the money from you once a week. Do you agree to pay Don Carlo?"

Don Carlo had little choice in the matter and reluctantly nodded his head.

"Good," said Andreo, "we'll return to Scanzano and allow the water to flow again" and, without further ado, the Cucinotta brothers urged their steeds downhill towards Godrano village. The charges for fresh water increased as the summer months progressed and relief only came in late October when the rains arrived and Don Carlo's own water supply was again assured.

During 1938 and 1939 the Cucinotta's frequently employed road blocks to harass and obstruct supply convoys moving northwards to Palermo. They had a semi-permanent obstruction at Portella Sant Agata and another at Ponte San Vito on the Corleone/Bolognetta road just south of Marineo. These nagging road blocks were a headache to the muleteers from Corleone and frequent skirmishes occurred between rival mafiosi. Don Carlo was able to help the Corleonese by diverting their mule trains across Godrano estate to Cefala and Villafrati, where they hooked-up with the main road from Agrigento, and were able to get their produce to Palermo's markets. A tense situation arose when Benito Mussolini invaded Albania on Good Friday 1939 and Sicily became a major training ground for Italian armies and a staging post for troops in transit to North Africa. After Nazi Germany's conquest of France, and Italy's inglorious entry into the war on

10th June 1940, the island became a virtual military fortress and Mafia activities had to be curtailed. In Sicily, Italian troops were favourably poised for the short dash across the sea to North Africa from the ports of Palermo, Trapani, Marsala and Agrigento and the inadequate inland roads were stretched to the limit with motorized convoys and troops constantly on the move. In the interests of national unity, and to maintain their anonymity, Mafia squabbles and Cosa Nostra activities were suspended between 1939 and 1944.

In the last week in October 1940 Don Carlo was summoned to Palazzo Sclafani to meet with Don Triddu Caminiti. After an exchange of courtesies he was ushered into an ornately-decorated loggia by the senior Capo.

"There is an urgent matter which needs attention and I rely on you to help me and my Family. Two young mafiosi came across from Naples four days ago. They're fugitives from the Italian army and wish to avoid military service. I am asking you to billet them at Godrano and hide them from the military police and Carabinieri. They are healthy, fit men and will work on your estate. You need a few extra men to run Godrano and they will take a lot of responsibility off your hands."

The two senior dons sat at a table sharing a bottle of acerbic local wine. They were both of similar age and treated each other with mutual respect. Don Carlo replied "I respect your wishes Don Triddu but I have three grown-up daughters. I am fearful these men might become too familiar with my girls and bring disgrazitsa on my family. This I will not tolerate."

"I understand your concern, Don Carlo, but I have to insist. There has been an upheaval in Naples. Don Fabio Caruso was eliminated last week for collaborating with the Tunica Negra and the new Capo is Fredo Gicanetti who has asked for my help with the two mafiosi. One of them is his own son, Franco, and the other a nephew named Salvatore Branco. Between these four walls I can tell you they were responsible for the execution of Don Caruso and they had to leave Naples in a hurry. I wish to keep in the good books of the new Capo in Naples and I have taken the boys under my wing. I considered sending them to Portella Sant Agata but Don Giovanni has three sons of his own, also avoiding military conscription. I will ensure the mafiosi are fully aware of the situation at your podere and that honore must be observed at all times."

Don Carlo had to accept.

"Your word is good enough for me, Padrone. I will take the mafiosi into my house."

"Good! Good!," the worried don exclaimed, "the boys are in hiding in the Albergheria and will join your convoy to Godrano tomorrow morning. Tonight you will be my guest at Palazzo Sclafani."

As soon as he uttered his acceptance Don Carlo had a premonition he would live to rue the day he took the mafiosi into his household. In the event the runaway renegades remained at Godrano for two and half years.

Dressed as muleteers the young mafiosi joined Don Carlo's mule train on their return journey to Godrano on the following day. Brash and loud-mouthed, they took delight in chattering and laughing together and chancing their arm with the military personnel and Carabinieri on the busy road. Franco was intent on insulting and goading the policemen and Don Carlo was immensely relieved when, after five hours on the congested main road, they reached Villafrati and veered-off on to the near-deserted dirt track to Cefala, and finally to Godrano. Long before they reached his podere Don Carlo had decided the young braggarts would be housed in the barn and only allowed in his house at mealtimes. He was determined to keep his daughters away from the young bucks as far as possible and, even before he reached Godrano, he was praying their stay at his podere would be short-lived.

It soon became evident that the young mafiosi were of no use in managing Don Carlo's estate and had no intention of learning about agriculture. The ringleader was Franco Giacanetti. The killing of Don Fabio Caruso, and a previous attempt to murder a crooked police inspector, had elevated him overnight to celebrity status and enhanced his reputation as a tough customer among the Neapolitan Mafia. Salvatore Branco, his sidekick, was dim-witted and completely under the influence of his compatriot. To get the mafiosi away from his house and daughters, Don Carlo equipped them with mules and a shotgun each. Italian wartime authorities had enforced a ban on non-military personnel carrying firearms in towns and on arterial roads but shotguns were allowed for peasants in rural areas for protection against armed robbers and for hunting to supplement the cooking pot. The two mafiosi were given a roving commission collecting taxes, checking on peasant work-schedules and wild-goat hunting on the Rocca Buscambra mountain range. There were occasional skirmishes, mainly aggressive posturing and verbal insults, with the Cucinotta's along the border road between the estates and more serious confrontations with bands of robbers who roamed the mountain ranges. Local Carabinieri soon became aware of the presence of strangers at Godrano but were easily bought-off with bottles of wine and olive oil. Not so the Tunica Negra, the Blackshirt secret police, who carried out snap raids on villages and farmhouses. In anticipation of unwelcome visitations, Franco established an emergency hideout in a cave at the top of a sharp incline in the road halfway between Godrano and Cefala and about a mile north of Don Carlo's mansion. By the end of 1942 Franco and his aide were openly challenging Don Carlo's authority. The main factor which prevented the renegades making an outright bid for control at Godrano was the increase in military and police activity as the war inexorably progressed and Sicily emerged in importance as a staging post for transportation of Italian and German troops to the battlefields in North Africa. Don Carlo also threw out hints that, if the mafiosi did not toe the line, he might expose them to the dreaded Tunica Negra. Don Carlo was a traditional Mafia di Vecchio Stampo and a staunch believer in secrecy and silence and this was an idle threat. He could never turn pertito and betray his unwelcome guests unless, of course, they transgressed the established code of honour of his Family. As winter approached Franco Giacanetti and Salvatore Branco became permanent residents in Don Carlo's podere and, much to the don's displeasure, they flirted openly with his daughters. Anna, the eldest and plainest, showed little interest in the young men but Gina, who had a pleasantly-rounded face and curvaceous body, sometimes reciprocated. She was 28 years of age and well-able to look after herself. Don Carlo's main concern was for 16 year old Carla who was headstrong and had never had contact with grown men. He feared she might succumb to Franco's crude charms and, like a cockerel protecting his hens, he strutted around the house making certain that meetings between Carla and the mafiosi were brief and at a superficial level.

During the second half of 1942 Italian and German reinforcements poured across the Straits of Messina into Sicily and the north-south highways were in constant use. The commissariat of these mobile columns soon realised there was a ready supply of fruit, oil, wine and vegetables at Godrano and foraging militia paid regular visits to purchase food supplies. The frequent presence of soldiery, and in particular German soldiers, made life difficult for Franco and his comrade. During daylight hours they kept well away from the farmhouse only returning at night to be fed and to sleep. Don Carlo fretted about the vulnerability of his daughters during these nightly visits and they needed his protection, but his health was failing. He was constantly tired and losing weight and a nagging pain in the pit of his stomach kept him awake at night. By morning he was exhausted and completely spent. He trusted 32 year old Anna to chaperone her sisters but she couldn't be everywhere at all times and Don Carlo suspected Gina and Carla were carrying-on with the mafiosi. For the women there was an air of mystery and excitement about the two renegades who came visiting after dark and were under constant threat of exposure and arrest.

In March and April 1943 the tide of troop movements changed and Axis forces were now moving from ιe south coast ports northwards to the Straits of Messina. American troops had landed in Oran in North Africa on 10th November 1942 and advanced from the west while General Montgomery's 8th Army pressed from the east. Axis forces were held in a pincers movement on Cape Bon Peninsula in Tunisia where, by April 1943, evacuation by sea from the port of Tunis was in full swing and the Sicilian roads from the south coast ports were jammed with men, tanks and vehicles making their way northwards. The retreating Germans sensed the Italians were on the verge of surrendering to the Allies and were downcast, brow-beaten and smarting at their defeat in North Africa. Gone was the bravado of their previous excursion to war across Sicily and, like the cornered rats they had been on Cape Bon, these men were dangerous. They did not barter for food supplies but simply took what they wanted and moved onwards. Despite his increasing lethargy Don Carlo was particularly vigilant when these dispirited soldiers were in the vicinity and confined his daughters to the kitchen and the cellar and Franco and Salvatore, dressed as peasant farmers, were sent packing to the fields. In the wake of retreating Axis forces, Allied planes straffed mobile columns and motorized convoys who took to moving under cover of darkness which added to the chaos on the already over-cluttered roads. After Tunis fell on 7thMay the traffic on the evacuation lines through Sicily dwindled to a trickle and finally ceased when Axis forces in Tunisia capitulated on May 12th 1943.

9th May 1943, Godrano.

The wizened, round-shouldered, sixty year old Padrone shuffled across a dirt road to the back a the red-roofed barn and took his seat on a worn, wooden bench in the shade of a eucalyptus tree. This was his favourite resting place, where he had a panoramic view of the undulating hills, citrus groves and vineyards of his lush Godrano estate. He had a glimpse of the rooftops and church spire in Godrano village, about a mile below his feet, and a partial view of the yellow earthen road which, like a coiled serpent, wound its way across the fertile, cultivated basin and gentle undulations of a bush-covered escarpment below his podere. From his vantage post he could keep a close eye on any vehicles or pedestrians approaching his farmhouse. Behind him the road bisected his property and then began a tortuous climb northwards, winding around a mountain, to the village of Cefala some two miles distant. Thereafter the road continued its undulating course eastwards to join the Agrigento/Palermo highway at Villafrati. Don Carlo Cecci had been Padrone of Godrano since 1920 and now, in May 943, the cares of the world seemed to rest on his thin, bony shoulders. Shading his watery eyes he surveyed his domain with pride and took a deep breath of the scented mountain air. Normally he would have been invigorated by the fresh air and scenic beauty before his eyes but today, and for the past two months, he was out of sorts, plagued by waves of nausea and the anguish of uncontrollable lethargy. There were important decisions to be made, very important, and it would be unwise to prevaricate much longer. Don Carlo's moment of truth had arrived. The eucalyptus tree provided partial shade and relief from the blazing sun but the gnawing pains in his stomach and waves of nausea continued unabated. His mouth was parched and his senses reeling. He was craving for a drink when he heard muffled footsteps on the yard behind his back and, within seconds, Carla stood at his side holding an earthenware pitcher. She placed one hand lightly on his bony-thin left shoulder and looked affectionately into her father's eyes.

"You must have something to drink, Papa. The sun is very hot and you must be thirsty. I have some lime juice here but, if you would prefer, I'll get you some goat's milk."

Don Carlo slowly turned his head and gestured to his daughter to sit beside him.

"Thank you Carla. The lime juice will do. I've been sitting here thinking what's best for my Family."

The frail old man took a sip of the juice and winced as the acidic fluid reached his stomach.

"I have decided to pay Don Triddu a visit tomorrow."

A look of concern and alarm crossed Carla's face "But Papa you are not in a fit state to make the journey to Palermo and return the same day. It will take you at least 6 hours to get there on the congested roads. It will be madness to go."

The don touched his daughter affectionately on her forearm.

"I must go. Don Triddu is an old friend and he will advise me. The future of Godrano is at stake and, besides, I will go and see a doctor in Palermo. I'm not feeling too well and I need some medicine."

Carla saw the logic in her father's proposal.

"Yes, Papa, we all wish you'd see a doctor. I will come with you to Palermo."

She made the last statement knowing full-well she would have to walk to Palermo and back beside her father's mule. Women were not allowed to ride astride horses, or mules, as such an act was an insult to their dignity and brought disgrazitsa on the Family. The Don refused point-blank.

"No, Carla! I will take my gabelotti and spare mules with me and we should get to Palermo and back in a day."

The young woman shuddered at the thought but knew better than to raise objections. Once her father's mind was made up wild horses would not change it and she knew better than to ask about his motives in visiting Don Triddu. She stood up to leave and walked briskly away from the shade of the eucalyptus tree. When she reached the driveway to the house a sudden thunderous roar heralded the approach of two fighter planes about 300 feet above her head. Carla held her head in her hands at the sudden, horrific noise and, as she glanced skywards, one of the planes dipped its wings in salute as it streaked in a flash northwards and out of sight behind the mountains above Cefala.

At crack of dawn on Monday 10th May 1943 Don Carlo, accompanied by Mario his senior gabelotti, set out astride mules and trailing two pack mules laden with food, water, wine and olive oil. At first they headed into the rising sun and then northwards from Villafrati where the highway became sporadically busy and, as the day wore on, a few motorized convoys and locals on mules passed them by. Don Carlo had to stop at the roadside at frequent intervals to retch and vomit foul-smelling bile and to drink sparingly from his flask of tepid water. The sky was strangely quiet. By mid-day they were two kilometres beyond Misilmeri and approaching the hamlet of Villabate when Don Carlo called a halt in an orange grove. Exhausted, he lay on the ground and dozed fitfully for a few minutes and was woken by the buzz of swarming bees settling on a flowering bush above his head. And then, in the far distance to the south, he heard a constant rumble which grew louder by the second. Don Carlo wondered if Mount Etna was erupting but the rumble was coming from the wrong direction. As he got to his feet the noise became an intense, deafening roar as two low-flying planes streaked westwards towards Palermo. Within half a minute of the fighter's disappearance a squadron of twelve Blenheim bombers flew overhead and, as the continuous rumble receded and they reached their target, the noise was replaced by the unmistakeable crump of clusters of exploding bombs. Forty bombs were dropped on Palermo's harbour area that morning and, as a final flourish, the Mosquito fighters, cannons ablaze, returned for one final strafe. The whole attack had lasted ten minutes and, when it was all over and the planes had gone, an eerie silence descended on the hamlet of Villabate.

It took nearly two hours for the travellers to reach Via Corso dei Mille on the eastern outskirts of Palermo where refugees from the dockland area were fleeing in their hundreds. Shrouded by a dense pall of smoke the mid-afternoon sun was only a dim, yellow, shadowy ball in the sky above their heads. Walking ahead of Mario and the mules Don Carlo struggled forwards down Via Roma and, near the smouldering cathedral of San Domenica, he came to the house of Professore Abrigo Natale. The harassed professor was in his surgery dealing with victims of the bombing and Don Carlo joined a long, hysterical queue whose length multiplied by the minute as casualties kept arriving from the devastated harbour. The injured screamed, cried and related exaggerated stories about hundreds of bombs dropping on the port, falling d?bris, houses collapsing and hordes of dead people lying among the rubble. At long last, after a two hour wait, Don Carlo's turn came and he was barely able to shuffle into the doctor's office. A teacher at Guiseppe Teatini University, Professore Natale sat behind a mahogany desk and looked haggard and drawn. He wore a blood-stained, white tunic and his hand was shaking as he removed his pince-nez glasses and glared at Don Carlo "And where are you injured old man? I hope you are not here to waste my time."

With an effort Don Carlo raised his head to stare at the specialist. His mouth was dry and he spoke in a croaky whisper "I am here because I feel unwell, Il Professore. I have ridden all day from Godrano and we witnessed the bombing from Villabate. I can see you're busy but please examine me. There's something seriously wrong with my stomach."

The professor sighed wearily, stroked his goatee beard, replaced his pince-nez glasses and looked at his timepiece.

"I can give you five minutes, Signore Cecci."

He took down a few details and, with a sweeping gesture, ordered Don Carlo to lie on the couch. Perfunctory and casual at first, his examination became more intense as he palpated and prodded Don Carlo's abdomen and his nimble and practiced fingers outlined the patient's internal organs. He examined Don Carlo's fingernails, tongue and eyeballs and finished with a rectal examination, an unpleasant and undignified experience for the patient. The consultation took twenty minutes and, at the end, Don Carlo had a premonition that something serious had been diagnosed by the Professor.

"What is wrong with me Il Professore?"

The thin-faced specialist readjusted the glasses on the tip of his nose and looked over the rims.

"I have to tell you some bad news, Signore Cecci. I am sorry to say you have cancer of the liver."

Don Carlo g lped and bowed his head.

"How bad is it Professore Natale?"

"It's fairly advanced but you still have good liver function," the specialist volunteered. Don Carlo sat up straight in his chair.

"Is there any treatment? Can an operation cure me?"

Professore Natale shook his head "Surgery will not cure you. I will give you a bottle of medicine which will help to control your pain. Arrange for one of your gabelotti to pick up supplies when they come to market. I'm sorry I cannot do more for you. I suggest you put your affairs in order."

Don Carlo Cecci stood to take his leave and, at the door, turned to face the medical specialist.

"How long have I got Professore Natale?"

"Six months, probably nine" the professor replied and added "you will know when things are getting out of hand when your skin and eyeballs go yellow."

The professor shook hands with Don Carlo who looked the specialist straight in the eye. "Thank you Doctore Natale."

The harassed professor immediately turned on his heel and rushed off to attend to the growing queue of clamouring casualties in his surgery.

Don Carlo trudged wearily along Via Roma and wondered why he had thanked the professor for giving him a life sentence? Utterly dejected, exhausted and short of breath he made a pathetic figure as he dragged himself slowly down Via Vittorio Emanuele, pulling two mules behind him. The Via was crowded with people who stared at Don Carlo but most were still in shock and, in the excitement of having survived the bombardment, a skinny old man and his rough-coated mules were of limited curiosity. He was all-in by the time he reached Palazzo Sclafani. In answer to his bell-ringing a guard opened the heavy door and, when he saw the scruffy peasant, made dismissive signs with his hands. Don Carlo propped himself against the door and again rang the bell until Don Triddu Caminiti himself appeared at the courtyard gateway.

"Goodness me Don Carlo. What on earth has happened to you?"

Don Carlo could not muster enough energy to reply. The guards carried him to a bedroom where he drank a generous dose from his laudanum bottle and, completely exhausted, he fell into a fitful sleep. The last thing he remembered was Don Triddu's distant voice proclaiming "We'll sort things out tomorrow."

It was nearly 10 o'clock in the morning before Don Carlo felt well enough to face Palermo's Capo de Tutti Capi. He refused food and a glass of wine for breakfast and drank a glass of plain water and another generous measure of his morphine-based medicine.

"You look terrible, Don Carlo. I have arranged for a doctor to call later this morning."

Don Carlo held up his hand.

"Thank you, Padrone. That will not be necessary. I saw Professore Abrigo Natale yesterday and he gave me some bad news. I have a cancer in my liver and only about six months to live."

Don Triddu's face dropped and, in a sympathetic whisper, he asked "Can anything be done?"

"No," Don Carlo replied, "the only treatment is this bottle of medicine which controls my pain."

There was a long, awkward pause broken by Don Triddu "What will happen at Godrano?"

"That's why I'm here and I need your advice. As you are aware I have three daughters and no males to inherit my estate. We need a strong man at Godrano. I'm sure the Corleonese would oblige but I don't want anything to do with them. Is there anyone in Palermo who might take over from me? Whatever happens it will need to be arranged in the next two or three months."

The Provincial Don was near to tears. He looked with sympathy at his ailing compatriot.

"You are a brave and loyal Family man Don Carlo Cecci and I honour you for thinking about the Cosa Nostra when you are so sick. For a year or two I've given thought to the future of Godrano. Your podere is, after all is said and done, the chief supplier to my markets in Vucciria and we need to keep Godrano in the Family. My main concern at the moment is with the Corleone dons who are making a bid to take over Palermo. You will recall Angelo Muzzi who ran Sant Agata? Well, he's now a real danger and the Corleonese are using him as a hitman. I dare not venture into their territory and guard myself at all times. Up to now Godrano has been a buffer state between Palermo and Corleone and you will see, therefore, that maintaining a sympathetic don at Godrano is in everyone's interest. Are you with me so far?"

Don Carlo sat up with a start. His head had been drooping and his shoulders sagging and he was halfway between consciousness and oblivion.

"I appreciate your situation Don Triddu. I also have a problem at Godrano. The mafiosi you asked me to protect two years ago are becoming a dangerous liability. They behave irresponsibly and are paying too much attention to my daughters. I am here to request their removal as I fear they may bring the mili ary police, or Tunica Negra agents, to Godrano. I hope you did not have these two in mind to replace me?"

Don Triddu sat in deep thought for a full minute.

"I shall arrange for your difficult mafiosi to be removed and sent elsewhere. As far as your replacement is concerned I wish to unite Sant Agata and Godrano estates. In order to keep your family interest in Godrano I propose your eldest daughter marry Giovanni Cucinotta's eldest boy who would then become Don of Godrano. Andreo is a Man of Honour and will make a good husband for Anna. At the same time you may wish to unite Gina with Santo, Don Giovanni's second son. I can see it would be a good match. With two married daughters to the Cucinotta's, and when Don Giovanni passes on, you will have your blood line in both estates. That can only be to the benefit of both Families and the Cosa Nostra.".

Don Carlo was speechless and the thought of uniting with the Cucinottas filled him with revulsion. He was breathing heavily and his parched mouth was wide open. He took a gulp of cold water and the waves of nausea returned with a vengeance. Eventually he heard himself say "This is a difficult decision to make. Can I have time to think it over?"

The Provincial Don's demeanour changed from sympathy to authority.

"No, Don Carlo! You know we don't have much time. You have

consulted me on this matter and my final decision is your daughters will unite in marriage with the Cucinotta brothers. That is an order."

Don Carlo understood the protocol and the interview was over. He stood unsteadily on his feet and started to sway. Don Triddu sprang to his side and led him gently back to his bedroom with the parting words "Rest again today, Don Carlo. We'll bring you some food and broth and I'm sure you'll be able to return to Godrano tomorrow."

When morning came Don Carlo was not well-enough to ride his mule and one of Don Triddu's lieutenants drove him to Godrano in a battered old Fiat. As the car was about to move off from Palazzo Sclafani, and certain he was seeing his lifelong comrade for the last time, Don Triddu kissed Don Carlo on both cheeks and whispered "Don't forget to make the arrangements we agreed as soon as possible."

Little did he realise at that moment the frail old man lying on the back seat of the rickety old Fiat would outlive him by seven months.

Sunday, 23rd May 1943.

Flanked by two of his lieutenants, and shepherding five of his womenfolk, Don Triddu Caminiti emerged into bright sunshine through a portico of Palermo's cathedral on to a marble, baroque-style landing. A cardinal stood outside the portico and solemnly shook hands with the Capo and escorted his entourage to the top of the thirty stone steps leading down to Via Papireto. As he walked along Don Triddu reflected he would have been worshiping at San Domenica on Via Roma that morning had Allied bombers not destroyed half the church during the 10th.May raid. He preferred the more serene atmosphere of San Domenica to the overpowering grandeur of the 14th century cathedral with its

Islamic façade and gloomy Gothic interior. He took a pair of tinted sunglasses from his coat pocket and began descending the steps. Ahead of him a milling throng of worshipers — men, women and children, all dressed in Sunday best — cluttered the steps, chattering and smoking in the warm sunshine. As Don Triddu approached they parted to allow his party to pass through. He stopped to readjust his sunglasses and, at that very moment, three well-dressed men holding sawn-off shotguns stood ten steps below the startled don. The screaming and shouting started instantaneously as the gunmen opened fire and the entire execution happened in the winking of an eye. Don Triddu was blown backwards by the first blasts and his two lieutenants fell at his side. The cardinal sank to his knees clutching his blood-stained cassock and Don Triddu's wife and her sister were thrown sideways by the fusillade of gunshots. The gunmen turned and fled down the steps into Via Vittorio Emanuele and disappeared into the Albergheria leaving behind a scene of carnage on the cathedral's blood-stained steps. Don Triddu and one of his lieutenants, both shot in the chest, lay dying. The second gabelotti had a shattered shoulder and the cardinal was on his knees, as if in prayer, clutching a gaping wound in his abdomen with blood streaming down his vermillion cassock. A priest was administering the last rites to Don Triddu's wife and another black-garbed female lay dead in pool of her own blood at the side of the kneeling, moaning cardinal. The once-happy Sunday worshipers were grim-faced and silent as the shock of seeing death at close quarters took effect and they began to hurry away from the scene of the massacre. Many had seen such incidents before and realised the killing they had witnessed that morning was a Mafia vendetta. Who had perpetrated it, and why, was none of their concern and they knew better than to poke their noses into Mafia business. In their heart of hearts they also knew the Cosa Nostra would close ranks and protect the identity of the assassins. Better to leave the mess for the Carabinieri to sort out and, as they slunk away, the police began arriving in large numbers but they were too late to apprehend the killers.

Angelo Muzzi and his companions arrived back triumphantly in Corleone on the Wednesday after the assassination. The dons who put out the contract on Don Triddu were immensely pleased by the success of their mission. By his actions Angelo Muzzi had achieved two goals. He had obtained personal revenge on Don Triddu Caminiti for evicting him from Portella Sant Agata and he had removed the main obstacle for a Corleonese takeover of Palermo Province. The date of the assassination, however, was ill-timed and, within two months of the atrocity, another major factor came into play. On 10th July 1943 the Allies invaded Sicily and another foreign power came to occupy the island for three years.

Don Carlo's recovery after his return from Palermo took longer than expected and for the first fortnight he was confined to bed. With judicious feeding, and Professore Natale's laudanum, he came downstairs in the first week in June and started taking an interest in the affairs of his messadria. The decisions he had to make were c nstantly on his mind. He could have used the murder of Don Triddu as an excuse to absolve him from the marriage pact but the agreement he shook hands on in Palazzo Scalfani was binding and sacrosanct. When he was bedridden Franco and Salvatore had moved into the big house lock, stock and barrel and mixed freely with his daughters. This Don Carlo could not tolerate and he ordered the mafiosi out of his house. They retreated to their hilltop hideout near Cefala and were only allowed back for supper, the main meal of the day. The one person concerned about their banishment was Carla. Now seventeen years of age, she was blossoming into womanhood and had developed a teenage crush on Franco, whom she idolised from afar. Given the opportunity Don Carlo feared she might allow matters to progress further. Dealing with the mafiosi was one of Don Carlo's headaches and the second was his word of honour to Don Triddu which entailed coming face to face with his hated neighbour at Portella Sant Agata. By mid-June Don Carlo made up his mind to pay a call on Giovanni Cucinotta with a double-marriage proposal.

After a thirteen-day aerial bombardment Italian forces on Pantelleria surrendered without a fight to a British seaborne landing, quickly followed by Lampedusa on 13th June 1943. In Sicily, where there were 230,000 Italian troops and 40,000 Germans including the XV Panzer Grenadier division, defenders were put on red alert and an Allied assault on the south coast was expected daily. Don Carlo Cecci's personal dilemma far outweighed his worries about an invasion and he came to a final decision at supper on Sunday 20th June. Sunday's evening meal was always an important occasion in the Cecci household. Don Carlo sat at the head of the wooden kitchen table, silent and brooding, as he listened to Franco's braggadocio and watched him openly flirting with Carla. His nerves were taut and his head ached as he toyed with a bowl of meat broth and a hunk of rye bread. Short-temperedly he pushed his soup plate aside and glared at his daughter and the mafioso.

"Tomorrow I shall call to see the Don at Sant Agata. You Franco and Salvatore will accompany me. We must set out at daybreak and I suggest you leave now. Goodnight." and he shuffled away from the table. He had only gone a few paces when Franco piped up with an expectant note in his voice "Will we be taking our shotguns Don Carlo?"

The old man paused and leant against the door frame.

"I see no reason to take guns. It will be a peaceful visit. In any case it will be unwise to go armed with all these Germans on the roads."

Franco was crestfallen. He was spoiling for a fight and the

Cucinotta boys were fair game. Covertly the young mafiosi agreed to carry knives strapped to their shins for their foray into 'enemy' territory. And now they had to leave the women. The old don was hovering near the doorway and would not budge until they had left through the back door. The elder sisters started clearing the table but Carla sat staring at Franco's vacated chair. Franco was becoming very aware of Carla's interest in him and, as they walked towards their hideout, he confided in Salvatore "I think Carla has a crush on me. Have you seen the way she sighs and looks at me? What do you think Salvatore? She's thin and bony but I love her dark-brown eyes. If I get a chance I'll have a go at her."

Not to be outdone in braggadocio, Salvatore replied "I like the other one, Gina. She's got a nice bottom and lovely breasts and she's a lot of fun. I could have a good time with Gina."

The mafiosi walked on in silence for a hundred yards engulfed in sexual fantasies about their respective paramours. Franco broke the silence "I wonder why the old man is going to see Don Giovanni. I hope it's nothing to do with us. If we play our cards right we could become bosses at Godrano. The old man is skin and bone and will soon pass on. Then we'll be the only mafiosi to run the place and we'll have the girls to ourselves." The slow-thinking Salvatore took a minute to digest his friend's words "I suppose you are right, Franco. We may find out tomorrow."

Astride their mules, the three men left as dawn was breaking and the sun's lukewarm rays were penetrating the fine mist which shrouded Godrano valley. Franco led the way and Salvatore brought up the rear with Don Carlo, hunched on his mule, riding between the mafiosi. Even at this early hour they passed silent figures on foot, or astride mules, workers on their way to the fields for another long day of back-breaking toil. By the time they reached Bivio Lupo and the Marineo/Corleone road the whole countryside was bathed in bright sunshine. Here they encountered their first military convoy, an Italian gun battery proceeding southwards to Corleone. After a mile they swung acutely northwards along Lake Scanzano's west bank and the road deviated and wound its way steeply uphill for four miles to Portella Sant Agata. At an acute bend, a mile north of the village, their progress was impeded by two armed Sicilians standing in the middle of the road barring their way. The smaller of the two men asked "Who are you and where do you go?"

Don Carlo lifted his head and spoke with authority "I am Don Carlo Cecci, Padrone of Godrano, and I'm on my way to see Don Giovanni Cucinotta."

The spokesman scowled "Are you armed?"

Don Carlo shrugged his shoulders.

"You can see we have no shotguns. My mission is peaceful. Let us through."

The hard-faced gabelotti relented.

"Very well. We will lead you to Don Giovanni's podere. We have an hour's climb uphill. Follow me."

Cucinotta's gabelotti hardly spoke a word on their journey uphill. They reached the gates of Sant Agata just before 10 o'clock. Don Carlo was all-in and was helped off his mule by Salvotre and, making a valiant effort to straighten up, he walked up the driveway to his adversary's front door. The armed gabelotti stood guard on each side of the gateway while Franco and Salvatore retreated to a citrus grove on the other side of the road and sat under a lime tree, glaring insolently at the guards and fingering their sheath knives and wishing they had been allowed to carry shotguns.

Smartly dressed in a clean white shirt and an embroidered waistcoat, Don Giovanni greeted his neighbour politely and, after a perfunctory handshake, guided Don Carlo by his matchstick-thin foreman through the cool interior of the house to a shaded patio where they sat three feet apart on each side of a wooden table. Never having met,they sized each other up for half a minute. Don

Giovanni had dark hair, balding at the crown, a pointed aquiline nose and deep-set, dark, darting eyes. On the other hand, Don Carlo had a weather-beaten, cracked face, dark-green eyes and a mop of unruly grey hair. Somewhere in his ancestry, Norman genes had been introduced into the Cecci lineage. Wine and pickled olives were offered and declined and Don Giovanni opened the batting

"And to what do I owe the honour of this visit, Don Carlo?"

The older man's lips and mouth were parched and an attempt to reply died in a throaty croak. He took a mouthful of tepid water and Don Giovanni spoke again before he could reply "I expect you've come to discuss plans of action if the Ami's, or the British,come to Sicily? I can see your predicament. Your gabelotti will take off the moment the soldiers arrive. I shall be guarded by my three sons and you'll be helpless at Godrano."

Don Carlo shook his head vigorously and gulped down a mouthful of water.

"I am not worried about the Americanis or the British. They may well be more sympathetic to us than Mussolin's Tunica Negra. My health is failing and I'm worried about the future of Godrano. Before his assassination Don Triddu proposed our families should unite. I am here to offer my two elder daughter's hands in marriage to your sons, Andreo and Santo, and Godrano and my blood will pass into your Family when I am gone. If we come to an agreement the weddings will have to be soon."

Don Giovanni's haughty demeanour mellowed rapidly. His main ambition when he moved into Sant Agata was to acquire Godrano estate for his Family and now he was being handed the property on a plate. He leant forwards and his piercing black eyes were alive with greed.

"Does your proposal include your three daughters?"

Don Carlo pondered the question for a few seconds.

"Anna and Gina have been running my household since the death of my wife and will make excellent brides for your eldest sons. Carla is but a girl and too young to marry. An engagement perhaps and marriage in a few years. Is this agreeable to you?"

The dons rose and clasped hands and a marriage pact was solemnised by the handshake. Don Carlo was on the point of passing out but forced himself to speak "I have an urgent matter at Godrano which needs attention. Two mafiosi, who are with me today, have an eye on Godrano and possibly my daughters. I discussed them with Don Triddu-------"

Eyes flashing, Don Giovanni interjected "I presume, Don Carlo, your daughters are virgins?"

Don Carlo was offended and replied in a hurt tone "I assure you I have protected their virginity. Franco Gicanetti and Salvatore Branco are an embarrassment and I must be rid of them before the weddings take place. Before he died Don Triddu was going to move them and, at the moment, they are out of my house but they show little inclination to leave Godrano."

The Sant Agata don was lost in thought for a full minute.

"Maybe the invasion, when it comes, will solve your problem. If not, and with your permission, I will send my gabelotti to Godrano to eject them. From what I've heard your mafiosi are full of braggadocio and we should have no trouble in sending them packing."

The dons shook hands again and agreed to keep their bargain a secret until the renegades were out of the way and in no position to ruin their plans.

In the heat of the mid-afternoon sun the journey back to Godrano was extremely taxing on Don Carlo's strength and temper. Franco kept bombarding him with questions but he remained tight-lipped and his daughters knew better than to probe into the reason for his visit to Portella Sant Agata. That was man's work and the outcome of the visit was in man's domain. Every morning the sick old don looked into a cracked mirror in his bedroom for the tell-tale signs of jaundice which would, almost certainly, herald his demise. Day after day he struggled on and prayed, hoping against hope his skin and sclerotics would remain white for a few weeks longer.

An air of anticipation and foreboding descended on Sicily during the first week in July 1943 and increasing air activity and bombing sorties on Catania, Messina and Palermo heightened the tension among the island's defenders. When would the Allies come and where would they strike? Anticipating trouble Franco and Salvatore retired to their hilltop cave. The workers in the fields became nervous and absenteeism was rife. Food convoys to Palermo ceased and tons of perishable goods went waste. The whole island was like a timebomb waiting to explode and the explosion came, with a big bang, at dawn on 10th July 1943.

`CHAPTER 3

Don Mario Deluca's gofer

THE SON OF SICILIAN IMMIGRANTS, Alphonse Rizzi was born in a three-roomed tenement flat in the Bronx in May 1922. His father worked in a meat-packing factor and became a semi-professional boxer, tipped by a few columnists to reach world championship level. Known as 'Kid Rizzi' he fought for New York State's welterweight championship in 1932. The fight was 'fixed' by a New Jersey syndicate and the Kid took a dive in the tenth round. Thereafter, managed and cheated by a succession of unscrupulous promoters, he began sliding into obscurity and his fights degenerated into small-time brawls and beatings became a regular occurrence. After his last bout in May 1934, when he was knocked senseless and remained in a coma for four days, Vittorio Rizzi constantly talked about a comeback but, by the time Alphonse was thirteen years of age, he was unemployed, punch-drunk and a drunkard. The Rizzi family had come full circle from poverty to relative wealth and back to poverty and were again destitute and penniless. Vittorio was killed in a hit-and-run car accident in 1936 and, thereafter, fourteen year old Alphonse became the breadwinner and supporter to his mother and two sisters. He reached maturity and responsibility at an early age.

By 1938 America was well-clear of a world recession but jobs were still at a premium and Alphonse had to compete with older men in the labour market. Casual jobs at a nearby meat-packing factory and a brewery were few and far between and his income came almost entirely from petty crime. Nicknamed 'Al the Wop', or simply ' The Wop', he was taller in stature and stockier than boys of his own age and commanded respect from his peers, becoming leader of an Italian neighbourhood gang. They roamed the streets at night, and at weekends, pilfering and offering protection for parked vehicles. Refusal to pay resulted in slashed tyres, smashed windshields or grit in petrol tanks. Clashes with the police were infrequent and most of Al's gang were street-wise and cunning and avoided arrest. Anyone caught by the Law was bound by a code of secrecy and, such was Al's influence over his Mob, no one grassed and he was never charged with any of the crimes he had committed. Other youth gangs operated in the Bronx and scuffles and fist-fights with Irish, Jewish and Polish hoodlums were frequent and governed by an unwritten law of conduct. Knives and firearms were taboo. Not so with the Hispanics and blacks in Haarlem where stabbings and gangland shootouts were commonplace. Increasingly disillusioned with returns from his criminal activities Al decided to operate on his own. His apprenticeship in the Bronx stood him in good stead and he became an expert in the 'tricks of thieving'. Al's speciality was car theft, not of the vehicle itself but any valuables left by a negligent owner inside the car or in the trunk. For the purposes of his trade, and for protection, he carried a stout jemmy strapped inside his left thigh.

Al's break into the bigtime came on one drizzly damp night in April 1939 He was patrolling the Brooklyn bank of East river, down a dimly-lit alley off Tillary Street, when he noticed a yellow and black Cadillac coupe parked 80 yards away from the main thoroughfare. A quick glance confirmed the alley was deserted and on the car's back seat he saw a lady's white fur jacket and a gent's grey Astrakhan, overcoat. To Al's amazement the car door was unlocked and, in a flash, he was inside the vehicle. He gathered up the coats and, using his jemmy, he prised open the trunk. Hidden underneath a thick woollen blanket he found two Thompson submachine guns and boxes of ammunition. He left the guns untouched and slammed the trunk shut. He then wrapped the fur coat inside the Astrakhan and beat a hasty retreat down the alley and up the main approach road to Brooklyn Bridge. Al was a scared young man. The Cadillac evidently belonged to a gangster and, if he were caught in possession of the goods, retribution could be swift and possibly fatal. He crossed into Manhatan and walked swiftly up Frankfort Street and, skirting to the east of Chinatown, he came to a busy sidewalk on Park Row. So far luck was with Al and he had avoided running into rival gangs or the police who regularly patrolled downtown Manhattan. But as he approached Duane Street he saw a group of thugs lounging nonchalantly under a lamp post on his side of the road. A sixth sense warned him there was trouble ahead and he needed to take evasive action. He dashed across the busy street and made a beeline for a brightly-lit restaurant at the junction of Chatham and Bowery, closely followed by three hoodlums. Breathless, and in a panic, he pushed his way through the frosted plate-glass door of Ristorante Berterelli.

Ristorante Berterelli is an old-established eating joint popular with inhabitants of the Italian quarter in Manhattan. Once inside the vestibule Al took stock of his surroundings. On his right hand side was a long bar with an array of optics and beer pumps and attended by two barmen. The body of the restaurant before him was cubicleised and a score of blue-aproned waiters scurried to and fro between the dining booths. Al stood transfixed. This was a classy joint and he had better get out and fast. He was retreating towards the entrance when a fat, round-faced, bald-headed barman,sporting a waxed moustache, bellowed "Hey, you bum! Whadda ya want? You can't come in here dressed like that!"

Al was about to apologise and leave when he thought 'What the hell I've got nothing to lose'.

"I wanna see the Boss."

The barman eyed him up and down.

"I'm the boss here buddy. So get lost!" and, as an afterthought, he added "Whadda ya got inside the overcoat?"

Al saw his chance.

"I've got a couple of classy coats here. Would you like to see them?"

The barman's curiosity was roused. He motioned Al to follow him into a dimly-lit stockroom packed from floor to ceiling with crates of beer and spirits and rack upon rack of neatly-stacked wine bottles.

"Show me buddy."

Al unwrapped his bundle. The barman inspected the goods.

"Are they the real McCoy? Where did ya get 'em?"

"They're genuine," Al replied, "the coats were left by my grandmother who died last week."

"Tell it to the friggin marines, sonny. I'll give fifty bucks for the mink and twenty-five for the overcoat."

Al was unsure of his bargaining power.

"I want two hundred for the mink and a hundred for the coat."

"Forget it" the barman replied with a shrug of his shoulders but, realizing they were two valuable garments, greed overcame his natural caution with money.

"Okay buddy! I'll make it two hundred bucks for the two."

"It's a deal" Al replied. As Al made his way to the exit, clutching the dollar bills in his breast pocket, the barman delivered a parting salvo "I don't wanna see you around here again, kid, unless you got some merchandise. If you call again get yourself a decent jacket. You stink!"

The barman had hardly resumed his position behind the bar-counter when he was summoned to an open-ended cubicle opposite the bar by a well-dressed, pear-shaped man dining alone.

"What was that all about, Joe?"

Joe stood in front of the fat man's table and replied "The hoodlum sold me two coats, Don Mario. I paid three hundred bucks for them. You can have them if you wanna, Padrone."

Don Mario Deluca waddled across to the stockroom and inspected the coats.

"You done well Joe. I'll take the mink for a friend and you can get rid of the Astrakhan. Did you know the minks' not a mink? It's ermine".

Joe was suitably impressed and pointed out an identification tab inside the Astrakhan – 'A.Andretti.' The fat man burst out laughing, his jowls and fatty abdominal folds shaking like jelly.

"That kid don't know how lucky he is. He's pulled a fast one on Antonio Andretti. Antonio will kill him if he finds out but we won't tell him will we Joe?" Don Mario queried as his laughter subsided and his voice became sharp and menacing.

"No, Padrone," Joe replied, "my lips are sealed."

Don Antonio Andretti was an unscrupulous Italian immigrant who was pushing to expand his empire from the Bronx into Manhattan where Don Mario Deluca owned two seedy hotels, a steam laundry and two restaurants. Berterellis', near Brooklyn Bridge, was his flagship. He resumed his cubicle seat and pondered why Andretti had been dining in the Chinese quarter in Manhattan? Was the weasel collaborating with the Chinks in order to gain a foothold in Manhattan? Don Mario levied money from all the Italian restaurants and enterprises on Manhattan Island and the Chinese had their own extortion syndicate. So far they had acted independently but if Andretti was nosing around he would have to nip matters in the bud. As Joe was about to leave the cubicle Don Mario asked "What's the kid's name, Joe?"

"I dunno,Boss. He was just a hoodlum off the street."

"Well," Don Mario said, "if he comes in again get his name. I wanna speak to him. Is he Italian?"

Joe confessed he did not know.

Within a week Al was back in Ristorante Berterelli. On this occasion he was smartly dressed in a baggy black suit with wide, padded shoulders, a white shirt and red necktie and black patent-leather shoes with white toecaps. He had purchased the whole ensemble from a Jewish pawnbroker for twelve dollars and, fully dressed, he resembled a miniature Al Capone. The restaurant was busy with evening diners and patrons, good- naturedly chattering and jostling around the crowded bar. Al pushed his way to the front and threw a 50 cent coin on to the shiny, mahogany counter. The bald- headed barman appeared in a flash.

"What'll it be?"

"Gimme a beer," Al requested. Joe pulled a pint of frothing lager and picked up the coin.

"Keep the change buddy" Al commanded.

"Sure thing" Joe replied and, suddenly recognising Al, "Hey kid what's up? Any merchandise?"

Al shook his head and took a generous gulp of his beer.

"What's your name, sonny?" the barman requested.

"Who wants to know?" Al retorted.

"Don't you come the wiseguy with me you friggin punk" the barman snarled as he moved down the bar to serve another customer. He was back in a few minutes and again faced Al "Look wiseguy! My boss wants to know your name."

Al knew he was getting the better of the big barman.

"In that case I'll give my name to your boss."

Don Mario Deluca sat alone in his favourite open-ended cubicle where he could keep an eye on his customers and staff. An empty plate lay in front of him and a Bolognese-stained napkin was tucked inside his white collar. He held a glass of wine in one hand and a fat cigar in the other. Joe pushed Al forwards into the cubicle.

"Boss. This is the guy you wanted to meet."

Don Mario removed the napkin at his throat, pushed his plate away and, at the same time, indicated with a wave of his cigar for Al to take a seat at his table.

"What do they call you son?"

"Alphonse Rizzi" Al replied nervously.

Don Mario's broad globular face creased in a quizzical smile

"Related to Kid Rizzi, the middleweight?"

"My father" Al replied.

"He was a good 'un," Don Mario continued, "I made a few bucks on his fights. So you're Italian."

"No, Sicilian" Al replied.

The Don's podgy face again broke into a wide grin as he recognised the youth's pride in his Sicilian ancestry though he had never set foot in Sicily, or Italy for that matter. Don Mario puffed at his cigar and inspected his manicured finger nails.

"I like your style Alphonse. How would you like to work for me as a gofer? The money's good."

Al could not believe his ears.

"Yes please,sir. When do I start?"

"Right now" the fat man replied and delved into a brief-case on the seat beside him and pushed a brown paper parcel, wrapped in string, across the dinner table.

"I wanna you deliver this package to the address on the card at 11 o'clock tomorrow morning. Here's ten bucks for your expenses. Don't come looking like a gangster and dress casual. Off you go kid."

Al pocketed the parcel and the ten dollar note and made a rapid exit from the booth. At the counter he called Joe and ordered another beer.

"Who's the big guy in the restaurant?"

"Don't you know him?" Joe asked in amazement "he's Mr Deluca. I guess you've heard of him?"

Al was dumbstruck. He knew Mr Deluca by name to be a notorious New York gangster. He walked home to the Bronx with buoyant steps continually mumbling to himself 'Yes siree! I'm working for Mr Deluca, the most powerful man in Manhattan, if not the whole of New York. Yes siree! I'm in the bigtime.'

Alphonese Rizzi was up early the following day and the 'valuable' package was secreted inside his underpants. Twice during the night he considered inspecting its contents but resisted temptation. The address on the package was a tenth floor penthouse apartment in a luxury block of flats in Howards, an upmarket residential district of Manhattan. The doorbell was answered by a swarthy young man dressed in a black suit and wearing sunglasses.

"Yeah. What d'ya want?"

"I was hired to deliver a package" Al said with trepidation.

"Come in. You're expected" and, without asking permission, the guard expertly frisked Al and removed his sheath knife.

"You won't be needing this, mister" the guard said and ordered Al to follow him into a spacious lounge with panoramic views over the Hudson River.

"Sit," the guard ordered and left the room. Ten minutes later he returned and flicked his thumb sideways, indicating Al to follow him through a side door into a darkened billiard room. Suddenly the billiard table was illuminated and Don Mario Deluca stood at one end, his corpulent eighteen stone frame covered by a gaudy, voluminous, red dressing gown. He held out his right hand in greeting and his gold and diamond signet rings sparkled in the phosphorescent light.

"You made it Alphonse. Gimme the packet."

Don Mario Deluca inspected the brown paper parcel minutely before exposing its contents – about fifty sheets of newsprint cut into the shape and size of dollar bills. He looked across at Al with a wicked glint in his eyes "Well done Alphonse! You've passed the test. I'll use you again as errand boy. By the way, how old are you?"

"Nineteen" Al lied, adding two years to his proper age. Don Mario produced a twenty dollar bill and threw it on the green baize table.

"Here's a few bucks for your delivery. Keep in touch with me at Berterelli's. Show Alphonse out Dino."

Dino returned Al's sheath-knife at the door and he was halfway down to the ground floor before he realised he had been subjected to a test of character by Mr Deluca. He mouthed a silent prayer of thanks he had not succumbed to the temptation of opening the package as, if he had done so, he suspected Deluca's gorilla would feature prominently in dishing out punishment. A potential wiseguy, or so he thought in his daydream, Alphonse strolled light-heartedly through Times Square and passed Madison Square Garden, where his father had featured in many boxing promotions, and into Central Park. He sat daydreaming on a wooden bench and ate a hotdog. His future was rosy and he saw himself and his mother and sisters moving from their grotty Bronx flat into a luxurious apartment on Manhattan Island. His daydreams, at least, cost him nothing.

For three and half years, from April 1939 to September 1942, Alphonse Rizzi acted as gofer and general factotum for Don Mario Deluca. His base was Ristorante Berterelli where the Boss dined four nights a week, mostly alone, sometimes with a smartly-dressed lady and sometimes with one or two of his ever- present henchmen. Very quickly Al became friendly with Giuseppe Falcone, otherwise known as Big Joe, who taught him the tricks of the trade, how to water down spirits, overcharge customers and extort tips from clients. Al was dependent on Don Mario for his income and Deluca was inordinately generous most of the time but, depending on his mood, he could be incredibly mean. Alphonse quickly learnt when to approach the Boss and when to steer clear and he avoided the smoke-filled cubicle when the Boss was entertaining strangers or one of his regular ladyfriends. As gofer he frequently delivered handguns and the odd grenade to various hotels and apartments in New York City and, on Fridays, he collected handouts and packages from bars and restaurants in Brooklyn and Manhattan and, occasionally, across the Hudson in New Jersey. When the European conflict broke out in September

1939 Alphonse was a regular doorman at Berterelli's. He wore a gold-braided navy cap and a long dark navy-blue overcoat with gleaming brass buttons. He had grown into a handsome dark-haired young man and caught the eye when dressed in his doorman's regalia. He helped guests out of their automobiles and ushered them into Berterelli's, invariably receiving a tip for his services. The big tippers were directed to Big Joe's station at the bar and Joe, in turn, made sure the diners were waited upon by his younger brother, Nico. They worked as a team, milking the wealthier customers and sharing the night's profits on a seniority basis, 50% for Big Joe, 35% for Nico Falcone and 15% for Al. In the event of trouble Joe has a concealed button underneath the bar which activated a buzzer in the Boss' private cubicle. When the buzzer sounded Don Mario and his guests left the cubicle immediately and locked themselves in a strongroom at the far end of the restaurant. During his apprenticeship Al saw no violence or shootings at the restaurant but stories of gangland warfare between Italians, Jews, Irish and Poles were rife. He soon came to realise his Boss was a big noise in New York's Mafia but information about the Mafia from Big Joe was not forthcoming. Joe and his brother Nico were both members of the Secret Society. Al had to be content with sitting on the sidelines. He dreamt one day of becoming a fully-fledged member of the Cosa Nostra and had grandiose visions of becoming Boss in Manhattan just like Don Mario Deluca, his mentor and paymaster at Berterelli's.

Alphonse Rizzi's blooding into the violence associated with Mafia gangsterism occurred one dark, misty November night in 1941. Sheltering from the rain under a blue and white canopy he was at his station outside the restaurant when a group of six inebriated naval cadets baled out of a taxi and came face to face with Al. One saluted him and asked for permission to come aboard which produced peals of raucous laughter from his buddies. Inside Berterelli's Al could hear their loud voices and merriment and half-wished he could be inside, out of the rain, in the company of the jolly sailors when Big Joe Falcone came through the door with a worried look on his f ce "Anything suspicious out here Al?"

"No," Al replied, "I can hardly see across the road. There's been a black limo parked under the lamp post outside Denman's store for over an hour. Are the sailors causing trouble? They were a bit high when I let them in."

"Yes and no," Joe replied, "one of the cadets is a bit out of line and we can't take any chances. The Boss is in tonight with a lady guest. Go to our garage and get the Boss' driver to bring a car to the back alley. Then get yourself inside the restaurant. Do that now."

Big Joe was worried about one of the naval cadets who claimed to be Antonio Andretti's nephew. Drunken and loud-mouthed the young officer was proclaiming in a loud voice "Uncle Antonio's moll is in here somewhere and he's out to get her. If we hang around guys there'll be some fireworks."

When Al re-entered Berterelli's Jo Falcone was at the Boss' cubicle door and motioned him to join two armed bodyguards, Don Mario Deluca and a strapping, busty bottle-blond hanging on to the Boss' forearm. The hooker was giggling and pleasantly drunk, not aware of the seriousness of her situation. Don Mario's podgy face was ashen and his sunken, deep-set black eyes were ablaze with anger. Big Joe Falcone assumed command and issued orders.

"Enzio and I will go first. You follow with Miss Cindy, Padrone, and Al and Vittorio will walk behind you. We're all going down to the strong room. Let's move now."

The small party shuffled down the aisle in a tightly-knit group. Some diners stopped eating and looked up inquisitively at the owner of Berterelli's with a giggling blonde by his side being shepherded towards the kitchen. Others looked away and continued their meal with disinterest whilst the inebriated cadet's voice was heard above the din "There goes the tart. There goes Miss Cindy. Ain't she got lovely legs and tits?"

His cronies burst into raucous laughter and started jeering.

Inside the locked strong room Big Joe reacted with haste. He ordered Al to remove his cap and put on Don Andretti's grey Astrakhan overcoat. The fit was nowhere near perfect but, with his own coat as an underlay, the larger coat merged with the contours of his muscular frame. The Boss' grey trilby was placed firmly on his head and, for effect, a half-smoked Havana cigar was thrust between his left index and forefinger. The Boss faced Al "Take Miss Cindy home. My driver knows where to go. Don't leave her at the kerbside but take her into her apartment and make sure she's locked in safely" and, turning towards his tiddly lady-friend, he said "Cindy honey! Al Rizzi will take you home. I'll ring you tomorrow."

The blonde goddess, swaying slightly and smiling inanely, tried to press her heavily-painted lips against the Don's cheek. He brushed her aside roughly and Al guided her by the elbow out through a steel delivery door into a back alleyway and into the back seat of a waiting Buick saloon. Before they had time to settle in their seats the automobile started off with a jerk and turned left alongside East River heading towards Queens. The Buick saloon was closely shadowed by a black limo which had been parked at the kerbside outside Denman's store.

Back in the strong room Don Mario eyed Big Joe "What's it all about Joe?"

"Andretti's boys are on the prowl. There's a sailor at the bar shouting his mouth off. Say's he's related to Andretti. Sounds as if Miss Cindy is Andretti's private property."

Don Mario's stern face relaxed "I guessed as much. Cindy's been knocking about for a while. I wonder if she was planted? Tell you what to do. Enzio and Vittorio will go to the back alley and you see if you can get the loud- mouthed son-of-a-bitch outside in ten minutes. Enzio and Vittorio will then take him for a ride and dump him outside Andretti's apartment. Now let's get o 1 with it" and, as an afterthought, he added "I wonder if young Rizzi can look after himself?"

Big Joe reassured his boss that the eager-faced gofer could cope with the situation. Joe Falcone returned to his bar and offered free drinks to the gallant naval officers which were accepted amid loud applause. The mouthy matelot was still shouting obscenities and Joe took him aside and whispered "I wouldn't drink no more, son. You'll want to be fit for the job ahead. One of my waitresses fancies you. She's off duty now and is waiting for you outside the restaurant. Don't keep her waiting. Her name's Louise."

The young cadet stood to attention, wiped a sliver of spittle from the corner of his mouth, picked up his cap and gave a mock naval salute.

"To the US Navy and USS Louise and all who sail in her" and, turning on his heel, he staggered out of Berterelli's. His fellow-cadets continued drinking and no one was overly concerned about the departure of their vociferous mate.

Outside the restaurant the drunken officer walked into Enzio's waiting arms.

"Where's Louise?" he stammered, just before Vittorio coshed the back of his head. They carried the unconscious cadet into the back of a saloon and drove at speed to Don Andrettis' apartment in the heart of the Bronx. With an expertise born from experience and, without ceremony, Vittorio applied steady pressure on the unconscious sailor's windpipe and, when life was extinct, the body was unceremoniously dumped at the foot of the steps leading up to Don Andretti's apartment. Within half an hour of the abduction Enzio and Vittorio were back at Ristorante Berterelli and reported their successful mission to Don Mario Deluca.

"That'll make Andretti think twice about messing me up. Well done boys! He'll wake up tomorrow and find his nephew like a cold plate of spaghetti outside his apartment."

The rear compartment of the Buick Continental was screened-off from the driver by a thick, sound-proof, plate-glass partition. Miss Cindy sidled up to Al and removed his trilby hat. Cupping his face in both hands she planted a firm kiss on his lips. Al was taken by surprise and, such was the ardour of Miss Cindy's kisses and tongue -probing, he soon gave up any pretence of resistance. The lady was now getting physical as she slid across the leather seat and crossed his thighs with her muscular left leg. Al was helpless. Miss Cindy gave a drunken squeal of delight "I'm sitting on something hard. Are you glad to see me big boy?!"

The innuendo was lost on Al. He forcibly lifted Cindy's thigh off his legs, delved deep into the pocket of his Boss' Astrakhan, and produced a Colt 45. Al stared at the gun in his hands. Miss Cindy leant across and took the gun from him.

"Is it yours Al?"

"Nope," Al replied.

"Let's not let the gat get in our way" and Cindy threw the gun on to the floor and, with serpentine leg movements, returned to business. Despite his bragging, Al Rizzi was a virgin but his partner in the back of the limousine was most certainly not. An experienced hooker, her probing sinewy fingers began exploring Al's genital region. Al restrained himself with difficulty, conscious of the fact the woman seducing him was the Boss' property but sexual lust was rapidly overcoming his inhibitions.

"We mustn't Miss Cindy. The Boss will kill me."

Cindy's lips stifled further protests and her probing, massaging fingers were now inside Al's zipper when, suddenly, the glass panel was pulled aside and the driver drawled over his shoulder "Were here folks. Time to get out."

Rearranging their clothing Al and Cindy walked up a few steps to the illuminated entrance to an apartment block. The driver called after Al "There's a limo following me. I'm taking off now. I'll be back later to pick you up" and, with a squeal of tyres, he sped off into the night.

Within a few seconds Al and the hooker were inside the lobby where Cindy exchanged a few flippant remarks with an ageing, cross-eyed caretaker. The old man was used to seeing her return home with a variety of 'clients' day and night but this one seemed different. He had a young man's face but his over-large overcoat and grey trilby suggested an older person. As they sped up to the 10th floor Cindy pinned Al against the elevator wall and, clutching each other, they ran along the corridor to apartment 1002. Once inside Cindy made a dash for the bedroom and rapidly undressed.

"Come on big boy. Come and take me."

Al undressed slowly in the lounge and again reconsidered the drastic leap into manhood he was about to take.

"I'm waiting honey" cried Cindy and, feeling self-conscious about his nudity, Al draped the Boss' Astrakhan coat around his shoulders. He then put out the light in the lounge and entered the semi-dark bedroom where, completely naked, Miss Cindy was lying on a king-sized bed. Her eyes were pleading and laughingly she asked "And what are you hiding under your coat big boy?"

Al blushed and turned off the main light in the bedroom. A thin pencil of light from the bathroom partially illuminated the bed and Cindy's curvaceous pelvis. Aroused again he took off the Astrakhan and laid it on the bed. He then lay down beside the expectant hooker not knowing how to proceed with his intention of ravishing her naked body. He need not have worried. Miss Cindy was an expert and directed foreplay, kissing and licking Al's erogenous areas and, at the same time, guiding his hands and tongue to her own stimulating trigger points. Al's erection was at bursting point when, at the crucial moment, he developed an overpowering desire to micturate.

"Cindy, honey, I have to pee."

"Okay, but don't be too long lover" Cindy replied. Al failed to urinate. He had been standing at the toilet for fully two minutes and only a trickle came out of his erect penis. His concentration was abruptly shattered by Cindy's scream from the bedroom followed rapidly by four gunshots and, after a few seconds' interval, two more. In a panic, Al turned out the light and bolted the bathroom door. He heard male voices in the bedroom "We've got the friggin bitch and that bastard Deluca."

"Yeah! We'll have some good friggin news for the Boss. Let's go!"

There was a sound of departing footsteps and then silence, complete silence. By that time Al had wet himself and his erection had subsided.

Alphonse Rizzi delayed for a minute before cautiously re-entering the bedroom. On turning on the light the sight that met his eyes was horrific. Cindy must have sat up in bed when the assassins fired at close range and her head and upper torso were splattered in a bloody, mangled mess over the bedhead and bedroom wall and pools of blood were gathering on the floor at the bedside. The murderers had also aimed two blasts at his Boss' overcoat whir 'l lay in shreds on the bed with a large, charred, smoking hole in the coat breast. Al shuddered at the thought of his narrow escape and his immediate reaction turned to self-preservation. He ran into the lounge and dressed rapidly and was tying his shoelace when the squint-eyed concierge appeared in the doorway, nervously holding a handgun.

"Keep 'em up buddy! You're in a hurry to get away. The cops will be here any minute."

Al complied with his request and stared at the older man "Did you see two guys coming up here? They shot their way into the apartment."

The old man was not communicative "Nope! You can tell it to the cops. Keep 'em up buddy."

The precinct police took ten minutes to arrive and came bursting into the apartment. They disarmed and dismissed the concierge, and handcuffed and searched Al. Ten n inutes later he was taken downstairs and driven to a precinct station where he was grilled all night by a chain-smoking, gum-chewing sergeant detective. Alphonse stuck to his story, insisting he had picked up the lady at the junction of Bowery and Duane Street and taken a yellow cab to her apartment in Queens. He had been in the can having a pee when the shooting started and the only voice he heard was the broad's scream. The half-destroyed Astrakhan on the bed was not his. The crafty sergeant tried all his wiles to make Al deviate from his story, but to no avail and at noon on the following day, he was released without charges. The cops regarded him as an unfortunate young buck who had been caught en flagrante with a prostitute. When questioned by the police, and to save his own skin, the concierge denied having seen anyone in the foyer after Miss Cindy and her gentleman friend went upstairs. In fact the armed hoodlums had come to his desk demanding Miss Cindy's apartment number and warned him to make himself scarce and keep his mouth shut. The old man recognised a genuine threat when he heard one and told the police the first hint of trouble was five or six muted gunshots from the tenth floor. He omitted to add he deliberately delayed rushing upstairs until the assassins left the building and only then did he call the cops. The mutilated Astrakhan overcoat still had Antonio Andretti's name tab on it but the mobster had a watertight alibi and was out of town when the murder happened. He admitted he was a frequent visitor to Miss Cindy's apartment and, on one occasion, left his coat in her flat. Within days of the incident the police had lost interest in the case which was categorized as a revenge killing by a person, or persons, unknown. Throughout the police grilling Al Rizzi protected Don Mario Deluca's name and made no mention of the car ride or the use of the Boss' charcoal- grey, Astrakhan overcoat.

In gratitude Don Mario promoted Al to lieutenant and made him under-manager of Ristorante Berterelli.

Alphonse Rizzi took up his new position on Sunday 14th December 1941, seven days after the Japanese attack on Pearl Harbour. He was now on probation with the Mafia and on their payroll and his new position entitled him to carry a pistol at all times. During the early months of 1942 Uncle Sam was actively recruiting and expanding his armed forces. Alphonse was just turning twenty years of age and received his call-up papers in February.

"These goddam sons of bitches want me in the army. I've a good mind to tear up the papers. What do you advise, Boss?"

Don Mario thought hard for a few moments and squinted once more at the official letter "You must obey their order, Alphonse. I see they want you for a medical at Fort Wadsworth on 24th April. Tell 'em you gotta backache and flat feet. That should keep you out of the army."

Despite his protestations about pain in his spine on bending, or twisting, and amateurish attempts to bamboozle the medical examiners, Alphonse passed out A1. His posting to a basic training camp at Albany in New York State came through in late August. Waving his draft papers he again consulted Don Mario "The jokers want me in Albany in late October. I'm gonna join a friggin cavalry regiment. That means tanks. I don't wanna go! I could easily get lost in the Bronx 'till the heat's off and the friggin war's over."

Don Mario usually objected to the use of expletives but ignored Al's oversight and replied without hesitation "No, Alphonse, you must go. The cops and military police are very hot on draft-dodgers and we don't wanna those guys snooping around. You won't be in for long. After all we've only got those goddam slant-eyed Japs to beat and, when you come out, there'll be a job waiting at Berterelli's."

"Thank you Boss" Al muttered with a resigned sigh.

A week before he left for Albany Al was invited to dine at Don Mario's apartment in Howard, a fashionable residential district near the Italian quarter of Manhattan. He turned up in a light-blue silk suit and sported a bright red necktie and black, patent-leather shoes. He was introduced to Signora Deluca, a shy, rather dowdy, female with grey hair and wearing an unflattering plain black dress. She spent most of the evening in the kitchen preparing a meal for her husband and his guest and Don Cario's daughters waited at table. The eldest was rather plain and retiring, cast in the same mould as her mother, but the younger daughter was a gorgeous creature and her father openly doted on her. Claudia had an oval face, an aristocratic nose and jet black eyes surmounted by long tresses of black hair, combed into ringlets at the nape of her neck. Her constant smile accentuated her full, generous mouth with inviting lips covering a perfect array of pearly-white teeth. Alphonse was smitten. Claudia flirted openly with him and Don Mario was content to allow the youngsters to enjoy the evening. She showed Al the family photograph album and they laughed long and loud at the sight of the Deluca sisters, aged three and five, 'de nada' in a bathtub. At the end of the evening Al plucked up courage to ask Don Mario's permission to take Claudia to a cinema and, after consultation with Signora Deluca, his request was granted.

On the night of the assignation the young couple, accompanied by Signora Deluca and a maiden aunt, went to see the long-running epic, 'Gone with the Wind,' at the Gaumont Theatre on Broadway. Hemmed in on either side by a chaperone Al sat next to Claudia. He was extremely nervous and twitchy and sensed Claudia was similarly affected. A brief flick of touching hands, or the momentary pressure from a knee 'accidentally' pressed against his own, sent barbs of electricity shooting through his body. He was sexually aroused and had to hold himself on a tight rein and his emotions were in conflict. On the one hand he wanted the film to end quickly to release him from the torture of sitting so close to the desirable, ravishing beauty. On the other hand he prayed the film's wind would blow forever and he could continue his chaperone-regulated courtship of Claudia. The evening ended formally with a lingering handshake and a promise form Signora Deluca the couple could walk out together again when Al was home on leave from the army.

Trooper Alphonse Rizzi came home for a seven day furlough in the first week in December 1942. He wore his uniform with pride and the good-looking muscular young trooper turned many a female head. But Al only had eyes for Claudia. They had corresponded regularly for the eight weeks at his training camp in Albany but, for fear of parental censorship, Al's letters did not contain material of an amorous nature. Before Al was allowed to take Claudia out on the town unchaperoned he had to face Don Mario in the billiard room at his Manhattan apartment.

"I wish to speak to you on a Family matter, Alphonse. By saying Family I include my wife and children and my brothers in the Cosa Nostra. If one of my Family is insulted my whole Family becomes involved and we are governed by the laws of our Society. One of the strictly held rules we abide by is female virginity before marriage. Men of Honour are duty-bound to observe this law and it is in this respect I am allowing you to take my Claudia to the cinema. You are not yet mafioso but, if you behave honourably, this will be put right in due course. If you keep this bargain I shall take steps to bring you and your family under my protection. Do you see what I'm getting at, Alphonse?"

Al immediately recognised he was being offered Claudia's hand in marriage and, at the same time, the prospect of becoming a member of the Cosa Nostra. He cleared his throat and blurted out "You honour me by allowing me to take Claudia to the flicks, Don Mario. You also extend the hand of friendship by offering to take my family under your wing. I accept both offers and swear I shall do nothing to break your Family code of behaviour."

Satisfied, Don Mario stretched out the back of his right hand.

"As a token of respect for me and Claudia and the Cosa Nostra you may kiss my hand."

Self-consciously, Al brushed his lips on the back of the Don's extended fingers. The interview was over and he was free to go. Dressed in a pale-pink, two piece suit, Claudia was ready and waiting in the lounge while her mother fussed and tut-tutted in the background, not at all pleased her precious daughter was walking out unchaperoned on the arm of a lusty American GI. She crossed herself twice as the ecstatic couple left the apartment.

The young lovers again went to see 'Gone with the Wind' only, on this occasion, they occupied two seats at the rear of the auditorium where kissing, cuddling and petting was the order of the day. Neither saw the film in its entirety. Al caught a glimpse of Rhet Butler and Scarlet O'Hara in a clinch but, in a flash, his excitable companion had him pinned to his seat as she thrust her turgid lips into the side of his neck and sucked ferociously producing a bruise which, by the next day, became an embarrassing and easily visible love bite. Al Rizzi survived the pleasant ordeal and returned Claudia, virgo intacta, to her parent's apartment each night. By the end of his six day furlough Al knew the film's dialogue by heart. He amused Claudia by quoting verbatim from Rhet Butler's speeches and, in jest, threatened to have plastic surgery to make his ears protrude just like Clark Gable, the hero of the celluloid masterpiece.

In mid-December Al's unit was transferred en bloc to a remote tank training depot outside Aberdeen in South Dakota, 2,000 miles and two days by train from New York City. He spent a lonely Christmas at the training depot. Unsure of his ability to express himself in writing he confined his communications with Claudia to a few postcards and a weekly telephone call which was frequently abruptly cut off by truculent telephone operators. He managed to speak to Claudia for a predestined 30 seconds on Christmas day and blew a kiss over the line which caused the young lady to blush. Her mother read the signs correctly and tut-tutted and crossed herself with eyes elevated heavenwards. Claudia burst into tears and retired to her bedroom to daydream about her handsome soldier boy.

Trooper First Class Alphonse Rizzi passed out as a Sherman Tank driver in the 7th South Dakota Armoured Regiment and, by March 1943, the unit was fully trained and ready to go to war. The call to action came in early April and the regiment transferred to a holding camp outside Boston. Embarkation, destination unknown, was planned for the last week of April and the troopers were sent on a week's furlough. Al spent his pre-embarkation leave in New York with Claudia. Her father loaned him a pink Cadillac coupe and the vehicle expanded the scope of the lover's enjoyment of their time together. They ferried across to Staten Island and drove to the seashore on Long Island and to Coney Beach resort. The days slipped by quickly and the lovers were becoming increasingly frustrated, Claudia more so than Alphonse. She became more adventurous during their torrid, endless kissing sessions on the back seat of the pink Cadillac and the American teenage custom of petting assumed a broader dimension. French kisses were eagerly exchanged and, during the frenetic petting sessions, Claudia insisted on removing articles of clothing which obstructed flesh-to-flesh contact. Al had to summon all his powers of resistance to bring their physical contacts to an end before penetration actually occurred. His insistence in stopping short at the brink often caused Claudia to burst into tears and wail "You don't really love me Al!" and reassurance by cuddling and further petting inevitably led to another crisis within five or ten minutes. His frustration was mounting but Al was able to keep his promise to Don Mario Deluca until their last night together when matters came to an explosive end. After dining at Berterelli's they drove to their favourite courting spot at Lookout Point on Long Island. Within ten minutes of their arrival they were lying side by side on the plush leather, rear seat of the pink Cadillac. Gentle at first, the petting was becoming frenetic and Claudia dug her nails into Al's shoulder. She was alternately sobbing and whimpering "Please take me Al."

"I can't honey. I promised your father on my honour and I can't break my promise."

Claudia inserted her hand inside Al's underpants and gently touched his semi-erect penis.

"Papa won't know. How can he tell?"

Claudia was now massaging his penis with increasing ferocity and Al felt himself slipping into submission. She purred in his ear "You'll be away tomorrow Al and I need something to remember you by when you're gone."

Al was in turmoil! The erotic sensation in his groin was rapidly overriding his dented willpower and his penis took control.

"Okay honey d'ya want it? You'll get it" and, with a thrustful lunge, he entered the sacred channel between her legs. Claudia stiffened and gasped in pain and then she relaxed allowing Al to pummel away. As he mindlessly thrashed and contorted his muscular body his pelvic nerves took over ending in a crescendo and a half-stifled, climactic bellow. The whole act of union was over in 80 seconds. Claudia lay beneath Al's limp body with a seraphic smile on her face. She had nailed her man but, if what she experienced was sex, it was grossly overrated. After the initial stab of pain the sex act was too quick to be pleasurable but it had served its purpose which was to satisfy Alphonse Rizzi.

"How was it Al?"

"Fantastic honey, just fantastic! Are you okay?"

"I'm fine honey, just fine" and a self-satisfied smirk on her face confirmed she had slipped comfortably from girlhood to womanhood on the Cadillac's soft, brown- leathered rear seat. Al knelt on the car floor and kissed Claudia tenderly. His eyes were troubled "I love you, honey, but promise one thing – never tell anyone about tonight."

"Have no worries Alphonse. It's our secret and no one will ever know. I love you too, Al. Come back to me in one piece and we'll do that again every night for the rest of our lives."

Claudia had planned the seduction and could tell that Al was a worried man. A maid in her father's household had told her about the 'safe period' and she had calculated she was due in two days time. Aware of her father's views on premarital virginity she was adamant about keeping the nights' escapade a secret between herself and Alphonse. Should Don Mario find out she would be ostracised by her family and, worse, Al would be severely dealt with and hounded out of New York. None of these results could justify the eighty seconds of minimal pleasure she had experienced on the back seat of the pink Cadillac coupe.

The following morning Don Mario Deluca and Claudia came to see Al off at Central Station. His departure among a milling throng of military personnel, their families and children, was brief and formal. Don Mario stood aside while the lovers shook hands and Al pecked Claudia on the cheek. As he did so he whispered "I love you."

Claudia responded with a barely audible "Me too."

Don Mario held on firmly to Al's hand "Come back soon, Alphonse. Don't get shot up. We need you at Berterelli's. Take this parcel and write to Claudia and let us know how you're getting along. Good luck son" and the two men embraced unashamedly in a cloud of spewing steam from the locomotive. At the end of the embrace Don Mario proffered his right hand and Al brushed the don's knuckles with his lips. Another quick embrace followed and, among a cacophony of whistles and 'all aboards,' Al got on the train and, klaxon blaring, the locomotive pulled slowly out of New York's Central Station.

Al's compartment was overcrowded with anxious-faced servicemen, all leaving their loved-ones and friend , on their way for embarkation to 'God knows where.' Some erupted into bouts of bravado but there was a pervading sense of sorrow and nostalgia at possibly seeing their families for the last time. Al sat motionless trying to recall events of the previous night and holding Don Mario's parcel in his lap. He remembered a few exotic seconds at the height of his climax but otherwise his memory was of groping in the pink Cadillac and an all pervading image of Rhet Butler in a passionate entanglement with Scarlet O'Hara. The troop train was well clear of Bridgeport before he started unpicking his Boss' parcel. Inside was a note in Don Mario Deluca's handwriting – 'Claudia wishes you to have the enclosed photograph. Also enclosed are fifty Cubans. I notice you've taken a shine to smoking the odd cigar lately! I've had printed a hundred business cards in your name. Wherever fate takes you, advertise Berterelli's on all occasions. It's all good for business. Good luck Alphonse and come back soon.' Al inspected a gilt-edged card with his name prominently displayed at the top and Ristorante Berterelli's full address beneath. Strangers, and excessively curious, his compatriots in the carriage were impressed by the business cards and vied to outdo each other with compliments about Claudia's photo – 'A smashin' broad! Some tits! A nice arse! and 'I bet the broad's a good lay!' Someone produced a bottle of Jack Daniels and Al handed out his cigars and, by the time they detrained in Boston, everyone in the compartment had a Berterelli business card in his wallet and a Cuban cigar in his breast pocket. Fortified by Jack Daniels whisky the valiant GI's were ready to go to war and face the enemy. By the next day most had changed their minds and were intent on draft-dodging if the opportunity presented itself .

CHAPTER 4

Alphonse Rizzi's war

AT A CASABLANCA CONFERENCE on 23rd and 24th January 1943 Winston Churchill and Franklin D Roosevelt agreed on a common policy for the conduct of the war in Europe after Axis forces had been driven out of North Africa. The political aims were to open a new front in Europe and alleviate pressure on the Russian theatre of war, to coerce Italy into an early armistice and to give Allied troops experience in seaborne landings. Winston Churchill pressed for an attack on Europe's soft underbelly via the toe of Italy and, as a direct result, Operation Husky was conceived. After establishing beachheads in southern Sicily the ultimate military objective was to capture Messina at the north eastern tip of the island, thereby cutting off the enemy's line of evacuation to the mainland. At the time of the invasion there were 230,000 Italian and 40,000 German troops in Sicily, including the XV Panzer Grenadier and the Herman Goering armoured divisions. Beach landings were made along a seventy mile stretch of coastline on July 10th, the British 8th Army and Canadians around Syracuse and General Omar Bradley's 7th American Army between Scoglitti and Licata in the south. The Americans were deployed as a shield to protect the British flank while Montgomery's forces, and a Canadian brigade, struck northwards towards Messina. Montgomery was held up at Catania by German Panzer Grenadiers but in the south General George Patton, an aggressive divisional commander, moved swiftly to take Agrigento and Marsla and his tanks then swung northwards to capture Palermo and liberate western Sicily. Disregarding pre-invasion speculation that Sicily would be unsuitable for tank warfare, the dashing general had landed his Second Armoured

Division in the vanguard of the invading forces. Patton then advanced eastwards along Sicily's northern coastline, by-passing enemy strongpoints, by transporting his tanks and infantry in barges and landing behind enemy lines. Catania eventually fell to the British 8th Army on August 5th and a race to be first in Messina developed between Patton's and Montgomery's forces. In the event American troops arrived in the city at 10.15 hours on 17th August, some four hours before the arrival of Montgomery's exhausted 'desert rats.' British forces involved in the Sicilian campaign continued their fight against retreating Axis forces on the Italian mainland while the bulk of American troops were withdrawn to Britain where they continued training for Operation Overlord, the Allied invasion of France in June 1944.

Saturday, 10th July 1943.

"Gimme a drag Hank."

Trooper Alphonse Rizzi, 'Al the Wop' to his friends, turned to beg a cigarette from his nearest neighbour. Together with 120 men of the US 2nd Armoured Division they were seated on wooden benches along the bulkheads of a tank landing craft. Three Stuart light tanks, one Sherman and two M113 armoured personnel carriers were securely chained to the floor in the hold. That the 16 ton Stuarts were securely stowed was a blessing. The shallow-drafted tank landing craft had been buffeted and unceremoniously thrown about by high seas on its 100 mile crossing from Cape Bon in Tunisia to the landing beaches at Licata in southern Sicily. The stench in the confined, dimly-lit hold was overwhelming-a mixture of diesel fumes, cigarette smoke, stale bilge water, overflowing bucket urinals and human vomitus. Al again repeated his request "Hey! What's up with you Hank? Gimme a light!"

Hank was retching over a bucket already over half-full with vomit. He wiped the corner of his mouth and, as the ship keeled over, he again thrust his head into the receptacle.

"Jees Al! Do you have to smoke? My lighters' in my tunic pocket."

Al lit a cigarette and leant back against the bulwark. He felt the waves pounding and thudding against the ship's hull and took stock of his surroundings. Most of his squadron, including his tank commander Lieutenant Conrad Bradley Jr., were vomiting into makeshift receptacles and some into tin helmets which would have to be worn when they hit the beaches. Before he started vomiting the lieutenant had read out General Patton's pre-battle message 'Officers and men of the 2nd Armoured Division. Operation Husky is the largest seaborne invasion in history and we have the honour to spearhead the assault. In a few hours we shall be hitting the beaches of southern Sicily. The prize is a city called Messina in the top left-hand corner. You will attack with all speed and make a dash for Messina. Though were going the long way round we must get there before Montgomery's 8th Army. I don't wish to hear reasons why you couldn't make it! Just improvise and beat the hell out of the Krauts and the Ities. I wish you luck and Godspeed in the battle ahead.'

Al had a brief mental picture of the three-star general, sporting two pearl-handled revolvers in his belt, gum chewing and with his jaw thrust out aggressively, and arrogantly strutting around mouthing obscenities at all and sundry. Idolised by his men, Patton's gung-ho approach to modern tank warfare was legendary. In his own words he was a 'goddamn tank man and a good 'un at that.' Despite his belligerency General Patton was not wallowing in the stench-filled cesspit but, as befitted his seniority, he was transported to the Sicilian beaches aboard the Rookwood, a British Hunt Class destroyer.

Men, tanks and vehicles of the US 2nd Armoured Regiment had crossed the Atlantic in April 1943. To avoid marauding

German U-Boats the convoy sailed southwards to the Caribbean and hit the west coast of Africa at Dakar. Five days later it passed through the Straits of Gibraltar and docked at Oran on 23rd April. Within eight days the 2nd Armoured's tanks were in Bizerta and, as fighting on Cape Bon was almost over, their tanks were kept in reserve and the regiment first went into action in Sicily. Untried rookies, this was to be the men's first blooding in battle and, so far, their introduction into the rigours of tank warfare had been a miserable fiasco. Al had a feeling they must be nearing the beachhead. Speaking through a loud-hailer the lieutenant issued his orders "You've got time for one last smoke before we hit the beach. In about ten minutes you will mount on my order. You will not start your engines until you get my signal. So let's go get 'em."

Al lit another cigarette and glanced at the indistinct silhouette of his Stuart tank, wondering if the tin can was as safe as a Sherman. Loaned by the British, the Stuart was considered more suitable and manoeuvrable than a Sherman on the hilly terrain and tortuous Sicilian roads. The Stuart was only lightly armoured with a 37mm cannon and two Browning machine guns, one mounted coaxially with the cannon and operated by the tank commander, and the other by a codriver who also acted as wireless operator. Al Rizzi was the troop commander's driver and his Texan codriver was Hank Schweitzer who, at that moment, was retching again and moaning "I wanna goddamn die!"

Al shuddered at the thought the damage from a German Tiger tank, or an 88mm anti-tank gun, might do to a Honey's flimsy armour plating. The British called their Stuart tanks 'Honeys.' He could not fathom why and their only saving grace was their manoeuvrability in tight corners. Al's reverie was rudely interrupted by three blasts on a klaxon, the three- minute warning. He placed his helmet firmly on his head and walked across to the canvas-covered, iron-clad monster. All around troopers were galvanised into action, tidying their clothing and strapping on equipment. At two blasts on the klaxon Al turned to Hank and shouted "What the hell are we doing here? Why in goddamn hell are we about to drive on to a frigging beach and get shot to bits? Answer me Hank?"

Chewing gum, Hank managed a wry smile.

"Were doing this for good old Uncle Sam, buddy."

Al calmed down a little. The klaxon blared once more and almost simultaneously, amid the deafening clatter of chains and hawsers, the front end of the landing craft hinged forwards and crashed on to a shelving, pebbly beach. Vehicles sprang to life and the hold filled rapidly with pungent, silvery-blue diesel fumes. Closely following the Sherman to his front, Al drove down the ramp and across a shingly beach to a metalled road. No shots were fired and the landing itself was an anticlimax. The beachhead was secured unopposed and defending Italian troops of 207 Coastal Defence withdrew rapidly on first sighting the Allied task force. During their first 14 hours ashore Al's squadron moved in fits and starts but, despite conflicting orders, made steady progress along 20 miles of coastal road until they were brought to a halt at Ponte di Mandranova. A vital bridge had been blown by the enemy after one Sherman had crossed and the rest of the heavy tanks were stranded on the road waiting arrival of engineers to span the gap. Colonel Jim Morrow took his squadron into an orange grove where they bivouacked for the night. On the following day the squadron crossed a Bailey bridge, constructed overnight, and pressed on to support an infantry attack on Agrigento. On the outskirts of the town they came across the burnt out Sherman and, when his own leading Honey was immobilized by a direct hit from an antitank gun, Colonel Morrow ordered his squadron to retire to a disused quarry about a mile to the rear where they sat for 24 hours waiting further instructions. In the meantime American GI's and paratroopers had invested Agrigento and were waiting tank support for the final assault.

Colonel Jim Morrow's indecision was dramatically resolved on the night of July 13th when General George Patton and his operations officer arrived unannounced. The entire bivouac heard the general's dressing down "Goddamnit Colonel Morrow, what the hell are you doing sitting on your butt? Didn't you get my friggin message in Tunis? You are ordered to proceed with all speed and take Palermo. So get off your goddamn arse and get moving. You will move out at first light and take Agrigento."

The belligerent old warhorse strode through the bivouac to the cheers of the tank men and, with his entourage, he disappeared into the dark towards the audible night battle in Agrigento.

Lieutenant Conrad Bradley's Honey led the cavalry charge into Agrigento. His tactics were a mixture of recklessness and extreme caution and, when the Honey reached the outskirts of the town, he battened down the hatch and ordered Al to stop. An American paratroop sergeant and a 7th Army G I came out of a building and thumbed a lift on Al's Honey. The little Stuart tank, carrying the exultant soldiers, then rumbled forwards into Agrigento town square to find that enemy forces had withdrawn under cover of darkness. Within an hour the Shermans arrived in force and took up the chase, one column continuing on the coast road towards Sciacca and the other swinging north on the main road from Agrigento to Palermo. Such is the injustice of wartime, Colonel Jim Morrow was decorated for his 'bold' action and hailed by his Regiment as the conqueror of Agrigento. Lieutenant Conrad Bradley Jr. got nothing.

Hauptman Rudolf Grenz, a veteran of Rommel's North Africa campaign, felt the world, and General Karl von Rudinger in particular, was against him. His regiment, the XVth Panzer Grenadiers based outside Catania, had moved to the south coast in anticipation of an Allied invasion which came on July 10th. He had been charged with covering withdrawal of Axis forces to northern Sicily and his 88mm antitank section, and remnants of the Italian 207th Coastal Defence, held Agrigento for two days. He was now ordered to take his depleted unit across Godrano valley to set up a road block at Villa- frati on the Agrigento to Palermo road to hold up American tanks advancing from the south. His effective firepower was down to two serviceable 88mm antitank guns and 28 Panzer Grenadiers. This was a suicide mission but an order was an order and there might be a Clasp to his Iron Cross, albeit posthumously, in the offing. General Rudinger's order to move came at teatime on19th July. A pursuing American armoured column was ten kilometres to the south, just approaching Corleone. He would have to move quickly but unruly Italian infantrymen, sunbathing and swimming in Lake Scanzano, delayed his departure for three vital hours and, by the time his column reached Godrano, mansion, darkness was descending. He ordered his men to bivouac for the night in the farmyard and strode across the road to the estate house.

Hauptman Grenz's prolonged banging on the sturdy oak door eventually provoked a response from Don Carlo Cecci who stared at the business end of a Schmeitzer machine pistol.

"Old man! I am commandeering two rooms in your house for the night. Get your wife to prepare a meal."

Don Carlo stared at the German officer who pushed his way into the hallway closely followed by Feldwebel Otto Schulz, also wielding a submachine gun. Don Carlo scurried to the kitchen and ordered Anna to prepare some food for the unwelcome visitors and urged his daughters to lock themselves in the cellar for the night. The Germans were up and about an hour before daybreak. From a vantage point near the barn the Hauptman could hear tracked vehicles moving around which left him in no doubt American tanks had reached Scanzano Lake during the night. It was time to move on. After formally thanking Don Carlo for his hospitality he mobilized his unit and they moved smartly up the dirt road towards Cefala. At a flat plateau on the mountain .ide Hauptman Grenz called a halt and scanned the winding road from Godrano and the estate house and cobblestone farmyard. Clouds of dust hung over the valley in the clear morning air and an American mobile column was making slow progress across the valley.

"Feldwebel Schulz. Can our 88's depress sufficiently to hit the road and that farmyard?"

Originally designed for antiaircraft defence, the German 88mm flack gun was renowned for its versatility and the Feldwebel had no hesitation in replying "Yes Herr Hauptman, it can be done. We have a firm base on the rock. Shall I order the guns up?"

"Yes, Herr Feldwebel, lets do that! We'll have a crack at the Amis when they get to the farmyard."

Hauptman Grenz was fully aware he was contravening General von Rudinger's instructions to make all speed to Villafrati but the chance of a pot shot at the enemy's tanks was too inviting. The guns were mounted side by side on the plateau and hurriedly camouflaged with wire netting.

Hauptman Rudolf Grenz's depleted unit awaited arrival of Lieutenant Conrad Bradley's mobile column and, when it came, the German could not believe his luck. The leading tank veered off the road and came to a sudden halt in the farmyard. A figure emerged form the tank and walked across the road to join a group of helmeted soldiers who were debusing from an armoured vehicle. At that range the American tank was a sitting duck. After a minor adjustment to the gun sight he gave the order "Feur eins" and, four seconds later, "Feur zwei." He saw the first high explosive shell burst under the front end of the stationary tank but the gun's recoil upset the standing of the second gun and its shell went flying over the farmyard to burst harmlessly in a tree-lined ravine. Three further shells were dispatched but the 88's alignments were inaccurate and they all exploded in the valley below the farmyard. As a result of the only direct hit black acrid smoke billowed out of the stricken tank. It was now time to beat a hasty retreat towards Cefala and onwards to Villafrati where the German kapitan led his men into the welcoming arms of a holding battalion of U S infantry. His Italian allies were delighted to lay down their arms and surrender to the Americans. Hauptman Grenz's war was over. He was not to know American forces had captured Villafrati, and 2,000 Italian prisoners, on the previous day and had advanced a further 20 kilometres northwards on their way to capture Palermo.

Godrano Estate House. 18th-20th July.

By 18th July 1943 Allied forces were well-established ashore in Sicily and General Patton's 2nd division had occupied most of the western territory on the island and was only days away form capturing Palermo. Ever since the invaders arrived Don Carlo Cecci spent his time sitting on a hard bench in the shade of an eucalyptus tree at the back of the red barn where he kept a watchful eye on his Godrano estate. Carla supplied him with water and milk and, twice a day, brought across a bowl of broth and a chunk of maize bread. He refused to allow his daughters to keep him company and his solitary vigil had its advantages. He could vomit and urinate without disturbing the household and he secretly disposed of most of Carla's food over the edge of a rock face about ten yards in front of his bench seat. The sounds of battle to the south crept ever nearer and high-flying bombers and strafing, low-level fighters barely produced a reaction in the tired old man. His rheumy, squinting eyes stared fixedly at his little empire as if daring anyone to come and dispossess him. Soon the grim reaper would intervene and his lands and estate house would pass to the Cucinotta's who would become the bosses at Godrano.

If only he had a son! And sooner still he would have to tell his daughters about the marriage arrangements with Don Giovanni's sons. Sicily was a patriarchal society and, being female, their very existence would fade into insignificance. At least he was rid of the two mafiosi who had been foisted upon him and, when Allied forces landed, Franco Gicanetti and Salvatore Branco moved permanently to their cave hideout outside Cefala.

"Good riddance" he muttered under his breath and pondered what the Americans and the British might bring to Sicily? Mussolini's regime had been harsh and oppressive but the Mafia had survived. And now Il Duce was in trouble from Italian communists and likely to be dethroned as dictator.

"Good riddance" he muttered for the second time in as many minutes.

At lunchtime Carla brought a pitcher of cool well-water and a gourd of goat's milk and sat beside her father "Papa, what's happening? We heard planes this morning but no shooting."

Don Carlo drank voraciously to slake his raging thirst. Water from the pitcher dribbled down the side of his mouth on to his shirt and formed a tepid pool on the wooden bench. "Mia Carla! I see my fields and orchards and no workers on them. I hear guns firing to the south and planes overhead. There is much activity and movement of vehicles around Lago Scanzano. Italian and German convoys are moving north and low-flying planes shoot at them from time to time and that's when we hear loud bangs. It looks as if our soldiers are running away and the Americani are close behind."

Don Carlo stopped speaking abruptly, his cracked lips almost sticking together as his overpowering thirst returned. He grabbed the pitcher and gulped rapidly and, within seconds, he was violently sick bringing up bile and most of the fluid he had drunk.

"Papa! Papa! You must come indoors into the shade. The strong sun will hurt you. Let me help you across the road."

Don Carlo smiled fleetingly at his daughter's concern "No, Carla! I will stay here and keep an eye out for trouble. Go my child and lock yourself in with your sisters. I will be in for supper."

Carla knew her stubborn, inflexible father inside out and was secretly pleased he refused to return to the house with her. Despite her sister's protestations she had been taking food and drink to the mafiosi's hideout for four days and now was her opportunity to visit the renegades. Carrying a gourd of fresh goat's milk and a haversack stuffed with rye bread, goat's cheese and crispelle she made her way uphill towards the cave. The date was Sunday 18th May and this was her fifth trip to the hideout.

Carla's sexual awakening declared itself when she was just sixteen years of age when she developed a crush on Franco Gicanetti. The mafiosi came into the big house for supper most evenings and Carla only had eyes for her handsome, dashing hero. She admired him from afar and amateurishly plied her wiles, acting coyly and sometimes aggressively in his presence with languid, sidelong glances and special attention in preparing, and presenting, his meals. Franco, in turn, felt the intensity of her attention and, to inflame the teenager, he flirted openly with Gina. All the while the suppers were sternly supervised by the ailing don and at the first sign of impropriety the mafiosi were sent packing and Carla was banished to her bedroom where, most nights, she dreamt about her paramour. Matters came to a head in May 1943 when Don Carlo began retiring early and the mafiosi took advantage and sometimes returned to the kitchen to join the women when teasing and flirting became more intense and serious and led to a few stolen kisses. In Gina's eyes Franco was a boastful braggart but Carla would have none of it. In her besotted state he was a Don Juan and a brave hero and, such was Franco's hold over her, she was persuaded to deliver food and drink to his cave hideout.

Salvatore spotted Carla as she started climbing the shepherd's path leading from the road to the shrub-covered hideout entrance.

"Here she comes Franco! We'll have someth' .g to eat in a minute."

Franco was lounging just inside the cave.

"I'm only hungry for one thing, Salvatore. I'm going to lie down. Bring Carla to me and tell her I'm not well. Once she's inside, stop her getting out."

For once Salvatore acted like a gentleman. He ga\ ɔ Carla a hand with the gourd and haversack and helped her on to the ledge outside the cave.

"Where's Franco?" she inquired.

"He's not well, Carla. He's in the cave. He wants to see you," Salvatore replied.

On her previous visits Carla had not been inside the cave. She was astounded by the darkness and coolness of the chamber and height of the ceiling and the cavern appeared to extend to infinity. Unaccustomed to the dark she whispered "Are you there Franco? I cannot see you in the dark."

A moan from the floor some ten yards ahead, and to her right, led Carla to Franco who was lying on a bed of sacking and straw. Franco whimpered "Carla mia! You have come to see me. Hold my hand."

They groped in the dark until their hands touched. Carla knelt on the floor at the cot side and, for a few seconds, the handclasp was tender and gentle. And then Franco's grip tightened and his voice hardened "Come here you bitch. I want you."

He sat up abruptly and pulled Carla towards him. At first she giggled and thought Franco was playacting but it soon became evident his intentions were entirely different. She struggled to contain Franco's assault but the muscular man was too powerful for her waif-like frame. In the background she could hear Salavtore clapping his hands and repeatedly asking "What's it like

Franco? Tell me what its like?", but Franco was too preoccupied with his own carnal desires to reply.

The rape, for rape it was, was brutal. In his frenzy Franco hit Carla's face and bit her neck and lips. He tore away her underclothes and showed no mercy to the helpless woman beneath him as he penetrated her womanhood with a violent lunge which produced a long shriek of agony and Carla was rendered semi-conscious by the pain. Mercifully the rape only lasted about forty seconds when Franco reached a premature climax with repeated shouts of 'Mamma mia.' A sudden, eerie silence descended inside the cave. Salvatore rushed forwards to help Franco to his feet and broke the silence "Bravissimo Franco! You were fantastic."

Rearranging his clothing Franco strode towards the exit leaving Salvatore kneeling beside the sobbing woman. With grubby hands he began gingerly exploring Carla's bloodstained thighs and crotch. She sat up abruptly, spat in his face, jumped to her feet and kicked him violently in his groin sending Salvatore spinning to the ground and holding on to his crotch. Arms akimbo, and smiling mockingly, Franco barred her way on the sunlit ledge "You enjoyed that, Carla mia?"

She again e· ploded into action, pummelling Franco's head and shoulders with her small fists. Still grinning broadly, he stepped backwards and tripped over a boulder and Carla darted past him and plunged down the shepherd's path, tearing her skirt on the sharp thorn bushes. Franco shouted after the tiny, fleeing figure "Bring more food and wine tomorrow, Carla mia. We'll have another go when you come. Salvatore wants a go too."

By this time Salvatore, still clutching his groin, was crouching by his side.

"She's a lively bit of fun isn't she Franco?"

"I've been wanting her for over a year, Salvo. It was great" and, in a louder voice, he repeatedly shouted "Bravissimo Carla mia" at the diminutive figure disappearing around the mountainside bend.

Carla paused for breath on the flat plateau overlooking Godrano estate. Panting, and hurting between her bloodied legs, she broke down and wept cascades of bitter, salty ears and, with faltering steps and heaving sobs, she descended towards the farmhouse. Carla entered the house through the rear gate leading from a walled vegetable garden and found her sisters busy in the kitchen. They were horrified at the sight of their distressed sister. A large bruise had appeared under her right eye and her lower lip was torn and bleeding and the blood on her bare legs had caked into serrated, brown patches. She haltingly described the rape while Anna attended to her wounds. Gina was unable to contain herself.

"How could the bastardos do this to you? I'll get evens with them. I'll go up there and shoot that bastardo Franco. I promise you I will, Carla."

Sobbing convulsively Carla asked "What shall we tell Papa?"

Gina replied promptly "We tell him nothing. He's too weak to do anything about it. You can wear my tinted glasses and we'll tell Papa you had an accident in the garden. Don't you agree Anna?"

Her elder sister nodded her head and Gina continued "Right, you look presentable now. I'll go and collect Papa for his supper. Leave this to me, Carla mia. I'll sort out that devil Franco and his stupid friend tomorrow."

With Franco's last words still ringing in her ears Carla pleaded "Please Gina, don't call me 'Carla mia'. I hate it! Just call me Carla."

Mid-morning on July 19th Don Carlo Cecci ordered the women into the cellar and, armed with his shotgun, he took up position in an upstairs window where he had a view of the courtyard and the farmyard across the road. Foot-slogging columns of straggling Italian infantry began arriving at around 4.00pm and it took three hours for the whole column to pass through on their way to Cefala. The infantrymen appeared to be in good spirits, laughing and joking amongst themselves and apparently anticipating an end to the fighting in Sicily. A couple of vehicles pulled into the yard and a few soldiers took water from the well in the courtyard. Much to Don Cecci's annoyance, one Garibaldini urinated against the courtyard wall in full view of the estate house. By early evening the traffic eased perceptibly and a last group of vehicles arrived at Godrano at 7.30pm. By their efficiency and general behaviour, Don Carlo realised they were a German unit. Satisfied the coast was clear to his rear, a German officer ordered his men to disembark and bunk down in the red barn. His vehicles and guns, three kubelwaggens, two troop carriers and two 88mm anti-tank guns, were parked overnight on the farmyard and the captain and his feldwebel came across to the house demanding food and shelter for the night. Don Carlo Cecci had little choice and, on July 19th, Hauptman Rudolf Grenz and Feldwebel Otto Schulz bunked down in the estate house at Godrano.

20th July 1943.

After their 'heroic' capture of Agrigento Colonel Morrow's squadron was placed in reserve and followed the Sherman's armoured thrust along the main coast road towards Sciacca. At a T-junction 12 kilometre short of the town Captain Mike Dangerfield, one of Morrow's troop commanders, was ordered to take Al's section up a winding unmade secondary road which would eventually get them to Palermo via Corleone. Captain Dangerfield's troop was made up of six Honeys, an armoured scout car, three DUKW personnel carriers, a paratroop sergeant and 42 7th Army GI's. Determined to be the first unit in Palermo Mad Mike Dangerfield led his mobile column in an armoured jeep but the pace of his advance was controlled by the speed of the Honeys and there where frequent delays to clear booby-trapped roadblocks and land mines. The tanks took three days to get to Corleone with the loss of five GI's and one Stuart tank en route. At Lake Scanzano, just beyond the hamlet of Fiou: za, the captain called a halt at a Y-junction in the road. He had reports that the retreating Germans had blown a bridge at Pont d'Arcera on the right limb of the Y but the left limb through Piana was still passable for tanks. Mad Mike was impatient to be on the move and had his sights on being first in Palermo. That's what the mad old general had decreed before they left Tunisia and ¡ lad Mike was out to ensure General Patton got what he ordered. Yes siree! - a dash through Piana was for him. At 0700 hrs on Monday 20th July, Major Mike Dangerfield, Lieutenant Conrad Bradley Jr. and six non-commissioned tank commanders were huddled over a map spread out on the bonnet of a jeep.

"At this point we are only forty kilometres from Palermo. I shall press on to Piana with three Honeys but I must protect my flank. Lieutenant Bradley will take twenty men, two Honeys and a DUKW along this secondary road from Bivio Lupo across this valley to Cefala and hit the main road to Palermo at Villafrati. Our Shermans from Agrigento may well be there by the time you arrive. If not, set up a road block to prevent the enemy retreating north. The distance you have to cover is 22 kilometres and I reckon you should hit Villafrati in eighteen hours. Any questions, Conrad?"

Proud to have been selected for the mission, Lieutenant Bradley Jr. drew himself up to his full height of 5ft 7ins in his stockinged feet.

"When do we hit the road sir?"

Captain Dangerfield looked at his crew with pride "We move out at 0800 hrs. I'll see you all in Palermo in a few days. Good Luck."

Bradley's troop left Fiouzza at precisely 0800 hour on 20thJuly. The lieutenant treated his mission as a dashing raid into enemy-held territory. In command of Al's tank he led his section, alternately opening and closing the Honey's hatch and scanning the countryside at any suspicious turnings, bushes or buildings that might harbour enemy troops or guns. Consequently his reluctance to advance, and the fact the secondary road proved to be no more than a dirt track, led to a two hour delay in crossing Godrano valley. One kilometre short of Godrano village he called for a ten minute halt for the umpteenth time and stood with his helmeted head sticking out of the hatch and scanning the area with his binoculars. Al and Hank sat impatiently below his feet in their cramped, sweltering, unbearably hot seats.

"What's up Lootenant?" Al asked.

"There's a small village ahead. I cain't see any movement. Rev up Rizzi and, when I say 'go,' give her full throttle."

The lieutenant closed the hatch firmly over his head and prodded Al between his shoulder blades with his toecap. Al knew the drill. He pushed the throttle to the floorboard and engaged both gear levers. The tank lurched forwards, slowly at first and then rapidly picked up speed as its caterpillar tracks dug into the soft earth and threw up clouds of dust and grit. Closely followed by the troop-carrying DUKW's, Al's tank raced uphill and along Godrano's main street. They passed a church on the village outskirts and continued uphill for a mile when, around a bend and some half a mile distant, a large house, surrounded by a walled enclosure, came into view. The cautious lieutenant scrutinised the building with his binoculars. The dirt road ran alongside the walled property and, across the road, he saw a cobblestone yard enclosed on three sides by red- roofed barns. Al grinned and winked at Hank Schweitzer "What the hell is he up to now? I think the goddamn Lootenant's found us a latrine to attack!"

Hank was not amused.

"Cut the crap you friggin Wop! Put your foot on the gas a let's get outa here."

At that very moment the lieutenant's toecap urged Al to move forwards and the Honey's tracks crunched and squealed as the sixteen-ton monster shuddered and lumbered its way to the cobblestone farmyard. Lieutenant Bradley traversed the yard and the big house with his periscope and, satisfied there was no immediate danger, he opened the hatch and got out of the tank. Pistol in hand he walked across the road to a wooden gate in the perimeter wall where he was joined by a dozen GI's. Peering through the driver's hatch Al saw his lieutenant march boldly up to the front door of the mansion, surrounded by the eager GI's clutching their carbines and submachine guns. He squinted at the clear blue sky and spoke, partly to himself and to no one in particular, "What in God's name is General Custer up to now?"

His question went unanswered. Instead there was a shrill whistling noise overhead and, a split second later, a thunderous crashing bang. Trooper Rizzi was knocked senseless by the concussion of the explosion and Trooper Hank Schweitzer was killed outright by the blast from the same shell.

When the shell exploded under the Stuart, Lieutenant Conrad Bradley was ten yards away from the stone steps leading to the weather-beaten door of the estate house. He instinctively threw himself forwards on to the gravel pathway, dislodging his tin helmet and pistol in the process. Five seconds later another shell went whistling overhead and exploded with a dull crump somewhere in the valley behind the red barn. Petrified further shelling might occur he held his position and, parrot-fashion, ran through the tank training manual he had learnt by heart at base camp in South Dakota – 'One, 'Look to the safety of your men' Two, 'Look to the safety of your vehicles,' or was it the other way round? He couldn't remember. Three, 'Identify source of attack' Four, 'Plan counterattack' and Five, 'Dig in or plan orderly retreat.' While he was reiterating these edicts two more shells went whistling harmlessly overhead. Lying face down, and clutching his hands to his ears, he could not make up his mind on the next move when he felt a sharp jab in the region of his left buttock. On turning his head sideways he saw a pair of brown canvas toecaps and, glancing upwards, the scowling, unshaven face of the paratroop sergeant who had attached himself to his troop.

"What are your orders sir?"

Lieutenant Bradley sat upright and mentally selected points 4 and 5 from his training manual.

"Tell the men to dig in and prepare for a counterattack."

The sergeant laughed outright.

"The ground's too hard for diggin'and the men don't carry friggin spades. No siree, were not diggin'in!"

The lieutenant was affronted by the rebuke but the sergeant continued "Our lead tanks' been hit. Jerry's guns are about a mile up the road and I suggest you get the men and vehicles under cover in the barn. Shall I get the men movin' sir?"

"Yes. Carry on sergeant" the lieutenant replied lamely and, in a gravely Texan accent, the sergeant shouted "Get off your arses you sons of bitches. Get across the road and under cover in the barn. Let's go NOW!"

The second Honey smashed its way into the barn and the DUKW's and jeeps followed suit. The sergeant rejoined Lieutenant Bradley, now crouching in an archway and scanning the road and mountainside for signs of enemy activity. He glanced across at the solitary tank quietly sizzling and brewing-up and extruding wisps of blackish diesel fumes spiralling skywards. Poor old Rizzi and Schweitzer were the first casualties under his command. What to do next? The time had come for Lieutenant Bradley to make his second decision and he was about to order a retreat when the paratroop sergeant nudged his elbow "Someone's alive in the Honey. I can hear shouting."

For once the lieutenant forgot personal safety and, together with the sergeant and two troopers, led the rush to get to the burning tank. From inside the Honey came a barely audible croak.

"I've been shot in my friggin butt. Get me out of here for God's sake."

The lieutenant peered through the drivers hatch "Is that you Rizzi?

"Yeah,it's me Lootenant! They got me up the arse and I am fixed to the seat. I think poor Hank has had it. The shell went off right under his friggin butt."

"Okay, hang on Rizzi! We'll have you out in a second."

One of the troopers climbed into the smoke- filled tank and managed to unscrew and remove the back of the driver's seat. Al was transfixed to the base of his seat by a jagged piece of shrapnel which had penetrated the back of his thigh and into the muscle mass in his left buttock. A spreading pool of fresh blood, both his and Hanks,' was collecting in the driver's well. Al was fluctuating in and out of consciousness and, when conscious, shrieked with pain made worse by attempts to remove him off his seat.

"It's my friggin left butt, guys. Someone's stuck a red hot poker up my arse. Jesus, just look at poor old Hank."

The violence of impact had blown Hank bodily upwards, almost severing his legs at thigh level, foreshortening his torso and squashing his skull into a messy pulp. Death had been instantaneous. A trooper administered a morphine shot and threaded a webbing sling around Al's chest and, aided by the second trooper, they dragged him out through the tank's turret. Al screamed in pain but, within seconds, he passed out and when he came to again he was lying on his side in a semi-darkened room and a G I medical orderly was inspecting his wound. Sergeant Heffner stood at the foot of the bed and, in the background, Lieutenant Bradley was attempting to converse with a Sicilian civilian, but without success. The morphine had taken effect and Al was much calmer and, despite his weakened state, he volunteered to translate for Lieutenant Bradley.

"The old man says the Germans were here last night and only left a couple of hours before we arrived. They had an officer and about forty men in trucks and two big guns. If you want to go after the Germans just leave me here. He says his daughters will look after me and I speak their lingo."

Back in the courtyard Lieutenant Bradley's briefing was rudely interrupted by a whooshing sound from the farmyard and a column of black smoke gushed forty feet in the air. The stricken tank's diesel reservoir burnt fiercely for a few minutes and, afterwards, billows of black acrid smoke belched through the open hatches. Trooper Hank Schweitzer's entombed body was cremated inside the hull of the burnt-out Honey. On returning to the house the lieutenant found three Sicilian women in Al's bedroom and the youngest, wearing dark glasses, was applying final touches to his dressing. In a feeble show of bravado Al managed a lopsided smile and a wink "These ladies are Signore Cecci's daughters, Lootenant. They're gonna look after me. I'll be okay here."

"Okay Rizzi! I'll send an ambulance to pick you up. I'll be seein' you trooper" but, as he was about to depart, Al called him closer and whispered "One of these dames, the pretty one with a round face and big knockers, asked me to give you a message. She says two enemy agents are holed out in a cave about a mile north of here. You'll see the cave above the road at the end of a curve on the hillside. They've caused a lot of trouble in the area and you would do everyone a favour if you could blow them away."

"Thanks Trooper Rizzi, I'll think about it."

Lieutenant Conrad Bradley Jr. beamed with delight. Here was a chance to avenge the death of one of his troop. He virtually ran out of the house to take his position in Sergeant Heffner's Honey and to lead his depleted unit eastwards to Villafrati. The Americans pulled out of Godrano just before midday leaving Al Rizzi in the care of Carla Cecci's daughters

On the day after his sexual encounter, Franco sat outside their cave half-expecting Carla to appear with food and for another session on the straw cot but, instead, foot-slogging Italian infantrymen came, making their way in dribs and drabs up the steep incline to Cefala. Military activity continued until the evening when the road became deserted once more. Dispirited, hungry and disappointed at Carla's non-appearance, the mafiosi retired to their hideout at nightfall. Early morning on the 20th Franco went to the plateau overlooking Godrano but hurriedly returned to the cave to alert Salvatore.

"Take cover Salvo! German troops are in Godrano and they'll be coming this way shortly. They're forming-up on the farmyard and they've got two big guns."

His mind on other things, Salvatore asked "Any signs of Carla with our food?"

"No you damned fool! Take this seriously. We mustn't get involved with the Germans."

Two hours elapsed before the mafiosi had evidence that the Germans were close at hand. When the first big bang came from behind the hill the shock was instantaneous.

"What the hell was that?" Salvatore screamed and threw himself to the ground.

"Mamma mia! That's another one. They're shelling Godrano" Franco shouted as he helped Salvatore to his feet and rushed him into the cave. The next three muted explosions were spread over five minutes and then an eerie silence descended on the hideout. Cringing in a corner Salvatore was shivering with fright and, though himself a little shaky, Franco plucked up courage to return to his concealed observation post on the ledge. In twenty minutes a German mobile column appeared around the hillside moving briskly towards Cefala.

"They're gone Salvo" Franco shouted into the cave.

"I'm staying here," Salvatore replied, "I don't like those big bangs."

"Do as you please Salvatore. The Americans will be here soon. Shall we surrender to the Amis?"

"You do as you please, Franco. I'm staying here until everyone's gone."

Franco was fully determined to surrender to the Americans and, when a tank with a silver star on its turret appeared around the hillside, he jumped to his feet and waved his arms.

Having negotiated a sharp bend on the mountainside, Lieutenant Bradley scanned the hill to his right and, 400 yards ahead and well above his head, a man stood on a ledge furiously waving his arms. 'Some agent,' thought the Lieutenant, 'there should be two guys.' Swivelling the turret in an arc he aimed the Honey's 37mm, 2-pounder gun at the target and, in all, three shells were fired as well as a few bursts from the Browning machine gun. Chunks of granite and limestone flew into the air and one shell hit the cave entrance bringing down the roof and burying Salvatore Branco in a mound of rubble. Sergeant Heffner and two troopers were sent up to the hideout and, after one look at the collapsed cave, they returned at the double. The sergeant reported "The goddamn cave's completely blocked. No one left alive Lootenant."

"Okay let's go," and the lieutenant ordered his troop to move on. Had Sergeant Heffner been more thorough he would have found Franco Gicanetti crouching in a crevasse in the rock face. As soon as the Americans were gone Franco walked eastwards cross country avoiding all roads and hamlets until, after three days, he found sanctuary with Don Genco Russo's family at Mussomeli.

Palermo fell to the Americans on the 23rd July. Mad Mike Dangerfield arrived a day later and missed out on a citation but Lieutenant Conrad Bradley Jr's Honey and two Shermans of the U S 2nd Armoured Division were the first tanks to reach the city centre. The Lieutenant was awarded a medal for his achievement in being the first American to liberate Sicily's capital city.

CHAPTER 5

A double wedding and a funeral

TROOPER ALPHONSE RIZZI'S INJURIIES were not as severe as was first feared and the searing pain in his left buttock settled, only to recur whenever iodine-soaked dressings were packed into his open wound. He was nursed face downwards with his buttocks and thighs exposed to the air. The Cecci sisters assumed individual roles in management of the wounded G I. A stickler for propriety, Anna was uncommunicative and kept out of sight but provided all Al's meals. The softly-rounded Gina was prone to histrionics and couldn't stand the sight of blood and gore. She was effusively attentive and held Al's hand, or cried to order, but in a practical sense she was useless. Al's favourite was seventeen year old Carla who nursed him with competence and stayed at his bedside most of the day and slept at night on a sofa in the kitchen to be near the wounded trooper. On his fourth day in the sick room Al got out of bed and, supported by Carla and Gina, he struggled painfully across the room and felt the thrill of the females' close proximity. With a smile and a wink he thanked the women profusely but, behind her tinted lenses, Carla's eyes remained inscrutable. That night Al returned Claudia's picture, which he had propped-up on his bedside locker, to his wallet and on the following day Carla was a different person. She removed her dark glasses and smiled readily and paid extra attention to dressing Al's wound. IIe told her stories and Carla laughed aloud, not at the content but at Al's amateurish attempts to converse in a Sicilian dialect. Despite her traumatic experience a week previously Carla was growing fond of the glamorous and amusing American soldier.

Carla was not a ravishing beauty. She had an oval-shaped face and her nose was too pointed to be deemed attractive. She had a wide mouth with full, generous lips though her right upper lip was bruised and swollen. Her eyes were her captivating feature. Deep-set, black, limpid pools they promised everything, gentle when she smiled and steely when she was annoyed. Her figure was that of a boy with flat muscular buttocks and flattened puerile breasts. Al was attracted towards her and couldn't rationally explain why. Was it the glamour of being a wounded hero in a foreign land or the traditional bond that is said to exist between a casualty of war and his nurse? Al did not know the answer, but of one thing he was certain, he was sexually attracted to the thin, boyish- looking woman.

On his eighth day at Godrano two men dressed in peasant clothing and carrying shotguns appeared in Al's bedroom. Don Carlo Cecci introduced them "These are the sons of Giovanni Cucinotta from our neighbouring estate. Andreo is the eldest and the young man is Giudo. They have come to see if we're safe and sound after last week's bombardment."

After an exchange of formalities Don Cecci and Andreo left the bedroom but the younger man lingered and suddenly blurted out "Tell me about America Signore Rizzi."

"Well, Giudo, I'm from New York City where we got the highest buildings in the world and we got Broadway for shows. For the best friggin grub in the world we got Little Italy. There's plenty of work and lots of good money to be made in New York. If you got over there kid," and fishing in his wallet Al produced one of his embossed business cards, "look me up at Berterelli's. I'll stake you for a glass of wine and a square meal."

Al's queer vocabulary startled Giudo and he snatched the business card and beat a hasty retreat from the sickroom. Al chuckled.

The true purpose of the Cucinotta's visit was revealed by Andreo in Don Cecci's parlour "I've come to speak on Family matters, Don Carlo. I know about the marriage pact and we think it's now an urgent matter."

Don Carlo felt bitter spittle regurgitating at the back of his throat followed by waves of unrelenting nausea. He took off his cloth cap and wiped his sweaty brow.

"Don Giovanni and I sealed an honourable pact and I shall abide by it. I also see a need for an urgent union of our families. Don Triddu Caminiti ordered such an arrangement before he was killed."

Andreo coughed and hoicked, expectorating a gelatinous globule into the unlit fireplace.

"I wish to see the three daughters you offer in marriage."

The old don stiffened.

"Three! Three? The agreement was for my two eldest, Anna and Gina. Carla is only a girl and not ready for marriage."

Just like a farmer at a cattle market, Andreo inspected Don Carlo's daughters lined up in the kitchen. Giudo fixed his malevolent gaze on Carla and, with a smirk on his face, played at the game of outstaring her. Giudo won hands down. Blushing bright red, Carla lowered her eyes and ran into the pantry. Giudo's arrogance reminded her of Franco and she burst into tears. Satisfied with his inspection Andreo barked "The Cuccinotta Family are pleased to make your acquaintance, signorina's" and the women were dismissed.

After the strangers had gone, pandemonium erupted in the kitchen. Stoic and sullen, Anna stood in the middle of the floor and Gina pranced around the slate-topped table, babbling hysterically, while Carla sat sobbing uncontrollably with her head resting on her forearms on the table. The cacophony ceased abruptly when Don Carlo appeared "I have made a marriage pact with Don Giovanni Cuccinotta. I have given him my word. You are to marry Don Giovanni's sons."

Carla screamed "No! No! I do not want to marry anyone."

Don Carlo persevered "Not you Carla. Anna will marry Andreo and Gina will marry Santo. You, Carla, will be betrothed to

Giudo. The weddings must take place soon, very soon. I will now go and lie down."

Anna was first to react "I don't like the look of Andreo but we must respect our father's decision."

She was nearly 32 years of age and realised this was her main chance of marriage. Gina, as usual, became hysterical "I have never seen Santo. Is he handsome? I want a family of my own and I hope he's a strong man."

Still sobbing, Carla interjected with bitterness in her voice "Giudo's got a sly look. I'll run away, or kill myself, before I marry him."

Her sisters tried to calm her but Carla was inconsolable. Al overheard the shouting and arguments in the kitchen and, when Carla came in to his bedroom later, she explained it was common practice in Sicily for the head of a Family to arrange marriages for his daughters. But when she came to mention Giudo she broke down again and nestled in Al's arms.

"Please take me to America, Signore Rizzi. I want to get away from this place."

At that moment Al's only desire was to placate the tearful girl. He kissed her gently on her face and lips.

"Of course, little Carla, I will take you with me to America when the war is over."

Her sobbing ceased and, exhausted, she dozed fitfully for a few minutes in his soothing embrace.

Two mornings later Don Carlo, Gina and Anna were at Godrano church making arrangements for a double wedding. Left alone in the estate house Carla romanticised about a new life in America and her passport to the New World was in the front bedroom. On impulse she decided to involve Alphonse in the only way she knew and made a beeline for his bedroom. Al was sitting gingerly on the edge of his bed when Carla took the initiative and pulled him backwards next to her writhing, sexually-aroused body.

Denied the pleasure of sex for over seven months Al's resistance was low and the next ten minutes were a blurr. He succumbed to his basic instincts and intercourse took place quite r aturally. Carla was still in a tender state and the first penetration was painful but, afterwards, it was pleasurable and Al took time to be gentle with the waif of a woman who was clinging to his body like a tendril to a vine. And then the questions started flowing "When will you take me to America, Alphonse? Tell me about New York, Alphonse. What work will I do in America? Will I live in your house,Alphonse?"

Al answered all her questions and kept stroking her thick black hair and kissing her upturned, tear-stained face. The sexual act had left Carla satisfied and very much in love with the worldly American but for Al it had been a physical necessity. To show his appreciation, and as a 'thank you', he presented Carla with one of his gold-embossed Berterelli business cards.

A US Army Tank Recovery Unit and an ambulance arrived at Godrano a few days later. A medical officer, a Bostonian and a Harvard graduate, diagnosed a partial rupture of the left sciatic nerve and was complimentary about the treatment Al had received at Godrano. He assured all and sundry that Al's wound was a homer and he would receive a Purple Heart, First Class. Al responded by dishing out business cards to the entire Unit with the promise of free grub at Berterelli's if they ever visited Manhattan. By now Don Carlo Cecci was in a parlous state and his 'goodbye' handshake at the door of the ambulance was limp and feather-light. An engineer officer pronounced the burnt-out Stuart unsalvageable and the blackened hulk, with its bizarre contents, was unceremoniously dumped off the road into a ravine outside Godrano village. After the War a simple cross and a plaque was erected in memory of 'Trooper Hank Schweitzer, aged 19, US 2nd Armoured Division. Killed in action at this spot on July 20th 1943.'

August 24th 1943

About thirty peasants descended on Godrano church to witness the Cecci women's double wedding to Don Giovanni's sons. Dressed in their Sunday best they had been given a day off work to join in the celebrations and they intended making the most of a rare occasion. Respected by his tenants, Carlo Cecci was a popular figure and the tongue-clicking village matriarchs empathised with the don who, due to the war and his own ill-health, had failed to allow the traditional four to five years of strictly-governed courtship to elapse before offering his daughter's hand in marriage. The Cecci brides knew little about their grooms from Sant Agata but were determined to be loyal to Don Carlo and, to show that at Godrano they were 'tutti cugini,' one cosy happy family. Godrano's womenfolk had been preparing for days before the wedding feast. An enormous cake, containing pasta real and marzipan, was baked and filled with picotta cream and decorated with almonds and glazed fruit. Tables had been set out in front of the village taverna for the wedding breakfast and one long table was laden with traditional Sicilian delicacies - freshly baked loaves, chunks of goats cheese and an abundant supply of locally-produced wine.

The Portella Sant Agata party arrived at Godrano on mules at midday. Dressed in dark suits and wearing black felt hats, Don Giovanni led his sons uphill to the church, closely attended by a shepherd playing scialpi romantica ballads on his sacciapensieri, an antiquated type of mouth organ. Meanwhile Don Cecci's bridal party wended its way sedately downhill to the church. Ahead of them a peasant violinist capered and pranced and played popular folk music. Don Carlo was supported at each elbow by the heavily-veiled brides while, ten paces behind bare-headed and dressed in plain white, Carla walked alone. Gasps of dismay greeted the party in the church when the Godranesi saw how emaciated their don had become. His ancient black suit hung around his meagre frame and the ensuing two hour mass, and wedding service, severely taxed his strength. Led by musicians the wedding party then made their way downhill to the village square. Don Carlo refused to be supported by anyone other than Carla and whispered through his dry, cracked lips "I'm glad that's over Carla. I shall now rest in peace. You will be married one day but I shall not see it. What do you think about Giudo?"

"He's all right Papa," she lied, not wishing to cause further anguish to her ailing father.

On Godrano's main square the newly-marrieds and their parents sat at a long table and a chair in the shade was found for Don Carlo. Giudo took a seat next to Carla. Don Giovanni and Andreo made a few flowery comments about unification of the Families but Santo Cucinotta surprised everyone. He refused to make a speech and, instead, in a rich baritone, he sang a love ballad to Gina. She beamed with pleasure and looked lovingly at her new husband. Unlike his father and brothers, Santo was prepared to laugh and joke at the slightest provocation and when a friscalettu, a reed flute, struck up a chord he readily joined in, much to the discomfiture of Andreo and his father. Wine flowed freely and dancing commenced on the square, men dancing with men, a relic of occupation by the Grecians many centuries ago. Giudo was getting rapidly drunk and made surreptitious advances on Carla and resorted to braggadocio, a boastful recital about his virility and sexual prowess. Carla tensed and stiffened as Giudo's fingers caressed her thigh.

"Take your hand off my leg."

"And what if I don't? What will you do about it? After all we are betrothed."

"I'll hit your face."

It would never do for the son of a 'Man of Honour' to have his face slapped in public by a woman from another Mafia family. Bur Giudo was past caring and increased pressure on Carla's thigh. Suddenly her father crashed face forwards on to the table and Carla's attempts to get to her feet were obstructed by Giudo grasping hand.

"Let me go! Can't you see Papa is unwell?"

Giudo sneered "My needs are greater than that old mans'."

Carla acted on impulse and snatching a fork from the table she thrust its prongs firmly into the back of Giudo's left hand. He gave a loud yelp and pulled his hand away. A combination of nausea, noise and heat had overcome Don Carlo and, despite his protestations, Carla got up to take him home. An offer to accompany them from Giudo was sternly rejected and he was left sitting at the table, in 'disgrazitsa,' nursing his bleeding and bandaged left hand.

At around 7 o'clock the constant beating of a tamureddu, a skin drum, heralded the departure of Santo and Gina and the Sant Agata party and, an hour later, a cirameddu, a goat-skin bagpipe, announced Andreo and Anna were leaving the wedding reception. Surrounded by well-wishers they slowly walked uphill, the cirameddu becoming louder and louder until, with a plaintive wheeze, it shut off abruptly outside the main entrance to Godrano estate house. Andrea Cuccinotta had arrived at his new fiefdom and a turbulent era was about to dawn at Godrano.

Friday 3rd September 1943

Ten days after the double wedding Don Carlo Cecci died. He never recovered after collapsing at the wedding breakfast and became progressively weaker and yellower. As predicted by Professore Abrigo Natale, a deep jaundice appeared five days before he slid into unconsciousness and passed away peacefully in his bed. The funeral of a popular don was usually attended by a crowd of Cosa Nostra mourners but the ongoing war, and lack of a Capo in Palermo, confined mourners to his immediate family, his newly-acquired in-laws and the faithful artisans of Godrano, who turned out in force and ensured Don Carlo had a grand send-off.

To the accompaniment of plaintive beats of a tamureddu drummer, the cortège walked from the estate house to the church. Don Giovanni Cucinotta, Andreo and Santo led the procession followed at a respectable distance by black-veiled family females. Godrano's peasant farmers, including two professional wailers, brought up the rear. In purdah after his behaviour at the double wedding, Giudo was conspicuous by his absence. Don Carlo Cecci was laid to rest in the family tomb at Godrano church and,afterwards, in the parlour at Godrano Don Giovanni, Santo and Andreo sat down to a light snack washed down with liberal quantities of white wine. Don Giovanni took the stage "By marriage this estate now belongs to our Family and we shall have two Cucinotta dons, myself at Portella Sant Agata and you, Andreo, here at Godrano. My consiglieri will be Santo and Giudo will be your lieutenant. Make sure he does not disgrace us further by pestering that vixen Carla. My word of honour to Don Carlo Cecci stands and Giudo will marry her and she must be a virgin on their wedding day."

Andrea bent forward and solemnly brushed the back of his father's hand.

"I swear I will work in harmony with you, Don Giovanni, and I will take good care Giudo does not step out of line."

They raised their glasses and drank a toast to the Cucinotta Family. When Carla heard of the new arrangements she was livid and retired to her bedroom where she lay staring abjectly at the ceiling, fingering Al Rizzi's business card and willing him to return and take her away from this hateful house.

From his very first day at Godrano Giudo proved a nuisance and a pest, touching Carla at every opportunity and subjecting her to his own particular brand of verbal braggadocio. Andreo took his brother's side and even accused Carla of being the instigator and calling her a 'puttita,' Sicilian parlance for a common whore.

Carla reacted violently but soon realised Don Andreo was not a gentleman and certainly not a 'Man of Honour.' On a few occasions he slapped her face and once, completely losing his temper in drink, gave her a physical beating. Thereafter Carla kept out of his way and out of Giudo's clutches as far as possible. Anna was not sympathetic to her plight and stuck by her husband and, within a month of her father's funeral, Carla was banished to the kitchen.

Apart from his behaviour in the house, Giudo was developing a bad reputation for himself as a ruthless gabelotti. In Don Carlo Cecci's days about twenty artisans farmed small plots of land at Godrano and produced fruit and vegetables for their own use. The benevolent don frequently waived rental from them in return for their labour at harvest time. After Giudo's arrival payment of these dues was demanded, 'or else', and the peasants soon learnt the meaning of 'or else' – an injury to their mules, arson of their outhouses or homes and, sometimes, physical maiming. Don Andreo readily condoned his brother's actions and, as Don of Godrano, he was sole arbiter of the Law. Complaints from peasant farmers were dismissed out of hand and frequently invited further retribution from Giudo's gabelotti. With their inborn resistance to oppression the Godranesi learnt to grin and bear it and to suffer in silence thus, inadvertently, upholding the Mafia tradition of 'omerta.'

A Mafia Council. 9th October, 1943.

In 1943 the U S government unofficially appointed Charles Lucky Luciano political advisor to American armed forces on Italian soil and, from gaol, he directed reconstruction of the Mafia hierarchy in Sicily and southern Italy. As his agent in the field Luciano promoted Vito Genovese, a former mobster colleague who had been forced to flee from New York to Italy in 1938 and had ingratiated himself with Mussolini and the Fascist regime. On instruction from Luciano, Genovese made certain that most political and influential posts in Sicily's interim wartime government went to loyal members of the Cosa Nostra.

By order of the U S officer commanding Palermo District the dons of Portella Sant Agata and Godrano were requested to attend a conference at the American military headquarters in Palermo on 9th October 1943. The American authorities were unaware of Don Carlo Cecci's death and Don Andreo represented the interests of Godrano estate. Palazzo dei Normanii was crawling with armed Marines and a sergeant, with multiple stripes on his left sleeve, checked everyone's name as they arrived. The Plazzo's loggia was packed with Sicilians dressed in their Sunday best and partaking of a cold lime cordial. Don Giovanni nodded formally to some of the delegates and whispered to Don Andreo "There's quite a few Dons here. I've seen the Barbera brothers from Corleone and Angelo Muzzi is with them. The Don from Agrigento is in the corner speaking to an American soldier and near the door I see Genco Russo from Mussomeli and the Maranzano's from Castellmmare. There's something important in the wind."

The Sala de Ruggero of the palazzo was a fitting location for the important conference. The twenty-eight strong delegation sat around an oblong table in the ornate salon with its hunting-scene frescoes and tall, stalactite ceiling. An American colonel took up position near an open fireplace and, lounging nonchalantly by his side stood a man in an ill-fitting military uniform without badges of rank and only displaying a blue armband. The Colonel addressed his audience "I am Colonel James Fairbrother of the U S Marines and on my right is Mister Vito Genovese. He is the United States Government's official liaison officer to Sicily. I regret my command of Italian is poor and Mister Genovese will translate for me if we're in difficulty."

The Colonel paused and mopped his brow.

"We are here to elect an interim administration for Sicily based here in Palermo. You have been selected as trustworthy candidates for election to the positions available. Before we start I will conduct a roll call. Please answer to your names and declare the regions you represent."

When the colonel's drawling voice called out 'Signore Carlo Cecci,' Don Andreo sprang to his feet "I am Andreo Cucinotta. I represent Carlo Cecci who is unable to be here."

A delegate riposted "Is it not his death that has prevented Carlo Cecci attending?"

Andreo was flustered and the smirks on some of the faces around the table inflamed his ego.

"I am now Boss at Godrano and let no one challenge it."

Don Giovanni came to his son's aid "Don Andreo has been properly inducted and is worthy of his position."

Colonel Fairbrother intervened "What is the problem? Am I to understand some of you wish Signore Cucinotta to leave? We will settle this by a show of hands."

Mostly designed as a slap in the face for the Corleonesi the voting went in Don Andreo's favour and the colonel continued "That's settled. Now ve'll get down to business. There are two important posts to fill. One is chief administrator for the whole of Sicily and the other is the office of Mayor of Palermo. I will now leave you to your deliberations and Mr Genovese will remain to see fair play."

Once the colonel was out of earshot Vito Genovese lit a cigarette and addressed his audience in a high-pitched drawl "All present here are cosche. I am a life-long friend of the American boss, Luciano, and between us we've decided who will run the show in Sicily. So let's see if you come up with the same friggin answer."

The delegates broke into a babble of confused conversation and argument, each don laying claim to one post or the other. The volume of noise increased as fingers were pointed and fists brandished. After ten minutes Vito Genovese banged the table "Enough! Enough! Written on this piece of paper is the American Boss' nomination for the main job. Pass it around. I'm going outside for five minutes and when I return I hope to find unanimous support for his selection. The man appointed will then select a mayor from among you all."

The folded piece of paper was passed from hand to hand and each delegate feigned surprise at the nomination with the exception of Don Calagero Vizzini whose face was wreathed in smiles. Vizzini was a minor don from Villalba, a small village plagued by absentee landlords and providing cheap labour for the fiefdom of Miccicho. Don Genco Russo, his neighbour from Mussomeli, was particularly incensed and realised the whole affair was a f'ait accompli. Vizzini's choice of a running partner caused more consternation than his own appointment. Angelo Muzzi, the Barbera brother's consiglieri at Corleone, was nominated for the office of mayor. On his return Colonel Fairbrother expressed pleasure at the speed with which the delegates had reached their decision. He was expecting a long day of haggling but it was all over in an hour and a half. In his concluding address the colonel thanked Signore Vito Genovese and summed up "And now it only remains for Signores Vizzini and Muzzi to get together to pick their administrative team. When this war is over there will be plenty of rebuilding and reorganizing to do and I am certain the team you have chosen today will serve Sicily with pride."

When the time came for the appointment of administrative officers Vito Genovese ensured the posts were filled by paid-up members of the Sicilian Cosa Nostra.

On their way home the Cucinotta dons, father and son, rested their mules on a ravine bridge at Punta del Moarda. Don Giovanni was perplexed "We witnessed a fix-up at Palazzo Normanni today, Andreo. I don't trust Genovese. He was friendly with Mussolini before the Americans came and rumour has it he supplied drugs to

Count Ciano, the Duce's son-in-law. But he now turns up as an adviser. I don't trust him at all. The Big Boss in America is in gaol and Luciano is not an old style mafioso like us. The modern mafiosi in America think nothing of dealing in drugs and prostitution."

As Don Giovanni prepared to remount his mule he paused "Calagero Vizzini's appointment was a shock but it was done to annoy Genco Russo who thought the job was his. To make Muzzi mayor of Palermo was a big mistake. He isn't, and never has been, a proper don and hasn't forgiven us for kicking him out of Portella Sant Agata. Vito Genovese was born in Corleone and I suspect he, together with the Barbera brothers, pushed Muzzi's appointment. Mark my words, Andreo, Muzzi will be a thorn in our flesh for a long time to come."

Don Andreo silently mulled over his father's comments. Don Giovanni was a Mafia di Vecchio Stampo, a traditional-style Mafioso, but Andreo had different ideas and intended treading a different pathway. His ambition was to unite the two estates and become Don of the largest masseria in Sicily and, when the time came, he might be in a position to bid for the top prize – Capo di Tutti Capi of the Sicilian Cosa Nostra. Then, and only then, would the sparks begin to fly.

CHAPTER 6

Return of a war hero

AFTER THREE WEEKS in a U S Field Hospital at Trapani, and convalescence at Netley Hospital on Southampton water in England, Alphonse Rizzi finally ended up in Massachusetts General in Boston before his final discharge from Uncle Sam's Army on December 4th 1943. Throughout his eight months absence on active service he had only written to Claudia on three occasions. His letters had not revealed his whereabouts and he made a point of not mentioning his shrapnel wound. He planned to surprise everyone by turning up in one piece or, at least, almost physically intact. As soon as Al arrived at Central Station in New York he made a beeline for the restaurant he had advertised at every opportunity in Sicily and England and on U S naval vessels on the high seas. At the latest count he only had twenty Berterelli business cards left in his wallet out of the original hundred he took to war. His supply of Cuban cigars were long gone.

"What do I owe you buddy?" Al asked as he clambered out of a yellow cab with difficulty and, supported by an elbow crutch, he stood in the teeming rain outside Berterelli's. A khaki rainsheet protected his uniform but, even so, rivulets coursed down the back of his neck and inside his shirt collar. He had hailed a cab at Central Station and, throughout the journey along the blacked-out streets of Manhattan, the cabbie had chatted incessantly about the weather, the war and the poor street lighting. The driver stuck his head out of the window and spoke through the side of his mouth in a strong Bronx accent "No charge buddy. I don't take bucks from a G I. Where were you hit?".

Al misunderstood the taxi driver

"I was hit in the friggin butt."

The cab driver snorted and guffawed.

"Jees! I mean, was it the Japs?"

"No," Al replied, "the Krauts got me in Sicily."

The cab driver withdrew his soaking-wet head and began winding up the window

"My grandfather was Sicilian and I'm half Irish. Good luck to you son."

The yellow cab moved rapidly away from the kerbside, its spinning wheels spraying Al's trousers. He chuckled to himself. New York cab drivers were the salt of the earth and a law unto themselves and their tough talk and brash manners concealed hearts of gold. He readjusted his crutch and swung his body crabwise towards the dimly-lit entrance to Ristorante Berterelli.

Berterelli's crowed bar room was noisy and the air polluted with cigarette smoke. The customers, many of them servicemen, made way for the rain-sodden G I struggling with his crutch and making his way towards the long bar. Joe Falcone instantly recognised Al "Jesus Christ Al! What have they done to you? We heard you'd gone across the pond to Europe. When did you get back to New York?"

Joe leant across the bar and they clasped hands and held each other in a firn grasp for half a minute.

"Let me get you a drink. One Heineken coming up pal."

Joe returned with a frothing pint of lager and Al took a generous gulp.

"Is the boss in tonight, Joe?"

"You should remember Al, he's never in Berterellis' on Fridays. Tomorrow night's his big night. I'll give the Boss a buzz in a minute but tell me first, what's with the crutch?"

Al related his story and Joe laughed aloud, his large frame convulsing and his moustache quivering.

"Show 'em your butt or your Purple Heart, Al. I wish Nico was here to see it. He's with the Marine Corps in Texas and they're on the way to the Pacific."

Giuseppe telephoned Mario Deluca and passed on a message. "The boss will see you tomorrow at his apartment in Howard. He says to get there lunchtime and say's he's glad y⁄ ur back in one friggin piece."

Saturday 5th December 1943 was a dank, blustery, wet day, threatening snow. Al was on Don Marios' doorstep promptly at 12 noon and the don himself answered the doorbell.

"What in God's name have they done to you Al?" he exclaimed when he saw the crutch.

"It's nothing Don Mario. I'm okay" and the two men embraced.

"Come in! Come in, son. We've been expecting you."

Signora Deluca and her daughters were seated in the lounge and Claudia's welcoming smile vanished abruptly when she saw Al's prop.

"I was shot in the leg. The medics tell me everything will be okay but I may end up with a limp. I feel fine in myself."

Signora Deluca crossed herself and Claudia burst out "Why didn't you write to us Al? We only got two letters and they told us nothing. We didn't know where you were, or if you were still alive."

Don Mario spoke sharply to his daughter.

"If I've told you once, Claudia, I've told you a hundred times. Soldiers on active service are not allowed to let on where they are for security reasons. Ain't that so Al?"

"Yes, Don Mario, that's law in the army."

After lunch Alphonse was seated in a comfortable chair in Don Mario's private study and the don, pulling hard on a freshly-lit cigar, was in a serious mood.

"Before you went away I hinted there might be a job in my enterprises on your return. I'm going to make you my consigliere. You will be my right hand man and run my organisation for me. I see you and Claudia are very close and I hope one day you will be united. You will then become tutti cugini with my Family and so will your mother and sisters. If you accept you will be introduced into the Cosa Nostra."

Al made up his mind in a flash and replied promptly "I am honoured to become your consigliere, Don Mario, and I accept with thanks."

Don Mario smiled. The young man was impetuous but completely trustworthy and the right type of recruit into his Family business.

"Very well! I'll give you some idea of how the Families operate in New York. Lucky Luciano was our Big Boss until his arrest in 1936 when Frank Costello took over. We all pay our respects to Frankie and he makes all decisions and settles Family disputes. Twenty per cent of our income goes to Costello and, for that, he gives us protection. It's a sort of insurance policy and we call it 'wetting the beak.' All the other dons in the city, and across the Hudson in New Jersey, do the same thing. I take the skim to Frank Costello's Long Island pad once a month. I'll take you to meet him one day when the time is right."

Don Mario paused to relight his Havana.

"I have six legit businesses in mid and downtown Manhattan – Berterellis', the Capri café on 31st West and Dino's Diner on Canal and Baxter in little Italy. I run two hotels- the Sorrento on 43rd West and the Barclay, in Barclay street near City Hall. My laundry is on 51st Street at the back of the Waldorf Astoria. In the 30's our Family was strongly opposed to taking money from prostitution but the war has changed all that. Hundreds of servicemen need sexual gratification and we provide for them at our hotels. My lieutenants collect protection money from restaurants and brothels in Manhattan and, every Saturday night, we have a meeting in the storeroom at Berterelli's when the skim is divided out and twenty per cent set aside for the Boss on Long Island and the Big Boss in Dannemora State Prison. My organisation operates in downtown Manhattan, south of 70th Street, and to the north of this line Antonio Andretti is Boss. He also operates across Triborough Bridge into the Bronx and Haarlem. The blacks in Haarlem are into drugs and Andretti is also flirting with Chinese drug racketeers. Promise me Alphonse you will never have nothing to do with drugs."

Don Mario looked inquiringly at Alphonse who answered mechanically "I swear I will never involve your Family in drugs."

Al's answer satisfied Don Mario Deluca.

"There are five important Families in New York City and two in New Jersey, all answerable to Frankie Costello. A powerful wiseguy in Brooklyn is Joe Adonis who runs Joe's Italian Kitchen where the Mob hang out most nights. Joe and Frankie Costello look after Lucky Luciano's interests while he is in Dannemora. Three or four times a year Costello has a meeting of all Family Bosses at Statten Island Ferry Hotel which can only be approached from the water and his lieutenants make certain none of the delegates are armed."

Don Mario got to his feet and poured two glasses of cognac.

"So, Alphonse, there you have it. As my consigliere you will collect protection money, oversee our loan sharking rackets, run my hotels and accompany me to the Mob's meetings. From time to time we may get an order from above to fulfil a contract on a mobster or on a member of one of the Families. Will you be able to carry out these duties?"

Al had listened intently to Don Mario and responded solemnly "I thank you, Don Mario, for the opportunity to serve your Family and I promise to obey the Bosses at all times. My time in the Army has taught me to toe the line" and Al bent forwards and lightly kissed the don's ring finger. Visibly moved Don Mario took a generous gulp of brandy. "The war has affected our income. Luciano has ordered us to cooperate with the government. His stretch in Dannemora is for a thirty to forty years but, by advising the Feds, he hopes to beat the rap and get parole. Our best earners are the hotels and, as long as the war continues, we shall get big bucks from prostitution and, even if the war should end, I cannot see a decrease in demand for this lucrative service."

That night Al Rizzi took Claudia to dinner and a Broadway show. They only sat through part of the first act. Their intimate proximity in the theatre seats aroused passions which flared into a deluge of uncontrollable desire. They hurriedly left the theatre and drove to a secluded spot in Battery Park. By now a seasoned campaigner, Al had no intention of waiting until his wedding night for the joys of intercourse and had equipped himself with a supply of army issue condoms which he kept in his wallet next to the embossed Berterelli business cards. They indulged in a prolonged and torrid sex session and, afterwards, pledged undying love for each other and agreed to marry. Later, when alone, Al compared Claudia's performance with Carla's at Godrano. He gave Carla six out of ten and Claudia passed with flying colours and a maximum score. The announcement that Al had proposed came as no surprise to the Deluca. Don Mario was over the moon but Signora Deluca had reservations about Al's background and the fact his father had be n a pugilist and a drunkard. Don Mario quickly reminded his wife she originated from an Italian ghetto in Brooklyn docks. Claudia's elder sister was jealous and, by protocol, Bella should be the first in the family to wed. She pouted and sulked and had to be firmly reminded by her father there was a war on. The wedding date was fixed for Easter Saturday 1944.

Don Mario Deluca was determined to make his daughter's Easter wedding a memorable event in New York's social calendar. The wedding ceremony and Mass was conducted by the Catholic Bishop of Manhattan at St Patrick's cathedral and the reception was held at Frank Costello's Long Island villa overlooking Hampton Bay. A hired fleet of twelve pink Cadillac's conveyed guests from the cathedral to the wedding reception. Four marquees had been erected on Costello's extensive lawns and 300 guests sat down for the wedding breakfast. Everyone who was anyone among New York's elite was present – the deputy mayor, a police chief, two high court judges and prominent and wealthy New York businessmen mingled with Mafia mobsters and movie starlets. Theatre celebrities were two a penny and a young Italian upstart called Frank Sinatra sang for the guests. In one marquee four musicians played traditional Sicilian and Italian folk songs on a flute, an oboe and a tamareddu drum producing nostalgic emotions among the hoodlums, most of whom had never set foot outside the USA. Wiseguy's unashamedly burst into tears and hugged each other in a vainglorious demonstration of false affection. New York's Family bosses attended the reception and Bottles Capone, brother of the notorious Al, and Johnny Torrio flew down from Chicago. Surprisingly the diverse mixture of government, legal, business, entertainment and mobster elements gelled into a harmonious gathering and enhanced Frank Costello's standing in the community. Part of the glory reflected on Don Mario Deluca and Alphonse Rizzi, the wartime hero and proud bearer of the Purple Heart.

When celebrations were at their height Frank Costello contrived to have a secret meeting with his New York mobster colleagues in his den in the villa. Known as Prime Minister of the Underworld, Costello was at his suave best.

"I am delighted to see you here on our big occasion. Don Mario is to be congratulated on the arrangements. He has given us a day to remember for a long time."

The audience clapped politely and Don Mario smiled at the compliment from his Boss. Physically, Frankie Costello was just half an inch taller that Don Mario and had the same rotund shape and sagging, double-chins. Always a natty dresser he had excelled himself for the wedding and wore a pale-blue, pinstripe suit with a blazing red, silk necktie and white, patent-leather shoes. A deliberate pause was prolonged as he swept his penetrating gaze around the table, eyeing each mobster in turn.

"But even on this happy day we must not forget business. I have two matters that need attention. The first concerns Antonio Andretti" and, fixing his beady eye on the Manhattan mobster, he continued "Our accountants tell me you have not paid any skim from your loansharking enterprises for four months and the Big Boss wants an answer."

Don Andretti was taken by surprise "I'm not aware you've been underpaid Padrone."

"Not just underpaid, Antonio, not paid at all in February and March. You will make up the arrears this month."

"Yes. Padrone, it will be done" the don from uptown Manhattan stammered. Some of the mobsters shuffled uncomfortably at the Boss' rebuke but most felt Andretti got all he deserved and showed their disapproval by audible tongue clicking.

Costello now invited Don Mario to speak on his behalf. Deluca cleared his throat

"I wish to thank Frankie Costello for allowing us to use his beautiful hom · for my daughter's wedding reception. It has been a wonderful day and I am very proud to see Claudia married to a handsome G I. Alphonse Rizzi is one of us. He comes from a Sicilian family and I propose him for membership of our Societa Honorata. He will become my underboss and consigliere."

Costello ordered Al brought into the crowded study and addressed the nervous bridegroom.

"We intend making you a 'made man' and a member of our Honourable Society. Do you accept the honour and pledge allegiance to me and my New York Families and our larger Family in the States? You must agree to keep the secrets of our Society and uphold our vows of honorata and Omerta at all times. Do you swear on your honour to do all this, Alphonse Rizzi?"

Alphonse did not hesitate and replied in a loud clear voice "I pledge my loyalty to your Family and the Cosa Nostra and I will strictly obey the Society's laws" and he bent forwards to kiss the back of Costello's right hand. The Prime Minister of the Underworld then led Al around the room to hug and shake hands with his newly-acquired Mafia brethren. Frankie Costello brought the meeting to a close "Let it be known that today we have accepted Alphonse Rizzi as a member of our Sacred Society and his appointment as consigliere to Don Mario D luca must be respected at all times. Anyone unjustly interfering with Alphonse Rizzi's position will be answerable to me."

The ten minute 'ceremony' was a pale imitation of a Sicilian induction ritual which usually lasted over an hour and involved swearing an oath on the Bible. The dons filed past the uncrowned Capo di Tutti Capi of New York and kissed him on both cheeks and hugged him as a token of fielty and respect. They then returned to the reception to mingle, drink and celebrate with the other wedding guests. Accompanied by a piper the newly-marrieds were escorted across the lawns at midnight to a seashore cottage where they spent their three-day honeymoon. Seated outside the bridal suite a drummer beat his tamureddu every minute until dawn's first rays brought nuptials to an end. At first the couple were acutely aware of the mournful drumbeat but after two hours torrid lovemaking they fell asleep, blissfully satiated and exhausted.

Don Mario Deluca's wedding gifts to the young couple were more than generous. In July his family moved into a villa at Oyster Bay on the north shore of Long Island and Al Rizzi's mother and sisters came to live with him at Deluca's apartment in Howard. Alphonse's cup was full to overflowing and, in one fell swoop, he had achieved two of his ambitions. He had married the girl of his dreams and had been accepted into the most powerful Family in New York. His third ambition, to eventually become

New York's top man, was one step nearer realisation. Everything was 'tutti cugini', comfortable and cosy, in the protective embrace of Frankie Costello and Don Mario Deluca. Alphonse Rizzi was well on the way to becoming an important mademan in New York's mobster fraternity.

CHAPTER 7

A kidnapping

A SISTER IN THE ORDER OF MERCY eventually responded to the insistent bell-ringing at Via Cavour's street entrance to the convent of St Giorgio d'Genovese in Palermo. Standing in a steady drizzle, and soaked to the skin, she found a short, thin woman dressed in black and carrying her worldly belongings in a canvas bag suspended on a pole over her shoulder. The woman in black addressed the Sister "I am hungry and have nowhere to sleep. Please Sister can I stay in your convent?"

The Sister readjusted her wimple and fingered the chunky wooden crucifix hanging around her waist. She stood aside "Come in child. We will shelter you for tonight."

By the light from a lantern she guided Carla through a maze of corridors into an austere, chilly reception room where she was ordered to sit on a wooden bench. The Sister nodded curtly and quickly left Carla, shivering uncontrollably, sitting in semi-darkness in her rain-sodden clothes. She was cold and hungry and her baby insisted on kicking inside her swollen abdomen. After her father's death life at Godrano had been unbearable. Don Andreo was aggressive and vindictive and, worse still, Anna had become swollen-headed by her elevation in status and took Andreo's part. Carla's only ally was her sister Gina, who had visited Godrano in early December and quickly noticed Carla's predicament.

"You're putting on weight, Carla. You'll have to watch what you eat."

Carla burst into tears and, in a flash, Gina understood the reason. "You're pregnant aren't you?"

The sobbing girl fell into Gina's arms and a reply was not necessary. Gina became hysterical "I should have murdered that 'good-for-nothing' Franco. This disgrazitsa would have killed poor Papa! You can't come to Sant Agata. Santo wouldn't mind but Don Giovanni will not have you."

Carla wailed "Where can I go? What will become of me?"

Gina thought things through for a full minute.

"As it is, you will be excommunicated by the village priest and then Don Andreo will throw you out of Godrano. Go to the Sisters of Mercy convent in Palermo. The Sisters will look after you. What you do with your child is your choice but I would have it adopted."

A fortnight after Gina's visit the bomb exploded and Anna's response was vehement "Disgrazitsa! Disgrazitsa to my husband and the Cucinotta's" and Don Andreo was more scathing "Woman! You have brought disgrazitsa on us. You will leave tomorrow and never return to Godrano. Giudo will not want you now. You're tarnished goods! I never wish to see you again."

Before daybreak the next day, and dressed in black to avoid male attention, Carla made her way northwards through Cefala and along the main road to Palermo. Just beyond Cefala it began to drizzle and, by the time she reached the convent in Palermo ten hours later, it was raining heavily and she was soaked to the skin.

A shaft of light flashing in the doorway roused Carla from her reverie and two black-garbed Sisters sidled silently into the room. Their pale impassive faces were accentuated by pristine, white guimpes which gave them an ethereal appearance. A Sister holding a lantern spoke softly "My child! You have asked for succour and we will take you and your unborn infant into our arms. You have sinned and we are bound by our faith to help all sinners to repent and return to the Lord's protection. Sister Helena will take you to a cell for tonight and tomorrow you will be accommodated in our hostel."

The senior Sister made a sign of the cross and withdrew and Sister Helena led Carla into a bare cell where she was issued with a rough flannel towel and an ankle-length, grey, gabardine smock.

Later she was given a bowl of broth, bread and cheese and she slept fitfully on a straw paliasse on the cell floor. Early next morning she was interviewed by the mother superior and her name and address duly entered on a register. The name of the father was demanded and Carla produced Alphonse Rizzi's business card and his details were recorded. This was the convent's first registered entry of an illegitimate pregnancy in the aftermath of the Allied occupation of Sicily and a prelude to a deluge of unwanted pregnancies which occurred in the ensuing months. In her heart of hearts Carla hoped Alphonse was the father of her unborn infant and, one day, he might return and take her, and her baby, away to the promised land on the other side of the world.

The Sisters of Mercy established a convent in the grounds of St Giogio d'Genovesi church in the late 1600's and provided an infirmary and a school for children of impoverished Palermian dockworkers. In 1820 a hostel for unmarried mothers, known as magdalenas, was built in one corner of the convent grounds with a windowless wall facing Via Francesco Crispi and a solid, permanently-locked, oak door leading on to Via Cavour. The downstairs had a large communal dining room, a kitchen, a bakery and a laundry and was supervised by two lay Sisters. The upstairs was divided into two dormitories each sleeping eight inmates and toilet's and ablution facilities were located in a wooden shed to the side of the hostel. Thirty four nuns lived in the convent and a variable number of unmarried mothers, usually a dozen or so, slept in the hostel. Trained midwives delivered the mothers at term and, after weaning, infants were fostered, or adopted, and mothers had to leave. Exceptionally a mother and her infant were allowed to continue living in the hostel until her child was of school age. Babies and infants were well-cared for by the Sisters but the errant mothers lived in penury and were expected to wash, clean, cook and sew for themselves and for the Sisters. Their day began at 5.00am during the summer months and at 6.00am in the winter.

Having attended to their personal ablutions the magdalenas, pregnant or otherwise, were dispatched to their tasks and were given a Spartan meal at 7.30am followed by an hour's prayers in the convent chapel. They continued with their chores until 4.00pm when they had their main meal of the day and, after prayers in the dormitory, they were in bed by 8.00pm, earlier in winter months. Sunday was their only day of rest. This inflexible routine applied in equal measure to novitiates into the Order of Mercy. Three days of complete rest followed childbirth and, afterwards, nursing mothers were only allowed a break from their chores to breast feed their babies. Though not strictly bound by a vow of silence the Sisters spoke sparingly, and in whispers, and discouraged idle conversation between the magdalenas.

On admission to the hostel Carla's long, black tresses were cut short by a lay Sister and a grey calvaria, a skull cap, was placed firmly on her head. Her first task was in the chapel where she joined three similarly-dressed pregnant women who were scrubbing the aisle. The girl kneeling next to her was a seventeen year old peasant housemaid from Mussomeli and, over the ensuing days, they became friendly. Sophia had been seduced by one of Don Genco Russo's gabelotti and was near term. One night she confided in Carla that another man had taken advantage of her when she was four months pregnant.

"He came to the Boss' estate house a few days after the American's passed through Mussomeli. He was a good-looking boy on the run from the militia and I felt sorry for him. He only stayed three weeks and then he was off. I knew I was pregnant when he was with me."

"Do you know who the father is, Sophia?" Carla asked.

"Yes, Giuseppe Autorino. The other man was from Calabria and called himself Franco."

Carla was poleaxed. Surely, the Franco she knew was dead? Sophia must be mistaken, but the thought kept her awake for several sleepless nights wondering if the father of the baby in her womb had survived the shelling near Cefala. Carla gave birth to a healthy 7lb male infant on 2nd April 1944 and he was registered under the name of Alfonzo Cecci. Despite pressure from the Sisters of Mercy to have him adopted she insisted on brining him up in the Convent. For nearly four years mother and child lived in the Convent of St Giorgio d' Genovesi and, despite unrelenting daily labour and spartan surroundings, these were the happiest times in Carla's life as she watched her precious infant grow into a healthy strong boy.

Dressed in their distinctive black habits, white wimples and coifs, the Sisters of Mercy were regularly seen on the streets of Palermo wandering in pairs and collecting alms from shopkeepers and marketeers. One day in May 1947 Santo and Gina Cucinotta were haggling with a shopkeeper in Vucciria market when, escorted by two Sisters, Carla walked by. When Gina saw her sister for the first time since she left Godrano in disgrace in December 1944, a pang of remorse hit her conscience and she decided to act. Later that day Carla was in the convent scrubbing a corridor when a Sister appeared and bent forwards to whisper. "There's someone to see you in reception. Come with me."

As soon as they entered Gina sprang to her feet and let out a stifled scream "What have they done to you, Carla? Where's your beautiful, black hair and where's your child?"

They hugged fiercely and wept openly. The stern-faced Sister shuffled in the background and then silently withdrew.

"Gina, I've missed you. Is Santo with you? Does he know I'm here?"

"Santo is in Vucciria market and he knows you're here. No one else knows."

Tears of gratitude streamed down Carla's cheeks.

"I thank God for that. Little Alfonzo is in nursery school. We're very happy here with the Sisters but one day we'll have to leave.

I'll worry about that when the time comes."

Carla paused and studied the ground "How's Anna?"

Gina stiffened and her voice hardened "Anna is completely under Don Andreo's thumb and stands by him at all times. Andreo is turning against Santo and me and, to a certain extent, his own father. Santo won't put up with it much longer and we're thinking about emigrating to England or America."

The two women lapsed into silence and the Sister returned and glided silently into the room.

"Its time to go Signora Cucinotta. It's against the rules to let anyone into the convent without an appointment."

Carla and Gina embraced and kissed and Gina whispered "I'll call and see you again Carla," but she never did. As Gina walked out of the convent a Sister was ushering four beautifully turned-out children across the road and she wondered which one might be Alfonzo. A bright-eyed, active little boy was straining at the leash to push ahead of the others. She took a step towards her nephew but realised this was unwise and, with a heavy heart and tears in her eyes, she walked along Via Francesco Crispi to Vucciria market.

In 1946 Charles 'Lucky' Luciano was released from Dannemora Prison, ostensibly for co-operating with American military authorities during the war. Deported to Italy, he settled in a luxury suite at Hotel de Palme and rapidly assumed control of Mafia organisations and interests in Naples. He then turned his attention to Calabria and Sicily and his aim was to replace the antiquated, traditional mafiosi, the Mafia di Vecchio Stampo, with American-style bosses of his own choosing. In this he succeeded in southern Italy but the Sicilian agrarian dons were another kettle of fish. In April 1948 Luciano invited representative dons from Sicily to a conference at Hotel Turistico in Naples' dockland. The meeting was a fiasco and broke up in disarray. Two factions emerged from among the Sicilian bosses. One group, representing the Mafia dei Cantieri from Catania, Messina and Syracuse and led by Calagero Vizzini and Angelo Muzzi of Palermo, were sympathetic to Luciano's aims and strongly supported by the ambitious Corleone dons. Don Genco Russo, also known as Zu Peppi Jencu, or Uncle Joe the Little Bull, represented the all-powerful agrarian dons and was strongly opposed to any changes. The Cucinotta dons, father and son, and the Boss from Castellammare Del Golfo sat on the fence and had their own secret ambitions for power and position in the Mafia infrastructure in Sicily. After the meeting Fredo Gicanetti, Naples' Capo and a front man for Lucky Luciano, cornered Andreo Cucinotta.

"Can we do a deal? My son Franco was a gabelotti at Godrano estate from 1940 until the Americans came in 1943. Don Carlo Cecci's daughter, Carla, became pregnant by him and her child would now be about four years old. Assist me in finding the boy and Luciano and I will support your plans to seize power in Palermo."

The dons embraced and shook hands, thus sealing a secret contract between them. Andreo was surprised to hear Franco Gicanetti was alive. According to local information he had been killed by American gunfire in the cave near Godrano. But Franco had survived and married soon after his return to Calabria and the couple had two daughters but no male heir. Don Fredo was desperate to have a grandson and would go to any lengths to ensure survival of the Gicanetti lineage.

On an overnight ferry from Naples to Palermo, Don Giovanni Cucinotta had a private meeting with Genco Russo who voiced his concern about Luciano's encroachment on the Sicilian fiefdoms.

"We must take steps to prevent him taking over our Sicilian Families. The dons in Catania and Messina, and Calagero Vizzini in Palermo, are already in his pocket and before long the Corleone dons and Angelo Muzzi will follow. I can see your position in

Portella Sant Agata and Godrano becoming difficult. We, the Mafia dei Giardini, must form an alliance to stop this happening. Do you agree Giovanni?"

Don Giovanni nodded and shook hands with Zu Peppi Jencu. The matter was next discussed with his sons over lunch at Portella Sant Agata two days later. Andreo and Giudo were in favour of confrontation but the gentler, non-militant Santo was against the use of force. His brother's aggression was too much for Santo who blurted out "I want nothing to do with this business. Gina and I wish to get out of Sicily."

Andreo reacted sharply "Get out of Sicily if you have to! There's no place in this Family for cowards. Unlike you, Giudo is prepared to fight for a just cause."

Still seething with rage Santo thought, 'The only 'just cause' Andreo subscribed to was his own glorification' and this made him more determined than ever to get away and start a new life abroad.

Don Giovanni calmed things down "Son's! Don't fight over this business. I'll decide what to do when the time comes."

Tempers cooled a little over lunch and, as he was departing for Godrano, Andreo invited Santo to walk with him to the main gate.

"Is Gina in touch with that woman, Carla? If you tell me where to find her I will help you and Gina get away from here."

Santo was completely taken off guard. Apart from Gina, Carla Cecci's name had not been mentioned by any of the Family for over three years. Santo desperately wanted to leave Sicily and Andreo was offering a way out, an offer too good to miss. Without thinking he jumped at the chance "I know where she is. Carla and her boy are with the Sisters of Mercy at St Giorgio's convent in Palermo. The boy is now nearly four and he's named Alfonzo."

As soon as he spoke Santo knew he had made a big mistake but the unfortunate deed could not be undone. Gina would not approve and he decided not to tell her and, in any event, the end result justified the means. They were now one step nearer to starting a new life in a new country far away from the strife and intrigue of their Mafia community. Andreo's message to Don Fredo Gicanetti in Naples was clear and concise 'Carla Cecci and her boy are sheltering in a Hostel for Fallen Women in the grounds of St Giorgio d' Genovesi convent in Palermo.'

Mid-Morning on June 9th 1948 Captain Tomaso Valente guided his fishing smack into La Cala harbour and berthed on the south mole. Aboard he had two crewmen and Franco Gicanetti and they had left the fishing port of Cetraro, on the Italian mainland, on the previous evening. Unlike a dozen or so boats tied-up on the quay, Valente's smack had no fish to unload on the congested wharf which was cluttered with crates and creels of fish and crustaceans and bustling porters pushing laden tumbrils to Vucciria market on the other side of Via Francesco Crispi. Around midday, the activity and babbled conversation on the quayside ceased and Franco ventured on deck. To all the world a shiphand going ashore, he was dressed in a rough blue flannel shirt and black calico trousers and, on his head, he wore a flat peaked cap. He made his way briskly to the main road and, within a mile, arrived at the church of Sant Giorgio d' Genovesi. He took up position in the church's shaded portico where he could keep the convent's doorway under observation. Franco intended gaining entry to the convent but 'Lady Luck' came to his rescue and eventually delivered Alfonzo into the kidnapper's clutches.

Over the next two hours three pairs of Sisters carrying provisions entered the convent and then, just before 3 o'clock, a rotund Sister shepherding four children, and fussing around her brood like a hen with a clutch of chicks, emerged through the doorway. Identically dressed in blue shirts and grey short trousers or skirts, with clean white plimsolls on their feet, the children carried buckets and spades. Sister Carmelita was taking her charges for an hour's recreation on La Cala beach. The toddlers hung on to the corpulent Sister's black habit but the eldest boy in the group forged ahead of the others. Sister Carmelita scolded him "Alfonzo! Come here immediately. If you don't behave I'll take you back to the convent."

"Yes, Sister Carmelita," the youngster replied, his dark-brown eyes spitting defiance. He obeyed up to a point but steadfastly refused to cling on to the Sister's habit and progress along the straight mile was punctuated by numerous stops and remonstrations from the breathless Sister. Franco followed the group at a respectable distance. At long last the party reached a deserted sandy beach wedged in an angle between the south mole of La Cala harbour and the main road. The children immediately started playing in the sand and, puffing and grunting, the perspiring Sister propped herself against a stone wall. Within a minute she had dozed off to sleep. In the meantime the older boy distanced himself from the younger children and walked along the seashore idly kicking a tin can through the surf. Attracted by cigarette smoke, curiosity drove him in Franco's direction and he stopped about ten feet away. Franco was sitting on a boulder at the foot of the stone steps leading up from the beach to the quayside.

"Ciaou little man! What's your name?"

The boy shuffled his bare feet in the sand and fixed his gaze on Franco "I'm going to be a sailor when I grow up. Are you a sailor?"

"Yes" Franco lied.

"Sailors can go fishing all day and sail far away. If I can't be a sailor I'll be a pirate. They rob people on ships and are very rich."

The boy waited expectantly for a reply.

"I've come here to look for a boy called Alfonzo. Do you know him?"

"I am Alfonzo. I live in Sister Carmelita's convent."

"What a bit of luck! You're the boy I'm looking for and I've come a long way to find you" Franco replied. In the prolonged silence that followed Franco could hear the squeals of the children playing with sandcastles and, in the background and about forty yards away, loud snores from the dozing Sister.

"I've got a boat in the harbour, Alfonzo, and a real captain to sail it. Shall we go fishing?"

"I would like to go fishing. I'll run across to tell Sister Carmelita that I'm going with you."

"No! That's not a good idea, Alfonzo. The fat old Sister is asleep. You can surprise her when we get back with a big swordfish to cook for supper."

Alfonzo's eyes lit up in anticipation. He took Franco's extended hand and they strolled off the beach, up the stone steps and on to the quay, now completely deserted in siesta hour. They were aboard the moored ketch in five minutes and Captain Valente gave the boy a hearty welcome and a mug of cold lemon juice.

"Right," shouted Franco, "let's go fishing! Take her out Captain! Full steam ahead!"

Their smack was the only vessel moving in the harbour at that time of day and Captain Valente steered her out of La Cala and plotted a course eastwards towards his home base at Cetraro on the Italian mainland

The crew made a fuss over Alfonzo and plied him with food and drink and gave him a flat-topped sailor's cap to wear on deck. He did not whimper or whine and his main concern was Sister Carmelita's reaction to his truancy. To amuse the boy the crew let out half a dozen hand lines and, much to Alfonzo's pleasure, they pulled in a dozen mullet as they cruised steadily eastwards towards the Italian coastline. The light was fading when Alfonzo asked for his mother and with promises she would be with them in the morning, he fell asleep on deck. Captain Tomaso Valente unerringly steered his boat to arrive at his home fishing port just before daybreak on 10th June. A car met them at the quayside and whisked them away to Franco Gicanetti's messadria on the foothills below the mountain village of Bisignano where Alfonzo met his 'new' family. For a whole month he cried himself to sleep each night and repeatedly asked for his mother and Sister Carmelita. Thereafter Alfonzo never mentioned them and adapted to his new surroundings like a duck to water. Within a few months the impressionable four year old had changed his ideas of becoming a sailor, or a fisherman, and now saw his future on the land, strutting around the countryside with a shotgun and bossing the poor peasants at work in the fields just like his newly-found Papa.

Sister Carmelita woke with a start from a fitful half-hour catnap. Her headdress was awry and her wimple crumpled and sweat-sodden and pins and needles radiated down her left arm. The hot sun beat down relentlessly on her generous frame and the sand inside her woollen stockings was uncomfortable and irritating. She cast a bleary eye in the direction of her charges and, with one exception, they were happily playing in a sand pit. Alfonzo was missing which, in itself, was not alarming as the boy often wandered off to play on his own. A sixth sense commanded her to check further and one of the playgroup reported seeing Alfonzo wandering off towards the steps. The fat Sister panicked and, gathering up her habit, waddled in an ungainly swagger up the steps to the main road. Alfonzo was nowhere to be seen. Sister Carmelita hurriedly ushered her brood down Via Crispi to the convent schoolroom to raise the alarm. Four Sisters of Mercy left to search the beach and Vucciria market which was, by now, getting busier and the number of searchers increased rapidly but no one found a lost little boy dressed in a blue linen shirt and shorts. Alfonzo's white plimsoll shoes were found at the water's edge. Sister Carmelita had the unpleasant duty of reporting Alfonzo's disappearance to his mother. Carla was sitting on the edge of her bed with her eyes downcast. She had a premonition something was badly amiss and, at the approach of the florid-faced

Sister, she stood up suddenly, her dark eyes pleading, "What's going on Sister? Where's my Alfonzo?"

"Little Alfonzo went missing off the beach this aft rnoon. I didn't see him go. The Carabinieri and the whole of Palermo are looking for him and I am certain he will be found and brought back to us safe and sound before it get's dark."

Carla did not weep and, head bowed, she stared fixedly at the wooden floor. Her mind was blank and all she saw was an image of Alfonzo's face engraved in the wooden floorboa. ds.

Carla Cecci had been a subservient resident in the Hostel for Fallen Women for nearly four years. She had put up with the rigours of convent life for Alfonzo's sake but, as the hours and days slipped by, she became morose and withdrawn and hardly went outside the convent's doors. Chaperoned excursions to the market with the Sisters ceased to offer relief and many Palermians, mainly married women, turned their backs on, or spat at, the grey-garbed Magdalenas from Sant Giorgio's Hostel. Latterly there had been veiled hints that, before the end of the year, she might have to leave the hostel and place Alfonzo in an orphanage. She was determined this would not happen and, come what may, she would never be separated from her precious little boy. And now the very reason for her existence had gone missing. At night she cried into her pillow and, for days on end she lay on her bed, staring at the ceiling and refusing to budge in response to visits from the Sisters who came to pray for Alfonzo's safe return. Her premonition that she would never see Alfonzo alive again became a reality when the Carabinieri gave up searching and presumed the boy had accidentally drowned. Her resolve suddenly snapped and she got out of bed and walked out of Sant Giorgio's convent on to the streets of Palermo.

CHAPTER 8

Giuliano and Giudo

WITH NO PLANS OF WHAT TO DO, or where to go, Carla Cecci walked out of St Giorgio's Convent an hour before sunset on 30th June 1948. Of one thing she was certain, she would not be returning now the reason for her being there no longer existed. She had progressed half a mile when she became acutely aware of hostile stares from passers-by not accustomed to seeing Magdalena's at large and unaccompanied by a Sister of Mercy. She removed her calvaria and made a detour off Via Francesco Crispi into the Chiese Madre, a maze of narrow interlocking alleyways in the poorer quarter of Palermo. Clothes lines were strung at intervals across the alleys from one dwelling to another obstructing Carla's progress and, from one of these lines, she stole a pair of trousers and a blue, serge shirt and pulled on the clothes over her pale-grey smock. A few yards further on Carla grabbed a cloth cap from a windowsill outside a peasant's hovel and clamped it firmly on her near-naked scalp. Thus attired she returned to mingle with the crowds on Via Crispi, to all intents and purposes a fisherman on his way to the harbour or one of the sleazy bars in Palermo's red-light district. On La Cala beach she gazed dolefully over the calm, blood-red sea reflecting the dying rays of the setting sun. She walked the whole length of the beach and up the row of stone steps leading to the quay. Halfway up there was a wooden platform and an open archway which led into a forty-foot square, windowless chamber which contained a variety of coiled ropes, buoys, placards and painting utensils. In one corner Carla fashioned a rough couch from ropes and canvas slings and, for three weeks, the louse-ridden chamber became her home. During daylight hours she kept out of sight for fear of bumping into the Sisters of Mercy and, from the wooden platform, she was able to keep an eye on the beach. After nightfall Carla went foraging. She appropriated a flask from the storeroom and, each night, filled it with drinking water from a fountain in Piazza San Domenico. After dark the empty market place proved a valuable source of over-ripe fruit, nuts, root vegetables and, occasionally, small fish and hunks of meat, sufficient to sustain her from day to day. Sunday was always a barren day when Vucciria market and Piazza San Domenico were not trading.

On her third Sunday of exile Giuliano came into Carla's life. She had retired early when, around ten o'clock, she was disturbed by someone moving around in the pitch-black chamber. The intruder was in close proximity to her makeshift litter and smelt strongly of alcohol and stale tobacco. A male voice at the entrance issued a command "Strike a match, Pietro."

Carla pushed her thin body into the couch and broke out in a cold sweat. By the light from the match Carla caught a glimpse of three men in the chamber and the bearded man spoke with authority "This place will do for tonight. Let's light a fire. I'm starving."

One of the men lit a candle and, in its flickering light, Pietro saw Carla cringing on her makeshift bed.

"Look out, Giuliano! There's someone in the corner."

Giuliano spun around and stared into Carla's petrified eyes.

"Who the hell are you?, he yelled, while his companions moved swiftly forwards towards Carla. She sat up with a jerk.

"I'm Carlo" she blurted out and crammed the cloth cap firmly on her head.

"What are you doing hiding in here son?" the bearded leader asked. Carla decided to lie "I'm hiding from the Carabinieri."

Giuliano burst out laughing, a raucous, coarse, mirthless laugh.

"That's not unusual. Most of us are trying to avoid the Carabinieri. Why are the bastards after you?"

"I killed a man, my husband."

Giuliano's face creased in perplexity.

"Your husband! Your husband? That means you're a woman" and, laughing aloud, he turned to the others "It seems we have a woman in our midst. What do you think of that lads?"

Pietro and Firenzo sniggered but remained silent. Carla was mortified, worried she was about to be raped again and memories of the cave at Cefala came flooding back. But Giuliano reacted unexpectedly. Known as a misogynist and abuser of women, he saw a funny side to the situation. He continued to laugh in a loud raucous bellow and spoke to his comrades in between gasps "Tell you what we'll do. We'll take this woman with us tomorrow and show her how we deal with the Carabinieri. Now let's eat! You can join us if you wish, Carla."

They sat around a camp fire and ate a meal of rye bread, goat's cheese and hard-boiled eggs and afterwards, despite her worries, Carla was allowed to sleep unmolested for the rest of the night.

On the following day, a Monday, Carla was given a practical demonstration of Giuliano in action. The target was a Carabinieri lieutenant and the place for a 'hit' was Vucciria market. Giuliano seemed to know the outlay of the market like the back of his hand.

"The market opens at six o'clock and customers start coming at eight. Our Lieutenant turns up around nine o'clock. After the hit we'll make our separate ways to Passo di Rogano."

Carla and her new-found comrades arrived at Vucciria market at around 8.30am and the place was already packed with jostling housewives and vendors pushing and shouting around the various stalls. Giuliano selected a fruit stall near an exit road for his strike and issued his instructions "Pietro! Go with Firenzo and stand near that stall and, at my signal, start a fight. When the Carabinieri get to you run away. You stick with me Carla and do as I say."

Accompanied by two policemen a Carabinieri lieutenant arrived on foot at ten minutes past nine and made his way around the market in a clockwise direction, stopping at each stall and covertly taking money from stallholders. When they were about twenty yards away a fracas broke out between Pietro and Firenzo and a crowd gathered around the scuffling men, who were gently wrestling each other and shouting obscenities and threats in loud voices. Baton in hand, the lieutenant rushed forwards and pushed his way through the onlookers towards the scuffle. Pulling Carla with him Giuliano inserted himself between the lieutenant and his attendant policeman and a few of the crowd followed his example. Within seconds the lieutenant was marooned in a sea of jostling humanity and the next minute was bedlam. Giuliano stabbed the officer twice under the ribs and brought him to his knees. He then grabbed the officer's helmet and, pulling his head sharply backwards, thrust the razor-sharp blade straight across his extended neck. The Carabinieri's shouts faded in a strangulated gurgle as his life blood gushed forth and sprayed over the cobblestones and feet of the screaming bystanders. He fell forwards on his face and rapidly expired in a pool of blood. His aides, who had been striving to get to their officer, now turned tail and fled across the piazza. Giuliano wiped his bloody blade on the Carabinieri's tunic and, with a fiendish grin on his face, addressed the crowd now silently melting away from the scene of the assassination.

"Let it be known that I, Giuliano, carried out the killing."

He seemed inordinately proud of his achievement and the onlookers became respectful as if, in the act of execution, he had created a work of art. Carla was both horrified and excited by the gory event and felt as if Giuliano's knife was repaying her for the misery she had suffered at Godrano and the recent loss of little Alfonzo. With a look of reverence she faced the murderer "That was fantastic Giuliano."

On their way to the rendezvous at Passo di Rogano, Giuliano couldn't stop talking "That lieutenant I killed in the market was collecting protection money from stallholders, money that belongs to the mayor of Palermo. Muzzi refused to use his own men to do the job. That's why I was called in" and, with a fleeting bemused smile, he added "I will kill anybody, anywhere for money."

The words were spoken simply and matter-of-factly without emotion or braggadocio and the killer believed he had a mission in life. The rights and wrongs of the case, and the politics and status of his victims, were of no concern to Giuliano as long as the money was good and paid in advance. And then, in a perverse way, he took great pleasure in distributing his ill-gotten gains among the poor and needy. Illegitimate by birth, Giuliano could never hope to attain membership of the Honoured Society. So he sold his services to the highest bidder. Ruthless and mentally unstable he became a champion of the poor, a latterday Robin Hood, and after the killing in Vucciria market Carla Cecci became one of his staunchest disciples.

By 1949 Giudo Cucinotta had become leader of a gang of notorious gabelotti who ruled Godrano and Sant Agata estates with an iron fist. A regular absentee from school in his younger days, Giudo's education had been disrupted by the Cucinotta's move from Calabria to Portella Sant Agata and he could hardly read or write. By the age of fourteen he carried a shotgun and spent days on end hunting wild goat in the mountains west of Portella Sant Agata. The European conflict brought an influx of Italian soldiers to Sicily which was used as a staging post for troop transfers to North Africa. A temporary camp was established on the banks of Lago del Scanzano and seventeen year old Giudo spent most of his time fraternizing with the soldiers who allowed him to experiment with their weaponry. In the spring of 1942 the easy-going Italians were replaced by German reinforcements for Rommel's Afrika Corps and Giudo became persona non grata but not before he had acquired two Italian carbines, a pistol and a stock of ammunition and hand grenades. The Allies' rapid conquest of Sicily in June 1943, the double wedding and his own betrothal to Carla Cecci in August and his promotion to gabelotti to his brother Andreo in September, all contributed to his transformation from a teenage loner to a man of authority and power. The main blot on his copybook was the disgrace he had brought on his Family at the double wedding and the subsequent indignity of a broken betrothal to Carla. By 1948 these events had faded into the background but, seven years later, in true Sicilian fashion, had not been forgotten. Santo, on the other hand, could not tolerate his Family's increasing involvement in crime and in September he took Gina to London where they settled in the Soho district and started a new life as restaurateurs. For a few years trouble had been brewing between the Cucinottas and the La Barbera Family of Corleone over a disputed right-of-way across Godrano estate for Corleonesi convoys to Palermo's markets. To a large extent Palermo depended on Godrano for its daily food supplies and, in effect, the Cucinottas held the city in a stranglehold. This state of affairs could not be allowed to continue and the action at Ponte Arcera brought matters to a head and involved the Big Boss in Naples and Calagero Vizzini, Palermo's Provincial Capo.

Shortly after Santo's departure Giudo committed his first execution and enjoyed the experience. Up to that point he had been involved in general beatings, face-slashing and kneecapping but had never killed a person in cold blood. The action on the bridge at Ponte Arcera, on the Corleone/Marineo road, started quite innocently. Stefano and Paulo, Giudo's lieutenants, stopped a Corleone muletrain from crossing the bridge. Giudo observed the ensuing slanging match from behind a clump of bushes and the muleteers began retreating slowly down the road. Suddenly an armed gabelotti came rushing forwards and fired at point-blank range hurling Stefano backwards on to the dirt road. Paulo retaliated and shot the nearest mule and the gabelotti gunman sprinted down the road avoiding Paulo's second shot. A few seconds later a startled mule, completely out of control, came charging up the road with another Corleone gabelotti on its back desperately trying to hang on to the headstrong animal. At a range of thirty feet Giudo let fly with both barrels. The wounded mule reared on its hind legs and crashed on its haunches pinning the injured gabelotti underneath its writhing, expiring body. Stefano had been mortally wounded and the left side of his face and his left shoulder were a shattered and a gory mess. Giudo knelt by his side "Stefo can you hear me?"

Stefano's half-mutilated head nodded and his words were lost in a gurgle of frothy blood trickling from his shattered mouth. Giudo felt a surge of cold hatred "I'll make the bastards pay for this."

Calmly he walked across to the fully- conscious gabelotti pinioned underneath his dead mule and looked straight into his eyes.

"Ciao bastardo."

Giudo fired three shots with his revolver. One through the victim's mouth and one through each eye socket. He then turned his attention to a lightly-wounded, unarmed muleteer whose legs had been peppered by Paulo's gunshot.

"Please signore! Please don't kill me. I have four bambinos. You will leave them without a father."

The unfortunate man's pleading fell on deaf years. With cold precision Giudo shot him through the back of his neck and the bullet exited through the muleteer's forehead, scattering fragments of blood, bone and brain on to the flank of his dead mule. Stephano was taken to his home in Marineo where he expired within the hour. The muleteer's corpses were dumped on the road at the boundary of Corleone estate and served as a warning to the La Barbera Family that the Cucinottas meant business. At Stefano's funeral Paulo asked Giudo the reason for shooting the gabelotti through his eye sockets.

"It's traditional, Paulo. We, the Mafia, believe that when a man dies his soul takes an image of the last thing he sees on earth with him to heaven. Shooting out the eyes destroys that image. That's why I did it to the Mafia gabelotti. It wasn't wortl wasting three bullets on the muleteer."

On the night of the incident at Ponte Arcera, Giudo Cucinotta slept soundly, the sleep of the 'just.' Despite his father's admonition that the action could lead to more trouble he felt all-important and all-powerful. The rule of the gun had reigned supreme that day and he had enjoyed the act of killing. On the bridge at Ponte Arcera he was transformed from a gun-toting mafioso to a budding assassin and he became determined at that moment to make this his future occupation.

The Ponte Arcera shootings had wider implications involving the Big Boss in Naples. The Cucinottas sat astride the supply routes from the south to Palermo and sat on a fence in their dealings with Lucky Luciano. He eventually concluded the answer was to remove the Godrano bottleneck and strengthen the bond between Corleone and Palermo. Luciano resolved to place his own men into Portella Sant Agata and Godrano and Don Giovanni and Don Andreo Cucinotta would have to go. A contract was passed on to Angelo Muzzi in Palermo and he, not wishing to expose his own hitmen, commissioned Giuliano to carry out the assassinations. Born illegitimately in Montelpre, Giuliano roamed the mountainous crags of the Buccadifalco range as a young man, robbing and plundering at will. Between 1938 and 1943 his main targets were Italian militia and, once Allied forces left Sicily in 1947, he played one Mafia family against another and took to a life of arson and murder until he himself was shot dead at Castelvetrano in 1950. Giuliano had lived alone for many years in a dilapidated Moorish-style house in the Chiese Madre district of medieval Montelpre. An unpretentious entrance from an alley led down a tunnelled corridor into an open courtyard with living rooms disbursed in two storeys around a quadrangle. Drinking water was provided from an artesian well in the centre of the open space. Montelpre was a 'dead' town, depopulated by mass emigration in the thirties to provide Sicilian cannon fodder for Maranzano's mobsters in New York. A link with the Maranzano Family of Castellammare del Golfo remained and Montelpre was part of their fiefdom. After the assassination of the police lieutenant in Vucciria market, Giuliano brought Carla to Montelpre. He seemed impervious to living conditions in his household. A layer of chalky-white dust covered the sparsely-furnished rooms and the bug-ridden bedding stank to high heaven. Giuliano did not believe in material comfort and his attitude towards Carla, and women in general, vacillated between occasional politeness to blasphemy and, in between, a brooding moroseness and silence which could last for days on end. As far as she was able to manage Carla kept out of his way in her own half of the courtyard. Visitors were few and far between. Firenzo and Pietro from Castellammare occasionally called and an old lady was allowed in once a week to attempt the hopeless task of tidying the living apartments. All in all, Carla's life had again become lonely and secluded and she remained in this state for over a year.

Carla was beginning to believe Giuliano regretted bringing a woman into his life and home when, one evening in May 1949, he burst into her quarters in a drunken and agitated state. His bearded face was flushed and his penetrating, bulging eyes sparkled like diamonds.

"Woman! I've been given a contract. We move out tomorrow. You will cut your hair and dress like a puttita again. We shall be gone a week."

Giuliano made it clear the arrangements were not negotiable.

"Grazie Giuliano" Carla replied and, with a slight tremble in her voice, she asked "What's a contract Giuliano?"

The bearded brigand burst out laughing.

"A contract is a Mafia word and we shall be doing the same thing as we did in Vucciria market."

Carla wanted to ask about their destination and target but she knew better and remained silent. She retired to her room and cut her black tresses. Dressed in her cloth cap, trousers and barathea jacket she looked like a young man but, equally, she could have been taken for a prostitue from Palermo's waterfront.

At the crack of dawn the following day Pietro and Firenzo appeared out of nowhere with six mules. Two pack mules carried their provisions, bedding, rifles and ammunition, in side saddles and wicker panniers and the other mules were ridden. Having trekked along mountain passes and shepherds' trails for two days they made camp on a hillside west of the Piana/Corleone road and overlooking the disused military encampment at the southern end of Lake Scanzano. Before daybreak the next day Firenzo was left in charge of the mules and Giuliano, Pietro and Carla crossed the main road to a concealed position on a rock-strewn hillock thirty yards away from a winding path leading down to the lakeside huts. The men were armed with Italian carbines and Carla carried a German army Mauser pistol tucked into her trouser belt. Giuliano was in one of his silent moods and Pietro had to drag information out of him.

"What are we looking for Giuliano?"

Giuliano snapped in reply "Giovanni Cucinotta, the Don of Portella Sant Agata. I'm told he has white hair."

Carla looked up sharply "I know Don Giovanni. I will identify him for you" and Giuliano accepted her offer without dissent.

At first light, workers came streaming down the main road to walk around the southern end of the lake and into Godrano's fertile fields and, about seven o'clock, someone came out of the wooden huts to relieve himself and fetch water from the lake. Carla was the first to hear the shuffling thud of hooves approaching at a brisk canter down the earthen path and three mounted, dark-suited gabelotti pulled up directly in front of their hideout. One of the riders removed his cap and mopped his sweaty brow. Carla whispered "The one with his cap off is Don Giovanni."

Giuliano was galvanized into action and ordered Pietro to shoot. Almost simultaneously, two bullets hit the grey-haired man toppling him off his mule on to the pathway. The riderless mule took fright and bolted towards the lake closely followed by the other two riders. After travelling thirty yards one of the mules reared violently throwing its rider to the ground and continued its onwards charge towards the sanctuary of the lakeside huts. Giuliano let fly another shot at the riderless mule and, wielding a pistol, sprang to his feet.

"Cover us Pietro. Come on Carla let's finish them off."

Giuliano made a beeline through the scrubland for the white-haired man lying in the middle of the path. Both bullets had smashed through the left side of his chest and Don Giovanni Cucinotta was dying by the time Giuliano reached him. The other gabelotti's body lay half on and half off the dirt road. When he was ejected off his mule his head struck a boulder and, by the time Carla got to him, he was slowly recovering consciousness. She let out a sharp gasp when she recognised the face of the seemingly dead man. Giudo Cucinotta! Her pent up hatred surged to the surface and she was about to pull the trigger when Giudo's eyelids fluttered and he gazed straight at her with uncomprehending eyes. In that brief second of consciousness his brain retained an image which was to haunt him for the rest of his life – an image of a clean-shaven, youthful man wearing a grey cloth cap. Carla hesitated. She could not bring herself to kill a 'dead' man.

From behind her back Giuliano shouted "Is he dead, Carla?" and, simultaneously, there were two revolver shots within four seconds of each other as Giuliano shot the dying Don in both eye sockets. Using the butt of her revolver Carla struck Giudo on his left temple and, reversing the gun, fired two bullets into the ground, one on each side of the unconscious man's head. She moved quickly away towards Giuliano.

"Did you shoot him through both eyes, Carla?"

"Yes Giuliano" she replied tersely as Pietro joined them on the path. Their departure from the scene was accelerated by gunshots from the direction of the lake and a peppery rustle of expended lead pellets in the undergrowth. The shooters were well out of range and showed no inclination to give chase. The exuberant trio ran up the path, crossed the Corleone/Piana road, and were soon out of sight on an escarpment where Firenzo was waiting with the mules for a rapid departure.

In the evening the gabelotti brought two bodies on muleback to Godrano estate house. Don Giovanni was laid out in the parlour and Giudo was put to bed in a front room where he waxed and waned in and out of consciousness for a week. During that time Don Giovanni Cucinotta was buried and Don Andreo assumed control of both estates. The assassination had all the hallmarks of a Mafia hit and the Corleonesi were the obvious culprits. Don Andreo instinctively planned retaliation and top of his hitlist were the La Barbera brothers and Luciano Liggio of Corleone followed by Angelo Muzzi in Palermo. As soon as he recovered fully, Giudo volunteered to honour his brother's vendetta and it was at this time in his life, at the age of 23 years, Giudo Cucinotta became a dedicated assassin.

The hamlet of Portella Sant Agata is perched at 600 ft on a sharp rise on the main road connecting Corleone with Piana. Its population of fifty souls live in quaint whitewashed cottages strewn on each side of a climbing, cobblestone road. Sant Agata estate house lies a mile west of the hamlet and the sizeable village of Piana degli Albanesi is four miles to the north. During Giudo's convalescence, Godrano and Sant Agata estate houses were virtual fortresses and occupied all of Don Andreo's available gabelotti. Road blocks at Ponte Arcera, Lake Scanzano and Ponte Agata lay unattended and the Corleonesi took advantage to push heavily-armed mule trains up to Palermo two, or three, times a week. By mid-September 1949 Giudo had recovered fully and was ready to honour his brother's vendetta. For his first ambush he selected a roadside cottage in Portella Sant Agata and, after three days' fruitless observation, his patience was rewarded. Guarded by armed gabelotti at the front and rear, ten heavily-laden pack mules came slowly uphill towards the sleepy hamlet. Giudo dispatched his own gabelotti to the village square and took up position at a curtained window in a roadside cottage. It was raining heavily and the muleteers pushed forwards on foot urging their charges up the slippery, cobblestone surface of the rutted lane. Sitting astride his mule, and ensheathed in a black, waterproof cloak, a solitary gabelotti brought up the rear, about twenty yards behind the mule train. Giudo stepped calmly out into the road in front of the rider who sat transfixed, staring in disbelief at the barrels of Guido's shotgun. For five seconds, like cat and mouse, they stood perfectly still and then, without provocation, Giudo let fly with both barrels from fifteen feet away. The blast blew the gabelotti off his mule and he landed in a tangled heap in a doorway across the road. The dead man's mule bolted uphill and ploughed into the main body of the mule train which became a mass of flailing legs and frightened muleteers and flasks of olive oil and wine came tumbling out of the panniers. In the confusion the leading Corleonesi gabelotti took flight and disappeared up the road towards Piana. Giudo bent to examine the corpse. Not able to recognise his victim he approached two muleteers cowering in a cottage doorway "Who is your gabelotti?"

There was no reply. Giudo let off a shot into the air.

"I ask again. Who is your gabelotti?"

Looking askance at his petrified comrade one muleteer stammered a reply "It's Antonio La Barbera, signore."

Giudo beamed a satisfied smile. He had hit the jackpot with his first real venture. He ordered his lieutenants to release the muleteers "Let them go. Confiscate their mules and packs. They can walk home to Corleone."

Antonio La Barbera was strapped to the back of a mule and the ambushers released the animal three miles south of Lake Scanzano at Corleone's estate boundary. Carrying its ghoulish cargo the animal found its way home where the arrival of his brother's corpse incensed Don Luigi La Barbera. He concluded that the he Cucinotta brothers had a lot to answer for and, if this was a reprisal for the death of their father, Don Luigi had no explanation. His Family had no part in the murder of Don Giovanni Cucinotta. But of one thing he was certain, the Cucinotta's had started a feud which would ultimately lead to their elimination.

For half a century the Maranzano Family of Castellammare del Golfo in northwest Sicily had arranged emigration to the New World and most émigrés ended up in the ghettos of Brooklyn, or downtown Manhattan, where they provided cannon fodder for New York's mobsters. The incumbent Don in 1949, Salvatore Maranzano, was wealthy beyond belief and had grandiose ideas of annexing Palermo Province, thus becoming the premier Capo for the whole of Sicily. From his stronghold in the Mafia-dominated village of Villalaba the current Palermian Capo, Calagero Vizzini, was fighting a losing battle to maintain control over the militant agrarian dons and had lost credence with the Big Boss in Naples who wanted him replaced. There were three main contenders for this prize; Luciano Liggio of Corleone, Don Genco Russo of Mussomeli and Don Salvatore Maranzano himself. Naples backed Liggio and Don Genco Russo had severed all contacts with Lucky Luciano while the ambitious Maranzano played his own game and only had his own interests at heart. The pot came to the boil in the spring of 1949 when it became evident that Liggio was about to make a move to overthrow Vizzini. Don Salvatore Maranzano acted unilaterally and two of his lieutenants and Giuliano were contracted to assassinate Luciano Liggio.

Giuliano's party took the best part of three days to accomplish the fifty kilometre trek from Montelpre to Liggio's mountain retreat four kilometres west of Corleone in the Coso San Filippo hills. As soon as they settled in a vintners hut, Giuliano left and was away for nearly 24 hours recceing the lie of the land. Luciano Liggio's fortified house stood on a promontory overlooking Ponte Arancio which carried the road from Corleone across the Frattina River. The estate was dependent on its large sheep and goat herds and its extensive vineyards on the lower slopes of the Coso San Filippo range. The castle walls were patrolled by armed gabelotti but, on his return, Giuliano reported finding a way into the fortified house and planned to make their move that night under cover of darkness. Pietro and Firenzo took the mules over Ponte Arancio and made their way northwards along the west bank of the Frattina to a point of confluence of two streams. Giuliano took Carla uphill to an unguarded back entrance into a walled vegetable garden and into a lean-to wooden shed in one corner. At first light Giuliano poir¹ed out two upright wodden structures astride a brook and about thirty yards from the back entrance to the house.

"Those are latrines. Liggio came out at around eight o'clock yesterday and was in one of them for half an hour. I think he's a man of habit and will do the same again today."

Crouching inside the cramped wooden shack they waited with mounting anticipation with their eyes glued on the kitchen door. With a clatter of bolts and locks a gabelotti carrying a shotgun emerged at around 7 o'clock and walked up the whole length of the garden to take up position outside the garden wall.

"Damn it!" Giuliano whispered, "this didn't happen yesterday."

At precisely 8 o'clock a tubby, balding man in shirtsleeves and red, cross–over braces emerged. Contentedly smoking a cigar, and carrying a wad of cut-up newspaper sheets in his left hand, he strode into one of the wooden, stand-up latrines.

"That's our man Carla. Give him a minute to settle in. You'll have to shoot him and I'll deal with the guard outside to clear the way for our escape."

At the count of thirty Giuliano dashed out of the shack followed by Carla a few seconds later. Giuliano was in luck and the unsuspecting guard stood idly smoking a cigarette with his shotgun propped against the garden wall. He barely had time to shout a warning before Giuliano thrust a knife under his ribs and, moving swiftly behind him, held the gabelotti in a stranglehold and slit his extended neck from ear to ear. Blood spurted in all directions as the victim valiantly struggled to get out of the headlock but, within half a minute, he lost consciousness and, as he slid to the floor, Giuliano heard gunshots from the garden. As Carla approached the occupied latrine, cigar smoke seeped from under the door and deep grunts from inside left no doubt the victim was busy going about his business. She flung the door wide open and stared straight into the startled, brown eyes of the seated man with his trousers and bright-red braces hanging limply about his knees. He took the cigar out of his mouth and looked with incredulity at the fresh-faced young man standing five feet away and brandishing a pistol. As he made an effort to get to his feet Carla's first bullet hit him fair and square in the centre of his forehead throwing his head violently backwards. Carla looked on with a mixture of horror and elation at her first execution in cold blood. Unable to look at the man's bloodied face she delivered the next two shots with eyes closed. The first bullet ploughed through the base of the victim's neck and the second into his upper chest. The seated man's cigar fell inside a fold in his trousers and started burning a hole in the cloth. Carla made a rapid exit from the latrine and met Giuliano on the garden path.

"It's done Giuliano! Signore Liggio is dead" and she burst out laughing, partly in relief but also remembering the incongruous sight of the fat don with his trousers draped about his knees. Together they ran over the crest of the hill and made a rapid descent into the narrow Frattina valley 600ft below. Giuliano led his party into a cave in the vastness of the Rocche di Rao Mountains and, after three days, the Corleonesi searchers gave up and the coast was clear for a return to Montelpre. But Giuliano's reputation was dented when it became known that the man they had assassinated in the latrine was a minor mobster on a visit from Agrigento. Don Luciano Liggio was very much alive and kicking and placed the blame for his colleague's murder fairly and squarely on the shoulders of the Cucinotta's of Godrano.

Calagero Vizzini's loss of control over the agrarian dons of Palermo Province stimulated Angelo Muzzi, the Mayor of Palermo, to establish stronger links with Naples and to import ruthless n'drangetta from the mainland to run his underhand enterprises and maintain his muscle-power in dealing with militant Dons. Under instruction from Naples, he instigated a confrontation and a take-over bid for Maranzano's empire at Castellammare in June. For decades the port had been a departure point for Sicilian émigrés and a lucrative source of income for the Maranzano Family, who denied Lucky Luciano a piece of the action. In October, Muzzi sent one of his n'drangetta lieutenants to infiltrate the Maranzano organisation and incite strikes among the dockworkers and, by the end of the year, Alberto Profaci was causing bedlam and had organised one-day stoppages and forced the Boss to increase the dockers' wages. He resorted to arson and collected levies from employees and émigrés who passed through the dockland gates. All attempts by Maranzano's gabelotti to curb the upstart met with failure and Giuliano was conscripted to undertake an execution on Alberto Profaci. The time and place for the hit were of no consequence to Don Salvatore Maranzano as long as he himself and his gabelotti were not implicated. in the

Giuliano and Carla moved into top floor rooms in a grotty Transit Hostel in Castellammare's dockland in the last week of November 1949 and, from the flat roof, Giuliano could observe the fishing harbour and the commercial dock offices. Alberto Profaci had negotiated mid-morning breaks for the dockers and used the opportunity to address the men. Profaci was a typical southern Italian - a short, wiry man with a dark, swarthy face and prominent, hooked nose. At the height of oratory he flailed his arms wildly, haranguing his audience in a piercing, high-pitched voice. The impromptu meetings in front of the dock offices usually ended in three loud hoorays and a clenched- fist salute from the dockers. A disturbing feature of Profaci's meetings was a ring of bribed Carabinieri around the piazza perimeter. Giuliano outlined his plan "I'll knock him out from the flat roof tomorrow morning when he speaks to the dockers."

Carla nodded and asked "What do you wish me to do, Giuliano?"

"Wear your black dress and, after the shooting, hide my rifle. The Carabinieri won't think of searching a woman. I'll meet you afterwards on the coast road at Alcamo. Ditch my rifle if you have to but it's very valuable and I would like it saved if possible."

Armed Carabinieri were in position around the periphery of the piazza at 11.00 am the following day and dockworkers came streaming out for their mid-morning break. Amid cheers, Profaci stood at the top of the steps outside the dock offices and started speaking in a penetrating, nasal accent. At a range of 250yds he made a perfect, unmissable target and Giuliano's bullet hit him in his left chest and flung him backwards into an office doorway. Unaware that Profaci was not playacting, a few bystanders laughed outright but others, including the Carabinieri, turned towards the hostel roof and pandemonium broke loose. Some men ran in circles and others flung themselves to the ground in an attempt to make their profile less of a target. Holding Giuliano's rifle across her chest Carla looked down from her bedroom on the terrified mob in the piazza. She smiled briefly and, suddenly, her hatred for men surfaced and, in a bout of uncontrollable frenzy, she let fly indiscriminately with the remaining five bullets. No apparent targets presented themselves but a police sergeant, still on his feet, was shot through his neck and spun to the ground in a lifeless heap. Another bullet passed through the abdomen of a kneeling docker and ploughed into the groin of a Carabinieri lying on the cobblestone piazza. Meanwhile Alberto Profaci lay dying in the office doorway, his life's blood pouring in spurts form a large hole in his chest and dribbles of frothy blood regurgitating from his speechless mouth. Carla experienced the height of ecstasy as she saw, and almost felt, the bullets tearing into human flesh and the carnage and confusion in the piazza. Her extra shots had given Giuliano the chance to clear the building and now it was time for her to go. She secreted the carbine lengthwise under her black dress and, mingling with curious hostel guests, she walked calmly down the stone staircase. On the first floor landing three Carabinieri came rushing upstairs, pushing their way through the onlookers. One shouted "Out of our way" and "Scuse Signora" and Carla, humbly, stood aside. The hostel lobby was crawling with policemen but no one took any notice of the thin, waif-like woman pushing her way politely towards the exit. She walked slowly out of town and, twenty minutes later, joined Giuliano at the roadside on the outskirts of Castellammare. He was more exited by his reunion with his trusted American rifle than by Carla's safe return. Investigating Carabinieri in Castellammare found six empty shell cases, one on the hostel's flat roof and five in an upper floor bedroom overlooking the dockyard piazza. The identity of the assassin was never established and Salvatore Maranzano's men, who would have been prime suspects, were never implicated.

By Christmastime 1949 Giuliano was again in the doldrums

and the presence of a female under the same roof increased his depression. Carla was not given a choice. Giuliano moved her lock, stock and barrel into a whitewashed labourer's cottage outside Baida on the pine-covered foothills of the Buccadifalco Mountains and three miles north of Monreale. The hamlet boasted eight Moorish-style hovels of which only three were occupied and Carla moved into the fourth. In common with the rest of Palermo Province, Baida had suffered from mass emigration to the New World in the thirties and had never recovered. A wizened old bachelor farmer lived next door and provided Carla with goat's milk, cheese and vegetables from his smallholding and, on his rare visits, Giuliano brought lamp oil, olive oil, flour and flasks of rough, local wine. Carla spent a long, lonely winter in her primitive abode and reverted to enjoying her own company and, in the spring, she cultivated a patch of arable land at the rear of her cottage.

The winter of 1949 was exceptionally mild and dry until heavy rains came in February and March 1950. Giuliano took advantage of the clement wintry weather to go on foray's along the coastal road between Palermo and Trapani. Living rough and off the land, he apprehended and robbed unwary travellers and distributed the proceeds among the local poor. Carla was never invited, or involved, in these activities and she wintered peacefully in her whitewashed cottage at Baida. Her life was basic, humdrum and uncomplicated and this state of affairs continued until one sunny spring morning in 1950 when Giuliano appeared out of the blue. Carla was shocked by his appearance and mental state. All his life a moody person, he was now severely depressed and melancholic.

"What's happened to you, Giuliano?"

The unshaven brigand stood shaking in the doorway, his bulging eyes glazed and vacant. Suddenly he took two steps forwards and burst into tears. Reluctantly Carla took him in her arms and cradled his head on her shoulder. His long matted hair and bristly beard smelt of stale wine and tobacco and, in between plaintive sobs, a torrent of words came tumbling out of his mouth "Last week Salvatore Maranzano gave me a contract on Angelo Muzzi."

His voice faltered and his thin body convulsed as he clung to Carla and stuttered "But Carla! How can I eliminate Muzzi? He's my father! I was told this in a bar at Castellammare."

After another bout of violent sobbing he calmed down and loosened himself from Carla's arms.

"You see Carla, I was brought up in an orphanage in Trapani and until yesterday I didn't know my parents. I still don't know who my mother was and I was fostered out on the Giuliano family and took their name. I hate my father. He must know who I am and where I live. So why hasn't he made contact with me?"

Carla tried to rationalize "Perhaps he's ashamed of you Giuliano," and then her own hatred for lustful men surfaced, "He's been a rotten father to you and should have taken you into his house years ago. By now you would be an important mafioso. He did nothing to help you and he deserves to die."

The troubled look faded from Giuliano's face and was supplanted by an angry determined glare.

"You're right Carla! Angelo Muzzi must die. He was never my father" and he spat on the floor. Miraculously his mood changed and he smiled as he unslung a canvas strap off his right shoulder.

"Look at this gun! I got it at Castellammare."

With pride he showed Carla his latest acquisition, a British Army Stengun complete with a loaded magazine. Carla was not impressed by the squat, bull-nosed weapon but Giuliano hastened to explain "It's lethal at close range and is easily dismantled into sections. Come outside and I'll show you."

In the watery, evening light Giuliano demonstrated the efficiency of his Stengun by shooting the head off a cactus plant in Carla's vegetable plot. As his enthusiasm and excitement waned so Giuliano's depression quickly returned and, in a half-whisper, he spoke to Carla "I'll kill Angelo Muzzi with this little gun."

Word arrived in Montelpre that Angelo Muzzi would be attending a religious service at his family shrine at Portella Ginestra on May 10th 1950. Giuliano knew the area well and together with Carla, Pietro and Firenzo, his faithful lieutenants from Castellammare, he moved across to Portella Ginestra two days before the commemoration service. Portello Ginestra lies on a hillside, sheltering underneath the 2,200ft high Sierra della Ginestra and about 12kms by mountain road due west of Piana. The Muzzi family shrine was a pillared mausoleum built by the Normans and set into the rock on a wooded hillside about a kilometre from Ginestra village. In the two days they lay under cover near the shrine Carla became concerned about Giuliano. He stayed out in the hot sun all day, staring fixedly into space, and ate and drank sparingly. He had no preconceived plan of action, merely muttering to himself from time to time, and it came as a great relief to the group when their patience was rewarded. At around 11 o'clock on 10th May a procession was seen wending its way on foot up the road from Portella Ginestra. An attendant holding a cross aloft led the parade followed by a priest dressed in white robes and ten paces behind, and flanked by four gabelotti, came a short, squat man in a black suit and a grey trilby hat. Further back six male relatives walked in line abreast and a group of black-garbed women and a few children brought up the rear. Finally, at a discrete distance behind the procession, a black Fiat saloon containing two armed mobsters crawled sedately along the road. For the first time in days a flickering smile of anticipation crossed Giuliano's face.

"Here he comes! Carla and I will hit him on the path. You two go through the woods to the road and, when you hear me shooting, open up on the Fiat."

Pietro and Firenzo departed immediately to take up their positions at the roadside. Carla had a query "What shall we do about the priest and the women and children?"

Without a seconds' hesitation Giuliano replied "Just shoot them if they get in the way."

The procession had to walk in pairs up the shepherds' path to the shrine and, when the cross-bearer and the priest were clear, Giuliano leapt out of the bushes and, at twelve paces, let fly with his Stengun. The men at the front end of the procession crumpled like a pack of cards and, Stengun at hip level and a fiendish grin on his face, Giuliano advanced on to the path and emptied his magazine at point blank range into the screaming, writhing bodies. The priest descended into the middle of the massacre and knelt to administer last rites to a dying gabelotti. Giuliano did not hesitate and ordered Carla to finish him off with her pistol. From the direction of the road a gun battle was audible above the screams where Pietro and Firenzo were heavily engaged with the two Mafia gabelotti in the black Fiat. Giuliano slammed a fresh magazine in his Sten and turned to Carla "Finish off these men. I'm going down to help Pietro."

On inspection three of the bodies on the ground, including the target, were dead and two were dying. One gabelotti was barely conscious and Carla shot him through the forehead. Giuliano's path downhill was barred by four peasants who resolutely refused to budge and acted as a protective screen for the women and children. Carried away by the killing power of his new toy, Giuliano opened fire and continued firing until none were left standing and his second magazine was empty. Stepping over the moaning, wounded and dying, victims and screaming children he called to Carla "Come on! Follow me down to the road."

Carla obeyed and thanked God she was wearing trousers and a cloth cap. She dared not look the wounded women in the eye and two lifeless children in the middle of the massacred bodies made her feel sick. With closed eyes she ran blindly down the pathway after Giuliano.

Evidently satisfied with themselves, Pietro and Firenzo stood beside the pellet-ridden Fiat and two dead gabelotti lay side by side on a grass verge. By now Giuliano was anxio is to make his getaway.

"Can anyone drive this Fiat?"

"I can," Firenzo volunteered and took the wheel. The black Fiat was driven at speed over the Sierra della Ginestra Mountains to San Cipirello and south on a tortuous road as far as Poggioreale where the engine blew up and the car had to be abandoned. Here the group split up and Pietro and Firenzo retraced their steps northwards while Giuliano and Carla made tracks for Mazara on the south coast. By this time Giuliano had made up his mind to flee Sicily and head for North Africa before the authorities caught up with him. After three days cross-country trekking over the hilly terrain they rested in a disused barn on the outskirts of Castelvetrano. News of the Ginestra massacre had spread like wildfire throughout the Province but it was not Giuliano's notoriety that led to his downfall. The depressed renegade went into a taverna in Castelvetrano where he became embroiled in an argument with three young mafiosi. Their leader was a member of the Accardo Family from Portanna and he insisted on inspecting Giuliano's Stengun. A scuffle spilled out to the street where Giuliano was beaten-up and his weapon forcibly removed from his grasp. He hit out at the nearest attacker and knocked him to the ground. Renewing their assault two mafiosi held him down and, unused to the gun's sensitive hair-trigger, their leader accidentally fired three rounds into Giuliano's exposed back. The mafiosi turned and fled and left him for dead. That he was able to stagger and crawl the two kilometres to his hideout was a miracle and he was dead on his feet on arrival. He fell into Carla's arms and she cradled his head on her lap. With the dying words, "Get my little gun back for me, Carla," he slipped into unconsciousness and stopped breathing. Carla removed a gold ring from his finger and a silver cross from around his neck and laid the body to rest on a bed of straw in a corner of the barn. With arms folded across his chest, and reverently clutching a red poppy, the corpse looked angelic in repose but, in view of all his atrocities, Carla doubted that Giuliano's soul had successfully made its journey to heaven.

The mysteries surrounding Giuliano's death were many. The mobster murdered at the Portella Ginestra massacre was a family connection and accorded Boss-status for the day by Angelo Muzzi who provided him with a Fiat saloon and bodyguards. There was a question as to how many hitmen were at the massacre with Giuliano and where they went afterwards. The murder of women and children transgressed the Mafia code of honour and the identity of the person who laid Giuliano's body to rest on a bed of straw at Castelvetrano remained unsolved. Unheralded, and without ceremony, Giuliano's body was interred in an unmarked paupers grave at Castelvetrano. His reputation as a latter-day Robin Hood was irreparably tarnished by the Ginestra incident but his legend lived on and, for years after his death, he was regarded with awe and reverence by the superstitious Sicilian peasantry. The identity of his fresh-faced, ever-present lieutenant was never established. Only Carla knew the true extent of Giuliano's munificence and criminal shortcomings. Her whereabouts were known only to Pietro and Firenzo and she retired to her whitewashed cottage in Baida, where she remained for the best part of four years, leading the life of a semi-recluse and eeking out a meagre existence from her smallholding.

Following the assassination of Antonio La Barbera in September 1949 a state of emergency existed between Corleone and Godrano estates. Giudo converted the small hamlet of Flouzza into a fortified camp, guarded by a garrison of well-paid gabelotti, and denying access northwards to Corleonesi food convoys. Though condoning his brother's actions, Don Andreo took no part in the ensuing skirmishes and was content to remain at Godrano protected by his personal guards. Angelo Muzzi in Palermo was running with the hare and the hounds and, while paying lip service to Corleonesi demands for action against Godrano, he continued to allow Don Andreo's farm produce to flood his Palermo markets and was paid handsomely for the franchise. In June 1950 Luciano Liggio of Corleone issued an ultimatum - either Muzzi acted against Godrano or he would be ousted from his position as mayor of Palermo. The all-powerful Corleonesi don won the day. Overnight, Don Andreo's convoys were intercepted at Piana, Bolognetta and Villafrati and those that managed to get through to Palermo were confiscated in the market with the result that Godrano's farm produce and crops lay withering in the fields. The whole area was like a time-bomb waiting to explode and, by July, seven gabelotti had lost their lives in local skirmishes.

On a hot summer's evening towards the end of July, Don Andreo and Giudo were seated on the old wooden bench overlooking Godrano valley. Don Andreo was a worried man "We can't carry on much longer, Giudo. We have no market for our grain and two wheat fields had to be burnt yesterday. Sant Agata's grape harvest is rotting and we may as well pour the wine into Lago Scanzano."

He paused to wipe his sweaty brow "There's only one answer. We'll have to get rid of Angelo Muzzi. When he's out of the way I'll make a deal with new don in Palermo."

Don Andreo omitted to add that, if his plans worked out, he might be the elected mayor to replace Muzzi. But first he had to make his peace with the Corleonesi and, for that to happen, Giudo would have to be out of the way. Giudo gave the matter a few seconds thought "I've heard Muzzi's heavily guarded since the Ginestra massacre. He knows he was the intended victim that day and getting to him will be difficult. But I'll work out a way to complete the job."

"We have no choice, Giudo. By the winter Godrano will be bankrupt. Once we fail to pay your Flouzza gabelotti they'll disappear or, worse still, they'll defect to the Corleonesi. When will you go?" Don Andreo asked.

"I'll leave in a few days and I'll go alone," Giudo announced. Fearing an internal revolt from Guido's militant gabelotti, Don Andreo looked up sharply "Shouldn't you take your gabelotti for protection?"

"No, Andreo. I want to do this job on my own."

Disguised as a muleteer Giudo spent the first week of August 1950 hanging around Vucciria market and La Cala harbour in Palermo. His vigil was rewarded on a Friday night in the old Mercato Ittico when Muzzi, accompanied by a bevy of bodyguards, dined in a converted warehouse on a disused wharf. He took over Ristorante Pescadore for the night while his armed gabelotti patrolled the area and denied access to all would-be diners. Fish on Friday is an acknowledged Catholic tradition and Angelo Muzzi was passionately fond of pasta and fish dishes. During siesta hour Giudo paid a visit to Mercato Ittico wharf. Built on wooden stanchions, the dilapidated pier jutted eighty yards into the harbour and its distal thirty yards was almost derelict. The windowless back wall of the restaurant supported a lean-to, wooden hut which served as a latrine for customers and had a frosted-glass window facing the harbour. The pier was a perfect place for an assassination but Giudo would have to persuade a fishing boat to take him to Mercato Ittico pier. Local fisherman could not be trusted and, for his purposes, he called on Don Salvatore Maranzano at Castellammare.

"And to what do I owe this honour, Signore Cucinotta?"

Giudo and the silver-haired don sat in a living room in an unpretentious town apartment next to the castle walls. Maranzano was suspicious of the Cucinotta mafioso's motives and, in fact, he mistrusted all other mafiosi in the region.

"I bring greetings from Don Andreo. I have been given a contract and I need to hire a fishing boat to take me to Mercato Ittico pier in La Cala harbour."

Don Salvatore was now very interested.

"And whom, might I ask, is the target?"

"Angelo Muzzi," Giudo replied, "I intend to ————."

At this point the Boss held up his hand and silenced Giudo.

"I don't need to know your plan of action. The ı ss I know the better. Captain Santiago takes a boat out of Alcamo twice a week and sometimes takes his catch to La Cala. So long as you don't involve the captain and his crew you may make use of their fishing boat. I wish you luck Signore Cucinotta."

The Maranzano boss could hardly conceal his excitement at the thought the aggressive young mafioso might succeed where his own gabelotti had failed miserably.

Captain Santiago's fishing boat, with Giudo aboard, berthed at the end of the derelict pier in Mercato Ittico an hour before dusk on the third Friday in August, just as Palermo's fishing vessels were phut-phutting out of the harbour on their way to the fishing grounds off Cape Gallo. It was dark by 9 o'clock when Giudo went on to the pier and picked his way carefully to the back of the restaurant. The latrine's frosted window was three-quarters open to allow the fetid stench of urine and carbolic to escape into the night air and, slung from a hook in the ceiling, a kerosene lamp provided illumination inside the smelly pissoir. After a forty minute wait in the shadows, the third visitor to the latrine was Angelo Muzzi. He was in his shirtsleeves and carried a pistol in a holster under his left armpit. With a self-satisfied smile of a well-fed man at peace with his conscience and surroundings he stood, legs apart, whistling and concentrating on directing his urinary stream into the hole-in-the-ground urinal. Giudo suddenly appeared at the window behind his back.

"Buenosera, Signore Muzzi!"

The startled don stopped whistling and his right hand instinctively left his dribbling penis and moved towards his holster. Giudo's first bullet hit him beneath his left shoulder blade and the second ploughed into the right side of his chest. Muzzi was thrown violently forwards against the latrine wall and then, in slow motion and clutching at the tiled wall of the pissoir, he slid slowly downwards to end in a disjointed heap on the urine-impregnated floor. Giudo pumped three more bullets into his writhing torso and, after pulling the frosted window shut, took to his heels and raced back to the boat. With all recognition lights doused, Captain Santiago nosed his boat out of La Cala harbour and,by the time the searchers got on to the pier, they were speeding past Molo Nord and beginning their overnight dash back to Castellammare.

Giudo had kept himself hidden in Captain Santiago's cottage at Alcamo for three days when Don Salvatore dropped in unexpectedly.

"My spies tell me you fixed Muzzi for good. His funeral will be tomorrow and I must be there. There will be questions asked and you may be a ϳrime suspect. There's a ship sailing for New York tomorrow morning and you must be on it. I've got immigration papers and a passport already prepared for you. Your new identity will be Giudo Ceserano."

Giudo had little choice in the matter.

"Grazie, Don Salvatore. I don't speak good English. I'm told this does not matter in America."

"Of course it doesn't," Maranzano reassured him, "my cousin, Joe Bonanno, will look after you when you get to New York."

The ruggedly-handsome, silver-haired don smiled briefly "I'll drive you across to our Transit Hostel in the docks. The Romanza leaves tomorrow at 7 o'clock. Now say your goodbyes to Captain Santiago and we'll be off."

The dye was cast. Giudo Cucinotta, alias Giudo Ceserano, would be leaving Sicily in the morning and, now he was a wanted man, there was every reason for defecting to the New World. But who was this Joe Bonanno, his contact in New York? Giudo didn't care for the sound of his name. In the seclusion of his spartan room in the Transit Hostel he took out Al Rizzi's gold-embossed business card. 'Ristorante Berterelli,' that sounded more promising than meeting with a man called Joe Bonanno.

CHAPTER 9

Saratoga Springs

DISAFFECTED IMMIGRANTS WHO FLOCKED in their thousands to New York between 1890 and 1940, not surprisingly, found themselves impoverished and unemployed in ethnic ghettos in the city. No more so than the Sicilians, many of whom were established mafiosi, who very rapidly formed themselves into clans, each with its own leader and territory and in open competition with Jewish, Irish and Polish mobsters. Unification of clans for added power and protection occurred in the 20's and, in 1928, a 43 year old leader emerged to become Boss of New York's Families. Having fled from Sicily on a murder charge, Giuseppe Masseria, otherwise known as Joe the Boss, was a Mustache Petes, full of Sicilian prejudices and upholding the Mafia traditions of his country of origin. One of his lieutenants was Charles 'Lucky' Luciano whose parents emigrated from Sicily to the USA in 1906 when he was nine years of age. Mafia organisations prospered during the bootlegging years in the 30's and Luciano, together with Jewish mobsters Bugsy Siegel and Meyer Lansky, were front runners in illicit trading in prohibited liquor. In 1929 Vito Cascio Ferro, the Sicilian Boss of Bosses, dispatched an emissary to New York with the objective of uniting all Mafia organisations throughout North America and it soon became evident to Salvatore Maranzano he could not achieve his goal without deposing Masseria. Both natives of Castellammare del Golfo in Sicily, open warfare developed between Masseria and Maranzano and over fifty small-time Sicilian mobsters were eliminated. Not content with Masseria's leadership Lucky Luciano planned a coup and, on April 15th 1931, he lured Maaseria to lunch at a Coney Island restaurant where he was shot six times while Luciano was in the men's room and denied any knowledge of, or involvement in, the murder. Maranzano took over as Boss of Bosses, promoted Luciano to underboss, and parcelled New York into five crime family territories. His reign over New York's Mafia only lasted five months. Using a Jewish hitsquad Luciano, Lansky and Three Fingers Brown Luchese arranged a counterplot on September 10th 1931 and hired Jewish gangsters to stab Maranzano to death in his office in Grand Central Buildings. Though he abhorred the title, Lucky Luciano went on to become a true Boss of Bosses for all Mafia organisations in the United States. He formed a National Crime Syndicate which controlled organised crime throughout the USA and ensured his Jewish and Polish colleagues were non-voting members of the Syndicate. The concept of a Cosa Nostra faded into the background and more importance was placed on the organisation of crime rather than the ritual jingoism of traditional Mafia practices. Imprisoned on prostitution charges in 1936, Luciano retained his influence over the Syndicate and, even after his deportation to Italy in 1946, he continued to receive regular handouts from his mobster colleagues. The concept of five major Mafia crime families in New York remains to this day though the Bosses have moved around, died, or been eliminated. Affectionately known as Prime Minister of the Underworld, and a friend of judges, police and politicians, Frank Costello became the undisputed Boss in New York during Luciano's imprisonment at Danemmora in upper New York State. A member of the Big Six, and tipped to become Boss of Bosses for all

American Families, Costello retired after an attempt on his life on May 2nd 1957. The retired don lived out his years as a Long Island squire and died of natural causes in 1973.

MV Romanza arrived in New York waters on 3rd September 1950. Commissioned in 1932 the 20,000 tonne Romanza, once a luxury passenger liner converted for trooping during the war, made the crossing in seven days. The upper decks were reserved for luxury class passengers and, in common with eighty eight immigrants, Giudo Ceserano travelled steerage. Women and children were segregated and he shared a cabin with three male members of the Minelli family from Montalta in Calabria. He spent his days on the aft-lower deck allocated for steerage passengers and dreaded returning at night to the stuffy, smelly cabin in the bowels of the ship. On their fourth night at sea the Minelli's were celebrating a birthday and had consumed a bottle of grappa when one turned to face Giudo lying on his bunk and pretending to be asleep "Where's your home Giudo?"

Giudo felt obliged to reply "I come from Godrano in Palermo Province."

"Godrano eh? Franco Gicanetti from Montalta was there during the war. Did you meet him?"

"Yes. I met him once. The Americani's killed him and his fat friend Branco near Godrano in 1943."

The Minelli man's face screwed up in disbelief.

"His friend may have been killed but Franco Gicanetti came back to a farm near us in Montalta. About two years ago he suddenly produced a four year old boy out of nowhere. No one knows where the little lad came from and they say Gicanetti kidnapped him in Sicily."

Giudo sat up with a start. He had often wondered what happened to Carla and her child and the story he just heard suggested a kidnapping. He stared at the inebriated Calabrian.

"I don't think we're speaking about the same Franco. The one I knew was definitely killed in the cave. I saw the body," he lied. He leant back on his pillow and closed his eyes. Someone must have informed Gicanetti of the boys' whereabouts and the only suspect at Godrano could be his own brother, Andreo. Despite his tough guy façade Giudo still adhered to some of the Mafia's traditional principles and he detested kidnapping. He vowed that one of these days Andreo and Franco Gicanetti would be made to pay a price for their perfidy.

On arrival in New York waters the steerage passengers were herded like cattle into an airless lower deck while the Romanza came up the Narrows and the Hudson estuary and berthed in Brooklyn's Port Hamilton to disembark the upper class passengers. American immigration officials and armed police came aboard and the liner retraced its course across Upper New York Bay to its final berth on Ellis Island on 3rd September 1950. As they came down the gangway in the fading autumn light the immigrants caught their first glimpse of the promised land - the Statue of Liberty two miles across the bay and, in the background, the highrise buildings and skyscrapers on Manhattan's unique skyline. The men were segregated and confined in compounds enclosed by an electrified wire fence and, after sundown, were locked inside communal dormitories. Interviews began in earnest the following day. The blue-uniformed officials were thorough and particularly fastidious about the health of the newly-arrived Sicilians. Many potential immigrants, including the entire Minelli family, were whisked away to an isolation block for rigorous medical check-ups. Giudo passed A1 and was categorized as Sicilian: General Labourer: Linguistic Category MI - monoglot Italian. He was issued with a ferry ticket, a taxi voucher and two ten dollar bills and given the address of a Sicilian hostel in Seaport Market in downtown Manhattan. When he set foot on Battery Park Ferry Terminal on 5th September Giudo Ceserano was officially in the United States and carried a photographed entry and work permit to prove it.

Marine Sergeant Nico Falcone and Al Rizzi were having lunch in

Don Mario Deluca's reserved booth at Berterelli's. The old don rarely came to town these days and had virtually handed over his Manhattan enterprises to his son-in-law. Claudia was pregnant for the third time and the Rizzi's were praying for a son and heir, a brother for their two daughters. Home on a weeks' furlough, and looking for a way to return to civilian life, Nico Falcone sat at the table sharing a bowl of fettuchini Siciliana and a bottle of full-bodied Chianti with Al Rizzi. Al placed his fork on the side of his plate of pasta.

"So you wanna out of the army, Nico? The best I can do is head waiter at Berterelli's. Your brother Joe is still top man here and I canna promote you over his head."

Proudly thrusting out his chest to fully display his campaign medals, the marine sergeant replied "I canna come back to humping friggin crockery. Will you make me a consiglieri or enforcer for Don Mario's businesses?"

Al took a generous gulp of his Chianti.

"That's an idea, Nico! I'll have a word with the Boss and I'll be in touch. Are you still in Milwakee?"

"Yeah, Boss! I'm still in friggin Milwakee."

No so ner had Nico left the restaurant than his brother, Giuseppe, appeared and placed a gold-embossed business card on the table. When he recognised the card Al's eyes lit up with curiosity. Since the war a few regimental chums had called at Berterelli's for a free meal and on one memorable occasion Mad Mike Dangerfield, now a full colonel, had dropped in for a chinwag about the good old days in Sicily. Joe fingered his apron strings "There's a strange-looking guy at the bar. By the way he's dressed I'd guess he's straight outa clink. He speaks very little English and looks like a friggin Siccy", Joe's abbreviated slang for a Sicilian. Al got to his feet "Make sure he's clean and bring him to my office in ten minutes. I'd like to look him over" and, picking up the embossed card, he limped his way to the storeroom at the far end of the restaurant.

Back at his station behind the bar Joe Falcone eyed the small-statured stranger standing stiffly to attention on the other side of the counter and refusing a drink. He wore a dark grey overcoat, a white starched collar and a black necktie and a flat cap. His face was ashen and his coal-black, sunken eyes stared fixedly at the array of liquor bottles and optics on the shelves behind Joe's back.

"Come here," Joe commanded in Italian, and the stranger pushed forwards to the counter.

"Identification," Joe barked. Giudo produced his documents and Joe read the details aloud "Giudo Ceserano. Italian/Sicilian. General Labourer. Capital MI! What does friggin MI mean?"

Giudo had no explanation and simply shrugged his shoulders. Five minutes later Joe ordered the visitor to follow him down the length of the restaurant into a toilet where he was frisked and then ushered into the storage room- cum- office where Al Rizzi was seated behind a trestle table.

"Mister Rizzi! This guy's clean, Boss, and he's a goddam Siccy all right. He calls himself Giudo Ceserano."

"Okay, Giuseppe, leave us now" and, in broken Italian, he continued "Sit down Signore Ceserano.I haven't seen one of these cards for months. Where did you get it?"

Giudo sat stiffly on an upright wooden chair.

"You may remember me Signore Rizzi. I am a Cucinotta, the son of Don Giovanni of Portella Sant Agata. My brother and I met you at Godrano after you had been wounded in the war."

Memories came flooding back and, as they did, so Al's left leg began to ache.

"I remember you and your brother. What happened at Godrano after I was taken away?"

Giudo took off his cap and placed it on the table. He made up his mind to tell the truth to the American who wasted opposite.

"Two months after you left Don Carlo Cecci died and my brother, Andreo, became Don at Godrano. And then, in 1948, my father was murdered by the Corleonesi and I became Andreo's lieutenant and, in retaliation, I killed one of the La Barbera brothers. This started a war between us and Corleone and many men from both sides were killed ending up a month ago when I shot Angelo Muzzi, the Mayor of Palermo and I had to get out of Sicily quickly. Signore Maranzano in Castellammare arranged my papers in the name of Ceserano and told me to contact a man in New York called Joe Bonanno."

Al was by now mentally reminiscing "Whatever became of the three girls at Godrano? They looked after me in 1943."

Giudo took a sip of iced water.

"Andreo and Santo married Anna and Gina. Anna is at Godrano with Don Andreo but, soon after my father's death, Santo and Gina moved to England."

"And what about Carla, the pretty dark one? What became of her?"

Guido's face screwed up in distaste "That puttita became pregnant and 'rought disgrazitsa on the Cecci's and Cucinotta's. The father of her child was Franco Gicanetti who was hiding at Godrano to avoid the military. We thought he'd been killed by your soldiers but he must have escaped back to his homeland in Calabria."

Al Rizzi was intrigued and had thoughts in the back of his mind that he might have fathered Carla's child.

"And where is Carla and her child now?"

Giudo hesitated and then volunteered the information he had gleaned on the Romanza "I don't know where the Cecci woman is living, or even if she is still alive. I heard on the ship that Franco Gicanetti runs a farm in Calabria and has a seven year old boy in his house. The rumour is he kidnapped Carla's boy from Palermo with help from someone in Sicily."

Alphonse Rizzi's whole body stiffened in anger.

"And who in Sicily helped the kidnappers?"

Guido hesitated again and then blurted out "It couldn't be anyone else but my brother Andreo."

Al remained silent for a whole minute weighing up the pros and cons. He had to decide what to do with the raw material that had, out of the blue, landed in his lap. Trained assassins were hard to come by, even in New York's violent underworld, and the Siccy sitting opposite him might well be a solution and ultimate answer to his prayers. Giudo Ceserano moved into Berterelli's that evening and slept on a couch in the store room at night. During the day he worked in the kitchens and was kept under wraps and out of sight of customers. The officer charged with keeping an eye on foreign immigrants called at William Street Market on a few occasions only to find the bird had flown. With a bemused smile, and a shrug of his shoulders, he assumed it was another case of a Wop disappearing into the cosmopolitan maelstrom of downtown Manhattan.

.   One frosty Sunday morning in October Al Rizzi paid his monthly visit to Don Mario

Deluca's mansion in Oyster Bay on Long Island Sound. After exchanging platitudes, and handing over a satchel of money, Al broached the subject "At the moment the number of contracts are getting out of hand. Thanks to Frankie Costello I don't need extra muscle for protection but I do need a reliable hitman. When Albert Anastasia's on the prowl victims get out of town and I can't use him for hits in New York. I've got a hot property at Berterelli's. He's a Sicilian and just come over from Castellammare del Golfo. I also have a backup man in mind. You'll remember Joe's brother at Berterelli's? Nico Falcone's now a sergeant in the Marines and wants out. Nico and this guy Ceserano could hide upstate and come into town for hits. And Nico could teach him English and the tricks of the trade. What do you say Boss?"

The old don fiddled with the stem of his wine glass "What's this Sicilian guy's pedigree?"

"He hit one of the La Barbera brothers from Corleone earlier this year and rubbed out Angelo Muzzi, a big noise in Palermo. That's the hit that upset the Sicilian Families and even the Big Boss in Naples has shown an interest in Little Cesare, as we call him at Berterelli's."

"If Lucky Luciano says okay, that's good enough for me. Fix it up Alphonse. Send them to the Adelphi in Saratoga Springs."

Sergeant Nico Falcone was given an honourable discharge from the Marines in the first week of December 1950. Most days he got together with Little Cesare and, after dark, they toured Manhattan's night-spots and bars. Nico relished the challenge of teaching Giudo basic English and gradually a genuine bond of friendship developed between the ex-Marine sergeant and the raw Sicilian hitman. On 6th January 1951 they travelled from New York Central to Saratoga Springs and, for two years, Nico fronted as the Adelphi Hotel's manager and Little Cesare acted as general factotum and handyman.

Centuries before European colonization of North America, Saratoga was a Mohawk India spa and a base for their hunting lodges. The Mohawks venerated the beneficial effects of Saratoga's sulphur springs. Historically, Saratoga was also the site of British General Burgoyne's surrender to rebel forces in the War for American Independence on 17th October 1777. Sir John Williams, and Indian agent, opened a trading post at Saratoga in the 1770's and, capitalising on the dubious effects of spa bathing, Gideon Putnam built a plush, temperance hotel at the turn of the century. Equidistant from New York and Boston the hotel was ideally placed and, within a few years, became a Mecca for the rich and famous. A profligate prize fighter and gambler named J M

Morrisey opened a racetrack in the sleepy little township in 1864 and, to satisfy the highrollers and punters, Mafia-controlled casinos were later introduced. The gambling and corruption got out of hand and, when the sulphur springs dried up in 1901, a religious reform group closed the casinos and Saratoga became a ghost town. To bolster trade from the health-giving natural springs, New York State re-established the spa and, by 1925, Saratoga was again a flourishing centre patronised by Bostonians and rich rail barons from Philadelphia. Mafia mobsters were quick to react and Dutch Schultz and Lucky Luciano reintroduced casinos and bordellos and these establishments provided a lucrative source of income for the National Crime Syndicate. Throughout its turbulent history Saratoga's racetrack has flourished and its meetings have established a niche in America's horseracing calendar. Hundreds of punters, mainly Boston Irish, descend on the City during the first week in August. Gambling at the racetrack and casinos was controlled by Mafia syndicates and the chances of a punter coming away from Saratoga with winnings in his pocket was very remote. With the deportation of Lucky Luciano to Italy in 1946, Frank Costello inherited the Adelphi Hotel and the Piping Hot Casino and bought a controlling share in the Gideon Putnam Hotel which henceforth had a liquor licence.

In January 1951 the whole of New York State, Vermont, and New Hampshire were covered in a thick blanket of snow which did not clear until April and only one main road and the railroad were passable in and out of Saratoga. The racetrack was under a four foot snowdrift and the adjacent Lake Sacandaga was frozen solid. The Gideon Putnam Spa Hotel was closed but the Adelphi kept its doors open throughout the interminable, cold spell. On their arrival Nico and Giudo were met in the lobby by a caretaker manager, a tubby, balding, bespectacled man in his fifties.

"I can't understand why New York has sent me extra staff at this time of the year. I've got six rooms open on the first floor and only two are taken. Still it's nice to have company."

Suddenly, remembering his status, the squat little manager pulled himself up to his full height of five foot five inches and coughed to clear his throat "Welcome to the Adelphi, gentlemen."

Nico responded "Mr Limberger, I presume."

The manager's shiny, bald pate tilted forwards in acquiescence and Nico continued "I am Nico Falcone and this is Giudo. I call him Little Cesare. He's just arrived from Sicily and speaks very little English. It's our job to teach him the ropes and he will help out doing odd jobs."

Little Cesare remained aloof and silent during the exchange of words and Nico took an immediate dislike to Mr Limberger.

"Come with me," Limberger commanded, "I'll show you round the hotel. It won't take long."

The podgy little manager ushered them through the restaurant and bars on the ground floor and the kitchens in the basement. On the first floor they were shown an opulent ballroom and the six functioning bedrooms in one wing. The top two floors and the penthouse suites were moth-balled and would be reopened at Easter. Once they were alone in their apartment on the ground floor Nico winked at Cesare "Did you notice all six bedrooms are in use but only two are entered in the register? This guy says he has twelve skeleton staff for the winter but, counting us, there are only five guys here. I think Mr Limberger is skimming the cream and we might have to get rid of him."

A telephone call to Berterelli's established that fourteen salaries were sent in cash each week to the Adelphi. A local resident, and with no Mafia connections, Mr Limberger had been appointed to give the Adelphi a squeaky-clean reputation and the bosses in New York were not well-pleased with Nico's information. Al Rizzi's instructions to get rid of the skimmer were clear and unambiguous and, within a fortnight, Nico Falcone became the

Adelphi's new manager.

Suspecting Nico and Cesare were New York auditors, Limberger relieved the heat at the hotel by taking his guests on local day trips in the Adelphi's courtesy Oldsmobile. One evening, on the way back from Glen's Falls, Nico called a halt five kilometres from Saratoga Springs.

"Isn't the Adelphi's fishing lodge near this spot, Limberger? I'd like to have a look at it."

They got out of the Oldsmobile and trudged along a snow-covered path for 200 yards into a thick belt of fir trees covering the sloping ground down to the lakeside. They were up to their knees in snowdrifts and it was beginning to snow heavily. Peering through his snow-covered lenses Limberger spoke up "We won't be able to make it to the boathouse. The drifts are too deep."

"This is as far as we go" Nico asserted and gave Cesare an imperceptible nod. In a flash Cesare had a wire garrotte around Limberger's neck and, pushing a knee into the wriggling man's spine, he expertly tightened the noose. Forty seconds later Limberger's arms and legs stopped flailing and he expired in Cesare's arms. The Sicilian's garrotting technique impressed Nico and the time spent teaching Cesare Marine drill had been worthwhile. Together they carried the corpse deeper into a thicket and hung the dead man by his neck from a branch. Further snowfalls erased all evidence that anyone had walked down the pathway to the Adelphi's boathouse. Mr Limberger's disappearance was reported to the police at midnight and Nico's story was watertight. He confirmed that, on their way back from Glen's Falls, Limberger had insisted on walking the last few kilometres into Saratoga. Known to be a keep-fit addict, Limberger took daily exercise and no amount of persuasion could put him off. A police officer attempted interviewing Cesare but Nico's assertion 'The Wop knows nuttin' quickly put him off. For three days the roadside between the lake and the Adelphi was searched but to no avail and Limberger's hanging body was eventually found when a thaw set in at Easter 1951.

Nico's first priority as manager was to sack the entire staff and reappoint a brand new skeleton workforce. Cesare's English improved by leaps and bounds and Nico began giving him driving lessons on the town's main road. The police were very helpful in providing a driving licence and Nico cultivated the law officers with bribes of free meals and, for Lieutenant James Murray, an occasional bottle of whisky wrapped in dollar bills. For these minor considerations the Police turned a blind eye to the use of the Adelphi's bedrooms as a brothel. In the winter months Saratoga boasted one functioning bordello in Bloomfield Street. Madame Jenny's was fully staffed with prostitutes during the holiday season, but was only occupied by the Madame and three 'country cousins' during the bleak, winter months and Nico and his hot-blooded Sicilian mate were frequent non-paying customers. On a quid-pro-quo basis Nico was not averse to arranging a 'lady-friend' to sleep with his guests as part of the Adelphi's services. Many hotel guests were bona fide commercial travellers but the majority were businessmen, out of town and away from their wives for a few days conference and with one thing in mind. Punters came from New York State and Vermont and, to cope with the influx of 'new' customers, ten rooms were opened on the Adelphi's second floor and Madame Jenny's complement of prostitutes increased to cater for the extra clients. Frank Costello was outwardly dead against prostitution but not averse to accepting Al Rizzi's handouts which increased dramatically as the weeks went by. Cesare's favourite at Madame Jenny's was an eighteen year old Puerto Rican immigrant. Lured into prostitution in a New York ghetto at the age of fourteen, Antonia stayed on in Madame Jenny's over the winter months and Little Cesare became one of her regular customers.

Tuesday was an important meeting night for New York's Mafia

bosses when Families gathered in restaurants and clubs and deals were struck over a meal and a bottle or two of wine. Afterwards, in the privacy of their own homes, the bosses ꞇontacted their lieutenants and issued orders and Nico was never far away from a telephone between ten o'clock and midnight on any Tuesday. He took a phone call from Al Rizzi on a Tuesday in March.

"How's business Nico?"

"We got sixteen guests in tonight. God only knows where they come from in this weather," Nico replied with pridꞇ.

"Has Limberger turned up?" Al asked, knowing full-well the corrupt manager had been put on ice permanent by his hitman.

"No," Nico replied, "Lieutenant Murray ain't found nuttin' and he thinks Limberger committed suicide. His father did the same thing years ago. The poor chap's disappeared into thin air" he added with an audible chuckle.

"Before you hang up, Boss, I have a question. I don't have keys for two locked rooms in the basement."

"A key is taped under the desk in your office. The code for the larger vault is HITMAN. Have a look inside when no one's about. Okay, Nico? Same time next week" and there was an audible click and the line went dead. Later, when all guests were abed and asleep, or otherwise occupied, Nico and Cesare entered one of the locked rooms in the basement. The shelved storeroom contained guns of all description and crates of ammunition, hand grenades and sticks of gelignite packed in padded boxes.

"Have you ever fired any of these guns, Cesare'?"

"No," Cesare replied with an expectant look on his face.

"Tell you what we'll do! When the thaw sets in we'll motor up to the Adirondaks for some shooting practice. Okay with you Cesare?"

"Okay with me, Nico!"

The big thaw commenced in earnest at the end of March when dark-grey buildings emerged from their white, wintry mantle and feeder streams into Lake Saratoga burst their banks flooding surrounding fields and most of the town's roads. Limberger's body was found hanging by a boatman and when Nico and Cesar returned from the Adirondaks the hotel foyer was crawling with police and curious townsfolk. Lieutenant James Murray promptly announced the deceased had committed suicide whilst the balance of his mind was disturbed, a verdict endorsed by a coroner's inquest a few days later. Nico attended Limberger's funeral and donated a wreath expressing sincere condolences from the management and staff of the Adelphi Hotel. Little Cesare had successfully concluded his first rubout on US soil.

The hit team's next call into action came in the second week of April 1951. They were contracted for an assassination on behalf of Abner 'Longy' Zwillman, otherwise known as the Al Capone of New Jersey and one-time member of the National Crime Syndicate. The target was Joe Palachi, Joe Adonis's underboss, who was muscling in on Zwillman's loan-sharking and numbers enterprises in Newark and insisting he was operating in 'open territory', but Longy did not see it that way. Zwillman's own hitman, Willie Moretti, and Palachi were bosom pals and Willie could not be relied on to keep his mouth shut. Al Rizzi brought his Saratoga hitmen to the Waldorf Astoria Hotel in New York and booked Tower Suite 405A in the name of Mr Bassani.

Together with a mobster carrying a canvas bag, Al Rizzi paid a call to Suite 405A late one evening

"Welcome to New York guys. You made two big mistakes already, Nico! You let us in without frisking us and you're both armed. Don't ever come into New York again carrying a friggin gun. Artillery for a hit will be provided."

Nico blushed at the reprimand from his Boss.

"What bum do we hit" he asked while Cesare unzipped the gymbag and laid its contents in a neat row on the bedcover. Al Rizzi produced a black and white photograph of a forty year old hoodlum with a pencil-thin moustache and wearing a white tuxedo and grey fedora.

"That's your guy! Joe Palachi hangs out most nights with his pal Willie Moretti at the Riviera Club on Palisades near George Washington Bridge. They're buddies with this crooner, Sinatra, and he's appearing in the Marine Room at the Riviera this week. The two wiseguys are sure to be there. Palachi stays on 'til daybreak and usually strolls through Palisades fruit market on his way home. He gets a kick from pinching fruit from market stalls. That's the place to hit him. Afterwards dump the ironmongery and get back to Saratoga. Don't hang about in New York."

Nico's surveillance of Palisades market and the Riviera Club paid dividends and, on the third night, a Friday, their hit went like clockwork.

A block away from the Riviera Club, Palisades' fruit market is transformed from a quiet backwater into a hive of activity at daybreak and trading continues until midday on six days a week. Delivery lorries arrive at intervals, marketeers set out their stalls and flat-capped porters in blue dungarees bustle around carrying baskets of fruit on top of their heads. For the purposes of the hit Nico had 'borrowed' a pair of blue dungarees and a flat cap and hired a yellow cab from a cooperative cabbie at Central Station. Standing beneath a neon-lighted hoarding announcing the personal appearance of Frank Sinatra in the Marine Room they awaited the appearance of their target. Easily recognisable by his grey fedora and white tuxedo Palachi and a bunch of hoodlums went into the Riviera Club at around midnight and Nico and Cesare retired to their taxi, parked in a narrow alley leading down to the fruit market. Daybreak came at 5.30am but it was a good hour later when Palachi and two hoodlums strolled past their cab and made their way into the Palisades. Dressed in his blue dungarees Cesare followed closely and, picking up a half full basket of oranges, he walked boldly into the milling throng.

Striding through the market place, and shadowed by his henchmen, Joe Palachi was obviously well-known to the stallholders and shouts of 'Look after your friggin fruit guys,' and 'Here comes the great white shark,' echoed around the square. Palachi revelled in the attention as he strolled among the stalls, squeezing oranges and sampling fruit at will. His protecting hoodlums helped themselves to bags-full of fresh fruit and were, by now, some way behind their boss when Little Cesare made his move. Emerging from behind a parked lorry, and clutching his .45 Magnum and silencer inside his dungarees, he edged gently forwards until he was within five yards of Palachi. He pretended to stumble and a cascade of golden Californian oranges came tumbling to the ground from his overhead basket. Some amused bystanders bent to pick them up and, with a stupid grin on his face, Palachi joined the scramblers.

"These friggin oranges gotta come from heaven! Help yourselves guys."

He had barely finished speaking when Cesare stuck his handgun under his ribs. There was a muted 'phutt' from the silencer which was drowned by the babble from the excited mob around the kneeling figure. Cesare fired twice more in quick succession and pocketed the gun. Clutching an orange in each hand, Joe Palachi fell slowly forwards and his grey fedora rolled off his balding pate. He was known to be a heavy drinker and bystanders assumed he had passed out and so did his henchmen when they arrived a few seconds later. One bodyguard picked up Joe's fedora and the other bent forwards to rouse his boss. It took fully a minute for them to realise they had a dying man on their hands and pandemonium broke loose. Porters, and men and women shoppers, ran in all directions and the confused mobsters ran in circles looking for an assassin. Meanwhile Cesare had walked away and, within a few strides, was out of sight between two parked lorries. He shoved his cap and dungarees into a rubbish bin and hid his Magnum under a pile of fresh fruit. By the time the shouting and commotion was at its height Cesare had joined Nico in the yellow cab and they moved sedately into an early morning queue of traffic waiting patiently to filter on to the approach road to George Washington Bridge. The assassination was only mentioned once by Cesare as they drove off the bridge and on to Manhattan Island.

"I hit him good, Nico."

Thereafter they drove in silence down Madison Avenue to Grand Central Station. As prearranged with the driver, Nico left the yellow cab at the rail terminal's parking lot and they boarded an express train to Saratoga Springs. By teatime on the Saturday they were celebrating with a glass of beer at the Adelphi.

In New York's underworld there was considerable speculation as to the identity of Joe Palachi's murderer. Willie Moretti was a non-starter and Albert Anastasia, the Brooklyn exterminator, was favourite but he had his hands full in a power struggle with the Mangano brothers. Anastasia won his fight and, on April 19th 1951, Phil Mangano's partially-clothed body was found in marshland in Sheepshead Bay in Brooklyn and his brother, Vince, became permanently missing. These murders had all the hallmarks of an Anastasia killing but, Al Rizzi and Frank Costello apart, no one in New York had an inkling that a new and ruthless exterminator had arrived on the scene and had been responsible for terminally dispatching Joe Palachi.

CHAPTER 10

Willie Moretti's rubout and Chicago buckwheats

FRANK COSTELLO, NEW YORK'S UNCROWNED BOSS OF BOSSES, and Joe Adonis, a member of the National Crime Syndicate, were relaxing in one of Adelphi's penthouse suites celebrating a successful day at Saratoga racetrack. Three of the seven races had been 'fixed' by the Syndicate, and betting returns were astronomical, but Costello had something else on his mind. He bit the end off an unlit cigar and sipped his brandy.

"I have to talk to ya about your onetime underboss, Willie Moretti. The Little Man," referring to Meyer Lansky,"and the Big Boss in Naples are worried about him. Willie and I were buddies in Prohibition days in East Haarlem and he's been a good soldier for all these years. But he's now a sick man and word on the street is he's gonna sing at the Kefauver hearings. Tony Accardo, Genovese and Greasy Thumb Guzik agree he has to go. It would be a mercy killing. Do you see it that way Joe?"

An illegal immigrant from Montemarano in Italy, and whose real name was Giuseppe Dotto, Joe Adonis smoothed down his well-oiled, black hair and placed his brandy glass on the coffee table. He was vainly proud of his good looks and had adopted the surname Adonis on a fancied resemblance to the handsome youth in Greek mythology. In 1944 he had moved from Brooklyn to New Jersey and presided over the Syndicate's affairs from his Mob headquarters in the famous Duke's Restaurant in Palisades Avenue, Cliffside Park where he maintained control over Vito Genovese and Longy Zwillman, two truculent and powerful mobster bosses in his New Jersey territory.

"What does Longy say?"

Costello puffed at his cigar and continued "Longy's coming round to our way of thinking. Four years ago Willie had forty guns at his disposal and was Longy's reliable enforcer. But recently Willie's mobsters have vanished and now he can't call on more than half a dozen. And then there's this Kefauver Lusiness."

Joe Adonis leant back in his chair and, with exaggerated panache, crossed his legs and smoothed the razor- sharp creases in his pinstripe trousers.

"In that case I'm all for a contract on Willie."

Satisfied he now had support from all his Syndicate colleagues; Costello flashed a radiant smile and immediately changed the subject to discuss the following days' racecard and 'certain' winners for the Syndicate.

Ever since postwar racing restarted in 1947 Costello reserved all penthouse suites on the fifth floor at the Adelphi for the whole of August and entertained fellow mobsters and much of the National Crime Syndicate's business was transacted. The entire fourth floor of the Adelphi was also reserved for lieutenants and soldiers of visiting bosses but there was one strict house rule – no firearms were allowed inside the hotel. The only armed personnel on the premises were Costello's lieutenants and Nico Salvatore who guarded access to the fourth floor and penthouse suites. When the hotel was invaded by underworld mobsters Little Cesare kept a low profile, lurking in the kitchens and occasionally serving as an extra waiter in the lounge bar. At Easter each year Saratoga Springs wakes up from its winter lethargy and the Municipal Spa starts operating and hotels then open their doors to visitors. By July the township is full to overflowing with guests seeking benefits from the healing waters and punters hoping to make their fortunes at the racecourse. Widows and wives of Philadelphia's rail and steel barons mingle with Boston Irish punters and, to cater for the gamblers and high-rollers, Costello had opened a private casino in a back room of the Hot Spot Restaurant. By 1949 the Mob-controlled casino brought in larger profits than the racecourse and New York's mobsters also had a stake in Madame

Jenny's bordello in Bloomfield Street. All in all the Syndicate had Saratoga Springs in its pocket and, during August race week, the pickings were exceptionally rich.

On the evening of his last day's stay at the Adelphi Frank Costello entertained Nico and Little Cesare in his penthouse suite. Full of good humour and largesse the immaculately dressed Boss stood with his back towards the fireplace and nodded casually towards two neatly-stacked bundles of hundred dollar bills on a low- lying mahogany coffee table.

"I wanna thank you boys for looking after me and my guests. I had a good day at the track with Tony Accardo and Jake Guzik. Those Chicago guys are something different! They bet heavy and we won big. I wanna you guys have a little skim from our profit."

Picking up a wad of notes he threw it across to Nico and turned his attention to Little Cesare.

"How's your English, Cesare? Al Rizzi tell's me you're doin' good business for the Syndicate."

The Sicilian only partially understood the fast –speaking Boss and stuttered a reply "I speak little English, Signore Costello. No very good."

"You're learning fast Cesare. It took me years to understand goddamn Yankee.! They speak multo rapido in New York!"

He bent forwards to the coffee table and tossed a bundle of notes in Cesare's direction.

"Thanks for what you've done for me."

Before he left Saratoga next day Costello took Nico into a locked room in the basement which contained row-upon-row of cardboard boxes full to the brim with dollar bills of all denominations. He deposited another cardboard box on one of the shelves.

"Only two persons have a key and know the combination of this vault, me and Greasy Thumb Guzik who will launder this money before next year's races. The Little Man may be in touch with you from time to time but your main contact is Al Rizzi. Don't do nuttin' without his say so."

Nico immediately recognised that the Little Man was Meyer Lansky from Miami.

By the last day of August 1951 Saratoga's high-rollers had departed for pastures new but a fringe element of part-time tipsters and avaricious punters remained, still hopeful of making a killing at the casino. Joseph Clancy, a small-time Irish undercover bookmaker from Boston, was one of the late season hangers-on. He had blown all his stake money on the first two days of the August festival and, relying on charity from his fellow Irishmen, he managed to hang on to a room at the Gideon Putnam Hotel. But Joseph was outliving his welcome and even the normally tolerant Irish were turning their backs and refusing credit to their truculent colleague. Well-built and muscular, and over six foot tall, Clancy had crinkly red hair, a round, open face and a ruddy complexion and two innocent, radiant blue eyes. With a ready smile he could charm the birds from the trees and the ladies adored him. When in funds he was generous to a fault but, in drink, he became violent and abusive. On the first Friday in September Clancy started drinking early in Alelphi's lounge bar. A misguided lucky Irish punter 'loaned' him 200 dollars and his capital was disappearing nearly as rapidly as his consumption of whisky. Not for the first time that week he became abusive to other customers and tried to pick a fight with a barman. Eventually his belligerency drove customers away and Joseph, with no one to confront, downed a doubler in one gulp, threw his empty glass at the stacked bottles behind the barman's back and, shouting at the top of his voice, "I'm outa here! This friggin place is dead," he staggered down Main Street to Madame Jenny's in Bloomfield Street. Out of all the voluptuous prostitutes on offer he selected Antonia and, in an upstairs room, she was subjected to an ordeal of sexual aggression for nearly an hour. Unable to achieve an erection Clancy resorted to physical beating and attempted rape and left Antonia with facial bruising, a black eye and bleeding from a split lip. And, to cap it all and declaring 'the whore's no friggin good,' he stormed out of the brothel without paying for Antonia's enforced services. For a further hour Clancy wandered from bar to bar looking for free drinks and spoiling for a fight. Eventually a group of Bostonians took him under their wing and, by 11 o'clock, they were in the Hot Spot Bar where his benefactors abandoned him to his own devices. Some of the customers were amused by the loud-mouthed roustabout's antics but most wanted him ejected. Luck sometimes favours drunks and around midnight, with a full glass of wine in one hand and a cigar in the other, Clancy walked straight past two doormen into the overfull private casino. Normally a house pass, or an introduction from an established member, was necessary to gain entry into the inner sanctum where gaming was a serious occupation. The Bostonian Irish were present in force and many knew Clancy by sight and reputation. Unfortunately a few, out for a bit of fun, urged him to further excesses. He staggered from table to table, jostling gamblers, throwing his money indiscriminately on the tables and shouting obscenities at the terrified croupiers. On his night off Nico was playing at the gaming tables and immediately left the salon priv? and rang the Adelphi from the restaurant foyer.

"Cesare! I'm at the Hot Spot Casino. Get over here and bring a cosh with you. No guns. There's a Mick causing trouble in the gaming rooms."

Nico was about to hang up when Cesare's agitated voice shouted over the phone "Madame Jenny's here. She want to speak to you."

The bordello Madame came on the line "We've had trouble at Bloomfield Street. About two hours ago a drunken Irishman called Clancy beat up Antonia. I couldn't go to the police so I came across to the Adelphi. Did I do the right thing Nico?"

Fearful the police might shut a valuable source of income for his

Boss, Nico replied "Yes. You did the right thing Jenny. Leave Clancy to me. Is Cesare still with you?"

"Yes," the Madame replied.

"Tell him to get over here pronto. I need some help. Does he know about Antonia?"

"Oh yes! He knows alright. He's itching to get his hands on Clancy. He says he'll kill the bastard when he get's hold of him."

As Nico slowly cradled the receiver he thought 'Okay, Little Cesare, you may get your wish sooner than you expect.'

Within three minutes Cesare arrived outside the Hot Spot Restaurant and Nico was waiting. "The man's inside the casino. I'll get him thrown out by the doormen in a coupla minutes. Once you get a chance, cosh him and rough him up a bit. Teach the Irish bum a lesson. Clancy's a big man so hit him hard".

Cesare's eyes were gleaming in anticipation.

"Okay Nico. I'll hit him hard. Leave it to me."

Nico was confident that Little Cesare would somehow do the job to perfection. Having mobilised four hefty doormen, Nico returned to the Casino to find Joseph Clancy still creating havoc, rampaging around, overturning tables and hitting out at anyone who got in his way. The casino floor was littered with dollar notes, ivory chips and playing cards and punters and croupiers watched in disbelief from the edge of the playing area. Nico and his four henchmen descended rapidly on the drunken Irishman. His arms were pinioned behind his back and his flailing legs were kicked from under him. Two doormen sat on Clancy and waited until he calmed down. Nico leaned forwards and whispered in his ear "Mister Clancy! We're taking you out now. If you start anything you'll get the same treatment and next time we'll break both your friggin legs. Got it punk?"

Clancy grunted and was dragged to his feet and manhandled out of the Hot Spot Casino. The gamblers raised a cheer and then returned to the difficult and contentious business of sorting out their dollar bills, ivory chips and playing cards.

Clutching a leather-covered truncheon in his right hand Cesare lurked in the shadow of a building across the road and watched Joseph Clancy being violently ejected from the Hot Spot Restaurant. The troublemaker got slowly to his feet and faced the four doormen standing in line at the top of the steps.

"Bastards!," he shouted and again, "Bloody bastards!" and he took a few unsteady steps towards the entrance. Changing his mind he turned about and staggered down Main Street, shadowed at a respectable distance by Cesare. As he trundled down the street he sang at the top of his voice "Oh Danny boy, the pipes, the pipes are calling from glen to glen and on the mountainside. The summer's gone and all the leaves are dying———— " and his voice faltered as his befuddled brain forgot the words and melody. Across the road from a petrol filling station there was a patch of open scrubland and derelict remains of a house which had burned to the ground a few years previously. Clancy veered off the road and, head bowed, commenced urinating against a pile of bricks and rubble in the centre of the disused plot. Seizing his chance Cesare came up behind the preoccupied Irishman, now concentrating on directing his urinary stream away from his trousers and shoes. Cesare's first blow bounced off Clancy's bent head and seemed to have no effect at all but his second strike produced an electrifying response. Clancy's body stiffened and he fell face forwards striking his head violently against a pile of bricks while his hot urinary flow continued to trickle down inside his left trouser leg. For good measure Cesare kicked him four times in the region of his lower ribs and left Clancy on the ground, lying on his back and breathing sterterously. Clancy might have survived were he not so drunk but, as he recovered consciousness, he vomited twice and inhaled the vomitus, choking miserably on his own gastric contents.

Joseph Clancy's body was found the following morning by two

boys playing baseball near the derelict house. Lieutenant James Murray was quickly on the scene and soon concluded the cause of death was vomit inhalation and the bumps on the back and sides of the deceased's head were due to a fall. An inquest three days later recorded a verdict of accidental death. Clancy's Bostonian friends neither attended the inquest nor the subsequent funeral in a pauper's cemetery. Such was his reputation with his brethren they did not bother to have Clancy's body transferred to Boston for a decent Catholic burial.

Back in New York from Saratoga Springs, Frank Costello turned up unannounced at Berterelli's on the second Wednesday in September 1951. Al led the balding, dandified, well-dressed New York Boss to a reserved central cubicle in the restaurant where they were alone and could converse freely.

"I've come for a bowl of your shellfish chowder. The best in New York I hear, Al."

Al Rizzi bowed his head but he knew there was something more than a bowl of fish soup on the Boss' mind. As they dined they talked about routine business and Costello's successful gambling venture in Saratoga and, over coffee and a cigar, The Boss abruptly changed the subject.

"I'm passing on a contract from the Syndicate on Willie Moretti. I was best man at Willie's wedding and he's been a good buddy over the years. But he's a sick man and everyone knows he got syphilis. Worse of all he's started singing to the Kefauver mob and maybe the FBI. I love that guy but he's a danger to the Syndicate. It's a mercy killing and it's gotta to be done."

Al Rizzi knew better than to probe further into the order. Once received the method, time and place of execution would be left to Al as would whether he used local hitmen or brought in out-of-town mobsters. Murder Inc's chief enforcer, Albert Anastasia, was an obvious choice but he was too well known in New Jersey and the sight of his henchmen on the prowl would soon alert potential victims. He resolved to recruit Little Cesare and his legman Nico Falcone for the hit.

Willie Moretti's New Jersey empire was crumbling fast. He had lost control of Pennsylvania's racetracks and the lucrative 'sawdust' parlours, also known as dice bars, in Pennsylvania. His hold on the Riviera Nightclub and Marine Room Casino in Bergen was tenuous and slowly, but surely, his income suffered. Even his protégé, singer Frank Sinatra from Hoboken, distanced himself from the onetime ruthless enforcer and, when his mobsters started defecting in droves, Willie began losing control over his empire. His tendency to 'sing' at the Kefauver hearings was the final straw and, though Costello had been able to protect his buddy for a few years, when the order came down from other Syndicate bosses, Willie Moretti was as good as dead. Al Rizzi first recruited a minor hoodlum, and onetime Moretti underboss, as an inside informer. Joe Sciacca revealed that Moretti was short on cash and looking for new outlets and that, of a dozen or so mobsters still hanging out with the New Jersey Boss, only two were totally loyal. Sciacca himself was on Genovese's payroll and had aspirations of acquiring Moretti's Philadelphia enterprises. He agreed to arrange a setup but declined personally to carry out the hit.

On the last day of September 1951 Nico Falcone and Little Cesare moved into a suite at the Morris and Sussex Hotel in Belmar, New Jersey. Moretti's photograph, handguns and ammunition, awaited their arrival and, on their second night in the hotel, Al Rizzi brought Sciacca along to outline the hitplan

"Moretti comes in from his house in Deal three or four times a week and he'll be at the Riviera Club this Friday for sure. His pal from Hoboken is singing there. There's a little restaurant called Luigi's downtown and Moretti eats there with a few of his soldiers before going on to the Riviera. That's the rubout place. The story is you're casino owners from upstate looking for a backer. Willie's short on cash and looking for some out-of-town action. All the guys outside Luigi's will be bought off and I'll take you inside to Moretti's table. He'll be expecting you and ready to do a Casino deal. It's up to you how many of the bums you hit and when to hit. Is that okay?"

Nico digested the plan for a few seconds.

"Won't we be frisked inside Luigi's?"

"No. Moretti will assume you've been searched by his men outside and won't know you guys are carrying."

Sciacca then took the hitmen to inspect the yellow-shuttered restaurant from outside. Owned by Luigi, and for want of a better name called Luigi's, the restaurant seated about thirty customers. The bar area was festooned with Italian hams and salamis and megalitre bottles of Chianti, encased in intricate wicker baskets, hung on the walls and from the ceiling. The wooden tables were covered with square-patterned oilcloth which matched the blue and white tiles on the mosaic floor. The whole effect was of a homely, well run bistro specializing in Italian cuisine and run by a genial restaurateur. Set amongst the grey concrete blocks and tenements of downtown New Jersey, the yellow gem had an air of unwarranted pretentiousness and attracted Italian customers from far and wide. Sciacca issued his final instructions "Wait in your room for my call between six and eight o'clock on Friday and drive down to Luigi's. I'll meet you outside and take you in. After that you're on your friggin own."

Sciacca's plan seemed quite simple but Nico did not wholly trust him and ran through the proposed hit with Cesare. But the Sicilian was impassive, poker-faced and silent, and already building up hatred against a person he had never met and whose life meant nothing to him. These were true characteristics of a professional assassin which allowed him to carry out brutal murders in cold blood and made Little Cesare a ruthless and pitiless rubout man.

Sciacca's telephone call came at 7.25 pm on Friday 4th

October. Nico drove past Luigi's Restaurant in their hired car and saw two Oldsmobile Sedans parked outside, with a kerbside space between them, and Sciacca shooing away potential parkers. Five hoodlums wearing long black coats and grey fedoras were stationed at intervals outside the frontage of the yellow-shuttered restaurant.

"This looks like a setup to me" Nico explained as he turned into a side street, "we'll park here and walk to Luigi's."

Strolling casually down the sidewalk the assassins arrived unexpectedly on foot. Indicating the parking spot with a wave of his hand, Sciacca complained "Goddamnit guys! I was expecting you in an automobile and kept a friggin parking space for you. Let's get goin'! The target's been inside for a friggin hour."

Sciacca turned towards the hoodlums on sentry duty "Okay you guys. Make yourselves scarce."

He then pushed his way into the dimly-lit restaurant, closely followed by Nico and Cesare. Three tables were occupied by early diners and, at the far end, Willie Moretti sat facing the entrance with his back to the wall and sharing a table with three henchmen. As they advanced slowly across the tiled floor Sciacca spoke from the side of his mouth "Look out for the guy sitting on Moretti's right. The other two are okay and know the score."

Sciacca arrived at Moretti's table.

"Here are the guys from New Hampshire, Boss. They wanna talk business."

Moretti took a large cigar from his mouth and wiped his lips with the back of his hand.

"Are they clean Sciacca?"

"Yes Boss," the mobster lied.

"Come and sit at the table" Moretti commanded, using his cigar like a conductor's baton. And then, realizing there were insufficient chairs, "Make yourself scarce, Sciacca, and take my two boys with you."

Nico and Cesare were then invited to join him in a glass of Frascasti. Using a fictitous name Nico introduced himself and referred to Cesare as Signore Gambarini, an Ital'an landowner recently arrived in the States. He explained that Signore Gambarini had bought a controlling interest in the Hot Spot Casino in Saratoga and, with his known experience in night club management, Moretti's name had been put forward as a possible interested party to run it. Willie Moretti was flattered. He lit a fresh cigar and sent a waitress scurrying to fetch another bottle of chilled Frascati. As she disappeared into the kitchen Nico's foot nudged Cesare's calf under the table. This was the signal for action. Asking politely for permission to remove his overcoat Cesare stood up and his right hand dipped inside his jacket and emerged holding a handgun. The executioner and the victim's eyes met for a brief second and Moretti was smiling as he was shot three times up-front in his chest. He was slammed backwards against the wall and his twitching body slid slowly sideways on to the blue and white mosaic floor. And all the while his eyes kept mocking Cesare, as if, he understood and somehow approved of the assassin's execution. Cesare's fourth shot, the coup de grace, was administered on the floor to the side of Moretti's head and he died in a pool of his own blood rapidly collecting on the blue and white tiled floor. Throughout the execution, which only lasted thirty seconds, Moretti's lieutenant sat impassively looking straight into the business end of Nico's Colt pistol.

"Okay buddy! What's it to be? Are you joining your Boss or will you work for Sciacca?"

The surly hoodlum shrugged his shoulders. Siano knew when he was beaten.

"You gimme no friggin choice. I'm Sciacca's man."

Nico disarmed the bodyguard and the three men walked rapidly out of the restaurant, leaving Moretti's twitching body on the mosaic floor. At the sound of the first shots the other diners beat a hasty retreat and, by the time Luigi emerged from the kitchen carrying a bottle of wine, all his customers had departed with the exception of Willie Moretti who was in no position to settle his bill. Luigi sighed and took his time in calling the police, allowing the Mafia hitmen ample space to get well away. He did not wish any more shooting on his premises and had the reputation of his restaurant at heart. He had spent a lifetime creating Luigi's Restaurant and another gun battle in his joint would be bad for business. On the kerbside outside the two black Oldsmobile Sedans were revving up for a quick getaway. Nico pushed Moretti's lieutenant into the back of the nearest car.

"He's all yours Sciacca. Do what you want with Siano."

The car door slammed and Sciacca and his mobsters moved off at speed. Nico and Cesare strolled casually round the corner to their hired automobile and drove slowly northwards along the west bank of the Hudson River and out of the City. Two hours later they disposed of their firearms into the river in the Catskills and spent a night in a motel in the mountains. Next day they proceeded northwards again to Albany where their hired car was abandoned and they completed their journey to Saratoga Springs by rail.

Sciacca's mobsters, and their newfound 'friend,' wasted little time in muscling into the vacuum left by Moretti's death and, within 24 hours, they were acting caretakers at the Riviera Club and Marine Room Casino in Bergen. Moretti's funeral was attended by 400 mourners from the eastern seaboards' underworld and prominent among the congregation were Frank Costello, Joe Adonis, Vito Genovese, Joe Bonanno and Longy Zwillman, Moretti's accomplice in Prohibition days and in most of his New Jersey enterprises. Meyer Lansky, the Little Man, flew in from Miami. The earth over Moretti's casket was still fresh when Vito Genovese sent his soldiers to occupy the Riviera Club and a running battle ensued in the Palisades between Genovese's hoodlums and Sciacca's gang. Outnumbered and outgunned the outcome was inevitable and Joe Sciacca was shot dead in a street battle very near Luigi's Restaurant. Fiore Siano escaped and joined forces with Genovese's hoodlums who now had a firm foothold in New Jersey and began encroaching on Longy Zwillman's empire. The National Crime Syndicate reacted by sending Albert Anastasia's notorious mobsters into New Jersey and, one by one, Genovese's men were either shot or bludgeoned to death. Vito Genovese, or Don Corleone as he ₁ referred to be called, saw the light but not before eight of his trusted lieutenants and one son were rendered permanently incapacitated. Six years were to elapse before Don Corleone again felt strong enough to challenge Frank Costello for ultimate control of the Mafia Families of New York and New Jersey. He made his bid at a Mafia mobster's conference at Apalachin in November 1957.

A long, cold, wintry spell hit Saratoga in December 1951 and, for ten solid weeks, the town was virtually isolated from the outside world. The Saratoga hitmen were called into action during the second week in March 1952. A thaw had set in and they were ordered to execute an out-of-town hit in Chicago. The target was William 'Action' Jackson, a fledgling Chicago mobster who was ruffling Anthony Joseph Accardo's feathers. Once a Capone enforcer and now a member of the National Crime Syndicate Accardo, otherwise known as 'Joe Batters' but not to his face, was elevated to Boss of Bosses in Chicago on Capone's death on January 25th 1947 and had diversified his interests to Florida, Cuba, the West Coast of America and Las Vegas. His main source of income in Chicago was the numbers game and Action Jackson and five young tearaway hoodlums were muscling in on his preserve and skimming his skim. On Christmas Eve 1951 Accardo put the finger on Action Jackson and enlisted the help of Frank Costello who obliged and activated the Saratoga hitmen. In order to frighten away other upstarts Accardo insisted Jackson should be 'hit buckwheats' which, in Mafia jargon, meant the victim was to be subjected to a slow and painful beating. In his younger days Accardo had been a specialist in this form of execution and his favourite weapon was a baseball bat, hence his sobriquet 'Joe Batters.'

The Saratoga hitmen travelled to Chicago on an overnight train and put up in a suite at the swanky Savoy Hotel. Action Jackson was known to be a keep fit fanatic and swam every day and worked out two or three times a week at Salvo's gymnasium in downtown Cicero. Fiore 'Fifi' Buccieri, Chicago Syndicate's killer, and his 'boys' and the Saratoga hitmen kept the gymnasium under observation for two days. Suitably dressed in track suits and carrying guns and a baseball bat in a gymbag, Nico and Cesare enrolled for a three hour session at Salvo's. On the third day they mingled with half a dozen sweaty businessmen using the facilities and, around six o'clock, Action Jackson came bounding in and made straight for the men's locker room closely followed by Nico and Cesare. Jackson began undressing and spoke to the strangers "You guys outa town? I ain't seen you at Salvo's before."

"Yeah, we'r in Chicago for a ball game. We're from Buffalo," Nico replied. Action Jackson sprang to his feet and made for the door.

"I'm gonna have a quick workout."

He never reached the door. Cesare struck him a glancing blow on his left temple and, partially immobilized, he fell to the floor. 'Action' sprang to his feet and Cesare missed with his second swipe with the baseball bat. True to his nickname Jackson became a veritable whirlwind. A blow to Cesare's chin put him on the floor and Jackson then grappled with Nico whose Marine Corps training stood him in good stead. He kicked Jackson's legs from under him and followed with a vicious chop to his windpipe. Wounded, and gasping for breath, Action sank on one knee clutching his throat. Cesare could not miss the victim's bowed head with his next strike and a sharp blow propelled him forwards, unconscious, on to the floor. Incensed at being kn(cked down by 'Action,' Cesare raised the baseball bat to deliver the coup de grace but Nico intervened "Hang on Cesare! The Chicago boys want him alive."

They quickly dressed the unconscious figure in his black overcoat and crammed a trilby
hat on his head to cover his bruised and bleeding scalp. Then, with Action Jackson propped securely between them, they carried him across the gymnasium floor to the exit, explaining to the curious keep-fitters their friend was unwell and had passed out. At the foot of the steps on the street the Chicago mobsters were waiting and bundled Jackson on to the rear seat of a Buick saloon which was driven away and Nico and Cesare followed in a second automobile.

About a mile from Salvo's gymnasium the cars drew up outside a dilapidated mansion and Jackson's inert body was manhandled into the basement. Fiore Buccieri's boys stripped him naked and suspended his manacled ankles form a meathook in the ceiling. The rush of blood to his brain brought Jackson back to life which was a pity from his point of view for he was fully awake for the ensuing buckwheats. Under instruction from Buccieri, Cesare and two mobsters repeatedly and systematically, beat him with baseball bats around his lower torso and genitalia and his face was carved up with a razor and, as a traditional token of Mafia vengeance, a third mobster gouged out both his eyes with a blow torch. William 'Action' Jackson took 55 minutes to die and his agony was prolonged by his tormentors for as long as possible. Accardo's hoodlums left his naked, mutilated carcass hanging from the meathook and it served as a final deterrent to other greedy mobsters from challenging Joe Batters' authority in Chicago. The presence of the Saratoga hitmen at the Chicago outfit's assassination of Jackson was a direct result of a favour owed to Tony Accardo by Frankie Costello and the buckwheats ritual was in the nature of a training exercise for the New Yorkers. They could not have had a more proficient tutor in the intricacies of delivering buckwheats than Fifi Buccieri, Joe Batter's disciple and star pupil. The gruesome execution sickened Nico but the bizarre ceremony excited Cesare who realised that 'buckwheats' was a powerful weapon in a Mafia enforcer's armamentarium. Everyone in the Chicago underworld knew Joe Batters had ordered the execution and that Accardo's outfit had administered the final coup de grace. But the identity of the two hitmen who expertly extricated William 'Action' Jackson from Salvo's gymnasium in Cicero was never established.

CHAPTER 11

The Saratoga scam and buckwheats at Joe's Diamond Diner

THE SIX-DAY RACE MEETING AT SARATOGA in August
1952 proved to be one of the biggest, and most successful, scams
in the history of horseracing. The Mob was taken for a ride by
Hymie Cohen, a small-time crook and underhand bookmaker from
Boston. Hymie had been a regular attender at Saratoga's August
meeting since the Second World War and, known as Mr Fixit, he
acted as intermediary between dollar-laden Mafia punters and
racehorse owners, trainers and jockeys. Hymie looked in on Frank
Costello each morning at the Adelphi with racing tips for the day
and gossip from the training stables. At least three races were
'fixed' by Cohen during raceweek when jockeys and trainers were
bribed to lose in favour of a rank outsider. Over the years these
'dead certs' earned the Mob millions of dollars. To protect the
chosen horses' odds, bets laid on the course and off-course bets,
were placed two or three minutes before the 'off'. Costello
regularly passed on hot tips to Walter Winchell, the New York
Times columnist and he, in turn, informed J Edgar Hoover the FBI
supremo and an addictive gambler. These contacts were
invaluable and kept Costello on the right side of the Press and the
FBI.

If God had it in mind to create a human weasel Hymie Cohen
would have been his prototype. Just over five feet in height,
pencil-thin and dapper, with a pointed nose, deep-set brown eyes
and crinkly black hair greying at the temples, the sixty year old
Jew was always nattily dressed and sported a red carnation in his
buttonhole. He had a conspirational, disarming manner and, over
the years, had ingratiated himself with Mafia bosses resident at the
Adelphi during August race meetings. At lunchtime on Saturday,
the last day of racing in August 1952, he was ushered into Frank

Costello's suite and found the Mafia boss in his shirt-sleeves tucking into a plateful of eggs and bacon.

"Mr Costello. I have two hot tips for this afternoon and one dead cert in the last race, the Saratoga Sunset Stakes."

Frank Costello took out a solid gold pencil and jotted down Hymie's tips on his shirt cuff. He glanced across at the fawning Jew sitting nervously on a lounger.

"Now Hymie, tell me about the dead cert."

"It's in the 6th race at 5.30" Hymie said, producing a racecard, "It's a two-miler and there are nine runners. The first and second favourites are heavily backed and the rest of the field stand no chance. Our cert, Tenessee Boy should start at 20 to 1 and this also applies to off-course prices."

"Okay, Hymie, I know the tricks" Costello explained and continued "As it's the last day of racing I expect you'll be off to Boston tomorrow. My friends appreciate your tips. Here's a few bucks for your expenses" and he threw a fistful of dollar bills on to the table. Mouthing his thanks as he went Hymie scooped up the money and hurriedly withdrew. A sixth sense warned Costello that the little Jew was unusually nervous as he took his leave but he dismissed his oncern with a shrug of his broad shoulders. Hymie had always been dependable and the source of undisclosed wealth for himself and his Mafia cronies. He sighed, picked up the telephone, and spoke to Walter Winchell in New York advising him to back Tenessee Boy big.

As a result of disasters at the gaming tables Hymie was desperately short of cash and, in return for a piece of action at the racetrack, he had accepted money from the Boston Irish contingent at the Gideon Putnam Hotel. To oblige the Bostonians, and to make a killing for himself, Hymie had 'fixed' another stock horse at odds of 12 to 1 to win the 5.30 race. The 'dead cert' in the Saratoga Sunset Stakes was now going to be Falcon's Flight and not Tenessee Boy and, to make the scam watertight, Hymie bribed the supervisor of Saratoga's telephone exchange to block incoming calls to the racetrack and only allow the Irish contingent from the Gideon Putnam to make outgoing calls f(r five minutes before the 'off'. During that vital period the Bostonians were able to place off-course bets on Falcon's Flight with bookmakers all over the major towns and cities of North America.

At the racetrack Frank Costello's party occupied their private box in the stand and had a run of good luck. Both of Hymie's hot tips came in first and another of his low-priced horses won the 4 o'clock race. Frank Costello's winnings at this stage were a modest 5,000 dollars but the icing on the cake was to come and he kept 25,000 dollars in reserve to bet on the Saratoga Sunset Stakes. As the horses approached the starting gate a dozen or so of Costello's mobsters simultaneously placed huge bets with bookmakers in the paddock and the price of Tenessee Boy plummeted on the course but, due to telephonic interruption, its price remained at 20 to 1 off-course until the 'off'. When his henchmen returned to Costello's box they reported that Irish money was going on Falcon's Flight who, by the 'off', was co-favourite for the race. Confident that Hymie had deliberately misled the Micks, Costello smiled to himself and turned towards one of his lieutenants.

"Did you get through to Winchell?"

"No Boss," he replied," all lines in and out of Saratoga are busy."

"The hell they are!" Costello exploded and, smelling a rat, he scanned the paddock looking for Hymie Cohen. The little weasel invariably kept station at the entrance to the parade ring but was nowhere to be seen. With that the race was off and Falcon's Flight won in a canter with Tenessee Boy plodding at the rear of the field. Costello burst into a violent rage.

"Find the friggin bum and bring him here."

His mobsters dispersed in all directions but were hampered in their searches by the jubilant Irish celebrating their mammoth win.

The crafty little weasel has made good his escape before the race was off. Frank Costello knew he had been done and what had to be done. The little Jew boy must not be allowed to get away with it! All in all he had failed to gather in half a million dollars on that one horse race, aptly called the Saratoga Sunset Stakes. That night at the Adelphi, Costello put out a contract on Hymie Cohen and Nico and Cesare were instructed to carry out the hit.

"No fuss. No bother. He's just a friggin Jewish bum. Blow the bastard away."

Back in New York Frank Costello let it be known to Syndicate members that he was interested in the whereabouts of one Hymie Cohen who had disappeared from Boston without trace. In late October Raymond Patriarca, New England's Boss of Bosses, came up with information that Hymie had changed his name to Harold Conn and was holed- out in an apartment in Nashua, New Hampshire. Furthermore he had resurrected his Jewish faith and was a regular attender, and benefactor, at Nashua's synagogue. No one could understand his religious renaissance as he had only attended a synagogue on rare occasions since his barmitzvah and then only at funerals of his Jewish underworld brethren.

Nico's plan of action was a model of simplicity. One drizzly Saturday morning in November he drove past Nashua's synagogue as the congregation were collecting on the sidewalk after Sabbath service. Prominent among the worshippers was Hymie, easily recognisable by a brand-new white kippor on his head. Within a minute Hymie and his amply-rounded wife detached themselves and walked towards their parked car in a side street. Holding his wife's elbow, and sheltering under a communal umbrella, Hymie guided her into the passenger seat of his Studebaker and was walking around the car towards the driver's seat when he came face to face with Cesare and the barrels of a sawn-off shotgun. Concealing the firearm underneath his raincoat, Cesare had followed the couple down the side street and, satisfied the coast was clear, he spat out the death sentence "Frank Costello sends his regards."

These were the last words Hymie heard before the two barrels were discharged in quick succession and at point blank range. The first gunshot was expertly directed at his left chest and the second blew off his pristine, white kippor taking the top half of his cranium in the process. Hymie Cohen was as good as dead and his lifeless body was flung on to the bonnet of the Studebaker. Shouting and screaming Mrs Cohen dived to the floor of the car and missed seeing Cesare walking casually away from the murder scene and Nico reversing the hitmobile down the road to pick him up. The hitmen sped away from the scene of the crime and were well out of sight by the time the wailing and distraught congregation gathered around their stricken brother and attempted to console his inconsolable wife. By the time the Rabbi got in touch with the police the assassins were well on their way to Manchester. That night Frank Costello was dining with Al Rizzi at Berterelli's when Nico telephoned with news of their successful hit. Frank Costello was over the moon.

"The little Jewish arsehole got what he friggin deserved. That guy Cesare is something special" and Al Rizzi was in full agreement with his Boss.

Frank Costello had a charming manner but, deep down, he was a vain and arrogant man. Nicknamed the Prime Minister of the Underworld, he cultivated powerful political contacts at Tammany Hall, with law enforcement officers in Manhattan and Brooklyn, with New York's judiciary and with Walter Winchell, one of America's most influential columnists and a contact with J Edgar Hoover, Director of the FBI. Costello's vanity was further bolstered when Vito Genovese asked him to issue a contract on one Steven Franse. Though he hated and despised Genovese, Costello accepted the contract aware that Don Corleone would be his main rival for ultimate power in New York and, in the Mafia underworld, it never went amiss to have one of your adversaries owing you a favour. The contract on Franse was passed on to Al Rizzi and automatically to Nico and Cesare in Saratoga.

Vito Genovese and Steven Franse had been buddies in the bootlegging business during Prohibition and, afterwards, became firm friends. Facing a murder charge, Genovese fled to Italy in 1937 and left his accumulated fortune and his newly-acquired wife in the hands of Steven Franse. His ill-gotten gains were safely protected but Franse failed to curb Genovese's wife's insatiable sexual appetite. On Genovese's return to the States in 1948 she was out of love with him and completely out of control in her tempestuous affairs with lovers of both sexes. By 1952 she was vindictively suing Genovese for an increase in her maintenance allowance and threatened to reveal the sources of his income to the Federal Taxation Department. The underworld expected Don Corleone to react and eliminate the stoolpigeon but he could not bring himself to issue a contract on his estranged wife. To save face he vented his spleen on Steven Franse who had, in his opinion, failed to keep a careful eye on his wife during his nine year's enfor ed exile in Italy. One of Vito Genovese's underbosses, Joe Valachi, was Francse's uncle and had recently opened a bistro-style restaurant in lower Brooklyn. Decorated with photographs of famous baseball players and displaying clusters of hanging baseball bats and paraphernalia, the bistro was aptly named the Diamond Diner. Valachi agreed to set up a hit which was arranged for the second week in May 1953 and the 'Saratoga boys' were briefed by Al Rizzi at Berterelli's. They were told Valachi had invited his nephew to dine at the Diamond Diner at 8.00 pm the following evening and two of Genovese's hitmen would also be present to ensure a successful outcome.

On the way across Brooklyn Bridge in a taxicab Nico was worried.

"I don't like it Cesare. We've had no time to case the friggin joint and quite a few things could go wrong. Too many guys are involved and we don't know who the other bums a e."

Sitting ramrod stiff and staring straight ahead Cesare replied "Don't worry, Nico. I can handle it. Al wants a spite-job and I'll give the bum buckwheats," glibly referring to Tony Accardo's favourite method of execution. Cesare continued discussing the merits and demerits of buckwheats in a cold, calculated manner just like a coach on a football field. Nico shuddered. His protégé had developed into a hardened and callous assassin with no thought, or pity, for his victims and Nico had helped to create a mindless mobster who was dangerous and out-of-control and enjoyed killing for killings' sake. Cesare had graduated into a dedicated Mafia assassin and his preferred execution techniques, and the one's that gave him most satisfaction, were garrotting and buckwheat's. In his mayhem-riddled world the common Mafia practice of shooting 'up-front' did not fully satisfy Little Cesare. For the first time in their relationship Nico suggested calling the whole thing off but Cesare would have none of it. He was pumped-up and raring to go and to use his favoured execution expertise.

The Saratoga hitmen dropped off at the Diamond Diner at 7.20pm and met Valachi at the bar. Joe was a portly, square-shouldered, fifty year old man with sagging double chins and black, curly hair greying at the temples. He held a glass of whisky in one hand and a lighted cigarette in the other. He was nervous and jumpy and beginning to sweat profusely. Nico opened the conversation "Al Rizzi sent us."

Valachi inspected the two men in turn and spoke in a gravelly undertone "I was only expecting one friggin hitman. Genovese's boys will be along soon. Have a drink while you're waitin'."

Nico accepted the invitation but Cesare refused and his eyes kept darting around the restaurant where only two tables were occupied by diners. Valachi's enterprise was obviously slow getting off the ground.

"Where you from guys?" the restaurateur asked.

"Across the water" Nico replied and Valachi stopped probing.

Just after 7.30pm two men, dressed in black overcoats and wearing grey fedoras, marched through the restaurant and disappeared into the kitchen at the rear, closely followed by Valachi. Nico recognised them as mobsters and again reiterated his concern "I don't like the look of this, Cesare."

Little Cesare's face was blank and unperturbed, his deep-set black eyes riveted on the kitchen door. Puffing nervously on a newly-lit cigarette Valachi wheezed his way back to the bar.

"One of you guys follow me to the kitchen. The other can make himself scarce."

"I'll sit this one out," Nico volunteered, and Cesare followed Valachi's bulky frame into the kitchen where three cooks in sleeveless vests were toiling away at gas-fired stoves preparing evening meals. Just inside the kitchen door the two mobsters, hatless but still in their long black coats, sat sipping coffee at a wooden table and a third seat had been reserved for Cesare. Valachi cleared his throat and made the introductions "These guys are Pat Pagano and Fiore Siano. What's your name son?"

"Cesare."

"I'll get a cup of coffee, Cesare. Get to know the boys. When I'm ready the cooks will disappear and, when that happens, you can expect Franse to come in. He'll then be all yours."

Valachi left the kitchen. The three cooks busied themselves at their culinary duties and Fiore Siano kept staring at Cesare.

"I seen you somewhere before, buddy. Where you from?"

" Upper New York State" Cesare replied and immediately regretted having spoken.

"Now I've got it!," Siano exclaimed," You were with another guy at Willie Moretti's party. Where's your friggin sidekick, buster? Is he the guy outa front?"

Uncertain what might come next, Cesare remained resolutely silent. Pat Pagano sat upright in his chair meticulously manicuring his nails with a pocket knife. The three remained in a strained silence while the minutes ticked inexorably by.

At five minutes to eight Joe Valachi was at the main entrance to his restaurant welcoming Steven Franse. He kissed his nephew on both cheeks and hugged him three times and led him by the arm to a preset table for two at the rear end of the dining room while Nico sat nonchalantly on a barstool listening, in on their conversation. They laughed heartily from time to time and were attended by a special waiter who opened two bottles of vintage Chianti at their table. After their main pasta dish they settled down to cognacs and coffee and lit up cigars. Just before 9 o'clock a group of diners were about to leave when Joe Valachi stood up and announced in a loud voice "And now, Stefano, I'll show you round my joint. We'll come back to our cigars later" and he gently guided Franse to the distant corner of the restaurant.

Cesare had been sitting in stony silence for threequarters of an hour. His two surly companions were uncommunicative and Siano seemed to derive great pleasure from outstaring him and making him feel uncomfortable. Waiters scurried in and out from time to time, picking up plates of food and depositing used cutlery and crockery. And then, just after 9 o'clock, the head waiter and three cooks disappeared through the service entrance at the rear and the next minute Joe Valachi's gravelly voice was heard outside the kitchen door "And now Stefano you must see my new kitchen."

Franse was propelled inside and the door slammed shut behind him. He came face to face with the three assassins, two of them wielding baseball bats and, in that instant, Steven Franse knew his number was up. He opened his mouth to yell for help but, in a flash, the experienced Pagano had him in an armlock and clasped a brawny hand over his mouth. His muted screams were drowned as Siano and Cesare took it in turns to beat him in the belly and genitalia and around his ribs and head. The pummelling was prolonged for a few minutes until Franse slipped from Pagano's vice-like grip and crashed, face first, to the kitchen floor. He was then formally dispatched by strangulation by a wire around his neck and suspended on a meat hook from the ceiling.

After Valachi had pushed his nephew into the kitchen he went around the occupied tables politely asking his customers to vacate the restaurant due to a small fire in a storeroom. He then joined Nico at the bar and, pointing his thumb towards the kitchen, remarked "We'll give the boys ten minutes. That should be enough friggin time for the job."

He lit another cigarette, inhaled deeply, poured himself a large whisky and closed his eyes. Nico thought he might be praying for the soul of his soon to be departed nephew but Valachi was a realist, a dreamer and a schemer, and had visions of one day becoming Top Boss in New York and tonight's events might help him in his plans. He had masterminded the hit for Don Corleone and Frank Costello's mobsters and had a stake in its execution, valuable favours which he could reclaim at a future date. Joe opened his ey s abruptly, gulped down his whisky in one, stubbed out his cigarette and prodded Nico in the chest with his forefinger.

"Okay, buddy, let's see what's cooking in the kitchen."

Suspended from the ceiling on a meathook, Stephen Franse's lower limbs jerked erratically from time to time and urine trickled down his trouser leg, collecting on the floor in a widening pool. His battered face was blue and black and his grossly-swollen tongue protruded from his open mouth. There was little, if any, blood on the corpse and only a few streaks in the collected fluid on the kitchen floor. The buckwheats had been clean and professionally executed and Valachi looked pleased with a neat job well done. He barely cast a glance at his dead nephew.

"Okay, you guys! I don't wanna the bum hanging around in my

kitchen. Lose him for me. Take him for a friggin ride."

Pagano and Siano cut Franse down, wrapped his body in tablecloths, and carried him to a waiting car outside the back entrance. The mobsters then busied themselves for ten minutes removing all traces of the slaughter and, before they drove away, Siano came up to Nico and spoke with a hint of venom in his voice "We're quits now buddy! You let me go at Moretti's hit and I let your pal go tonight. Next time we meet look out for your friggin' selves."

On the taxi journey back to their hotel Nico expressed his worries "That guy Siano will need watching. I wonder if he knows where we hang out?"

But Cesare was totally unconcerned. He sat in the back seat of the taxi with a seraphic smile on his face and made no comment. He was basking in the glory of administering the buckwheat's, and the thrill it has given him, and it took a week before his feet were again planted firmly on the ground.

Steven Franse's body was discovered the next day on a municipal rubbish tip near Brooklyn dockyard. Though the police found laundry marks on a tablecloth implicating the Diamond Diner, Joe Valachi vehemently denied any knowledge of the killing and, as it was just another hoodlum murder, Homicide Squad were only too pleased to drop the case. Walter Winchell, the columnist and himself closely connected with the underworld, dismissed Franse as a second-rate mobster with no class or standing in New York's Mafia and not important enough to warrant coverage in the New York Times. Franse's death was put down to a victim of one of a multitude of gangland killings prevalent in New York at the time.

By the summer of 1953 Nico Falcone and Little Cesare had been operating partners for over two years and the partnership was beginning to sour. In the early days Cesare had been receptive and eager to learn but, by the latter months of 1952 and since his involvement in the Franse rubout, he had become morose and introspective. He had always been humourless and uncommunicative but, by now, he was psychopathic and aggressive and spent days reliving past successes as an assassin. Back at the Adelphi he refused to work in the kitchens and demanded a suite for his own use where he whiled out his days in isolation. His meals were delivered to his room and for female companionship, he paid Antonia for her services once or twice a week. He also started drinking heavily and Nico's visits only served to aggravate the situation. So much so that Nico made up his mind to opt out of the alliance as soon as possible and his first opportunity came at Saratoga's annual August race meeting in 1953.

As usual Don Costello and his entourage and guests invaded the Adelphi Hotel for Saratoga's race meeting in the first week of August. Costello himself occupied the master penthouse suite and two adjacent suites were reserved for Vito Genovese and his sons, Santino and Micheli, and their wives. Recognising that Genovese was a strong candidate for his position in New York, Costello's invitation was in the nature of a bribe and, adhering to the Mafia code of honour, Don Corleone would owe him a favour. To accommodate all the guests Cesare was ejected from the penthouse floor and the Sicilian reacted badly and broke into a torrent of verbal abuse which led to a prolonged and heated argument with Nico. Cesare stormed into a guest room on the second floor and locked himself in. By the time Frank Costello and his party arrived Vito Genovese and his family were established in their adjacent penthouse suites. Nico ushered New York's Boss of Bosses upstairs and, in the privacy of his master-suite, he unburdened his worries "Don Corleone and his boys are already here. Their suites are bugged and the receivers are in the basement. Santino and Micheli Genovese refused to surrender their guns and so did two of the Don's lieutenants on the fourth floor."

Frank Costello thought hard for a few seconds.

"Whaddya know? I'll deal with Genovese and you'll have to get the guns off his boys. By the way, who are his lieutenants?"

"Jimmy Squillante and Pat Pagano. I know Pagano. He was in on Franse's hit in May. They're in Rooms 410 and 412."

By now Frank Costello was a worried man.

"Hell, Nico! Them guys are Genovese's top hiti.,en. I smell a goddam plot hatching. Where's Cesare? Have they seen Little Cesare yet?"

"No Boss," Nico replied, "I was about to tell you about Cesare. I think he's blown his top. We had a big bust up last Thursday and since then he's locked himself in Room 209 and won't come out or speak to anyone."

Frank Costello took off his grey, silk jacket and sat heavily on the edge of the bed. He lit a cigarette and inhaled deeply.

"Here's what we do. You go to the armoury and wire-in on Genovese's suite. I'll go round there in ten minutes and do some probing. We'll see if we can find out what's goin' on."

Don Corleone was entertaining his sons in his suite when Frank Costello paid a courtesy call. The senior dons embraced and kissed each other twice on each cheek. Costello accepted a glass of chilled white wine and lit a Cuban cigar and, gathered around a mahogany coffee table, they exchanged pleasantries. Eventually Costello brought up the question of firearms.

"The hotel manager informs me that Santino and Micheli and two of your lieutenants have not handed in their guns. The Adelphi has a strict rule. No one is allowed to carry inside the hotel. I hope you will be able to assist me in this matter, Vito."

"My dear Frankie! We are your guests and will cooperate" and he ordered his sons to hand over their guns without question. Genovese continued "And who are my boys on the fourth floor?"

"Squillante and Pagano were mentioned."

"Okay, Frankie,I'll fix it."

Costello then changed the conversation to the forthcoming race meeting and, after a second glass of wine, he pocketed the mobster's firearms and returned to his private suite.

At his listening post down below in the basement Nico had heard all the conversation up to date. After Frank Costello departed Santino asked his father "Do you think the old fart is on to something? Micheli and I have spare guns in our luggage. Do you wanna the boys to disarm?"

"I wanna talk to them now. Get the guys up here."

For the next five minutes the clinking of glasses and desultory conversation dominated the background noises and then came the voices of two newcomers. Don Corleone's voice came through loud and clear "Has anyone seen the targets?"

Someone replied "When we came through the hotel lobby I saw the guy Nico near the bar. You know the bum, Boss? He's one of Al Rizzi's boys and he was at our buckwheats in Joe Valachi's kitchen."

"And what about the Siccy they call Cesare?"

There was ι ɔ reply and Don Corleone continued "He's the guy we wanna rubout. The Sicilian's taken over from Anastasia and I wanna him permanently on ice. Take him for a ride but make the hit away from this Hotel. Do buckwheats if you can but, if not, strangulation or hanging will do. One other point – carrying in this hotel is forbidden. So hand over your guns to Costello's soldiers."

"Okay Boss" a voice replied amidst a babble of loud chuckles and the meeting broke up on a light-hearted note. Startled by what he had heard, Nico rushed to Frank Costello's suite to report and the New York Boss immediately telephoned Al Rizzi at his Manhattan apartment.

"There's a contract out on Little Cesare and possibly Nico

Salvatore. Genovese's men are here at the Adelphi as my guests and their plans were overheard. What do you wanna do with the boys?"

Al Rizzi did not hesitate "Get them out tonight, Boss. They can go to our hideout on Lake Placid. Don Corleone's boys won't find them there."

"There's one snag, Al. Little Cesare is down in the dumps and is locked in a room on the second floor."

"Okay! Leave Cesare to me, Boss. Give me his room number and he'll be ready to move out in an hour."

"Room 209. We'll load up Nico's car and they'll be outa here by midnight."

Ever since he arrived in New York Giudo Cucinotta, alias Giudo Ceserano, alias Little Cesare had trusted Al Rizzi implicitly and was quickly persuaded to depart with Nico without further delay. He was smuggled to the ground floor and out through a back entrance to a waiting car at the rear of the hotel. The car had already been loaded with provisions and an arsenal of hand guns, shotguns, rifles and ammunition. With Nico at the wheel they sped westwards through the night and arrived at Lake Placid as dawn was breaking the following morning.

Back at the Adelphi Frank Costello treated his mobster guests royally. They were wined and dined and won consistently at the racetrack. Vito Genovese's polite enquiries about the lobby manager were expertly parried by Costello who insisted he had been suddenly taken ill. The true reason for Nico's disappearance, and the non-appearance of Little Cesare, became apparent when, on their last night at the Adelphi, Santino discovered a 'bug' planted inside an ornate Chinese vase in Don Corleone's suite. Vito Genovese realised he had been duped and would have to return to New Jersey empty handed and without hitting Costello's top enforcers. As Costello's guest he was in no position to complain about unfair treatment and took his medicine like a man.

CHAPTER 12

Joe Adonis' party

IN COMPLETE SILENCE, NICO FALCONE AND LITTLE CESARE drove along Route 87 from Saratoga Springs to their destination at Lake Placid. They left their vehicle in Hotel Marcy's carpark in town and, carrying their belongings and firearms in gymbags, made their way to Lake Placid's jetty and, at daybreak, a lodge caretaker rowed them across to Hawk Island. A desirable summer resort in New York State, Lake Placid was a favourite hideout for Mafia mobsters in the 50's and the 60's. Frank Costello's Family owned two lodges on the lake – one on Hawk Island and the other on Moose Island. The great advantage of these hideouts was complete privacy and security as the lodges could only be approached by boat. Visitors, friendly or hostile, could be spotted a mile away. Hawk Island Lodge was run in summer months by resident caretakers. Joe and Emily were both in their mid-fifties but, though they lived and slept together, they were not married. Joe had a wry sense of humour but Emily was a strict disciplinarian ınd ruled the Lodge, and Joe, with an iron rod. She objected to smoking and drinking and Joe, on the other hand, smoked at every opportunity and was very fond of his tipple, especially rye whisky. When they were safely ashore Joe broke the silence "Welcome to Hawk Island folks. It's the only Lodge on this island and we ain't had no guests for over a month. How long will be you staying?"

Nico responded to the weather-beaten caretaker's greeting "Glad to be here, Joe. My name is Nico and this is Cesare. We'll be around for two or three weeks."

Joe's smile faded quickly when he saw the impassive, stern expression on Cesare's face. The Sicilian grunted and Nico winked at the caretaker.

"Take no notice of Cesare. He's had a bad night."

The guns and ammunition were stashed away under floorboards in the cabin and Joe expressed no surprise a the visitors' 'baggage'. Most guests to Hawk Island Lodge carried firearms and he had learned not to be inquisitive. He was well-paid for his services and had Emily for a bedmate and companion all through the summer. In the winter months, when the lake was frozen solid, the Lodge was mothballed and he moved into his sister's house in town. Widowed at an early age, Emily lived in her own house in Lake Placid and the two hardly spoke to each other during the ice-bound winter months. But, come April, they crossed the lake together to open up the lodge and tongues started wagging. With a nod and a wink the gregarious Joe took local gossip in his stride but the pious Emily stood on her dignity asserting she was a cook at the Lodge, and nothing else, and her relationship with Joe was purely platonic. But underneath her crusty exterior Emily's body was aching for male comfort which Joe provided in abundance. Come the spring her heart-strings thrummed though, outwardly, she maintained her dignified and forbidding demeanour.

Nico soon realised that living in a confined space with Cesare was going to be a severe trial. In Saratoga he could get away on his own at will but on Hawk Island there was nowhere to escape. He disliked the demanding way Cesare ordered Joe and Emily about and his tendency to fly off the handle at the least provocation. Cesare preferred his own company most days and occasionally took a rowing boat out fishing, but none of these distractions improved his depression. On the island there was no means of communication with the outside world apart from a boat trip to town but Cesare was forbidden use of this escape route from boredom. Every Tuesday, under cover of darkness, Nico went across to Hotel Marcy in Main Street to speak with Al Rizzi in New York and expressed his misgivings about Little Cesare. Al urged him to stand fast and protect their piece of hot property and continued to belabour his orders "The heat is still on and you've gotta lie low for a coupla months. Don Corleone's hoodlums are still on the prowl."

"That's all very well, Al, but I have to live with him and I can't friggin stand it much longer. I wanna be back in the bright lights."

"All in due course Nico," Al replied, "you'll be back here by Christmas."

A long, pregnant silence was broken by Nico "Do you realise this bloody lake freezes over in November and the only way across will be on skates!"

"I know, I know," Al's tired voice replied, "we'll fix something before you get iced up" and, throughout September and October, conversations between the two rarely varied. Joe tried his best to get Cesare out of his shell with little success. On the other hand, Emily made a few inroads and, recognising Cesare's depression, she mothered him and prepared his favourite Sicilian dishes. On Sundays she even persuaded Cesare to join her in prayer and to listen to readings from the Bible and got him to refrain from smoking inside the lodge. Cesare was not a habitual drinker but prone to drinking bouts which lasted two or three days and, in Joe the caretaker, he had a ready compatriot. At such times Emily was in constant attendance and, by prayer and persuasion, she helped to moderate their drinking habits.

By the end of the second week in November Joe was getting restless and constantly inspecting the leaden skies overhead.

"The weather's breaking up. Last night was well below zero and there was a snow flurry early this morning. By this time we've normally packed up the Lodge and moved across to town. I reckon we got about a fortnight before the lake freezes over."

Nico communicated Joe's prediction to Al by telephone.

"Yes! It's getting colder down here too. Genovese's boys are still looking. Move from the Lodge in the next few days and make for Martha Riley's Homestead just outside Stowe. Vermont will be a safe place for the winter and they've got a telephone."

Nico protested "I can't take it any longer. I want out."

Al's voice hardened "If you wanna become my consiglieri you'll do as I say. Is that clear, Nico?"

"Yes, Boss" Nico replied lamely but, inwardly, he was in a turmoil at the thought of spending a long winter with his melancholic partner. Five days of November 1953 were left when Nico and Cesare packed their bags and departed from snow-covered Hawk Island Lodge. Joe saw them off in Lake Placid and Emily had packed a parcel of Cesare's favourite Sicilian crispelle. They journeyed eastwards along the Ausable River, through Jay and Clintonville, and to Port Kent, where they ferried across Lake Champlain to Winooski, and on to Burlington in Vermont. A Mafia-owned hideout, Martha Riley's Homestead was situated four miles north of Stowe and approached from Route 100 by a crumbling, mile-long, earthen track. Located in the Hyde Park district, the homestead was some forty miles east of Burlington and thirty miles due north of Montpelier, Vermont's state capital. The nearest village store was in Morrisville, three miles to the north along Route 100. Sturdily-built, timber-framed and roofed, with a two acre paddock at the rear and stables for a dozen horses, the homestead was no longer a working ranch. The property straddled a freshwater stream, a tributary of the Lomoille River, and pine-covered Vermont hills rose steeply at the rear of the paddock. Invisible from Route 100 it was an excellent hideaway and, by virtue of its only approach by a dirt track, a near-impregnable fortress. Previous occupants had moved out in late July and the larder was still well-stocked with tinned foods and beer cans and a neatly-stacked pile of firewood lay in an outhouse. There was an abundant supply of lamp oil in one of the stables and, much to Nico's relief, the telephone was in working order. Nico had been warned to use it sparingly, and only in an emergency, as incoming and outgoing calls were relayed through a manually-operated exchange in Stowe and the telephonists were prone to listen in on conversations.

At Christmastime 1953 the snow started falling in earnest and most days were dull and grey with persistent snowfalls from dark, leaden skies. On other days the sun shone brightly from clear blue skies but the temperature hardly ever rose above zero degrees centigrade. The worst falls came with brisk northerly winds in January and, on frequent occasions, snowdrifts isolated the homestead from the main road. The relatively sheltered ranch escaped the main ravages of the blizzards and the men spent most of their daylight hours keeping the farmyard clear and struggling to maintain a passageway to Route 100 which was itself obstructed by snowdrifts from time to time. Once a week the pair drove into Stowe, or Morrisville, for provisions and for replenishing their cigarette and alcohol stocks. The hard spade work and car trips mellowed Cesare a little but he still had a tendency to withdraw into his shell and to drink alone in his locked room. Nico had to put up with his moods and ill-temper and, when the phone line was damaged by snowdrifts in late January, he lost his ability to communicate with the outside world. Though warned not to use a telephone in t· wn, in desperation, he rang Al Rizzi from the Stowe Plaza Hotel one Tuesday evening in March.

"I've just about had it. It's snowing like hell outside and I'll be friggin lucky to get back to the ranch before the roads get blocked again. The telephone lines to the homestead are still down. As soon as the friggin thaw sets in I'm coming to New York with, or without, Little Cesare."

Al Rizzi was silent for a few seconds.

"Al! Al! Are you still there? The friggin line's gone dead again" Nico yelled.

"Yeah, I'm still here. The heat's off so you can come in. Dump the automobile and use the railroad. Contact me at Berterelli's when you hit New York."

Al Rizzi's orders lifted a great weight off Nico's shoulders but produced little reaction from Cesare. He was again in a melancholic mood and merely shrugged his shoulders, accepting what fate might bring.

The long-awaited thaw started in late March and then came the floods. The brook streaming through the farmyard became a raging torrent overnight which washed away part of the track to the main road and completely flooded the paddock. For two days Route 100 into Stowe was impassable. The floodwaters delayed their departure and they eventually drove into Stowe on 2nd. April 1954. Their firearms were discarded in Waterburg Reservoir on the way to Montpelier where, having removed the number plates they abandoned their automobile in a disused parking lot. They then took an express train to New York Central Station. On contacting Al at Berterelli's Nico was informed that a suite had been reserved for them at the Waldorf Towers under the name of Ricconi and they were to remain in their rooms to await further instructions.

New York's Mafia mobsters were having a Friday night out in a private booth at Madison Square Garden to see a long-awaited rematch between Jake La Motta and Sugar Ray Robinson. Jimmy Norris, the Garden's owner and founder of the International Boxing Club, acted as host and Al Rizzi, Frank Costello and Longy Zwillman, all members of the NBC, were benefactors from his crooked dealings. Joe Bonanno was an invited guest and Frank Carbo joined the group. Known as 'Mr Grey' for his habit of constantly wearing a grey fedora, Carbo was the Mob's pugilistic 'Mr Fixit' and both fighters in the main bout were his 'property'. The wine flowed, and tongues wagged freely, in the secluded booth.

"What's the odds on Sugar Ray, Frank?" Costello enquired.

Carbo readjusted his grey fedora and, puffing avidly on a large cigar, replied "La Motta and Sugar know the friggin score. Sugar Ray and Jake are broke and need a good win to pay the taxman. The Bronx Bull will take a dive in the seventh."

A compulsive gambler, Costello had a wide grin on his face.

"I've already put a few grand on Sugar Ray to win. I'll stake another twenty on La Motta taking a dive in the seventh."

Al Rizzi was more cautious and not a heavy gambler. He loved the fight game and was a regular attender at Madison Square where his father, Kid Rizzi, had fought many futile and 'fixed' bouts in the late thirties and during the War. For the ageing and punch-drunk La Motta this was to be his final fight and the Syndicate expected to make a fortune on his predicted knockout. In the relaxed atmosphere of the pre-fight entertainment conversation became animated as alcohol loosened tongues. Costello spoke to Al Rizzi "Nico Falcone would enjoy tonight's fight. I hear the boys are back in Town."

"Yes, Frankie, they're at the Waldorf" Al replied and then, realising his mistake, he rapidly switched the conversation back to the supporting bouts before the big fight. One man in the group was quick to pick up the titbit of information. Intent on keeping his foot in both camps and, later in the privacy of his own home, Joe Bonanno passed on the information to Vito Genovese. Don Corleone immediately activated his hitmen and the search was on again for Nico Falcone and, in particular, Little Cesare.

The fight at the Garden did not go as planned. As predicted Sugar Ray floored La Motta in the seventh round but, against all odds, the durable Bronx Bull sprang to his feet and subjected his opponent to a horrendous battering, disregarding his seconds' advice to go down and stay down. The raging Bull was so incensed with Sugar Ray that, for five more rounds, he continued attacking furiously until, out of steam and unable to defend himself, he failed to come out for the thirteenth round. La Motta was carried out of the ring never to fight again, a punch-drunk vegetable for the rest of his life. Robinson was reinstated as World Champion and, bruised battered and facially disfigured, he had to be helped to his changing room. The Syndicate lost big money on the fight and the only winners that night were the ringside bookmakers and the US Internal Revenue Service who confiscated all 100,000 dollars of Sugar Ray's purse. Frank Carbo attempted to explain the debacle to the disconsolate mobsters "That friggin bum, La Motta, aint got it upstairs. He lost count of the rounds and was told not to rough up Sugar Ray. His brain is p. .kled! I'll see to it he'll friggin suffer for letting us all down."

After the fight was over, Joe Bonanno approached Frank Costello in the men's washroom. Having lost a small fortune at the fight Costello was in a foul mood but Joe took his chance.

"My Family in Sicily urgently need a hitman to cross the pond. It's a Family affair and they don't wanna use local wiseguys."

Costello owed Bonanno a favour and Nico and Little Cesare sprang immediately to mind.

"I understand, Joe. I'll see what I can do. Who's the target?"

"I don't know, Frankie. I only know my nephew, Angelo Maranzano, urgently needs a friggin hitman in Castellammare."

Frank Costello was certain Joe Bonanno knew the identity of the target but was not letting on. He wondered if it could be the Corleonesi or the Don at Sant Agata who was a thorn in the flesh of the Castellammarese and Palermians and, indirectly, with Lucky Luciano in Naples. While the heat was on in New York it would be sensible to send Little Cesare and Nico to Sicily and he would be helping his lifetime friend in Naples to settle a feud which threatened to upset the Cosa Nostra's stability in Palermo Province.

Nico Falcone was bored. He had been holed out with Little Cesare in their private suite at the Waldorf Towers for three days with no news from Al Rizzi and his buddy was again becoming withdrawn and uncooperative. They had free access to room service but Nico was longing for a smokey bar and the taste of a rare, ribeye steak and a quart of pump-drawn ale. Around 8 o'clock on the third night he took matters into his own hands.

"Cesare. I'm going out for an hour. If the Boss rings, I'll call him back."

Cesare merely fixed him with a blank stare. Nico put on a full-length black raincoat and a grey felt hat and picked up an umbrella from the hallstand on his way out. Sandwiched between 49 and 50th Streets and Lexington and Park Avenues, Waldorf Towers is an exclusive annexe on the Park Avenue side of Waldorf Astoria hotel. Its entrance is off Astoria's lobby and manned at all times by a private concierge. The Towers has its own reception area and bell-station and access to the upper floors is by a man-operated elevator. A stairway to the upper levels is unobtrusively concealed on the right side of the elevator shaft. On his illicit outing Nico used the stairway from the second floor and brushed past the concierge who greeted him "Good evening, Mr Ricconi. Have a nice   night!"

Nico grunted and the officious head porter made an obscene gesture behin. his back as he strode across the busy main lobby and through the ornate, revolving glass doors. Out on Park Avenue's sidewalk Nico took a deep breath of polluted air before opening his umbrella and, crouching against the driving rain, he walked briskly around the block to Smith and Welowski's Steakhouse at the junction of Lexington and 49th Street. He failed to notice another raincoated man following him from the Waldorf and perching on a barstool in the restaurant. The same man shadowed him when, an hour later, he retraced his steps back to Waldorf Towers. In suite 209 Nico found Cesare flat on his back, snoring loudly, and an almost-empty bottle of bourbon at his bedside. He rang room service and forbade them to supply further alcoholic drinks to Suite 209 unless he, Mr Ricconi, personally ordered it. Meanwhile, having bribed the truculent concierge with a fifty dollar bill, his mysterious shadower learned that Signore Ricconi and a male companion occupied Suite 2(9. That same night Don Corleone was informed and he set his killer hounds loose. Pat Pagano and Fiore Siano, his top hitmen, were dispatched to Waldorf Astoria's lobby to keep the Towers under observation and to hit Suite 209 at the first opportunity.

Joe Adonis, New Jersey's crime boss and owner of Duke's Restaurant - a favourite mobster haunt in Cliffside Park, - had reserved the Stardust Room at the Waldorf Astoria for a dinner to celebrate the first anniversary of his release from Penitentiary. Born Joseph Doto at Montemarano in Italy in 1902, Adonis was incredibly vain and appropriated his surname as evidence of his handsome good looks. In his younger days he was a ruthless killer and, during Prohibition, led the Brooklyn Mob which, in later life, gave him a high position on the National Crime Syndicate. Imprisoned in 1951 for violation of State gambling laws he served 18 months and was released on 9th April 1953. Everyone who was anyone in New York's crime world attended Joe's celebration party and his guests included a Deputy Police Chief, three members of the judiciary and stars and starlets of stage and screen. Guests entered the Waldorf through an entrance half way down 49th Street and the road was jam-packed with parked cars and mafiosi who patrolled the sidewalk and entrance to the magnificent ballroom. At around 10 o'clock Al Rizzi excused himself from Frankie Costello's table and, accompanied by two henchmen, made his way through hotel corridors to the main lobby. He slipped unobtrusively through the entrance to the Towers and tipped a bellhop to take him, and his minders, to Suite 209 on the second floor. The door was opened by Nico who was delighted to see his Boss and embraced him warmly.

"Good to see ya, Boss! You're dressed to kill! What's up?"

Carefully smoothing his tuxedo lapels, Al sat down on a comfortable chair while his lieutenants stood guard outside the suite. He faced Cesare "How are things with you Cesare?"

"Okay Boss," came the curt reply.

"I'm below in the ballroom at Joe Adonis's party. All the Mob are downstairs, Vito Genovese, Joe Bonanno, Joe Vallachi and Longy Zwillman are all there. I came to tell you you'll be outa here in a few days. I've got a hit in mind for you. See me at Berterelli's the day after tomorrow."

Cesare immediately perked up at the prospect of some action but Nico looked troubled.

"I'm not so sure I wanna go on Boss. Can't you find me a job here in New York? I've taught Cesare all I know and he can look after himself."

"Out of the question, Nico.! You boys are the best friggin hitmen in the business. You're a perfect combination. Well, I must get back to the party before they miss me."

Nico walked his boss the door.

"Is it quiet in the lobby downstairs?"

"Yeah! There's few people about but 49th Street is blocked by automobiles and mobsters. Why do you ask?"

"I thought I'd go out for some fresh air" Nico explained.

"Why not? Just steer clear of 49th Street," Al replied.

"I'll do that Boss. Enjoy your party."

"I will, Nico. Why not take Cesare with you? Some fresh air will do him good."

When Nico asked, Cesare refused point blank to leave the sanctuary of Suite 209 and the prospect of drinking alone from his secret supplies of bourbon. Neither Al Rizzi nor his lieutenants noticed two dark-suited 'businessmen' seated at a low coffee-table in the hotel lobby. Pat Pagano and Fiore Siano had consumed innumerable cups of coffee during their prolonged vigil. Siano was the ringleader.

"Rizzi's gone back to the party. Now's a good time to get upstairs and flush out the bums and hit 'em good."

Pat Pagano stood up.

"I'll go get our automobile. We'll need a quick getaway."

Fingering a gun in his shoulder holster, and releasing its catch, Siano sat waiting for Pagano's return. As the time for action approached he felt the excitement mounting and the hairs on the back of his neck standing on end. He strolled casually towards the front hall desk and bent to pick up a magazine. Pret nding to read, he flicked through the pages and, all the while, his eyes were riveted on the entrance to the Waldorf Towers and, miraculously, one of his targets presented himself on a plate.

Nico's abduction was attributable to a large element of luck and opportunism. Siano had his face buried in a street map of Manhattan when Nico passed within twelve feet and turned to his right towards the main exit. Inside the revolving doors he suddenly came face to face with a startled Pat Pagano. Recognition was instant and both mobsters made frantic efforts to reach for their guns. In the confusion Nico felt the sharp end of a Mauser digging into his ribs from behind and Siano's voice hissing in his ear "Get outside you friggin bum! We meet again. We're gonna take a ride."

Nico was unceremoniously bundled into the back seat of a black limousine parked at the kerbside with its engine running and a legman sitting behind the wheel. He was disarmed and, wedged in between Siano and Pagano, the black limo was driven at speed down Park Avenue. His abduction was achieved without arousing suspicion among hotel customers in the lobby and kerbside strollers outside the Waldorf Astoria. Only the concierge and the bellboy observed the scuffle and they were well-versed in turning a blind eye to any unsavoury incidents. They knew full-well that giving evidence in such cases inevitably brought retribution from the Mob and, almost certainly, they would end up floating in the

Hudson River. When questioned later they religiously stuck to a stock phrase 'We ain't seen nuttin.'

Nico was taken for a ride in true Mafia fashion. The hitmobile proceeded across 12th Avenue and down 49th Street to a deserted pier on the west bank of the Hudson. He was made to stand facing a brick wall and Pagano moved in closer to tie his wrists behind his back. With a sudden lunge Nico dropped on one knee, whipped out a Derringer strapped inside his left calf, and let fly two bullets at point blank range. The first ploughed into the fleshy part of Pagano's left shoulder and the second penetrated his left groin and embedded itself in the side of his aorta. As Pagano fell sideways on to the ground Siano moved in and struck Nico's crouching figure on the temple with the butt of his revolver. Poleaxed, Nico fell senseless on to his face next to Pagano's writhing body. Clutching his left shoulder Pagano was in agony and bellowing obscenities.

"Shoot the friggin son-of-bitch, Fiore! He's hit me bad."

"Where you been hit, Pat?"

"My shoulder hurts like hell and there's a slug near my left ball but it don't hurt. Why don't you friggin-well bump him off Fiore?"

"I'm gonna work him over first. Then I'll take you downtown to the Municipal."

With the legman's help Siano tied Nico's wrists and ankles together and left him lying on the ground. Slowly Nico stirred and opened his eyes. Siano crouched in front of him and, wielding a razor-sharp stiletto dagger, demanded an answer "Where's your sidekick scumbag?"

"Frig off Siano."

"This will help your memory" Siano hissed and slowly pushed the stiletto blade upwards under Nico's chin. Nico screamed and the scream died in a gurgle as his mouth and pharynx filled with blood. Siano withdrew the dagger.

"Okay! Let's start again. Where's the friggin bastard you call Little Cesare?"

Nico shook his head and the sharp-pointed knife again transfixed his jaw and bright-red blood spurted out of his wide open mouth. He lapsed into unconsciousness. Siano was outraged. The punk was a challenge to his torturing skills and Pagano's incessant groaning, and pleading to be taken to hospital, was driving him mad.

"Shut your friggin trap, Pat. You've only got a bit of lead in your shoulder. I wanna do a good job on this friggin arsehole, something to make Don Corleone proud."

Siano lifted up Nico's face by his hair and, at that moment, the victim's eyes flickered open and Siano sensed the hatred and defiance in his gaze. Already infuriated by Pagano's antics, Siano saw red and lost control. In true Mafia fashion he deliberately shot Nico through both eye sockets. The young mafioso driver turned aside and vomited. Siano slapped him on the back.

"Okay son? That's a good job done. Gimme a hand to get Pat into the limo and then get a blanket. We'll truss up this friggin son-of-a-bitch and put him in the trunk. Let's go!"

"To the Municipal Hospital, Boss?" the driver asked.

"No damnit! We must finish the job. Make for Berterelli's first and then we'll take Pat to the Municipal."

The hitmobile sped through Greenwich Village and, in the rear seat, Pagano kept complaining and groaning but, after Nico's body had been unceremoniously dumped in a gutter outside Berterelli's, he became ominously quiet. On the way up Broadway, towards the Municipal Hospital, Siano broke the silence "Hey Pat! How's it going, buddy?"

There was no reply from the rear seat.

"Pull into the kerb" Siano ordered and jumped into the back of the limousine where Pat Pagano lay sprawled on the floor, his thighs surrounded by a large pool of congealed blood. Siano felt for a pulse and then calmly got out of the back of the car and resumed his place next to the ashen-faced driver.

"Forget the hospital! Drive to Joe Valachi's apartment in Queens. I'll have some bad news for Pagano's widow. She's a lovely broad and will need some consoling."

Fiore Siano exhibited no remorse, or sympathy, towards his dead comrade. To him it was all in a day's work. Pat Pagano was dead but he could be replaced by younger mafiosi who were queuing up for the honour of being hitmen for Vito Genovese. Joe Valachi received the dead body of his nephew's hitman into his apartment and, to the Honoured Society, and the criminal fraternity at large, he put on a brave face asserting Pat Pagano had died in his apartment from a natural heart bang. A week later he paid for a grand funeral for Pagano, a traditional Mafia send off and almost as lavish as that accorded to senior bosses of the Cosa Nostra.

At Joe Adonis' celebration party Old Blue Eyes was entertaining his guests in Waldorf Astoria's ballroom. Sinatra had been 'discovered' by Willie Moretti and Joe Adonis in the 40's and, in gratitude, had flown in from Chicago to entertain at Joe's party. Before an adoring audience he was on stage singing a duet with Joe. The air was thick with cigar smoke and the tables covered with dinner plates and empty champagne bottles. A scarlet-coated bell-captain threaded his way carefully through the exuberant revellers and handed a portable telephone to Al Rizzi.

"Yeah, Al here."

The man on the other end of the line was sobbing and spoke haltingly and in a whisper "This is Joe Falcone from Berterelli's. The bastards have hit my brother and dumped his body outside on the sidewalk. I've brought Nico in to the office" and Falcone's voice faded. Al paled and leaned towards Frank Costello.

"Something's up at Berterelli's. I have to go."

Costello simply nodded and turned his attention once more to the performers on stage and joined in the applause. Al Rizzi and three lieutenants hurriedly left Costello's table and, as they passed Genovese's party, Al had the distinct impression that Don Corleone was smiling triumphantly.

Al Rizzi organised Cesare's evacuation from suite 209 Waldorf Towers like a military operation. Pretending to be an FBI agent one of his lieutenants ordered everyone out of the Towers' foyer. Flanked by two lieutenants he went up to Suite 209 and, after an interminable wait, the door was opened by the inebriated Sicilian. Al burst into the room.

"Grab your things Cesare. We're outa here now."

Surrounded by Al's henchmen Cesare was unceremoniously hustled downstairs and into a waiting Cadillac on Park Avenue. His new hideout was the Remington, a seedy Mafia-owned hotel in Park Street, just off Broadway and a mile from Berterelli's. He was again confined to a hotel bedroom and one of Costello's lieutenants stayed with him as bodyguard. Al was about to leave for Berterelli's when Cesare asked a question "Where's Nico, Boss?"

"He's gone away for keeps. He's been hit good. Stay here with Leonardo until you're wanted."

Within 24 hours Al knew that Vito Genovese has ordered the hit and Little Cesare was still in grave danger. His decision was immediate. He would send Cesare out of the country. Joe Bonanno was an elder statesman in New York's underworld and undisputed Boss of Williamsburgh waterfront mobsters. He had his origins in Castellammare del Golfo in Sicily and was a close relative of the powerful Maranzano Family. For a decade after the end of the War he was active in importing illegal Sicilians and Italian immigrants into the States. Consequently he had a ready source of untrained and ruthless mobsters for whom he provided false papers and identities. This was a lucrative business and Bonanno had the trade in his pocket. When Ellis Island ceased operating as the main immigration centre in 1953 Joe brought immigrants directly into Williamsburgh docks. There they were processed by corrupt immigration officials who turned a blind eye to their pedigree and origins. Al Rizzi used Bonanno's services in reverse to export Little Cesare to Sicily under an assumed name. Frank Costello approved and saw his chance to kill two birds with one stone and return Joe Bonanno's favour. He telephoned Joe "I gotta hitman for the Sicilian job. Al will be in touch. Just fix the paperwork, Joe!"

CHAPTER 13

Return to Sicily

BY 1954 SALVATORE LUCIANA, otherwise known as Charles 'Lucky' Luciano, was running out of luck and his power over the National Crime Syndicate in the States, which he created in the 30's, began to wane. Underworld warring factions in America were all striving for ultimate control and excluded Luciano from their financial calculations. He had to rely on his old and trusted friends, Meyer Lansky and Frank Costello, to provide him with hand-outs from the Mafia's various enterprises. His appointed successor in New York was Frank Costello who was engaged in a running battle with Vito Genovese and, should the latter succeed, Luciano's main source of income would be effectively cut out. Things were no brighter on the Italian mainland and in Sicily. Deported from the States in 1946, Luciano immediately assumed control over Mafia Families in southern Italy and Sicily. By 1954 his appointed boss in Naples, one Fredo Gicanetti, paid lip service to Luciano but, just like Mafia mobsters in Rome, Milan and Turin, Gicanetti wanted a cut from the Sicilian drug market which was becoming a lucrative, worldwide business largely under control of Genco Russo of Mussomeli. Installed in Castello Manfredonico on an impregnable crag overlooking desolate farmlands Don Genco, also known as Zi Peppi Jencu or Uncle Joe the Little Bull, had secured control over most fiefdoms in Palermo Province excluding Andreo Cucinotta's Godrano and Sant Agata estates. The illiterate, uncouth, fat little Sicilian had developed a taste for wealth and political intrigue and, despite the fact he was a proponent of the Mafia dei Giardini, he rapidly became ringleader in drug trafficking throughout Sicily. Nineteen fifty four became a watershed in Zi Peppi Jencu's destiny when he exerted pressure on Luciano's puppet don in Palermo. Living the life of a recluse in Villalba, Don Calagero Vizzini was given an ultimatum. He could either retire and submit to the will of Uncle Joe the Little Bull or face a show of force which would retire him permanently. In the event Vizzini's death from natural causes was materially hastened by Russo's threats and, ipso facto, Don Genco became senior Capo of Palermo and the uncrowned Capo di Tutti Capi for the whole of Sicily. By the same token Lucky Luciano's tenuous control over Sicilian Mafia affairs was shattered. Luciano also had a problem in Naples where Fredo Giacanetti was flirting with Zi Peppi Jencu and, now that Russo had the majority of Sicily in his grasp, made moves for further integration with the Sicilian, particularly in drug-trafficking which Luciano vehemently opposed. Luciano was mortally offended and decided to teach Genco Russo a lesson. He ordered a hit on Don Andreo Cucinotta as a warning to Russo that he would be next in line. Luciano's only remaining ally in Sicily was the Don at Castellammare del Golfo. Forty four year old Angelo Maranzano also had grandiose ideas of becoming senior Capo of Palermo Province and profiting from the wealth that went with that position. Angelo neither had a wish to use his own mobsters for a hit, nor to import quarrelsome n'drangetta from Naples. He passed the contract out of Sicily to his uncle Joe Bonanno in New York. As a result, and armed with false identity papers in the name of Giudo Incutti - a New York businessman - Cesare left Williamsburgh Docks on a Jamaican banana boat bound for Naples at the end of May 1954.

Don Angelo Maranzano's cousins and lieutenants, Pietro and Firenzo, sat smoking a cigarette in the shade of the Customs House on the main pier in Castellammare harbour. A Jamaican banana boat had berthed two hours previously and they were there to meet a passenger off the boat and escort him to Don Angelo's apartment in the street below the castle. As soon as a gangway was lowered there was no mistaking the well-dressed visitor who strode purposefully down the quayside. He stuck out like a sore thumb. Despite the hot midday sunshine Cesare wore a full-length, black gabardine overcoat and a pearl-grey fedora. Firenzo's eyes sparkled as he hastened forward; to meet the newcomer and exclaimed "That's our man."

Pietro chuckled "It may well be. He's definitely an Americani."

"Signore Incutti?" Firenzo politely inquired but Cesare ignored him.

"Follow me," Firenzo commanded, and led Cesare into the Customs House where a well-bribed official waved them through after a perfunctory glance at Cesare's papers. Cesare was then driven to Don Angelo Maranzano's apartment.

In his early forties, Castellammare's Boss had inherited the Maranzano empire on the death of his father in October 1953. He had the austere, handsome face of the Maranzano's marred by a large, protuberant nose which was a constant source of irritation to its owner who frequently dabbed it with a white, silk handkerchief. This innocuous habit made strangers believe Don Angelo was effeminate but nothing could be further from the truth. He was a tough, ruthless, uncompromising mobster. He stood in the middle of his apartment eyeing his visitor from head to toe.

"Signore Incutti! Uncle Joe Bonanno recommends you highly."

Cesare did not reply. The Don touched the side of his nostril and partook of a pinch of snuff, inhaling nosily into his capacious proboscis.

"You know why you've come to Castellammare.?"

Cesare removed his fedora and remained standing.

"Yes, Don Angelo. I'm here to do a hit. Who's the target and when do I get to work?"

"All in good time," Maranzano replied, "now take off your coat and join me at the table for a meal."

With traditional Sicilian hospitality an elaborate lunch had been prepared for the American visitor. For an entrée they ate seppie, a mixture of octopus and cuttlefish baked in a black bean sauce and garnished with garlic, raisins and pinenuts. The main course was stigghiola, grilled goats' intestines stuffed with onions, cheese and parsley. The white wine from Marsala was chilled to perfection and, as the meal progressed, Cesare began to unwind. He had come off the Jamaican boat in a state of trepidation, uncertain about his reception and wary of the Don's lieutenants. But they turned out to be pleasant hosts though too inquisitive for his liking. They were avid for news about New York and about Uncle Joe Bonanno and his setup in Brooklyn. The two-hour lunch was rounded off with another Sicilian delicacy, fritella pancakes made of cornmeal and filled with almonds and marinated peaches. When the small cups of acrid coffee arrived Maranzano dismissed his lieutenants and Cesare and the Don took seats on a balcony overlooking the port. After nearly four years' absence Cesare was reminded how much he had missed the sounds, sights and smells of his native Sicily, particularly the street odours of cooking in olive oil and garlic and the heavenly smell of freshly baked bread. He was quickly forgetting his uncomfortable voyage on the banana boat when his reverie was interrupted by Don Angelo "We both know why you're here, Cesare. The Big Boss in Naples wants a local don eliminated because he's stepping out of line. But it's none of your business to know why we want him neutralised. You only have to worry about getting the job done."

"Who is the target, Don Angelo?"

"He has a messadria granda fifty miles from here. His name is Andreo Cucinotta."

Cesare's face became ashen-white and he drew in a sharp breath.

"Do you know this Don?" Maranzano asked. Cesare reacted slowly and shook his head but, inwardly, he was in turmoil. Al Rizzi had sent him all this way to rubout his own brother! Would he be able to pull the trigger and, at the same time, look Andreo in the eye? The answer had to be 'yes.' He was a hired assassin and duty-bound to fulfil a Mafia contract. And, after all, Andreo had not been too helpful when he was forced to flee from Sicily. Don Angelo relit his cigar and attended to his nose with his snuff-stained handkerchief.

"The setup is this. Andreo Cucinotta rarely leaves his messadria at Godrano and is looked after by a housekeeper. His wife lives on the Sant Agata estate. Rumour has it the housekeeper arranges for young girls to be brought to Godrano to sleep with her Boss. The place to hit him will be in the estate house."

"When can I do the hit?" Cesare inquired.

"As soon as you are ready, Cesare. Firenzo knows a person who will help you get into Godrano estate house."

Cesare bristled.

"I work alone, Don Angelo. Let your men take me as near to Godrano as they can. I'll do the rest."

"As you wish, Signore Incutti," the Don replied with a sardonic grin and a shrug of his shoulders.

Next day Cesare was kitted out in a rough flannel shirt and dark, baggy trousers and was taken to a barn on the outskirts of Castellammare to take his pick from Maranzano's hidden arsenal. Accompanied by Pietro and Firenzo, he was driven northwards in a battered old Fiat in the direction of Palermo. After an hour they were approaching Montelpre and Cesare was getting anxious.

"Hey, you guys! Is this the road to Palermo?"

"No, it's not," replied Firenzo with a disarming grin, "Don Angelo wishes you to meet someone who knows Godrano."

Still dubious about being taken for a ride Cesare unclipped the holster under his left armpit and kept a wary eye on his surroundings and the gabelotti seated in the front of the Fiat. A short distance outside Montelpre they passed an impressive building perched on the mountainside and surrounded by lush pine trees.

"That's the Benedictine Abbey of San Martino. Over a hundred monks live there" Firenzo explained. They skirted around the base of the mountain and the road then rose sharply to pass through the elevated village of Boccadifalco with its squat, ugly Gothic church and, a mile further up the mountain, they came to a fertile plateau hemmed in on three sides by dense pine forests. In the middle of an open glade, four whitewashed cottages were clustered at the roadside. Firenzo again explained "This is Baida. That's Arabic for 'white.' The person you're going to meet lives here."

The Fiat pulled up in a cloud of dust outside the end cottage of the four.

Carla Cecci was, at that time, twenty eight years old. Since Giuliano's death she had lived in semi-isolation in Baida attending to a smallholding which provided her with vegetables and fruit and her chickens and goats produced eggs, milk and cheese. At first a kindly octogenarian lived next door but he died in the winter of 1953 and his cottage was now vacant. Her only neighbours were a pair of middle-aged, bachelor shepherds who rarely spoke to Carla. She spent her days in her allotment and drinking water had to be carried from an artesian well some four hundred yards from her cottage. I 'ck of social contacts had made her slovenly in her dress and, at the risk of being called a puttita or prostitute, she wore trousers and a woven, woollen cap on her head day in and day out. About once a month Firenzo called rent-collecting but, by order of Don Angelo Maranzano, Carla was exempt from payment. With his muscular frame, florid, drooping moustaches and pearly white teeth, Firenzo was a handsome man and tried to take advantage of Carla on more than one occasion, but she resisted his advances. When Maranzano's lieutenant's came to call they brought provisions – flour, sugar, tea, cooking oil and table wine. In return Carla bartered for these commodities with eggs, vegetables and fresh fruit from her allotment.

On the day that changed her life, when the gabelotti

unexpectedly called, Carla was crouched hoeing a bed of aubergine in her vegetable patch. It was well past noon when she heard the chugging of a vehicle approaching lowly up the mountain road. The car skidded to a halt opposite her cottage throwing clouds of fine, limestone dust into the air which completely obliterated the vehicle from view for a few seconds. Out of the dusty canopy a figure approached and she immediately recognised Firenzo. He greeted her with a toothsome smile "I have brought a man to see you, Carla."

Alarm bells suddenly started ringing and she tightened her grip on the hoe. Two figures appeared from the dust cloud, Pietro from the front of the car and a stranger, dressed in farmer's clothes, from the rear seat. When they were ten feet apart they were both struck by instant recognition. Carla knew immediately she was looking at Giudo Cucinotta but Cesare's brain was reeling! Where had he seen this fresh-faced young man before? This was the face that recurred in his vivid nightmares. Quick as a flash it came to him! He was looking at the 'boy' who aimed a pistol at his head and let him off the hook on the day his father was assassinated. He instinctively went for his gun but Firenzo placed a restraining hand on his forearm.

"Signore Incutti! This is Signorigna Carla Cecci."

Cesare's head was spinning! Was Firenzo out of his mind and was this a trap? He looked over his shoulder and was gratified to see Pietro lounging nonchalantly against the Fiat and smoking a cigarette. By the time his gaze returned to face the blazing deep-set, black eyes of the 'young man' in the aubergine patch, Carla had removed her cloth cap and allowed her black tresses to cascade over her shoulders. Then, and only then, did he recognise Carla Cecci, the girl who had been promised to him in marriage and the woman who became pregnant and brought disgrazitsa on their Family and was regarded by the villagers as a puttita. Cesare lowered his gaze.

"I am honoured to meet you Signorigna Cecci."

In a fluster, Carla turned her attention to Firenzo "I was not expecting you today. The plums are nearly ripe and you can have as many aubergine as you wish."

"No, Carla. I have not come to collect the rent. Can you make us a pot of tea and I'll explain inside the cottage."

Under the questioning gaze of the reclusive shepherds two cottages away, the men trooped behind Carla into her spartan, one-roomed hovel.

Over a cup of tea Firenzo explained their mission "Signore Incutti has a vendetta against the Don at Godrano. You've lived there and can help us get into the estate house."

Carla did not ponder for long "Yes, I know a way into the house through the vegetable back-garden. Will my sister be there?"

"No! Anna stays permanently at Portella Sant Agata."

"In that case I will do it. In fact, I will do the shooting myself."

Cesare's gaze had not left Carla's face but, when he saw the bitterness and hatred flashing in her eyes, he knew this formidable woman meant every word. Chivalry and Mafia honour prevailed "No, Signorigna! I shall do the execution."

Carla turned away to hide her feelings. This man, who now called himself Cesare, was contracted to assassinate his own brother. She had no feelings whatever either for him or for Don Andreo Cucinotta except hatred and she would have great pleasure in killing the man who had caused her so much suffering and anguish during her illegitimate pregnancy. She decided there and then to do the killing on her own but, to salve Cesare's conscience and save face, she insisted it would be a joint venture and her main role would be to guide him into Godrano estate house. Reluctantly Cesare accepted "That's agreed Signorigna. We'll do the hit together."

Their eyes met again and, demurely, Carla lowered her gaze and blushed "Please, Signore Incutti, call me Carla."

The men planned to leave for Godrano on the following morning and moved into the empty cottage next door for the night. During the late evening Carla and Cesare strolled down to the well to fetch water and, on their return journey, Carla suddenly asked "How's life in America, Giudo Cucinotta? I'm surprised to see you after all these years."

Startled to hear his real name, Cesare replied "If I had known the hit was on Andreo I would not be here."

"I'll take care of Andreo. As far as Pietro and Firenzo are concerned you will be the killer."

Cesare started to protest but Carla cut him short "I know more about Andreo than you think. He has a passion for watermelons and young girls. Dressed as a puttita I will get into the house carrying a basket of fruit but I will need you to look after the gabelotti guards."

"Okay, Carla, we'll work out a plan together" Cesare agreed and, as they walked along, he rubbed the still-tender scar on the left side of his temple.

"I have to thank you for sparing my life at Lago del Scanzano."

Carla looked at him sternly "I don't know what you're talking about. I haven't seen you since my sister's wedding" and, abruptly changing the subject, "Why did you leave Sant Agata so suddenly?"

Completely confused, it was now Cesare's turn to tell a lie "I wanted to see America. I met Al Rizzi in New York."

A sudden flood of tenderness engulfed Carla. She asked coyly "And how was he Cesare?"

"He walks with a limp. He's an important man in New York and owns restaurants and hotels. He's married with two daughters."

"Sounds as if he's done well for himself. I've still got his card in my cottage" Carla replied.

After exchanging 'buena nottes', Cesare returned next door where Firenzo became inquisitive and, with a flashing smile and suggestive wink, he asked "How are you getting on with little Carla? You want to watch out for her. She's a man-eater!"

Cesare glared at him in distaste and ignored the innuendo. Carla had changed since he first knew her. She was now a mature woman and, in a stark way, very attractive. Life had dealt her a harsh blow and his own brother was largely to blame for her misery. He was strongly attracted to this waif-like woman, who dressed and behaved like a man, but resolved not to get too deeply involved until he had fulfilled his contract. And then, perhaps, he would make a move and allow matters to take their natural course.

Mid-morning the following day the strike party left Baida. Carla had transformed herself overnight and now wore a black skirt and a white blouse, tensely stretched across her puerile breasts, and her hair was held in place by a red bandana covered over by a black, silk scarf. Her personal belongings were packed into a canvas valise and she took along an empty wicker basket. As they left the hamlet the inquisitive shepherds appeared on their doorstep and eyed the departing car with curiosity. Firenzo and Pietro sat in the front while Carla and Cesare sat pressed together on the back seat of the little Fiat. As they negotiated tight bends their thighs were squeezed against each other, sending reverberations of pleasure through Cesare's tense body. Skirting Palermo City, they drove eastwards to Missilmeri and then southwards on the Palermo/Agrigento road, for 25 miles to Villafrati. The secondary road to Godrano was a mere dirt track and, just short of Cefala, Carla spotted a field peppered with watermelons. She disembarked to return with a basketful of golden-yellow peaches and two juicy melons. She scooped the flesh from inside the melons and secreted her .45 Biretta in one and a silencer in the other. The Fiat passed slowly through Cefala and pulled up on the rising ground overlooking Godrano valley and roughly two kilometres from the estate house. Carla outlined her plan to her companions "I will lead Cesare through the olive groves on the right side of the road to the back gate of the estate house. Afterwards we will make our way back to the road and you drive down and pick us up."

Firenzo nodded.

"Do you wish me to go with you?"

Carla looked at Cesare. He muttered "No! No, Carla and I will do the job. Keep your eyes on the road up from Godrano. If you hear shooting drive down fast with all guns blazing and shoot the hell out of them."

Carla and Cesare lay close to each other in a larch copse strewn with fragrant oleander bushes and about fifty yards from Godrano's rear entrance into a walled garden. Nestling a shotgun in the crook of his right elbow a chain-smoking gabelotti lolled in the shade under an archway leading into the walled garden. Cesare was excited at the prospect of going into action with this business-like woman by his side. He cast a sideways glance at his partner. Her thin, bird-like face, aquiline nose and deep-set black eyes were fixed in a steely stare, concentrating on the entrance to Godrano's back-garden, and her facial features were offset to perfection by the red bandana around her jet black hair. She spoke with authority "In a minute I will walk out of here and get the gabelotti to take me into the garden. When he comes out again you'll have to see to him. Are you ready, Cesare?"

"Yes, let's go" Cesare whispered, inadvertently using the popular American idiom.

Carrying her fruit basket, Carla calmly strolled down a well-trodden footpath used by farmhands to get to their orchards and olive groves. The gabelotti saw her coming and, warily cocking his shotgun, stood on the pathway.

"Hey there my beauty! Where do you think you're going?"

"I have brought fruit for Don Andreo. My sister normally comes but she is unwell. Can you take me to the house, please?"

Accustomed to seeing young ladies visiting the lecherous don, the gabelotti stepped aside to let Carla pass. This one, he thought, was older and more mature than most of the don's female visitors. "I'd better check your basket."

He pocketed two peaches and prodded a melon with his forefinger. Satisfied, he led the way through the archway into the garden.

"Come with me my beauty! You do know Don Andreo wants something more than fruit? If the Boss doesn't come up to scratch I'll give you an hour's fun when you come out."

Carla gave him a faint smile and the hint of a wink.

In response to the gabelotti's knocking a wizened, grey-haired woman, completely dressed in black, opened the back door to the estate house.

"The signorigna has brought some fruit for the Boss. Show her where to go signora. It's her first time and she's standing in for her sick sister."

The housekeeper was also familiar with strange females visiting her Don. Francesca led Carla through the kitchen down a familiar dark corridor and tapped three times on the study door before entering the dimly-lit room.

"A signorigna from the village has brought you some fruit, Don Andreo."

Buried in the depths of a leather armchair a shadowy figure shook himself and sat upright. He had been disturbed in his siesta and an empty wine bottle lay at his feet.

"I wasn't expecting anyone today but I could do with some female company. Place the basket on the desk and come and sit by me. That will be all Francesca" and the black- garbed old woman was dismissed from the study.

"I've brought you a dozen peaches and two beautiful melons from a field near Lago del Scanzano."

As she spoke with her back to the Don, Carla removed the Biretta from inside the melon and fitted a silencer to the end of the barrel.

Don Andreo was getting impatient.

"Leave the melon, woman! I can have the fruit after we've finished our business. Turn up the desk lamp so I c in have a good look at you."

Carla turned up the wick on the oil lamp and held it aloft in her left hand and, with the loaded Biretta in her right hand, she faced Don Andreo who was now standing unsteadily on his feet. Carla's voice was cool and cutting "Do you not recognise me Andreo? I am Carla Cecci, the girl you betrayed and called ⸗ puttita in this very house during the war."

Bemused, and hands outstretched, the don took a step forwards and a look of disbelief crossed his face when he saw a gun pointing straight at his chest.

"Don't shoot! Please don't shoot," he squealed, "I didn't mean to hurt you, Carla."

Engulfed with rage, and only intent on revenge, Carla coolly pulled the trigger twice. There were two muted phutts as the bullets ploughed into Don Andreo's chest hurling him backwards on to a leather couch where he lay sprawled and moaning loudly. The dying man's eyes were still open as Carla thrust the Biretta's muzzle into his open, protesting mouth and pulled the trigger twice more. By the time she left the study Don Andreo was dead and his body lay in a disjointed heap on the leather settee. Out in the kitchen she came face to face with Francesca cowering in a corner and fingering a rosary with a look of terror in her rheumy, old eyes. Carla had never shot a woman before in her life and her determination failed her at the last moment. Using the butt of her Biretta she struck the old lady on her temple and Francesca fell in an unconscious heap on to the floor. Carla stepped over the inert body and ran into the garden where, at the far end, Cesare was waving his arms and waiting for her.

As soon as the gabelotti guard entered the garden with Carla, Cesare sprinted to the covered archway entrance gate. Sucking loudly on a juicy peach, the guard reappeared a minute later and Cesare stepped behind him and slipped a garrotte around his neck. Kicking and writhing the gabelotti took over a minute to stop struggling and eventually succumbed and slipped lifeless on to the ground. Cesare dug a peach from one of his pockets and thrust it into the dead man's wide-open mouth. A few minutes later Carla was beside him and they made a dash for cover into the oleander-scented larch copse. They then made a rapid retreat through the orchards, olive groves and scrubland to the Cefala road. They were like two school children playing truant and the enormity of their actions was lost in the compulsive pleasure they both had derived from the act of killing. In this exuberant state Cesare got carried away and took hold of Carla's hand "Carla mia! Will you come back to America with me?"

She looked at him coyly, but replied instantly "Yes I will, but not as a puttita. If you want me, Cesare, it will be as your wife."

"Yes, Carla. Remember we were betrothed once? We'll get married."

The memory of that painful occasion during the war, when they were young and fancy-free, sobered them for a while and then Carla smiled and squeezed Cesare's hand.

"I thought I had a good reason for not shooting you near Lake Scanzano. Now I know why! I was keeping you for this! What will we do in America, Cesare?"

It was now Cesare's turn to smile.

"America is a land of opportunity. We can do anything we like there. There's nothing to stop us carrying on with the job we did today."

"I would like that" Carla replied and, by this time, they were at the roadside and the getaway Fiat came racing down to pick them up. Five minutes later they were speeding through Cefala and away from the assassination scene.

An hour after the assassins had left a gabelotti wandered into the kitchen for a glass of water and found Francesca, semiconscious and incoherent, on the floor with a gaping scalp wound and a pool of congealed blood around her head. Outside the garden gate he found the dead gabelotti with a fresh peach stuffed into his wide-open, speechless mouth. Fearing the worse he let off two warning shots and raced back into the house where he found the dead body of his Capo in the study. By this time the assassins were long gone. It took a week before Signora Francesca could recall events and the Godranesi could not believe that the visitor, and probable assassin, was a woman. The killing had the unmistakeable stamp of a Mafia execution and there were no female operatives in the Sicilian Cosa Nostra. But they reckoned without including Carla Cecci on their list of potential 'hitmen.'

On the day after the assassination the hit squad were back in Don Angelo's apartment in Castellammare. Angelo Maranzano was highly pleased with the 'hit' but there was disturbing news from Montelpre. The two reclusive shepherds from Baida had been spreading rumours at the open market about a stranger, and Maranzano's lieutenants, visiting the puttita in her cottage. Carla evidently could not return to Baida and Cesare, likewise, would have to go under cover. Don Angelo outlined his plan "I have a small podere at Visicari on Mount Sparagia. The farmhouse has a good view of the only approach road and the nearest podere is two miles away. You will be isolated but safe. Pietro and Firenzo will keep you supplied with provisions" and, with a benign smile, he added "You won't, of course, be expected to pay rent."

Cesare thanked Don Angelo and took hold of Carla's hand.

"Carla and I wish to get married. I will take her to the States when it's safe for us to go."

Don Angelo was lost in thought for a few moments "A priest at Fraginesi is a family friend and will marry you. I will make arrangements. And now you'll have to leave here in the next hour.

It will take you all of two hours to get to Visicari before nightfall."

A month later Carla and Cesare were married in a private ceremony at Fraginesi church. Don Angelo Maranzano gave the bride away and Firenzo acted as best man. The wedding breakfast was a simple picnic alongside the steep, winding road leading up to Visicari. The guests from Castellammare departed in their cars at teatime leaving the married couple to ride on mules uphill to their podere. Despite his arrogant nature, and the lax morals he had encountered in America, Cesare did not force his attentions on Carla during their premarital cohabitation under the same roof. In a peculiar way he still adhered to the Mafia belief in premarital virginity even though he knew Carla had borne a child. The marriage was consummated on their wedding night and the next twelve months were the happiest time of their lives. Carla cultivated a smallholding and grew vegetables and sweetcorn and milked their goatherd. An orchard provided peaches, plums and oranges and Cesare shepherded the goats and went hunting wild ibex on Mount Sparagia. Once or twice a month Pietro, or Firenzo, brought essential supplies but, otherwise, they had no contact with humans for weeks on end. Happy and content in their mountain retreat, their idyllic existence was interrupted in June 1955 by a visit from Al Rizzi.

CHAPTER 14

Hits in Napoli and Brooklyn

ALPHONSE RIZZI AND HIS WIFE CLAUDIA were the only guests at Frank Costello's Central Park apartment on a fogbound, peasouper of a night in February 1955. Despite having known Al for fifteen years, and a sponsor of his elevation into New York's Mafia, Costello still insisted on propriety and h. , guests were formally dressed and dined by candlelight. The ladies were excused at the end of the meal and Costello and Al sat at the dining table smoking cigars and sipping a five-star cognac. Al sensed the Boss had something on his mind.

"I wanna you and Claudia take a holiday to Napoli."

Al did not reply and waited for the Boss to continue "Luciano is having trouble and has lost control of Palermo Province to a lardass don called Genco Russo. They also call him Uncle Joe the Little Bull. The Don in Naples is also two-timing the Big Boss and he wants a hit on Fredo Gicanetti. That's why I wanna you take a holiday and set up a contract for Luciano. You can take his skim across with you when you go. That broad, Virginia Hill, has gotten the FBI on her tail and can't do the business at the moment."

This was an order and not a request. Al replied "Okay, Frankie. Maybe there'll be a chance to drop into Sicily to visit my wartime battlefields?"

"I'm sure there will be, Alphonse. Now let's join the ladies and break the news to Claudia. She'll be thrilled to have a trip to Napoli."

Al Rizzi and Claudia crossed the Atlantic first class on an Italian luxury liner during the last week in May 1955. Two pieces in their luggage were stuffed with dollar bills, money from the National Crime Syndicate and Costello, to wet Luciano's beak. On arrival Luciano took them sightseeing around Naples, visiting

Pompeii and Vesuvius and then on to an isolated podere north of Naples halfway between the hamlets of Nola and Avellino. Virginia Hill was a house guest. A woman of loose morals and a gangster's moll, she was on affectionate terms with Lucky Luciano and the Rizzi's spent a week in their company at the secluded farmhouse. One evening Luciano put his cards on the table.

"I wanna that friggin Gicanetti rubbed out. I wanna ship someone from the States to do a hit."

Al was prepared for this request.

"I can get a hitman from Sicily to do the job. The same guy hit the Godrano don and he's still about in Sicily."

Lucky Luciano smiled broadly which, due to the scar in his right cheek and his drooping, immobile lower eyelid, gave him a sinister appearance.

"That'll be friggin great! A hitman from Sicily will bring these friggin guys in Naples to their senses."

For the second week of their visit Luciano loaned the Rizzi's his luxury apartment off Via Scarlatti in the Vomero district of Naples and, with a twist of irony, arranged for Fredo Gicanetti to show them ar und. An import from Calabria, and after profligate years as Capo in Naples, Gicanetti had become grossly overweight and his once handsome face was florid, pockmarked and pugugly. His manner matched his appearance. Coarse and uncouth he ate noisily and voraciously, gulping down his food and, in drink, he became lewd and boastful. He was obsessed with food and, during the week, took Al and Claudia twice to his favourite restaurant on the waterfront in the shadow of the medieval Castell del 'Ovo. By New York standards Ristorante Bersagliera was a dump but the food was excellent and the ambience homely. Gicanetti was obviously a valued customer and the Padrone fussed over his every need. His favourite dish was Scaloppe alla Bersagliera, veal with mozzarella cheese and pickle, and he proudly boasted that, on

Tuesdays and Fridays, he reserved the entire upper floor to entertain his family and fellow mobsters. With a suggestive wink he confided that the Padrone also allowed him exclusive use of a service lift and the staff toilet on the ground floor. Less favoured customers, and members of his Family, were obliged to go down a rickety, spiral staircase to a grotty toilet in the basement. Al Rizzi pretended to be impressed and, all the while, he was assimilating information which the boastful Gicanetti provided in abundance. At Gicanetti's suggestion Al and Claudia used Luciano's sea-going, pleasure yacht for a two-day cruise and they docked overnight in Castellammare del Golfo in Sicily. Within ten minutes of a phone call next morning, and conscious of the importance of his visitor, Don Angelo Maranzano arrived at the dockside in a limousine and whisked Al away leaving Claudia to twiddle her thumbs and spend the day sunbathing on the yacht. The black automobile headed straight towards Mount Sparagia.

June the fourteenth was yet another blazing-hot, sunny day. Earlier that morning Cesare had shepherded his goats to a patch of lush grazing on the lower reaches of Mount Sparagia and, having tethered the dominant female, he climbed higher up the mountain in search of wild ibex. The endemic wild goat of Sicily is extremely shy of humans and a successful kill is a rare event but, on this day, Cesare's luck was 'in' and he bagged a healthy buck. He was carrying his kill across his shoulders downhill when he saw a black limousine threading its way slowly uphill towards his podere. Hanging the ibex carcass in the fork of an olive tree, he hastened down to the farmhouse and was relieved to see Firenzo and Pietro sitting on a stone wall enjoying a cigarette. Firenzo immediately recognised Cesare.

"Thank God you didn't shoot us, Cesare! There's someone in the house to see you."

Cesare dropped his rifle and, as he walked briskly across the yard, a familiar figure limped out of the cottage to meet him. Al Rizzi held him in a fierce embrace.

"What have you been up to you crazy guy? I didn't send you over here to snatch a broad. Congratulations Cesare!"

They entered the one-storey, two-roomed cottage together. In the cool, dark living room Carla was fussing over a boiling kettle on an open hearth and Don Angelo was perched on a wooden stool contentedly puffing on a cigar. Carla looked adoringly at Cesare and held his hand.

"Signore Rizzi has told me about New York and how he will look after us when we get there. But first he has a job for us on the mainland."

Cesare was silent for a moment "A job for US on the mainland? I don't need you with me, Carla."

Carla bristled and her dark eyes blazed.

"Make no mistake, Cesare, you're not going without me. We now work as a team."

"Cut it out!," Al interjected, "both of you will go to Naples and afterwards on to the States. Now let me tell you about the contract."

As soon as A' named the target Carla became agitated and paced around the living room.

"That man, Fredo Gicanetti. Is he the father of a gabelotti called Franco who was killed by the Americanis near Godrano during the war? You remember Franco don't you Cesare? He had a fat friend called Salvatore Branco who was also killed."

Cesare remembered Franco and Salvatore very well and had been involved in minor skirmishes with the renegades on more that one occasion. What is more, he had heard that Franco Gicanetti had survived the blast and was living on a messadria in a remote part of Calabria. But now was not the time to let Carla into his confidence. She was still in an agitated state and pacing around the room.

"If the Gicanetti in Naples is Franco's father," and she spat out the words, "he deserves to die. I will kill the bastardo!"

She calmed down over a cup of tea and Al outlined his orders "You will need papers to get to New York. Don Angelo will send a car for you when your papers are ready. And now we have to get back to Castellammare. I must clear the harbour before sunset and the next time we meet will be in Berterelli's in New York."

Al Rizzi and Don Angelo got up to take their leave. Rummaging around in a tin box on the mantelshelf, Carla produced one of Al Rizzi's gilt-edged wartime cards. Al smiled as waves of nostalgia came flooding back and, acting on impulse, he kissed Carla on both cheeks. She blushed and then the visitors drove away. For minutes after their departure she sat alone at the hearth, sobbing quietly, remembering those last days of her youth when the American army and Alphonse Rizzi came to Godrano and completely changed her life. And then she suffered again the violence of her rape and loss of her virginity by a loathsome n'drangetta. She burst into a flood of tears when she thought about little Alfonzo, her beloved son, who had been cruelly snatched away from her. But realisation she might soon be able to exact revenge from the Gicanetti's lifted her spirits and, by the time Cesare returned from tethering his goats for the night, she was dry-eyed and cheerful. She confronted Cesare "I can't wait to get at that man in Naples."

"No, Carla mia! It's agreed by Al Rizzi and Don Angelo that I am the one to kill Fredo Giacanetti."

With false papers, and named Spiteri, Carla and Cesare crossed on an overnight ferry from Castellammare to Naples on the seventh day of July 1955. To their fellow-travellers Cesare was a newly-married seafarer on his honeymoon. All their worldly possessions were packed into a battered suitcase and two revolvers and ammunition were hidden among their belongings. They found cheap lodgings in the rundown Quartieri Spagnola district and, like two honeymooners, spent two days sightseeing around Naples. Posing as an out-of-work merchant seaman, Cesare went down alone to the dockside at Porto San Lucia on a Monday and, at midday, stood outside Ristorante Bersagliera. Drawing appreciatively on a cigarette, a portly, bald-headed, bespectacled man, in a white short-sleeved shirt and wearing a blue and white striped apron, emerged from the restaurant and strolled up and down the quayside. Cesare intercepted him "Scusa Signore! Is this an expensive café?"

The man stopped in his tracks and smiled broadly.

"Yes it is! It's the best restaurant in Naples. I should know! I'm the proprietor. Why do you ask?"

"I'm from Sicily. I'm waiting for a ship and have been out of work for a month. Is there a job for me in your restaurant?"

The podgy padrone drew deeply on his cigarette.

"What experience do you have in the restaurant business?"

"I worked in the ship's galley on my last voyage," Cesare lied. The Padrone chuckled "Both my chefs are cordon-bleu trained and local waiters are queuing up to work for me. I could do with help in the scullery washing cutlery and dishes. I pay by the hour and you get paid at the end of each day. Do you want the job?"

Cesare accepted with alacrity "When do I start?"

"Report to me at 11 o'clock tomorrow morning. You'll be kitted out with a white tunic and trousers. I run the best restaurant in Naples and I have to keep up appearances."

The pleasant padrone glanced at his wrist watch and flicked his cigarette over the parapet into the sea.

"Ah, its lunchtime already! My customers will start arriving soon. When you report tomorrow ask for Signore Cantoni."

"Gracie, Signore Cantoni."

Ristorante Bersagliera was a two-storey brick and wooden structure built on a spit of land jutting into the sea with spectacular views of the Gulf of Naples. Its main approach was by a slipway which, within a hundred yards, joined Via Parlenope running alongside the seafront. Customers were served on two floors and, on a busy night, the restaurant could accommodate 140 diners. Visitors' toilets were in the basement and staff toilets were on the ground floor near the kitchens and scullery at the rear of the restaurant. On the following morning, a Tuesday, Cesare reported for duty. He was kitted out in 'whites' and shown the layout of the restaurant and the helpful padrone explained what was expected of him "I have ten redcoat waiters working on each floor. Ground floor staff will bring used cutlery and crockery to your scullery and upstairs waiters send them down in a service lift. When we're busy my chefs won't have anyone near their kitchen. So keep clear! Only use the staff toilet in an emergency. If you break anything it will be deducted from your wages and, I must warn you, some of the dishes and plates are very expensive."

Apart from an hour's break teatime, Cesare toiled all day in the scullery on his first day at Ristorante Bersagliera. Just after 10 o'clock the restaurant was clear of most of its customers when a green light appeared over the service lift hatch indicating another load of soiled crockery and utensils was on its way down from upstairs. Cesare moved across the corridor to the service lift when, much to his surprise, the door opened to reveal a man tightly packed into the lift, sitting on his haunches and with his knees drawn up under his chin. He struggled out of the lift, belched, touched the side of his nose, winked and then dashed into the staff toilet. He was in such a hurry he neglected to close the toilet door behind him and Cesare clearly heard him relieving himself and, at the same time, humming a few bars of 'O Sole Mio'. Cesare returned to his scullery and it was after midnight when he went to collect his wages and found Signore Cantoni pleasantly inebriated and in a talkative mood "Did you see that expensive lot of crockery that came down from the first floor about 10 o'clock?"

Cesare nodded.

"He's my best customer. Signore Fredo has a great sense of humour and it amuses his friends to see him squeezing into the service lift. I don't know why he does it! He's too fat and not as young as he used to be."

'On Friday night I'll fix his sense of humour once and for all' Cesare thought to himself and, with a polite grin, he bade the garrulous padrone 'goodnight'.

For the first time since Nico Falcone's death, Cesare had to plan Gicanetti's rubout on his own and his preparations were methodical and thorough. At Statzione Cumana, on Piazza del Gesu, he purchased two rail sleeper tickets on the Ligurian Express leaving Naples for Marseillaise at 11.30pm every night. Carla was instructed to settle their account at the pensione and arrange for a taxi to be waiting at 10.00pm outside a designated café on Piazza del Moritiri. On Wednesday he deliberately scalded his hand and came to work on Thursday swathed in bandages, concealing his silencer, and his revolver was strapped inside his trouser leg. He hid the loaded gun in a recess in the depths of his locker. By F·iday he was ready for action and a successful outcome depended entirely on Don Fredo being a creature of habit and having a predictable bladder capacity. Friday night's festivities upstairs started at around 8.00pm and Gicanetti's armed n'drangetta patrolled the slipway in front of the restaurant. Two of his men stood on the main staircase only allowing access to the upper floor to the waiters and Signore Cantoni. At around 9.30pm Cesare took his gun from the locker, screwed on the silencer, and thrust it inside his waistband underneath his tunic. It had been a hectic night in the kitchen but, by 10.15 pm, the chefs had executed their last orders and retired from their oven-hot stoves to the open air outside the back door. At around 10.40pm a green light indicated the service lift was descending and, on this occasion, it contained a human load. In a squashed position, with his head bent forwards and his knees up under his chin, Don Fredo presented an unmissable target and was a proverbial sitting duck. As if inviting Cesare to help him to his feet, Gicanetti extended his right arm but Cesare's own arm was also extended and he fired his gun four times at point blank range. Two bullets entered Don Fredo's torso from the front and, as his head fell forwards on his chest, two more ploughed through the back of his neck. Don Fredo Gicanetti was not quite dead when Cesare left his crumpled, impaled body in the service lift. His right leg kept jerking involuntarily but, within a minute, all signs of life were extinct.

Cesare moved rapidly after the rubout. He removed his white trousers and tunic, pulled on a cloth cap, and went through the kitchen area to the rear exit depositing his gun in a stockpot of bolognese sauce on his way out. The chefs were sitting on a parapet outside the back door relaxing, smoking and chatting.

"Leaving early tonight Spiteri?"

"Yeah! Padrone told me to go home. He wants me in early tomorrow. Ciaou!"

Cesare strolled unchallenged past Gicanetti's n'drangetta and tossed the silencer over a parapet into the sea. He then proceeded briskly across Via Parlenope and up Via Morelli to Piazza del Moritiri where Carla and a taxi driver were waiting at a kerbside café. The short drive to Statzione Cumana was covered in 10 minutes and the Ligurian Express pulled out of the terminal dead on time with Carla and Cesare safely on board. By that time Gicanetti's mobsters had been frantically scouring Porto San Lucia and the Quartieri Spagnoli district looking for a Sicilian seaman called Spiteri, but the assassin was safely tucked up in a bunk on the Ligurian Express.

The Neapolitan Carabinieri were not involved in an investigation into Don Fredo Gicanetti's sudden death. A Mafia-sponsored doctor pronounced Don Fredo's death was from a heart attack, a popular diagnosis in cases of Mafia murders, and the police steered clear of trouble and left the mobsters to their own devices. The Neapolitan underworld suspected Luciano was behind the hit but he was away from Naples at the time and they could not prove anything. Of one thing they were certain, the assassin was a vagrant Sicilian seaman and there the matter rested.

A month after Gicanetti's funeral Lucky Luciano convened a meeting of underbosses to select a successor for the murdered Don and, bolstered by promises of support from a few Neapolitan Families, Gicanetti's son put in a bid for the position. Franco Gicanetti managed a messadria in Calabria and lived on the farm with his wife and two daughters and his mysteriously-acquired son, Alfonzo. At thirty years of age he was still good-looking with crinkly, black hair and a boyish face. Luciano took an immediate dislike to the young upstart who, like his father, was arrogant and loud-mouthed but he seemed to satisfy the needs and aspirations of the Neapolitan Mafia. Much to Luciano's disapproval and concern about his own decline in status, Franco was unanimously voted into his father's shoes. Sicily was already a lost cause and now the Neapolitans, and the rest of the Italian Mafia, were rebelling against him. The feeling of isolation produced a predictable reaction in the Big Boss. He reverted to what he did best which was to plot and counter-plot between Families and to step in and arrange contracts when all else failed. In the latter respect he was, at least, still supremo. In common with Meyer Lansky, Tony Accardo, Frank Costello and Carlo Gambino he was held in high esteem by the Mafia underworld in the States and, after all was said and done, he was the undisputed founder of the National Crime Syndicate in the USA all those years ago.

Cesare Spiteri brought his bride to the United States on the good ship Laura Keene in August 1955, on the very same liner which transported Lucky Luciano to his exile in Naples in 1946.

On the eight day voyage from Marseillaise, Cesare received some unwelcome attention from Frank 'Don Cheech' Scalise who, with his twenty year old blonde lady-friend, was travelling first class and spotted Cesare as a fellow-mobster. Originally a member of the Mangano crime family, Don Cheech had defected to Anastasia's camp when his boss was eliminated by Anastasia. Scalise was heavily involved in drug trafficking and had been to Naples and Palermo, setting up drug deals. Affable and outgoing, Scalise kept pumping for information but Cesare stuck to a story that he had crossed the Atlantic to visit his ailing mother and marry Carla, his childhood fiancé. Scalise bribed an assistant ship's purser who had access to the safe deposit box in the purser's office and confirmed Cesare was travelling with three sets of papers and passports in the name of Spiteri, Incutti and Ceserano and he had a valid marriage certificate to Carla, nee Cecci. Don Cheech put two and two together and concluded his fellow-passenger was none other than Little Cesare, Costello's legendary hitman. As soon as they reached New York Scalise was on the blower to Anastasia "Hey, Albert, that lardass Little Cesare was on the Laura Keene. He's married a broad in Sicily and they call themselves Spiteri."

Anastasia's interest was immediately aroused. Arrogant in the extreme he was acutely jealous of his title, 'Lord High Executioner for Murder Inc.', and Little Cesare might usurp his authority. With his sidekicks, Scalise and Carlo Gambino, Anastasia had over two hundred killings to his credit and one more rubout was neither here or there. After Genovese's attempt to get him rubbed out eighteen months previously, Little Cesare had disappeared into thin air but, now the little Sicilian was back in New York, The Lord High Executioner would personally arrange to administer the coup de grace.

By the mid-fifties, 63 year old Frank Costello was gradually opting out of day-to-day running of his Manhattan enterprises but still maintained his position on the Board of the National Crime Syndicate. Al Rizzi took over his Family interests and with it came responsibility for arranging contracts. Since Little Cesare's enforced exile in Sicily he had been short of a reliable hitman. Albert Anastasia could no longer be trusted and it was a great relief for Rizzi when the Laura Keene docked at the end of August and brought his trusty assasin back to New York. On disembarkation the Spiteri's made a beeline for Berterelli's and were given a hearty welcome by Al Rizzi. Over a meal he outlined his plans for them "I have a contract which is overdue and I must honour it quickly. I'll keep you under wraps at my Long Island villa until the hit is set up. It will happen soon."

Cesare was unconcerned, almost indifferent "That's okay by me, Boss. I can stand my own company but I hope Carla will get to see Manhattan. I've told her all about the place."

"Yes, Claudia will see to that."

There was a long pause and Cesare was obviously uncertain about something.

"Tell me, Boss, what exactly did happen to Nico? It's been on my mind all the time. Nico was a good buddy."

"He was taken for a ride from Waldorf Towers by Fiore Siano and Pat Pagano. Pagano got hit good in a shootout with Nico but Siano is still around. He's top of my urgent hit list."

Cesare scowled.

"It will be a pleasure to rub him out. I owe it to Nico" and, within a fortnight of arriving back in New York, Cesare had his opportunity to strike.

Despite his vile character, Fiore Siano was a proud father to four boys and a devout family man. On Wednesday nights he dispensed with bodyguards and dined en famile at his first floor apartment in Brooklyn. Siano presided at the head of the candlelit table, flanked by his young sons, with Mamma Siano seated near the kitchen door. They were well into their main course when their noisy chatter was rudely interrupted by three rings on the doorbell.

"See whose there, Silvano."

His nine year old boy opened the door wide. Dre ,sed in a black overcoat and a grey fedora, Cesare stood in the dimly-lit passageway. Accustomed to seeing similarly-dressed men at the apartment quite frequently the young boy was not unduly perturbed but he was unaware that this one carried a loaded sawn-off shotgun under his black coat.

"There's a man here to see you, Papa" Silvano shouted.

"Who is it?" his father asked but the youth had no chance to reply. Cesare surged through the open door and into the dining room, his sawn-off shotgun grasped firmly in both hands. Siano jumped to his feet knocking a candlestick to the floor. Mama screamed and the seated boys looked on in horror. Siano instinctively dived to his right as Cesare's first shot took the tip off his left shoulder and he fell sideways and overturned the dining table. Cesare had to advance three strides to bring his second shot to bear on the screaming, writhing target on the floor. He hissed "This is from Nico, you lardass" and pulled the trigger just as Siano's thirteen year old son flung himself forwards in front of his father. The gunshot caught the youth in mid-air, blowing a gaping hole in the side of his neck and he fell in a bleeding heap on top of his father, showering him with cascades of bright-red blood, as the youth's life force rapidly ebbed away. Stupefied, Cesare looked on in dismay and disbelief and Mama Siano stopped screaming and now broke into a heart-rending wail. Cesare's resolve to finish the job vanished. He threw the shotgun into a corner and, turning on his heel, ran out of the apartment and fled out to the street, leaving the Siano family wailing over the dead body of their eldest son. Luckily for Cesare the shouting, screaming and gunshots caused little alarm among other residents of the apartment block. Over the years they had become immune to Siano's drunken outbursts and a discharge of firearms was not an unusual event.

They only became aware of a tragedy when an ambulance arrived to cart Siano to hospital and to convey his son's body to the city morgue.

On his journey back to Long Island, Cesare had much to think about. In the first place he had failed in his mission and, secondly, he had transgressed one of the unwritten laws of the Mafia fraternity which strictly forbade the killing of Family women and children. The disaster in Siano's apartment was to remain on his conscience for the rest of his life and radically changed his approach to professional assassinations. Cesare's botched attempt, and the accidental murder of Siano's eldest son, caused violent repercussions in the underworld. Genovese's mobsters went on the rampage and were baying for the assassin's blood. Having vowed to 'hit that little Sicilian bum' Anastasia contracted a notorious 'fixer' to search for Cesare. Born Anthony Strollo, Tony Bender had a chequered career alternating between the Costello and Genovese crime families and selling his services to the highest bidder. With Bender on their tail, the Spiteri's again became 'hot property'. Within 24 hours of the Siano debacle Al Rizzi was forced to smuggle Carla and Cesare out of his luxury villa on Long Island. Under cover of darkness they were taken by motor boat to Statten Island Terminal and, mingling with early morning workers, they ferried across to Battery Park at first light. Arranged by Al Rizzi, an automobile picked them up outside Battery Park's subway station and, by early evening, they were in Martha Riley's Homestead in Vermont where Cesare began a second period of banishment from New York which lasted nineteen months. Continually haunted by his unfortunate experience in Fiore Siano's apartment Cesare's depression reappeared with a vengeance. It was at this point in their married life Carla took over and assumed a lead in all decisions. She became the dominant force in their domestic and professional partnership.

CHAPTER 15

Charlie Lucky's dilemma and Don Corleone's downfall

BY THE SPRING OF 1956 LUCKY LUCIANO was facing a crisis in the continuing power struggle for control over the Neapolitan Mafia. Franco Gicanetti's power over Naples' fractious Crime Families had increased, rather than diminished, and his loud-mouthed, swashbuckling style of leadership, his drinking excesses and his whoring, seemed to commend itself to his mobster brethren. The sense of power had gone to his head and he was openly negotiating with Don Genco Russo for a handout from Sicily's drug-trafficking trade. The Neapolitan boss was hailed as a success by loyal mobsters who were promised untold wealth from Sicily's drug trade if they pledged fielty to Franco Gicanetti.

In public Franco was a boisterous, larger-than-life character with oodles of crude charm but, in practice, he was a tyrannical husband and father. Of Calabrian peasant stock his wife was a doormat and, by her, Franco had two girls aged twelve and fifteen and the kidnapped Alfonzo, now aged eleven, completed his family. For a year after his ascendancy to power in Naples Franco led a bachelor's existence in his father's waterfront apartment and his insatiable sexual appetite and over-fondness for wine and grappa had reduced him to a haggard, debauched man with telltale purple patches on his once-handsome face. He was so immersed in his new lifestyle he failed to change his ways when the family from Calabria arrived to join him at Easter 1956. Constantly drunk, Franco took to beating his wife and venting his spleen on his unfortunate son. Alfonzo had grown into a good-looking, dark-haired youth with a thin, wiry body and dark-brown eyes. Temperamentally he was quiet and submissive and his main interests were painting and music. He had taken little interest in riding, hunting and shooting on the farm in Calabria and was more content to sit with his music, books and paints. To compound Alfonzo's misery his stepmother favoured her daughters and the transportation of this timid youth from the tranquil Calabrian foothills to the hustle and bustle of Naple's waterfront was a callous mistake. The boy could not take it. He retired to his lonely room only emerging at mealtimes and when ordered to do so by his violent, blasphemous father when a physical beating was almost as inevitable as night follows day.

The Gicanetti's had been in residence for three weeks when, on the pretext of calling on Franco, Lucky Luciano turned up unannounced in the apartment. Signora Gicanetti did not recognise him but realised by his dress and presence he must be an important person. Reluctantly she invited him into her apartment. Lucky was appalled by what he saw in the lounge- two broken armchairs, a bare electricity bulb hanging on a wire thread, dirt and grime on the carpet and scraps of putrefying food and two empty wine bottles on a grease-covered table. Lucky Luciano looked around the room with distaste. The girls were seated at a grimy window playing with their dolls and Alfonzo was nowhere to be seen.

"Don Franco tells me there is a boy."

Signora Gicanetti gave a sly glance towards the closed bedroom door.

"Is he in there?" Luciano asked and, uninvited, strode into a darkened room where, curled up on a cot in one corner, he could just make out the outline of a human figure. He spoke kindly "Your name is Alfonzo isn't it? Come out where I can get a good look at you. I'm your Uncle Charlie" and the petrified little body uncurled itself and followed the tall man into the lounge. Alfonzo's blotchy face was fixed in a grimace in an attempt to hold back his tears. He looked pathetic and forlorn and Luciano, who was childless, was touched.

"Are you unwell, Alfonzo?"

The urchin shook his head. Luciano turned towards the stepmother "Is the boy not well, Signora?"

"There's nothing wrong with him that a good hiding won't put right."

Alfonzo burst into tears and Luciano touched him on the shoulder "Look at me Alfonzo."

The boy looked up at the man with a drooping right eyelid towering above his head and saw concern and compassion in his lopsided face. He stammered and, in a whisper, pleaded "Please take me away from here Signore. I hate Naples."

At that moment Franco Gicanetti came bustling into the lounge. Red-faced and flustered, and smelling of alcohol, he embraced Luciano.

"Please forgive me for not being here to receive you, Padrone. Is the boy bothering you? Go to your room immediately, Alfonzo, and stay there until I call you!"

Lucky Luciano held up his right hand.

"No! Alfonzo stays here. Come with me Gicanetti" and Luciano led the way into the bedroom and locked the door.

"I wanna know what's friggin-well goin' on here."

"Nothing I can't handle" Franco replied.

"You've had a month to sort things out. Your flat is filthy and that boy is very unhappy. He asked me to take him away."

A shrewd look came into Franco's shifty, bloodshot eyes.

"That's a good idea, Boss. If you take him to your apartment in Vomero I can see him every day."

"No," Luciano replied, "I'll take him out of Naples and look after him and see to his education."

On the very same day Lucky Luciano transported Alfonzo and his meagre belongings to his rented villa on Anacapri. He showered the boy with gifts and arranged for a tutor to come across from Sorrento each day. Franco Gicanetti only paid one visit to see his son and then found excuses to avoid trips to Anacapri. Besotted by the fleshpots of Naples, he eventually sent his family packing back to Calabria and Alfonzo never saw his stepmother and stepsisters again. Once free of family restrictions, Franco burnt the candle at both ends until eventually, by the beginning of 1957, the Big Boss in Naples requested an emissary from New York to come and sort out his problems. Having previously been on a mission to Naples, Alphonse Rizzi was Frankie Costello's automatic choice.

Al Rizzi disembarked in Naples on 20th April 1957 and the Big Boss himself was there to meet him at the quayside. The smartly-dressed, black-haired, beetle-browed man, with a lazy-lidded right eye, was easily recognisable as he nonchalantly leant against a green Oldsmobile with 1948 New Jersey number plates and with Bello, his enormous German shepherd dog, stretched out on the rear seat. Lucky personally chauffeured Al around town and their first call was at Luciano's 'office' in Hotel Turistico where they shared coffee and cakes with Signore Fantoccio, the hotel manager. The Big Boss' handout from America was deposited in a vault in the basement, followed by a two-hour lunch break at Ristorante Da Giacomino, one of Luciano's favourite eateries. After lunch they motored for 22 miles along the coastal road to Sorrento and, on the journey, Lucky Luciano unburdened his soul. Gone was the bonhomie and excitement of their morning in Naples and the soporific effects of their alcoholic lunch at Ristorante Da Giacomino. Charlie Lucky was a worried man and, unprompted, broke into a lengthy catalogue of his cares and woes.

"Gawd! I miss America," he blurted out, "and I donna like Italy and the friggin Wops are crap. I love their food and that's the best part of living in this goddamn country. Do you know, Al, they've had me tailed since 1948 and there's always a cop keeping an eye on me? They're behind us now and tonight you'll see them hanging around my villa on Capri. I'll tell you one thing, Al. With all these cops around I donna need bodyguards!"   He flashed a fleeting smile and continued "But I got nuttin' to hide. So why doesn't that arsehole Judge Anslinger get me back to Brooklyn and put me on a stand? It's all baloney! They took away my friggin passport in 1950 and I'm banned from goin' to Rome. I can go anywhere else in Italy but not to Rome or Sicily. It's all baloney! I get propositions every day of the week but I turn them down. I got contacts in Trieste, Turin, Rome and Anzio and all over Italy but all I do is put guys in touch. I don't handle dope myself and I keep my nose clean."

Lucky Luciano paused for breath. Al quickly realised the Big Boss had a persecution complex and his repeated denials of involvement in the drug trade did not ring true and were not at all convincing.   He did not seem to appreciate that putting drug peddlers in touch with each other constituted a felony and he had no scruples in accepting money from the profits of drug trafficking.

Luciano swung the Oldsmobile off the highway and swept down the approach road to Sorrento harbour. Two hundred yards in their wake a police Fiat executed the same manoeuvre. Luciano glanced in his rear-view mirror.

"The friggin cops are still on our tail. I'm pretty certain my villa is bugged and I wanna tell you something before we get there. Do you remember Don Fredo Gicanetti, the guy your triggerman put on ice? Well, his son Franco has taken over in Naples and is big in dope. He's openly trading with Genco Russo, the Sicilian frigger who calls himself Uncle Joe the Little Bull and whose a fat little hen and full of crap. Russo's called a conference in Palermo and its all gonna be about dope. I canna get to Sicily but Franco will be there and I canna trust him. You gotta go to Palermo and tell the guys you represent me and our American Families. Well old buddy, here we are."

The large green limousine crunched to a halt at the quayside in Sorrento and Al and Luciano boarded the ferry for the twenty minute crossing to Capri. They were closely followed by two men and, to Al's trained eye, there was no mistaking the fact they were plain-clothes policemen. Lucky Luciano went one better – with an engaging grin on his lopsided face, and tongue in cheek, he welcomed them aboard and wished them a safe crossing.

Alfonzo was delighted to see his 'Uncle Charlie' and it was evident that a firm bond had developed between them. They laughed and joked together and Luciano exhibited all the traits of a doting parent. The twelve year old took to Al from the beginning, jesting about their common christian name and asking about New York and the American way of life. The boy's austere, bird-like features reminded him of Carla and the longer he looked at the youth the more convinced he became that Alfonzo could be his own flesh and blood. He spent three happy days in Alfonzo's company on Anacapri and then it was time to depart for the Sicilian conference.

Ostensibly to discuss Mafia business, but primarily to deal with drug-trafficking worldwide, Don Genco Russo convened a meeting at H tel de Palme in Palermo on April 29th 1957. Joe Bonanno and his trusted underboss, Carmine Galante, headed the American Mafia delegation. Russo presided and Luciano Liggio, Padrone of Corleone and Palermo's boss, officiated at the summit which created a cupola to establish a heroin franchise for Sicily, including importation and distribution of drugs throughout Europe and the States. Sicily emerged as a strategic centre for drugs and illegal arms distribution and income from these enterprises was laundered through the so-called Pizza Parlours in Europe and America. Acting as spokesman for the Americans Carmine Galante approved the Sicilian plan and Franco Gicanetti pressed for Naples to become a major drug importation centre. Al cited Luciano's objections but the arrogant Sicilian dons had no respect for the views of an American interloper. When Al reported back on 2nd May, Lucky Luciano was furious.

"I'm surprised Joe Bonanno and that punk Galante were there and I told you to look out for Franco Gicanetti. Anyone would think the frigger is Big Boss in Naples. It's baloney! I'm the Big Boss here. I'll have to cut the punk down to size. Is that guy who did his father still in business?"

"Yeah Boss! He's in hiding in Vermont. He'll be okay to come across and do a hit for you."

"That'll do.! I can wait a while" but Luciano did not realise at the time he would have to hang on for over a year for his contract to be fulfilled.

The very next day a cablegram arrived from New York with news that an attempt had been made on Frank Costello's life and he was in hospital in a critical condition. Though terrified of flying, Al Rizzi packed his bags in a hurry and crossed the Atlantic on an American airliner to be at the bedside of his stricken boss. Frank Costello's 'accident', or attempted rubout to be more precise, was not as critical as Al Rizzi feared. He found his Boss sitting up in a hospital bed, smoking a cigarette, and full of joy at his miraculous escape. Apparently, at around 8 o'clock on 2nd May, Costello was entering his apartment building in Central Park West when a huge fat man in a black overcoat ran past him into the vestibule. As Costello was approaching the elevator, the man-mountain emerged from behind a pillar and shouting "This is for you Frank" he fired at point blank range. The bullet grazed the right side of Costello's temple and sent him spinning to the floor. Convinced he had killed the Prime Minister of the Underworld, the would-be assassin ran out of the building. At Costello's bedside Al Rizzi asked the vital question "Who done it, Boss?"

"I have no doubt Genovese ordered the hit and the hitman was definitely Vincent 'The Chin' Gigante."

"Hitting The Chin should be easy. Do you wanna Little Cesare on the job?" Al inquired

"No, Al, don't hit The Chin. We'll keep him for later. The first guy I wanna rub out is Don Cheech who set up my hit. Bumping off Scalise will be a warning to Vito Genovese. As it is I owe him a favour and, to demonstrate my goodwill, I'll deny ever seeing The Chin."

Al was perturbed to hear his Boss bending over backwards to appease Genovese. It was normal practice among gangsters to assassinate the opposition's most powerful underboss before going after the Big Boss himself and Al was concerned the tactic might work in reverse. Now that Genovese's hitman had failed in his mission to take out the main target he might turn his attention to the underboss, that is, Al himself. He shuddered at the thought. He would have to mind his back and, in the meantime, he had to fix Don 'Cheech' Scalise's rubout and satisfy Lucky Luciano's demands for a hitman in Naples. It was time to activate his No 1 hit-team from Vermont and the most pressing need for their services was to deal with the worsening situation among New York's warring Mafia mobsters.

Carla and Little Cesare had remained hidden away in Martha Riley's Homestead for the best part of two years until they were ordered to return to New York in May 1957. The ranch had changed little since Cesare was there with Nico in 1954. The telephone lines were now permanently down and the battered old station waggon was just usable to drive into Stowe, or Morrisville, to collect provisions and make phone calls to Berterelli's. A farm girl at heart, Carla soon had the log cabin ship-shape and, in the summer months, she developed a vegetable garden at the rear of the farmhouse. During the Fall her allotment produced late crops of beet and large, bulbous onions which were stored on hemp strands in an outhouse. And in January, like clockwork, the snows came and remained on the ground until a thaw in March or early

April. A return to the simple life, without worries or cares, suited Carla down to the ground. Gone were the memories of her hardships in Sicily and her renegade years with Giuliano. But most nights in bed she suffered vivid recollections of her four year old boy with his large, dark, doleful eyes and entertained a faint hope he might still be alive. She silently prayed that God, in his munificence, might reveal Alfonzo's fate.

Within a few weeks of their arrival at the Homestead, Cesare's schizoid personality resurfaced with a vengeance. Nightmares and vivid recollections of shooting the youth in Siano's apartment assailed him and, for days on end, he stayed indoors, morose and monosyllabic and drinking heavily. He had lost his nerve and dreaded a weekly phone call to New York for fear he might be called back to do a job and doubted if he could ever again carry out another assassination. Carla was aware of this and, in his torment and suffering, she was a tower of strength. She humoured and nursed him through two harsh winters and encouraged him to go on shooting and fishing expeditions in the summer and forced him to drive her into Stowe to make weekly contact with Al Rizzi at Berterelli's. The recall to action came out of the blue on the first Tuesday in May 1957. Al instructed them to close up the homestead, pack their bags, and be ready to be picked up next day at noon outside Stowe Plaza Hotel. At home in their own private ranch, just as they had been at their podere on the foothills of Mount Sparagia in Sicily, Carla was dismayed at the suddenness of their departure. But she was a realist and recognised Cesare's only talent was as a hitman and all the privileges they now enjoyed were entirely due to his proficiency in this field. She was aware that she, herself, had considerable expertise in the same occupation and, together, they made a formidable assassination team. Over the next two years their services were in frequent demand in New York and along America's eastern seaboard.

The imminence of a hit on Don Cheech Scalise came home to Carla and Cesare when they found Al Rizzi awaiting their arrival at the Remington Hotel in Manhattan to deposit a gymbag of firearms in their bedroom. Through his underworld contacts Al discovered that, on occasional evenings in the week, Don Cheech came down a fire escape from his third floor tenement apartment in the Bronx to a back street cul-de-sac where he bartered for fresh fruit at Luigi's open-air fruit stall. Thrifty by nature, Scalise always haggled with the fruiterer and delayed his visits until after dark when many stallholders were packing up for the night and selling their perishable produce at discounted prices. Al stressed the urgency for Scalise's hit and finally added "He's seen you on the boat from Sicily. You'll have to go in disguise."

Carla and Cesare made a daylight recce of the Bronx backstreets the following day. The cul-de-sac was about eighty yards long and fruit and vegetable stalls were set in an orderly fashion on the sidewalk. A fire escape from Scalise's apartment block came to ground between Luigi's stall and a bakery. The market operated from daybreak until lunchtime and again in the evening between teatime and dusk when the stalls were illuminated by spluttering kerosene lamps suspended from poles. As a disguise Cesare wore a false moustache and sunglasses and substituted a flat cloth cap for his customary fedora, while Carla's black tresses were collected in a bun under a broad-brimmed cap and, over her dress, she wore a flannel jacket and baggy, calico trousers. Thus attired they strode nonchalantly in and out of the cul-de-sac and loitered at street corners and, on the second night of vigilance, their patience was rewarded. Many stall-keepers were crating their unsold produce, and Luigi had fired his kerosene lamp and was hoisting it up on a pole, when a man in shirt-sleeves descended a fire escape into the alley and emerged near Patrinella's stall. By the bright glare of the overhead lamp Cesare recognised Scalise.

"Quick, Carla! I'll follow you down to the stall. After I hit the bum put out that lamp on the pole."

Cool as a cucumber Carla strolled towards the fri it stall and, as she approached, she could hear Don Cheech haggling with Luigi "Hey Lou, you let me have a dozen of those friggin oranges for a buck last week."

"I know Frankie. These arrived from Jamaica only this morning. They're worth every cent of your money."

Carla sidled up to the stall and stood three feet away from Scalise. She picked up an orange and started prodding it with her forefinger. Luigi turned his attention to Carla "Hey there you little punk! Don't manhandle the friggin goods if you're not buyin'."

Carla replaced the orange neatly on the stall and, at that moment, Cesare came walking rapidly from the blind end of the cul-de-sac. A sixth sense seemed to warn Scalise of impending danger and, as he stepped backwards, he bumped into the 'young man' standing behind him. Scalise's body tensed and his eyes were glued on the approaching stranger and then he relaxed as Cesare walked straight past without looking to his right or left. Only a foot away from the perspiring gangster, Carla took matters into her own hands. Snatching a pistol from her waistband she fired four bullets in quick succession, three into the back of Scalise's trunk and one into the gangster's left temple after he hit the ground. He slid, almost gracefully, on to the sidewalk pulling a shower of oranges after him. Scalise's jerking body finally came to rest in a widening pool of blood and Luigi's Jamaican oranges were strewn all over the sidewalk. Carla's fifth bullet extinguished the kerosene lamp above Patrinella's perspiring scalp and then, in semi-darkness, she thrust her pistol into a barrel of bananas and calmly left the cul-de-sac. She found Cesare shaking uncontrollably and cowering in an alleyway. Realising he had lost his nerve at the last minute, and had a guilt complex about his failure, she took him in her arms to comfort him. She was exhilarated by her night's work but, for the moment, her main concern was to make a clean getaway. She kissed Cesare's sweaty brow. "Together we did it, Cesare. Now let's get out of here."

Carla removed her jacket, trousers and cap and stuffed them into a canvas bag. Releasing her tresses she made Cesare remove his moustache and sunglasses. Then arm in arm, and the epitome of a loving couple, they strolled away from the Bronx and down a crowded Madison Avenue to their own little haven at the Remington Hotel.

The slaughter of Don 'Cheech' Scalise did little, or nothing, to curb Albert Anastasia's lust for power. His ambitions in New York and New Jersey apart, he pressed ahead with plans to infiltrate Meyer Lansky's gambling rackets in Las Vegas and Miami and that was a major miscalculation. Supported by Lucky Luciano and Carlo Gambino, the infuriated Lansky issued a contract on Anastasia in May 1957. Gambino was a cunning operator and had his eye on Anastasia's enterprises in New York and New Jersey. Often used as a gofer by underworld Bosses, the short, ferret-like, hooked-nosed Gambino had his finger in most pies in Mafia underhand activities. Technically he was Genovese's underboss but, in practical terms, he ran with the 'hare and the hounds' and it was little wonder he was ordered to mastermind Anastasia's rubout. In this he had full support from Vito Genovese who wanted Anastasia 'put on ice permanent'. The setup was delegated to master hoods Tony Bender and Joe Profaci and Al Rizzi was ordered to provide executioners. At this time Carla and Little Cesare were his top 'hitmen' and Al had no hesitation in nominating them for the job.

Albert Anastasia had jumped ship in New York in 1920. An uncouth and uneducated Italian he soon blustered and shot his way up the ladder in Brooklyn's Longshoremen's Union. With a penchant for killing as a means of coercion he, and Louis 'Lepke' Buchalter, became the main enforcers for Murder Inc., the

National Crime Syndicate's enforcement arm. They were credited with around 200 killings in the 30's and 40's. Throughout his violent career Anastasia had remained loyal to Lucl y Luciano and Frank Costello but, by the summer of 1957, there was a contract out on the master enforcer himself and Carla and Little Cesare were the elected executioners.

As ever, Tony Bender and Carlo Gambino's set up was impeccable. Every two weeks, regular as clockwork, Anastasia had his hair trimmed at a barber's salon in a shopping precinct inside the Park Sheraton Hotel. On October 25th his bodyguard and driver went to park their Cadillac in the hotel's basement but all available parking spaces were occupied by Gambino's henchmen. Failing to park their limousine they returned to street level where they were immediately arrested by bogus policemen. Meanwhile, safely inside the hotel or so he thought, Anastasia went to the salon where he was effusively welcomed by his regular barber, one Arthur Grasso. Anastasia settled comfortably in the barber's chair and closed his eyes in anticipation of the facial pampering to come as Grasso packed his face with hot towels. Bender and Carlo Gambino's brief was to deliver the victim to the barber's shop and the execution was entirely up to Al Rizzi's gunmen. For two days prior to the hit Carla and Cesare were booked into a second floor room at the Park Sheraton under an assumed name. Once Anastasia was in the barber's shop, and the coast was clear, Al telephoned their room and delivered a prearranged message 'Mr and Mrs Valenti. You'll get a good view today from the top of the Empire State Building'. Cesare and Carla hurried down to the shopping arcade off the main entrance hall and, to avoid recognition, they covered their faces with scarves. Guns in hand they burst into the barber's shop. Anastasia was the only customer and the barber was crouched over his client lathering his face. Cesare pushed Grasso aside and spun the swivel chair. The hitmen stood one on each side of the awestruck wiseguy.

"Okay, now!" Cesare yelled and six shots reverberated in quick succession inside the cosy salon. After the first volley, Anastasia jumped to his feet and made an effort to attack his own reflection in the barber's mirror but, slowly, he sank to his knees as four more bullets entered his exposed back. Anastasia's inert body slipped on to the shop floor on top of Artie Grasso who was laying flat on his face and clasping his bald head in his hands. One final bullet, the coup de grace, was delivered into the back of Anastasia's head and the hitmen beat a hasty retreat to their bedroom where Carla immediately transformed herself into a female. Five minutes later she walked hand in hand with Cesare down to the hotel's main exit. The foyer was in chaos and crawling with city police. In reply to Cesare's innocuous question about the cause of the commotion a police officer replied "Some arsehole has gotten himself shot. We think he's a Mafia hoodlum. Move on, sir!"

Pleased with their morning's work, and with Cesare's active participation, Carla gave his hand an affectionate squeeze as they proceeded along the sidewalk.

"We did it together, Cesare."

He smiled briefly and remarked "It's a pity we couldn't buckwheat's him. As it is we didn't hit him up-front," referring to the traditional Mafia send-off by shooting victims in the face while their eyes were fully open. Carla shuddered and withdrew her hand from his grasp. Little Cesare was a perfectionist and, not satisfied with a straight shooting, he hankered after the more gruesome practices of his profession. She wondered if he would ever overcome his sadistic tendencies. And, as they walked along the busy sidewalk, Cesare's smile, which had been evident a minute before, was now replaced by a cold, vacant, distant stare.

As a result of Anastasia's murder Carlo Gambino took over

the control of his Brooklyn Family which pleased Genovese who expected fielty from his underboss. Vincent 'The Chin' Gigante's failed attempt on Frank Costello's life in May 195£ had adversely affected Genovese's popularity with the Mob and his chances of becoming Boss in New York. But, now Anastasia was 'gone permanent,' he perceived his way was clear to re-declare his interest and, to achieve his ambition, Don Corleone had to count on support from Carlo Gambino. Therein lay his difficulty. The cunning, two-faced old fox nursed his own aml.tions and, in conjunction with Costello, Lansky and Luciano in Naples, started plotting to get rid of Genovese.

By the summer of 1957 Vito Genovese, the self styled Don Corleone, was at the zenith of his power. He had established his headquarters in Atlantic Highlands, New Jersey where, a month after Anastasia's assassination, he invited New York's crime bosses to congregate to demonstrate unity for his nationwide ambitions. A notable defaulter was Augie Pisano, a small-time mobster from the upper Bronx, who was one of Costello's Underbosses and boyhood friend. Pisano had worked his way through the ranks in Brooklyn but overstepped the mark when, in the early 50's, he moved into 'open territory' in Miami and attempted to take control of Meyer Lansky's rackets in that State. Pisano's non-attendance at Genovese's mobster meeting marked him down as a likely candidate for a future rubout. At that meeting Genovese made a deal with Costello and allowed the latter to keep his Manhattan empire and to readmit Pisano into the fold in exchange for their support nationally. After winning over the Mob in New York, Genovese felt strong enough to convene a national conference at the end of November 1957. The ill-fated convention was planned to take place at Joseph Barbara's mansion in the Apalachin Hills in upper New York State. Barbara's arrangements for police protection had been watertight over the years but for Genovese's conference security was grossly inadequate. Heads of major Families throughout the States had been invited but Frank Costello made his excuses, Meyer Lansky pleaded a throat condition and Al Rizzi and Joe Bonanno arranged to arrive a day late. The convention kicked off with drinks at Barbara's mansion but the party became a fiasco and the hacienda was surrounded by federal agents and state troopers. Fifty eight arrests were made including Trafficante from Tampa, Genovese himself, Profaci, and Gambino from New York and Magaddino from Buffalo. Of those arrested 35 had previous convictions, 23 had served prison sentences and 18 had been involved in murder investigations. There had obviously been a 'leak' to the Feds and Genovese lost all credibility for failing to ensure security for his fellow-mobsters. Nearly all delegates were released after 48 hours claiming they had come to Apalachin to visit Joseph Barbara who was known to have a serious heart condition. Carlo Gambino escaped unscathed and, protesting his loyalty to Vito Genovese, immediately began moves to depose his Boss and, in this, he had allies in Frank Costello, Meyer Lansky and Lucky Luciano in faraway Italy. After collapse of the Apalachin Conference, Genovese was relentless in his pursuit of the culprit who grassed to the Feds and he became convinced that Frank Costello and Augie Pisano were behind the frame-up. By the end of the year he had concrete evidence that Pisano, the scar-faced, small-time hoodlum from the Upper Bronx, was responsible but Genovese's hands were tied and he was unable to order a 'hit'. At the same time a counterplot was being hatched by Costello to 'fix' Genovese and, for this purpose, he employed the services of two master-fixers - Carlo Gambino and Tony Bender.

A native of Puerto Rico, Nelson Cantellops had come up the hard way. Born of mixed parentage in the slums of San Juan he developed into a handsome young Lothario with drooping moustaches, two rows of prominent, pearly-white teeth and a ready, disarming smile which hid the violent beast within. He has a string of killings by stabbing to his credit but had avoided arrest and conviction and, at the age of thirty, was a distribution agent for a cartel of drug barons in Puerto Rico. A vain character, he always wore a white tuxedo and black tie and chain-smoked slim, sweet-smelling cheroots. Dressed in his finery Nelson Cantellops presented a plausible picture but underneath, like a coiled spring, was a panther ready to pounce. On a humid May evening Cantellops was entertaining Tony Bender to dinner at a waterfront restaurant in San Juan. Grinning broadly, and eyes flashing, he relit a cheroot and gazed inquisitively at the mobster.

"Come now, Senor Bender, what is the true purpose of your visit?"

Tony Bender wiped the condensation off his sunglasses and marvelled how the Puerto Rican looked so cool in the humidity.

"I've told you, Nelson. I'm a tourist interested in importing snow to the States. I've been given your name as a contact."

Nelson Cantellops looked interested.

"Perhaps I can help. What quantity are we talking about?"

"A kilo, or two, for inspection."

The Puerto Rican burst out laughing "A kilo isn't worth a shit. It had better be more or there's no deal."

"My Bosses want to inspect the goods. If it's okay we may take a hundred kilos a month."

"That's more like it, Senor Bender. My heroin is pure snow. Who are your Bosses?"

"They're big wiseguys in New York. Bring a kilo of your best snow to Boston and there'll be a nice pick-up for your trouble."

"Si senor! I can do that, but why Boston and not New York?"

Tony Bender got up to leave "There's no need for you to friggin know. Good night Senor Cantellops."

Carlo Gambino and Al Rizzi were guests at Costello's Long

Island retreat and the Prime Minister of the Underworld outlined his proposals for 'fixing' Vito Genovese "The Little Man in Miami and the Big Boss in Naples are in on our 'fix' and so is Sam Giancana in Chicago. Tony Bender went hunting in Puerto Rico and he's come up with a stoolpigeon who'll bring the goods to Boston. Carlo will get one of Genovese's sons interested in the deal. The important thing is that the agent from Puerto Rico must think he's dealing with Vito Genovese's boys. Okay guys? I'll leave details to Al. When the time is right Carlo will bring in Genovese's mob for a piece of the action."

Carlo Gambino nodded and Al asked "Who's paying and where do we meet the Puerto Rican?"

"The Syndicate is putting up the dough and you'll have 20,000 dollars to pay upfront for the dope. Tony Bender will fix the first meet in Boston and Augie Pisano will be the legman. You must provide a bagman to carry the dough."

Al was not entirely happy "Can we trust Tony Bender, Boss?"

Carlo Gambino spoke up "Yeah, Al! I've got the twister in my pocket and he owe's me a few friggin favours."

Frank Costello followed his limping underboss to the door "Don't worry about Bender or Gambino, Alphonse. They're both one hundred percenters."

Vincent Charles Teresa was commissioned by Tony Bender to arrange a meeting place with Nelson Cantellops in Boston in May 1958. Twenty nine year old 'Fat Vinnie' was one of Patriarca's less salubrious protégés and had an undeserved reputation as a Mafia 'fixer'. Self ranked No 3 in line for Patriarca's territory in New England, Teresa had pushed himself forwards by bribery and corruption to become a wiseguy in Bostonian Mafia circles. A loud-mouthed hoodlum, involved in all rackets under the sun, he had no stomach for the physical side of his business. He knew everyone and everything in Boston's underworld and, likewise, everyone including the police and the judiciary knew Fat Vinnie and regarded him as a likeable, if somewhat eccentric, buffoon. Teresa arranged for a secret meeting to take place in a bedroom on the fourth floor of the Bostonian Hotel which was bugged for sound and had 'eyes in the sky' for observers on the floor above to watch proceedings. The meeting with Nelson Cantellops finally materialized during the last week in May 1958. Stationed at the 'eyes in the sky' above the bugged bedroom, Al Rizzi observed Little Augie Pisano and Cesare arrive for their meeting with Nelson Cantellops. Handcuffed to his left wrist Cesare had a brief case containing 20,000 dollars in used notes and took up a strategic position with his back to a wall and a Biretta held firmly in his right hand. The two sat silently for a while until Little Augie, obviously in a state of nervous tension, blurted out "Don't say nuttin' Cesare! Leave all the friggin dealin' to me."

Cesare merely grunted and stared fixedly at the bedroom door. Twenty minutes later Tony Bender ushered in the Puerto Rican and two hefty black bodyguards. Like a smiling angel Cantellops waltzed into the room while his armed black minders took up their positions, one outside and one inside the locked bedroom door. Cantellops introduced himself and threw a brown paper bag on the bed.

"That's pure snow man! Sniff it and see. I guarantee quality and that's what you'll get when you buy from me. Who's buying anyway? Who am I dealin' with?"

"You're dealing with me you friggin arsehole. Maybe you've heard of my cousin Vito Genovese? He's also known as Don Corleone" Pisano replied in a threatening tone. Nelson Cantellops body stiffened at the mention of Don Corleone and Pisano continued "Now here's the deal. You get 20,000 dollars today and the rest when the first shipment arrives in New Jersey. Have we got a friggin deal?"

The Puerto Rican nodded his head and simply said "Si."

Cesare unlocked the briefcase and Cantellops was allowed to

count the money and stuff 20,000 dollars, in 100 dollar bills, inside his white tuxedo. The two men solemnly shook hands and the chastened Puerto Rican prepared to leave.

"I expect you to keep your part of the bargain, Cantellops. If you friggin-well don't we'll get at you even in Puerto Rico. Don't be tempted to pull out of this friggin deal."

"Don't worry Senor Genovese. I will not let you down" and, tapping the wad of notes in his pocket, Cantellops bestowed a wide toothsome grin on the New York mobster and, protected by his minders, he strode out of the room Ten minutes later Al Rizzi moved into the bugged bedroom.

"Well done Augie! You did fine! Cantellops has taken the bait." Pisano grinned.

"He's certainly taken your friggin money, Boss!"

Al laughed outright.

"That's a chance we take in life. I think it'll work out."

An hour later they cleared out of the Bostonian Hotel and drove back to New York. The following day Al spoke to Frank Costello at his Long Island villa "Did everything go to plan?" Costello asked.

"Yes, Boss! I've just bought us twenty grand's worth of dope" Al replied with a satisfied grin, adding "The Puerto Rican took the bait hook, line and sinker. The goods should be here in a coupla weeks."

In the first week in October 1958 the long-awaited Jamaican banana boat arrived in New Jersey docks and, to underline his dubious honesty, the Puerto Rican drug-pusher personally accompanied the delivery. Nelson Cantellops' motives for keeping his word were heavily influenced by greed and the prospects of further dope deals with Genovese's mobsters. Anonymously forewarned by Augie Pisano, the dockside was crawling with police and federal agents disguised as longshoremen and dockers. Backed up by a dozen mobsters,

Santino Genovese and Vinnie 'The Chin' Gigante arrived to collect the goods and were immediately arrested, together with Nelson Cantellops and the entire ship's crew. Tl.e case against Vito Genovese was flimsy but the Feds held a trump card which they used to full advantage. When confronted by defence lawyers Cantellops steadfastly maintained his Boston contact was with a Genovese lieutenant. The trial came to court in January 1959 and Don Corleone was gaoled for 15 years and his henchmen received varying stretches. Silvano Genovese and 'The Chin' were put away for 7 years and Costello achieved revenge for the attempt on his life by Gigante in 1955. Carlo Gambino moved in and took over Genovese's empire and effectively became New Jersey's crime boss. Gripped by paranoia about his frame-up Don Corleone attempted to run his rackets from behind prison bars employing Jerry Catena and Tony Bender as his outside agents until he suspected Bender was implicated in the plot against him. He issued a contract on Bender who was not given the 'Mafia handshake' until four years later, on 8th Aprl1962. Vito Genovese did not survive his prison sentence in Danemmora and he died of natural causes in 1969.

The 'hits' on Scalise and Anastasia led New York's underworld community to conclude there were two expert enforcers in Town and their identity confused the Mob who were looking for two young wiseguys. By the summer of 1958, the scent was getting warmer and quite a few unwelcome hoodlums, including Fiore Siano, had their eye on the Remington Hotel. Al Rizzi was forced to move his hit-team to a 'safe house' in the fashionable Brooklyn Heights district of New York. Carla was happy in her new surroundings but Cesare again became depressed and hardly ever ventured outside. Inactivity merely seemed to deepen his depression and it came as a great relief when Sam Giancana of Chicago requested hitmen for a contract in Phoenix and specifically asked for a female to accompany the party. The Mafia never employed women to do their dirty business but Al's Boss owed Sam Giancana a favour and whatever Costello ordered was law in Al Rizzi's eyes. The woman selected for the job was naturally Carla.

Three mobsters from Boston came through Brooklyn and picked up Carla and Cesare in a black Cadillac hitmobile in the second week in November 1958. The drivers alternated regularly on the 2,200 mile journey to Phoenix which took the party three days to complete. Their companions from Boston were immature and bombastic mafioso, almost trainee hitmen, and treated the trip as a leisurely Sunday outing. The elder statesman among them, who could hardly have been 22 years old, explained their mission "We're out to hit a friggin Jewish bum. He's been two-timing my Bosses and Tony Accardo and Sam Giancana wanna him to sleep permanent. Greenbaum worked for them at the Riviera Club in Las Vegas but he stepped outa line and he was skimming the friggin skim. They wanna make an example of Mr friggin Greenbaum and we're the guys to do it."

"And why do we need a woman on the hit?" Cesare asked.

"She'll get us into his property. The Jewish lardass has a soft spot for dames."

In his day Gus Greenbaum had amassed, and wasted, millions of dollars. Mafia organisations undoubtedly profited vastly from his expertise in casino management but his compulsive weakness for women, gambling, alcohol and drugs led him into serious debt which he tried to resolve by skimming the skim at the Mob's expense. Eventually he was forced out and absconded to a small house on the outskirts of Phoenix where he was confident his former employers would never find him. But his confidence was misplaced and the hitsquad had little difficulty in locating his house. His name 'G Greenbaum' was boldly displayed on a brass-plated mailbox at the roadside at the end of his drive.

Mid-morning on a Monday the Chicago mobsters parked their Cadillac about a hundred yards from Greenbaum's drive and concealed themselves in a hawthorn copse near the house. Carla walked alone up the drive to the front door. A blousy, middle-aged bottle-blonde, smelling strongly of alcohol and dressed in a stained, pink nightdress, answered the doorbell.

"Yes honey! What can I do for you?"

"My auto has broken down. May I use your telephone?"

"Yes honey! Come in" and she led the way into a lounge, pointed at the telephone, and shouted from the foot of the stairs "Hey Gussy! We gotta visitor. She's a good-looking broad."

"I'll be down in a minute. Offer her a drink."

Mrs Greenbaum turned towards Carla who was now pretending to dial a number on the telephone.

"What'll it be honey? Bourbon, or vodka, or bourbon and coffee?

"Just coffee, please" Carla replied as she surveyed the filthy, unkempt state of the lounge with empty liquor bottles and cigarette stubs littering the floor. Gus Greenbaum shuffled unsteadily into the room. His thin frame was bent at the shoulders and his dark eyes shone like beacons from beneath a crop of frizzly, grey hair. With trembling hands he poured himself a glass of vodka and his covetous eyes weighed up Carla from head to toe. To dampen his ardour Carla spoke first "The repair men are on their way, Mr Greenbaum. Your wife is kindly getting me a coffee."

"That's okay," the wizened little man replied, "time enough for a quick cuddle."

To Carla's surprise Gus Greenbaum advanced unsteadily towards her with a lustful glare and she backed off to a corner of the room. At that moment Gus's wife emerged from the kitchen carrying two mugs of coffee. She quickly defused the situation "Leave the poor girl alone, Gus. Let her have her coffee first."

Gus backed off and reluctantly slumped into an armchair. Two minutes later the doorbell rang.

"That'll be the repair man" Carla exclaimed and hurried to open the front door. Cesare and the Boston mafiosi came rushing into the lounge and for the next twenty minutes Carla was witness to a most horrific slaughter which made her physically ill.

Boston's hoodlums went about their business in a cool, calculated, clinical fashion and even described their actions in detail as they performed their gruesome task. The Greenbaum's were securely gagged and tied into two upright, wooden chairs. The mobsters then produced cut-throat razors and, standing behind their victims with their necks extended they slowly, and deliberately, cut across their windpipes. Cesare was mesmerised. Pushing a mobster aside, he took up the role of executioner on Gus Greenbaum. The razor slashes slowly deepened and the purple ooze from their necks became a pulsating torrent of spurting red blood which sprayed on to the coffee table and the grime-covered floor. The victims' gasping attempts to breathe were released in horrific frothy gushes as their tracheas were finally transected. The gurgling and mini-cascades of blood continued with diminishing force until all life was extinct in the seated victims. Carla was amazed at the time it took for the Greenbaums to expire and horrified t the sadistic pleasure Cesare had derived from the slaughter. Throughout the execution he had behaved like a demented madman with a frenzied look on his face. The executioners wiped their razors clean on a grubby tablecloth and, without a further glance at their victims, they walked down Greenbaum's drive to their Cadillac.

Mr and Mrs Greenbaum's bodies were discovered three days later and, by that time, the execution party was safely in New York. The Phoenix police attributed the deaths to a possible suicide pact, though how the Greenbaums managed to slit their own throats with their hands partially tied was never explained and neither was the absence of 'suicide' weapons at the scene of the crime. Their fate reverberated throughout the underworld like a clap of thunder and served as a warning to potential skimmers and wiseguys. The Bostonian mobsters had transgressed a Mafia code of ethics in murdering a female, and a Jewish woman at that, and this did not please Meyer Lansky who had sanctioned the hit on his Jewish clansman in the first place. The Chicago bosses explained their actions by pointing out that the Greenbaums did not warrant a shooting up-front and the Mafia credo -'Cheat us and we'll pay you back with interest' was justified and had been upheld in all respects.

CHAPTER 16

Fat Vinnie cook's Cesare's goose

THE TRIAL AND CONVICTION OF VITO GENOVESE on a
bum narcotics charge caused havoc among the New World's
Mafia. Mobsters reviewed their security measures and,
temporarily, curbed many of their underhand rackets. Looking
over their shoulders they suspected everyone, and trusted no one,
constantly expecting a knock on the door and a visit from the Feds.
Bribes to the police and judiciary ceased abruptly. The Mob were
jittery and on the run and one Family boss who suffered loss of
nerve more than most was Abner 'Longy' Zwillman, whose fall
from grace had been rapid in recent months. Zwillman was
founder of the 'Jewish Mafia' and a member of Luciano's all-
powerful National Crime Syndicate in the thirties. At the zenith of
his power he was hailed as the 'Al Capone' of New Jersey and had
senior politicians and police in that city in his pocket. And then a
McClelland committee investigation targeted Zwillman's rackets
for special attention and Longy began to crack. The attempted
murder of his life-long friend, Costello, and the assassination of
Anastasia heightened his nervousness and he sidled into deep
depression. Sick and washed-out, he retired to his luxurious
mansion in West Orange, New Jersey and, by January 1959,
rumour had it that Zwillman was on the point of singing to the
Feds in exchange for immunity from prosecution. Alarm bells rang
throughout the criminal underworld which forced Meyer Lansky,
and Carlo Gambino, to approve an urgent contract on Zwillman.
As Longy was not true mafioso, Costello ruled out a Mob killing
and supported a policy of coercion and pressure on Zwillman to
terminate his own life and this was the order passed on to Al Rizzi.
Alphonse Rizzi and Augie Pisano called at Little Cesare's
apartment in Brooklyn Heights in the middle of a heavy February

snowstorm. Over a cup of coffee Al outlined the reason for their unexpected visit "Carla! I've fixed you a position as housekeeper to Longy Zwillman. He's a sick man and the bosses want him chopped, but with no violence. See if you can help him out with an overdose of medicine. The Zwillmans are short of a housekeeper and you start tomorrow."

Cesare looked puzzled.

"Why can't we bump him off, Boss?"

"He's too big in the Mob and the Little Man in Miami and the Big Boss in Naples are dead against a traditional hit. No! It'll have to be a drug overdose or self-topping."

"Perhaps I could persuade him to hang himself," Cesare offered, and Little Augie butted in "You'd be friggin lucky to handle him on your own. He aint called Longy for nuttin'. He's well over six foot and you'll need help" and Al agreed with the experienced fixer.

Within a few days Carla had assessed the situation in Zwillman's household. Longy rested in his bedroom most of the day but, dressed in a red, silk dressing gown, he was up and about in the early hours chain-smoking and roaming around the house. At sixty years of age Longy, who for several years had been a lover of the actress Jean Harlow, was still handsome but his face was haggard and drawn and his depression made him introverted and withdrawn. Presumably repaying him for his wanton years of debauchery, his wife slept at night in an isolated wing of the house when Longy retired to the basement where he sat playing with a gigantic model railway layout and drinking innumerable cups of lemon tea which he brewed for himself on an open gas ring. Carla felt sorry for the remote, morose man and, within a few days, came to a conclusion she would need outside help to perform an execution on the forlorn mobster.

Longy Zwillman's fortified villa in West Orange was completely surrounded by a 15ft wall and an electrified fence and the entrance gate to his drive was electronically controlled and manned by a gatekeeper during the day. Two vicious Doberman Pinscher guard dogs roamed the grounds during the night and all ground-floor steel doors were triple locked and alarmed from inside the house. Carla worked on a scheme to neutralise the Dobermans and, at precisely 11 o'clock each night, she fed the dogs outside the kitchen door. Being creatures of habit they appeared regularly for their food. Before retiring each night Carla also made a point of taking a tray of digestive biscuits and a flask of lemon tea to the lonely, depressed man in the basement. Her preparations now complete she communicated a date, and time of execution, to Al Rizzi at Ristorante Berterelli.

By 11.15pm on 27th February 1959 Carla had turned off power to the electrified fence and internal alarm system and fed the Dobermans with meat containing a strong sedative. The hounds were now dozing on a mat outside the kitchen door and Cesare and Augie Pisano were due to come over the wall in ten minutes. It was time for her to go to the basement to enact her final chore. She found Zwillman, in deep concentration, hunched over his model railway.

"I'm sorry t disturb you, sir. I've brought you a flask of fresh tea and some biscuits."

Longy looked up vacantly and a fleeting smile crossed his face.

"Thank you, Miss Carla. Put the tray down. I've already brewed myself a mug."

Carla did as she was told.

"Will you need me again tonight, Mr Zwillman?"

"No thanks, Miss Carla. Goodnight to you."

'And goodbye to you' thought Carla and felt a pang of genuine remorse and pity for the depressed ex-mobster. She withdrew demurely down a corridor to an outside patio door which opened on to a swimming pool and the snow-covered lawn. The night was intensely cold and pitch black and, peering into the gloom, Carla saw a flash of light from a pencil torch near the boundary fence. A few seconds later Cesare and Little Augie arrived at the open door.

"The dogs are asleep and you've got about thirty minutes to finish the job. Zwillman's in the basement. Follow me," Carla whispered, and led the hitmen up the corridor to the basement playroom.

When Cesare and Little Augie burst in on Longy Zwillman he was still hunched over the model railtrack. H. immediately recognised Pisano but did not move a muscle, or protest, as Little Augie put him in an armlock and clamped a gag firmly over his mouth. Cesare tied his ankles and wrists together and a nylon noose was placed around his neck. Zwillman was then manhandled on to a table and the end of the nylon rope was tied to a beam in the ceiling. Strangely, Longy offered little resistance and seemed prepared, and almost relieved, to accept his fate. The final act was to topple the table and Longy Zwillman jerked and struggled his way, sedately and silently, into oblivion. The whole macabre incident had taken ten minutes. It was an achievement for the two slightly-built five-footers to manhandle an 18 stone six-footer on to a table and they could not have managed it without the victim's partial cooperation. Pisano stood in front of the hanging corpse and commented with a broad grin on his face "We friggin done it, Cesare. I think the frigger wanted to croak and get outa here. Now let's tidy up and go."

Solemnly they shook hands and then went about removing the gag and the wrist and ankle ties. After they left the premises the way they had come in, Carla barred and locked the patio door, tidied the playroom and reactivated the alarm system and the electric fence. Finally she turned on the gas ring in the basement before retiring to her bedroom.

The dogs raised the alarm on the following morning when the gatekeeper found them scratching and barking outside the patio door. Zwillman's body was found hanging from a beam in the gas-filled basement. Longy's face was black and bloated and his swollen, purple tongue protruded from his wide-open mouth. His pyjama front and dressing gown was soaking wet and a moccasin slipper off his right foot lay in a pool of dark-yellow urine on the floor. Zwillman's wife had been expecting something to happen and she was not overtly upset by his sudden death. A coroner recorded a suicide verdict while the balance of his mind was disturbed and, in accordance with Jewish practice, Zwillman was buried in a New Orange cemetery within 48 hours of his death. Frank Costello, Carlo Gambino, Al Rizzi and Augie Pisano were the Mob's sole representatives at the funeral and Meyer Lansky sent a large wreath. Carla left Zwillman's villa a week after Longy's funeral and, never happy or comfortable in New Jersey, his wife moved lock, stock and barrel to a retirement home in Florida.

The void in New Jersey's underworld was immediately filled by Carlo Gambino who was steadily, but surely, on his way to becoming New York's premier Boss. Another repercussion of Longy Zwillman's forced 'suicide' by the Mob was more far-reaching and l d to a damaging rift in relationships between Lucky Luciano and Meyer Lansky. Luciano was displeased with the lack of effort Lansky made on Longy's behalf and Lansky, who held the purse strings, retaliated by curbing Luciano's skim from the Mob's profit. The rift became a chasm and, within a year, ended the life-long partnership between two surviving founder members of the National Crime Syndicate.

Vito Genovese's trial and subsequent fifteen year sentence, Anastasia's assassination, and Longy Zwillman's alleged suicide, were soon forgotten by July 1959 when Tony Bender, and his co-fixer Augie Pisano, produced positive evidence that Vincent Charles Teresa of Boston was cooperating with the police.

Unhappy with his treatment from New England's crime boss, Fat Vinnie was making approaches to Boston's police force. Raymond Patriarca was a worried man and enlisted Frank Costello's help.

"Fat Vinnie daren't touch me but he may blow the gaffe on Genovese's frame-up and I don't know if he's already spilt the beans. Vinnie likes a good living and won't care two farts if his dough comes from the cops. The game is in your ballpark Frankie."

"Thanks, but no thanks," Frank Costello replied. This was, indeed, a worrying development and Vincent Teresa's evidence might lead to a retrial and Genovese's release from Danemmora penitentiary. And a free Don Corleone, hell-bent on revenge for false imprisonment, would be a troublesome handful. Fat Vinnie was a well-known mobster in Cambridge, home of Harvard University and the Massachusetts Institute of Technology. He was a larger-than-life character and waddled around his territory in a white, silk suit, throwing his money around with gay abandon. To attain an air of respectability, and curry favour with the authorities, he endorsed a 1,000 dollar bursary to Harvard for research into urban crime among Boston's poorer classes. Al Rizzi's instructions to Little Cesare were brief and straight to the point "Get up to Boston and hit the greaseball. I canna make it more urgent. Hit the lardass and hit him good."

In a battered old Oldsmobile the Cesaranos motored to Boston and booked a room at the Charles Hotel in Harvard Square. Passing as tourists, Carla and Cesare strolled around Harvard University campus the following day. Near a bronze statue of the University's founder, with its burnished, shiny, 'good-luck' toecap, workmen were erecting a platform. A notice board nearby proclaimed an end of semester degree presentation ceremony at 11.00am on Saturday morning. Among a list of scholarship donors Mr Vincent Teresa's name appeared together with the value of his donation to the University for 1,000 dollars per annum.

Cesare politely enquired of a passing student "Tell me, young man, is this ceremony open to visitors?"

"Yes Sir!," the bright-eyed freshman replied, "it's a big occasion, just like a Presidential Inauguration."

"How long does it last?"

"About two hours, Sir, and there's free drinks and a buffet in the Great Hall afterwards."

At 10.0'clock on Saturday morning Cesare booked out of the Charles Hotel. Carla wore her baggy trousers and her blue, cloth cap and they hailed a yellow cab in Brattle Street. Cesare did a deal with the driver "I wanna hire you for three hours. How much?"

"Depends on how far" the cab driver replied.

"It's a short ride."

"I make it twenty dollars an hour."

"That's okay," Cesare confirmed, "here's a hundred bucks. Keep the change."

Charles Banoccio was overjoyed with his fare and his face broke into a broad grin "For a hundred smackeroos I'll drive you guys to Chicago and back."

"Lets hope ou don't have to" Cesare commented with a wry smile.

The cab pulled up at a kerbside in Massachusetts Avenue about a hundred yards beyond an archway entrance to a tunnel into Harvard's main quadrangle. Carla remained with the driver and the presentation ceremony was well under way by the time Cesare arrived and stood behind the seated audience. Gowned graduates, and formally-dressed parents, sat in rows on the quadrangle lawn and on the platform, dressed in their regalia, an ermine-collared Chancellor, the College Dean, the Mayor of Cambridge, a senior judge and six sponsors were seated in a row. Guarded by two plain-clothes bodyguards Vincent Teresa sat among the dignitaries and Cesare took a good look at his target. Fat Vinnie was an apt title for the Bostonian mobster. He was grossly obese, over twenty stones in weight, bulging out of his white tuxedo and constantly dabbing his sweaty brow with a silk handkerchief despite a cool, balmy morning.

The ceremony itself was boring. A Master of Ceremonies called graduates in alphabetical order to the dais to receive an inscripted scroll and a handshake from the Chancellor and the applause for successful students was continuous and deafening. In common with other benefactors Vincent Teresa presented his bursary to a thin, weedy, bespectacled freshman and made an impassioned speech about his family's humble, immigrant origins and, ironically, his concern about organised violence among Boston's slum minorities. The freshman receiving Fat Vinnie's bursary was named Patriarca and Cesare realised Teresa was merely redistributing his Family's wealth. After a rendering of Stars and Stripes and the Harvard hymn, the Chancellor brought proceedings to a close. Adhering to an age-old custom, and accompanied by boos, catcalls and firecrackers, the students surrounded the platform dignitaries and, one by one, herded them through the dark tunnel and on to Massachusetts Avenue. Cesare joined a large group of jostling freshmen surrounding Fat Vinnie who, with his police minders, was being pushed gently, but firmly, towards the exit from Harvard's quadrangle.

Cesare's opportunity to strike came inside the semi-dark archway tunnel. He was being squeezed tighter by the students when someone let off a cracker which produced a deafening roar in the confined space. Progress along the tunnel was reduced to a snail's pace but Cesare managed to push himself to within three feet of the back of Fat Vinnie's white tuxedo, which stood out like an illuminated beacon. Cesare drew his handgun and, a second before he fired, a firecracker went off and a startled student accidentally nudged his right elbow. Cesare's bullet missed Teresa and ploughed into the back of his bodyguard's skull emerging through his left eye-socket. Poleaxed, the minder fell forwards against the students immediately in front and then collapsed, face downwards, on to the concrete floor. Assuming the visitor was entering into the spirit of the occasion by reacting to the firework's bang, the students laughed and hooted and the first to react was Fat Vinnie's second bodyguard. Gun in hand he swivelled around to face the scrambling mob but, in the confusion, Cesare had slipped through the archway and was mingling with happy graduates and proud parents at the kerbside on Massachusetts Avenue. Back in the tunnel the laughter and banter were replaced by shrieks and screams of terror as the freshmen realised someone had been shot. The policeman bodyguard took charge of the chaotic situation.

"Captain Munro's been hit. Everyone stay exactly where you are. And for gawd's sake stop hollering!"

Cowering against the tunnel wall, his white tuxedo spattered with the dead policeman's blood, Vincent Teresa was shaking like a jelly and convinced the bullet was meant for him. Captain Munro's fate did not bother Vinnie one iota and he realised that protection by Boston's police force was not sufficient to guarantee his safety for much longer. He knew the Mob was definitely after his blood and there was only one solution - he had to quit Boston and take a long vacation somewhere in the country, or abroad.

Jeanette Brown, a pretty seven year old girl from Lexington, was being gently pushed and nudged by the good- natured crowd on Massachusetts Avenue and, ten feet away, her parents were proudly hugging and kissing her brother Joseph, one of the successful graduates presented that morning with his diploma. Suddenly the hubbub and laughter from within the tunnel turned into screams and shouts. Jeanette dropped her parasol in fright. Dating back from her grandmother's days, she stooped to pick up the family heirloom when a man in a hurry trod on the precious sunshade and there was a loud snap. From her crouched position Jeanette saw the man thrusting a handpistol into his waistband and edging forwards through the crowd until he broke clear and hurried down the pavement towards a parked yellow cab. At that moment a wave of hysteria swept through the crowd as news of the shooting spread like wildfire. Realising what she had witnessed Jeanette gave vent to a shriek "There he goes! That man's got a gun."

A breathless policeman arrived at her side just in time to see Cesare being bundled into a parked yellow cab by a young man wearing a blue cloth cap. The police officer blew his whistle three times to summon a squad car which screeched to a halt at the kerbside. The officer ordered the driver to follow the yellow taxi which was, by now, speeding away down Massachusetts Avenue towards Harvard Bridge. Claxon blaring, and headlights flashing, the police squad car gave chase.

In the cab the driver at first refused to budge "I aint friggin movin' buddy until you tell me what's goin' on."

He turned around to face the back and looked straight at the business end of Carla's .38 Biretta. With no choice he shrugged his shoulders "I guess you're the friggin boss!"

As they approached Massachusetts Institute of Technology traffic became denser and their progress was impeded. Claxon wailing and headlights blazing, the police car wove its way through the congestion some 400 yards behind the taxi. Carla prodded the driver with her Biretta and Cesare spat out an order "Faster! Faster you arsehole! Turn on your headlights and step on the gas."

"I'm doin' my friggin damndest! We'll be across Harvard Bridge in a minute."

But traffic on the bridge was almost at a standstill and a passageway for cars was reduced to two outer lanes. Two inner lanes were cordoned off and reserved for MIT students rehearsing a Smoot Ceremony for ragweek. The Smoot Ceremony originated in a student prank when Oliver Reed Smoot, a 5ft 6ins freshman, was used as a yardstick to measure the length of Harvard Bridge.

He was laid bodily on the road and the bridge marked off into 5ft 6ins sections, or 'smoots.' About 300 students had progressed to within a hundred yards of the Boston end of the bridge when, after two abrupt stops in the traffic queue, Cesare panicked "Get off the bridge you friggin arsehole and do it now!"

"I canna buddy. I just canna."

Cesare spotted the empty kerbside lanes.

"Get across to the right lanes and put your foot down."

The driver swung through the flimsy exclusion tapes and, tooting his horn, sped down the empty inner lanes but had to pull-up some thirty yards short of the milling crowd of Smoot Ceremony freshmen who would not budge an inch. With no sympathy for the student body obstructing their escape, Cesare prodded the driver in the chest with his handgun.

"Keep your finger on the friggin horn and force your way through."

"I canna do that! My son is a freshman at MIT!"

"Okay! If you won't do what you're friggin told, hit him Carla."

Carla's dumdum bullet from her .45 Biretta entered the back of the cabbie's head and blew the front of his skull through the shattered windscreen. He slumped across his steering wheel. Without a backwards glance Carla and Cesare got out of the yellow cab and, threading their way through the noisy students, hurried off Harvard Bridge.

The freshmen's suspicions that something was amiss were aroused when a police squad car came to a shuddering halt in their reserved lane and two armed officers cautiously approached the marooned yellow cab. Some thought it was a raid and scampered off the bridge while others were nosier and watched in awe as they pulled a dead, almost faceless, man out through the cab's shattered windscreen. Questioned by an inspector a few minutes later many students recalled two men in a hurry walking away from the cab and off the bridge into Boston. The inspector raced back to his squad car and radioed headquarters "Two suspects seen leaving Harvard Bridge into Boston. One young man wearing a blue cap and the second, a male Caucasian about thirty years of age, probably Latin-American. Cab driver, Charles Banoccio, shot dead on bridge. Cab probably hijacked after shooting at Harvard University. Suspects believed to be still in Boston. Request UPP."

An Urgent Police Priority meant all bus stations, railway terminals and airports in Boston would be under surveillance and random road blocks would be set up at major road junctions. Police authorities were not too concerned about an attempt on Vincent Teresa's life but were hell-bent on tracking down Captain Munro's murderers and therein lay their difficulty. Their suspects were two Caucasian males and the fact that one of the 'men' was a female never entered into their deliberations.

Once clear of Harvard Bridge, Cesare led Carla into a pedestrian subway which emerged on the south bank of Charles River and close to a bus station. The very first coach to pull out was heading for New Brunswick in Maine and, within two minutes of boarding, the fleeing couple were travelling eastwards out of Boston, across the Charles River Dam, skirting Cambridge and then northwards along the coastal road. Ten minutes later a cordon of road blocks were thrown around Boston but by that time the escapees were approaching Danvers and, four hours later, the bus pulled into Kennebunkport in Maine. Cesare decided to put up for a night at a local inn but, as it transpired, it was an unfortunate choice for an overnight stay.

CHAPTER 17

The Sleeping Sentinel

IN THE 50'S KENNEBUNKPORT was home to a thriving fishing industry serving the State of Maine. Kennebunk town spread along the banks of three creeks and the hotel chosen by Little Cesare, The Village Cove Inn, was a privately-owned, wooden building lying in a fork on the main creek. The hotel receptionist was mildly curious the guests had no visible means of transport and no luggage but he was immune to such surprises. Village Cove Inn was a frequent one-night stopover for honeymooners, runaways and elopers and, as long as they paid in advance, he had learnt to turn a blind eye. Cesare registered as Mr and Mrs Spiteri and, after a light supper in their room, they retired for the night just after 8.00pm.

Frank Drago and Charles Spencer were FBI undercover agents working for Boston's Narcotics Bureau and, posing as deep-sea fishermen, they had been resident at the Inn for two months. At around 10.30pm Cesare was awaken from a deep sleep by their arrival back from a stakeout. Easily heard through the flimsy partition between adjacent rooms, Charlie Spencer had a loud, booming voice "I checked with Boston, Frankie. There's a Liberian freighter out of Naples making her way down from Canadian waters and she should be with us mid-morning. The Chief thinks she's gotta a few kilos coke aboard and say's 'take a look at her.'"

There was a pause and then the booming voice continued "Boston also issued an UPP on two guys who shot Bill Munro at Harvard College and a cab driver on Harvard Bridge. You knew Bill, didn't you Frankie?"

"Yeah! I worked with him on the crime squad for two years. Poor bastard!"

"The hitmen are on the run. One's a thirty year old Latino guy and his youngster pal wears a blue beret. Do we respond to the UPP or do we go after the friggin Liberian freighter?"

Senior of the two officers, Frank Drago replied after a few moments' consideration "We're here to hit drug-runners, Charlie. It's hardly likely the runaways will come to this godforsaken town. We'll put the UPP on hold."

Cesare's position was painfully clear. In his attempted hit on Vinnie Teresa he had accidentally killed a high-ranking police officer in the tunnel at Harvard and, now, the hounds were baying for his blood. He slept fitfully and was ready to leave by daybreak but the Feds next door were already up and about, rummaging around their room and making preparations for their stakeout on the high seas. At 8.15am they went to the hotel dining room for breakfast and Carla and Cesare hurriedly scampered down the corridor, across the hotel forecourt and down a tree-lined lane alongside the main creek leading to Kennebunkport. Cesare needed an automobile to make a quick getaway and fast. He remembered Nico Falcone's advice in Saratoga 'If you need wheels in any small town, just hang around a bank or a village store. Someone in a hurry nearly always leaves their automobile unattended with the keys in the ignition. So you just help yourself,' which is precisely what Cesare did. At that time of the morning not many vehicles were around but, just after 9.00am, a Lovat-green Buick Convertible with sky-blue upholstery, pulled up outside the bank. A middle-aged lady with blue-rinsed hair emerged from the passenger seat dragging a matching, violet-dyed poodle behind her and teetered unsteadily on her high heels along the sidewalk. A portly gentleman puffed and panted his way out of the driver's seat and, hugging a black brief case, made his way up a few steps into the bank. As soon as the painted lady and her poodle turned the corner into Main Street the side road was empty except for the green convertible. The fat little man not only left his keys in the ignition but the 8-litre engine was also ticking over. The chance was too good to miss and, in a flash, Cesare was behind the wheel. With Carla by his side he sped over a swingbridge and out of Kennebunkport. Just outside town they took a left fork and headed west, and inland, towards New Hampshire.

The undercover FBI agents arrived at Kennebunkport police station to find the place in pandemonium and a sergeant being harassed by a fat little man supported by a purple-haired wife holding an excitable, snappy poodle whose tightly-curled coat was dyed in matching colours to its mistress' hair.

"Who the hell has stolen my Buick, Sergeant? Why don't you get out there and give chase?"

The wife joined in "It's my favourite car and the interior matches my hairstyle."

The police sergeant looked perplexed and, as boss and owner of Kennebunkport Fisheries, the irate man was stressing his importance in Town. An import from Bridlington in England he had lost none of his Yorkshire accent, guile or cussedness. Mr Postlethwaite called a spade a spade and he was not about to change character.

"But Mr Postlethwaite, unless you give me details of the Buick I canna put out a search call."

"Details! Details? You blithering idiot! You know my bloody car! It's the only green Buick tourer with blue upholstery in the whole of Maine and New Hampshire. A blind man could spot it a mile away."

"What's the registration, Mr Postlethwaite?"

"How should I know you bloody fool?"

His wife interjected timidly "I think it was registered in Boston."

"You keep out of this Vera. It's this buffoon's job to find out. Why the hell do we pay taxes?"

Sensing his master's rage the poodle yelped even louder.

"Shut that little pygmy up, Vera, before I kick its arse."

Vera now became hysterical.

"Don't you touch my little Fifi you monster" and she cradled the yelping dog in her arms. The situation was farcical and the FBI agents, who knew the sergeant well, stood aside smiling at his discomfiture. Suddenly, a breathless newspaper boy came running into the police station.

"I saw two men driving away in Mr Postlethwaite's Buick. The boy next to the driver was my age and was wearing a blue, cloth cap. They went over the swingbridge."

Frank Drago immediately took notice. He pushed up to the counter and flashed his FBI badge.

"I'll take care of this, Sergeant. What direction were they going?"

"North, sir" the paper-boy replied and, suddenly, the UPP became more significant than Drago's projected task for the day.

"Fill up the Mustang, Charlie. I'm gonna ring the Chief."

"At last something's happening" Mr Postlethwaite barked as Vera made futile attempts to soothe the overexcited poodle.

"There, there my little one! Papa doesn't mean to harm you."

The highly-strung dog lost control and bit her hand.

"There, there little Fifi! You didn't mean to do that did you?"

The poodle bit her hand again.

"Get rid of the bloody ferret" Mr Postlethwaite shouted and Vera burst into tears.

"Special agent Drago here, Sir. UPP suspects seen leaving Town in a stolen Buick Convertible"— Sergeant Drago was on the line to Boston Police HQ speaking to the inspector leading Captain Munro's murder investigation.

"Where the hell are you Drago?"

"I'm on a special narcotics stakeout with agent Charlie Spencer in Kennebunkport."

"Kennebunkport? That's in Maine aint it?"

"Yes, Sir! The suspects were going north when last seen."

The inspector paused to scan a chart on his wall "I'll alert our stations at Portland, Brunswick and Bangor Maine. Where else can they go?"

He paused again to look at his map.

"Christ! They've got at least six roads up north to the Canadian border. Take highway 302 to North Conway and give me details of the stolen vehicle."

"It's an 8 litre, green, Buick Tourer with blue interior, registered in Boston, Mass. It may smell of dog shit!"

"Pardon me, Drago. What did you say?"

"Last comment not relevant, Sir" said Drago with a wry smile. He met Mr Postlethwaite on his way out "We've got a lead on you car, Sir. I hope to get it back to you in few hours."

Postlethwaite drew himself up to his full height of 5ft 4inches.

"Thank God for the FBI! That bloody sergeant doesn't know his arse from his elbow."

The sergeant's face coloured in anger but he bit his tongue and remained silent. As the undercover agents sped away in their underpowered Ford Mustang, Mr Postlethwaite had grave doubts whether their scrapheap had a chance of catching his 8-litre monster. By now he had another problem on his hands. Vera was sulking and their penitent poodle was vigorously licking her salty, tear-stained face.

"Bloody hell, Vera!" was Mr Postlethwaite's sarcastic comment.

Little Cesare felt at ease at the wheel of the powerful green convertible. Without reference to a road map, he instinctively avoided Highway 302 and drove north-westwards along an interlocking network of secondary roads, skirting the northern boundary of Franconia National Park and dropping down alongside Moore Reservoir and into the hamlet of Bath where he called a halt. They had been motoring solidly for five hours and Cesare needed a rest. Boasting a multi-purpose village store, a

Presbyterian church, a traditional covered, wooden bridge and little else, Bath is a hamlet on the east bank of Wells River. Cesare parked the Buick out of sight near the river bank aɪ d lay down on the back seat while Carla went shopping in Brick Store. An inquisitive storekeeper got little change out of the strange-looking youth in a blue, cloth cap but he was helpful in informing Carla that interstate highway 302 from Franconia to Montpelier was only two miles down the road and Barre was a further 30 miles west. Cesare was fully awake by the time Carla returned to the car.

"We can't go on the highway in daylight. This old bobbydazzler will stick out like a sore thumb. We'll start out again when it gets dark" Cesare explained. Carla climbed into the back seat and nuzzled up beside Cesare. She felt safe and confident in his arms and they dozed fitfully until the light started fading and it was time to depart.

Whistling tunelessly to himself, Brick Store's owner was having a smoke on his veranda when a large green car suddenly appeared from behind his emporium and accelerated rapidly away. The Buick's powerful headlights partially blinded him but he distinctly saw his afternoon's customer, the young man wearing a blue cap, in the passenger seat. He shrugged his shoulders and went back into his store. One mile from Bath, on the slipway leading to Highway 302, Cesare pulled off the road and parked out of sight in a clump of larch trees and well clear of the motorway.

"It's not dark enough yet. We'll give it another forty minutes and then we'll make a dash for Barre and on to Martha Riley's Homestead."

Cesare lit a cigarette and held Carla's hand in the gathering gloom. They were preoccupied with their own thoughts and took no notice of a battered old Ford Mustang racing up the slip road and speeding westwards on Highway 302.

Agents Spencer and Drago had experienced a long and frustrating day's driving. Instead of using their skills in apprehending drug smugglers they had been sent on a wild goose chase from Maine, across New Hampshire and now, in the enveloping darkness, into Vermont. Lack of a radio transmitter in the Mustang meant frequent stops and delays on the way to report to Boston HQ from roadside telephone kiosks. They had followed Highway 302 most of the way but at Franconia Notch, Frank Drago had an idea and ordered Charlie Spencer "Take 117 and we'll avoid the 302 loop around The Old Man of the Mountain and Indian Head. According to this map we get to 302 again just outside a place called Bath."

Later, when agents Spencer and Drago received their citations for bravery, Charlie insisted that Frank's decision had been an inspiration but nothing could be further from the truth. Frank Drago was fed up to the back teeth with the whole exercise and wanted a change of scenery. They eventually arrived in Bath as daylight began to fade.

"Hey, Charlie, pull up here! I wanna packet of cigs and a few cans of beer. I've gotta feeling we're in for a long night."

Charlie Spencer brought the Mustang to a skidding halt outside Brick Store. Frank went inside and bought his purchases and added a sliced loaf and a pound of home-cured Vermont ham. The storekeeper was chatty "That ham ain't travelled far. It's as fresh as the morning dew and only crossed the river this afternoon. Did you know you're standing in New Hampshire in my store but across the Wells you'd be in Vermont?"

"You don't say?" Frank commented disinterestedly, and then, as an afterthought, he added "You ain't very busy tonight."

Counting out Frank's change the storekeeper moved sideways and glanced through the open door.

"That's a '48 Mustang ain't it?"

"Yep," Frank replied, picking up his loose coins and turning to leave.

"The car that left here a quarter ago was a beaut, a green '52

Buick Tourer."

Frank Drago spun around, his voice full of urgency "Did you see the guys in the convertible?"

"Yeah," the storekeeper replied, "one passenger came into my store this evening to buy provisions. He asked how far to Barre."

"Tell me! Was the young guy wearing a cap?"

"Come to think of it, he was, a flat blue beret."

Frank Drago flashed his FBI badge.

"Get me a telephone!"

"It ain't working" the storekeeper replied with a note of sarcasm and a hint of pleasure in his voice.

"Frig it," Drago shouted, "where's the nearest phone?"

"You'll be lucky to find a functioning kiosk between here and Barre. Yep! Barre's your best bet. It's thirty miles west on 302."

Drago was out of the store in a flash and into the Ford Mustang.

"Step on the gas, Charlie. The suspects left here about twenty minutes ago. I think they're taking 302 west to Barre."

Speeding along the highway Frank Drago had his eyes glued on the road ahead praying for a glimpse of a green Buick convertible. Contrary to popular belief Drago was an efficient federal agent who specialized in placing himself in the criminal's position. Scanning a road map by torchlight he gave vent to his thoughts "Tell you what he's up to Charlie! He'll keep on 302 to Burlington and up 89 to the Canadian border. If he gets to Philipville in Canada we've lost him. For Christ's sake, Charlie, put your friggin foot down and overtake this load of crap in front."

An overloaded lorry was holding them back.

"I'm on a long bend, Frankie."

"For once in your life take a friggin chance and go for it."

Charlie Spencer stepped on the gas and overtook the lorry.

Boston HQ's UPP had reached Barre police station late morning but there had been no sightings of a green Buick Tourer all day. Drago again put himself in the criminal's position and assumed, correctly, the glitzy Tourer had been taken off 302 to await total darkness before it made its final dash for the Canadian border along the main Highway. If he was wrong in his assumption then he, and Charlie Spencer, would suffer the consequences. Barre's police force was thin on the ground but Drago managed to muster three policemen and four vehicles with drivers to form a road block. He selected a spot four miles outside Groton where Highway 302 ran through a dense pine forest for an inclined, straight mile and a half. The highway's edges at this point were steeply cambered and there were no side roads, or exits, leading off the main road. Halfway along the straight mile, and on the left hand side of the road, a manmade lay-by had been cut out of the pine forest and a granite statue, The Sleeping Sentinel, had been erected by the citizens of Groton in memory of a local farmboy, one John Scott, who had been sentenced to death for falling asleep on sentry duty during the American Civil War. A last minute reprieve from President Abraham Lincoln saved his life, hence the popular usage of his name in the saying 'going Scott free'. John Scott's luck did not last long, however, and he was killed in battle a year later. Having placed a barrier of vehicles across Highwy 302 at the Barre end of the rising straight road, Drago and Spencer advanced 800 yards to their present position at the base of the Sleeping Sentinel and now, sharing a can of beer, awaited the possible arrival of Mr Postlethwaite's Buick Convertible. Frank Drago was calm and collected but Spencer was edgy and jumpy.

"I spotted this place, Charlie, as we made our run for Barre. It's the only turning point on this stretch for three thousand yards. When he sees the roadblock he'll either go for it or pull in here, maybe to turn around. That'll be our chance to jump them. Are you okay, Charlie?"

Charlie Spencer was a little nervous and feeling sick. This would be his first action using live bullets on live targets and the tension was getting to him.

"I'm okay, Frankie," he replied with exaggerated bravado.

Cesare waited for complete darkness to descent before edging the Tourer out of the larch copse on to Highway 302. The road ahead was brilliantly illuminated by the Buick's powerful headlamps and, between Bath and Groton, they passed a dozen vehicles travelling in the opposite direction. Two miles beyond Groton, Highway 302 took a sharp left turn and Cesare accelerated into a gently rising tree-lined, straight road. He had only gone half a mile when he became aware of a row of lights stretching across the road in the far distance and possibly blocking the Highway. He reduced speed and started cruising and, eventually, brought the Buick gently to a halt. The sudden deceleration roused Carla from a daydream and she sat up abruptly "What's wrong Cesare?"

"I think there's trouble ahead. Do you see those lights across the road? It may be a road block. We'd better turn around and get off this highway."

In the beam of the car's headlights Carla pointed to a layby 200 hundred yards ahead on the left side of the road "Look, Cesare, pull in there."

"Okay," Cesare agreed, "I need to go to the john anyway."

The Buick coasted slowly off the road on to the gravel layby and came to a stop opposite the Sleeping Sentinel monument. Cesare doused the headlights, flung open the car door and, leaving the engine turning over, stepped outside and went behind the granite statue. He undid his zip and commenced to urinate.

Frank Drago and Charlie Spencer had been lying in wait ten yards inside the pine forest when the big Tourer pulled into the Silent Sentinel's layby. They could not believe their eyes as the car door opened and a man got out and walked towards them, finally standing with his back to the hidden agents and urinating against the statue's plinth. In the courtesy light inside the car Drago saw a second seated figure, wearing a blue cap, in the passenger seat. He nudged Charlie "These are our guys," he hissed from the side of his mouth, "let's go get 'em."

Guns in hand, the FBI agents rushed at the dim outline of the suspect.

"Okay buddy! Hands over your head" Drago commanded. In mid-process of directing his urinary stream this order was a physical impossibility and, still holding his penis in one hand, Cesare turned to pee in the agent's direction. It was at this point, and Charlie Spencer swore it was true, he suspected the man held a gun in his hand. Charlie lost his nerve and began firing at Cesare's silhouette. Drago had no option but to join in and, all in all, nine bullets entered Cesare's body while he was erect and falling to the ground. Ironically, one bullet ploughed into his exposed penis, later described as the mobster's 'handgun' by the jubilant Charlie Spencer. Cesare's death was almost instantaneous. He finally lay in a crumpled heap at the foot of the Sleeping Sentinel, surrounded by a widening circle of blood and urine as his bladder continued discharging in spurts down his trouser leg. Reverberations from the gunshots had hardly died away when Drago shouted "Come on Charlie let's get the guy in the auto" but, by the time they got to the front of the statue, the Buick was back on the road and moving away with screeching tyres.

On hearing gunshots Carla, who had never driven a vehicle in her life, slid across to the driver's seat, released the handbrake, crashed the gears and pressed down hard on the accelerator. The powerful machine screamed into action and surged down 302 towards the police barricade. The federal agents fired three more bullets at the disappearing vehicle which had advanced 300 hundred yards down the road, swerving and swaying in an erratic fashion. Clinging to the steering wheel for dear life, Carla groped for the main beam switch and, at that moment, lost control of the car. The Tourer slewed sideways throwing Carla out on to a gravel path at the roadside and then careered to the right in a straight line crossing Highway 302 and plunged twenty feet into a rock strewn gully. A complete write-off, Mr Postlethwaite's prize possession ended up in a mangled heap of green metal and chrome in a dry-river bed off Highway 302. The FBI agents and the Barre cops arrived at the crash scene at the same time. Frank Drago breathlessly announced "The younger guy got away in the Tourer but we got a few shots off and he's probably dead inside the limo. Let's take a look."

But there were no bodies in Mr Postelthwaite's convertible only a blue cloth cap and a fully-loaded, unfired Biretta .38. There were no signs of the dead mobster's 'boy' and, despite prolonged searches by Barre police over the following week, the owner of the blue cloth cap was never found and apprehended.

CHAPTER 18

Little Augie Pisano and Mrs Drake

DON CORLEONE SAT SWELTERING in an oven-hot cell in Danemmora Penitentiary reflecting on where things had gone wrong. By August 1959 he had served five months of his 15 year sentence on a 'bum' narcotics rap which had delivered him, like a trussed chicken, into the hands of the Federal authorities. Twelve of his Family, including his son Santino and Vincent 'The Chin' Gigante, had been put away for shorter sentences. Genovese was paranoid about his frame-up and suspected everybody and everyone but, in the end, he came up with one name – Little Augie Pisano. Though incarcerated, Genovese had no intention of loosening his grip on his Family's affairs and appointed Carlo Gambino and Tony Bender as his external agents. He suspected all along that Frank Costello masterminded his frame-up but, in a clever counterplot, he nominated Costello to oversee a 'hit' on Pisano, his most loyal lieutenant and lifelong friend. In order to put his own Family in Don Corleone's good books, and to allay suspicion about his involvement in Genovese's stitch-up, Costello agreed to supervise the hit and made Carlo Gambino and Tony Bender linkmen and Al Rizzi was nominated to provide a triggerman. And therein lay Al's difficulty. His prize hitman was lying stone-cold in a paupers cemetery at Barre and Carla was missing, believed killed, somewhere in the impenetrable forests alongside Highway 302 in Vermont. Added to all this Lucky Luciano in Naples was going berserk and hounding Costello with repeated requests for an urgent hit on Franco Gicanetti, the troublesome Neapolitan Capo. And then, out of the blue, a telephone call on September 17th solved all Rizzi's problems and enabled him to kill two birds with one stone.

Carla stood in a public callbox in Barre holding Al Rizzi's

dog-eared business card in one hand and, with trembling fingers, she dialled Berterelli's. Through the glass panels she could see Jake smoking a cigarette and leaning against the trunk of a battered old station wagon station waggon. A tall red-haired man with a florid face and calloused, ham-like fists Jake was an employee of the mining company where Carla had been sheltering for the past two months. Her escape from the fatal ambush, and scene of her accident, had been a miracle and a nightmare. For the first hour she plunged through forest undergrowth, stopping and listening at intervals for the sounds of a pursuit, but none came. Eventually, around midnight and utterly exhausted, she fell asleep propped up against a fallen tree trunk. At around 5.00 am the canopy above her head became lighter and she pressed forwards following a brook running in a westerly direction. After a mile the stream passed under a man-made, wooden bridge and a path upwards, and around a bend, led her to a mining encampment in a clearing in the forest. An awry, wooden board announced she had arrived at the Palermo Granite Mining Company and the smell of fried bacon directed her to a mess hut where a dozen miners where breakfasting. A large blonde lady wearing a blue and white, striped apron came to her aid. Carla's skirt and blouse were torn and she had facial abrasions and her hair was matted with thick mud and thorns. Fat Mamma swallowed Carla's concocted story that she had been abducted from Montpellier by a commercial traveller and ran away to avoid being raped. The miners were none too anxious to report any incident, or her unexpected arrival, to the police. They had two illicit liquor stills in the hills behind the encampment and the presence of law officers, at any time, was distinctly unwelcome.

On her first trip out of the encampment Carla was nervous and wary and her driver was getting restless for another reason. The Palermo bosses paid the miners 'pick time' and Jake was losing money hanging around with Carla in Barre. He tapped the glass and indicated with his enormous thumb it was time to depart. At that moment the ringing tone ceased and a deep voice came on the line "Berterelli's! Salvatore speaking. What can I do for ya?"

Carla crouched over the phone and spoke in a whisper "I wish to speak to Signore Rizzi."

"Yeah! Everyone wants to speak to the Boss. Who's asking?"

"Tell him it's Carla."

"Jesus, Carla, where are you? Hang on! The Boss is right here." Al snatched the phone.

"Carla! Carla! Are you okay?"

"Yes, Signore Rizzi. I'm in a kiosk in Barre."

There was a long pause at the other end.

"Barre! That's a bit of luck. My cousin is in business there. His name is also Alphonse Rizzi. Go and see him and he'll fix you up. I'll let him know to expect you. You'll find his place next to Aldinifratti and Berganti stonemasons on Main Street. Salvatore says he's sorry to hear about Cesare. So am I, Carla."

"Gracie Signore Rizzi" and Carla hung up.

Outside the telephone booth Jake was sitting impatiently behind the wheel of his station waggon, revving the engine and anxious to get moving.

"I'm not going back with you Jake. Thank Mamma for taking care of me. I'll call around one day and thank her myself."

"Goddamnit woman!" Jake exploded and slammed the waggon into gear leaving Carla standing forlornly outside the empty phone kiosk.

Al Rizzi and Carla were sitting together in the study of his Long Island mansion. Since her return from Barre on September 17th Carla had been quiet and withdrawn and still in shock after Cesare's murder and her own harrowing experiences on Highway 302. Al was a good judge of character and felt the time was ripe to prepare Carla for her last assignment in New York before returning to Italy. He laid his cigar aside in an ashtray and stared at the morose woman.

"Have you had enough of America?.," he inquired. Carla simply nodded her head in assent.

"You can return to Italy, or Sicily, but first I have a contract here in New York. Are you aware the attempt on Vinnie Teresa in Boston failed because there was a leak? We now know the squealer and we want him hit."

Carla's mask-like face hardened and a steely glint appeared in her deep-set brown eyes. Whomsoever squealed was equally responsible for killing Fat Vinnie's armed police bodyguard and, indirectly, for Cesare's murder. She was not aware Al Rizzi had made up the story but she knew she wanted to avenge Cesare's assassination by the Feds.

"Tell me who did it Signore Rizzi?"

Carla could not get around to calling Al – Boss, Don Rizzi, or simply Alphonse.

"It was the hitman with Cesare at Zwillman's place in West Orange."

Carla's face registered disbelief "Little Augie! I can't believe it! He's such a likeable man."

But she remembered there was nothing pleasant about him when he went to work on Abner 'Longy' Zwillman in the basement of his house in West Orange.

"Yes, he's charming, but he has a tongue as long as Triborough Bridge. He's the stoolpigeon."

Carla simply said "I'll do it, Signore Rizzi."

Claudia took Carla shopping at Bloomingdales a few days later and purchased expensive, matching suitcases and half a dozen haute couture dresses and accessories. Al produced two American passports, one in Carla's maiden name of Cecci, and the second in the name of Carla Ceserano, her married title. And then it was a question of waiting at Rizzi's Long Island mansion for a call to blow away Augie Pisano.

On September 29th 1959 Tony Bender arranged to dine with Little Augie Pisano at Marino's Restaurant in the same avenue as the famous Copacabana Club. Little Augie was not alone and had brought along the wife of a well-known New York comedian as a paramour and companion. They were about to start their meal when Bender excused himself and telephoned Carlo Gambino.

"I'm with Little Augie and his moll at Marino's Restaurant. We're just sitting down to eat and we'll be here for a coupla hours. The little man ain't got no protection and he's knocking back the booze."

"Damn it!," Gambino swore, "we don't want a hooker in the way, but the hit goes on."

Carlo Gambino passed on details to Al Rizzi at Berterelli's and he, in turn, raced across to Long Island to pick up Carla and dropped her outside the Copacabana Club. He then rang Marino's Restaurant from a telephone kiosk and asked to speak to Augie Pisano. The three diners were at the coffee and brandy stage when the head waiter came to their table "Excuse me, Mr Pisano, you're wanted on the telephone."

Little Augie followed the maitre-d' to a booth at the back of the premises.

"Sorry to disturb your meal, Augie."

"Yeah! That's okay. What's up, Boss?"

"A soldier has been dropped outside the Copacabana Club by mistake and is needed in up-town Brooklyn in fifty minutes."

A lifelong member of Costello's Family, Little Augie had every faith in Alphonse Rizzi and did not question the orders.

"Okay, Boss. But I gotta friggin dame with me."

"It's urgent, Augie. Dump her if you have to."

"Okay, I'll do that in case there's friggin fireworks. Who's the soldier, Boss?"

"She was with you at Longy's mansion in West Orange."

"Carla! Little Cesare's dame?"

"The same broad. Get on with it Augie."

. As the pick-up package had turned out to be Carla, Little Augie felt safe enough to take his lover along for the joy-ride. He returned to the table and spoke to his paramour "Shake your butt, Honey! We're outa here to pick-up a friggin broad outside The Copacabana."

Mrs Drake rose unsteadily to her feet and giggl d when Little Augie slapped a horny hand on her right buttock. Tony Bender rose and embraced Pisano in a bear hug and they kissed each other on the cheek and, finally, fully on the lips. Little Augie missed the significance of that final goodbye kiss. In a Mafia fraternity it usually meant a final farewell before passage to another world. With apologies to Bender they hurriedly left Marino's Restaurant with Mrs Janice Drake hanging on lovingly to Little Augie's elbow and teetering unsteadily on her high heels.

In a plain black overcoat Carla was waiting at the kerbside outside the Copacabana Club and immediately recognised the short, well-dressed mobster with a tall, blonde hustler, draped in a mink coat, clinging to his right arm. The randy little man could certainly pick the best-lookers in Town and Mrs Drake was no exception. At 5ft. 10ins, and with her high heels and beehive hairstyle, she towered a good two feet above the diminutive mobster.

"Good evening, Signore Pisano."

"Hi there, Carla! My Cadillac's parked just around the corner. Where's we goin'?"

"To Ebbets Field parking lot. Just drop me there."

In the black Cadillac Mrs Drake sat almost in Little Augie's lap and the top of her bouffant hairdo extended at least twelve inches above his balding pate. Carla had not been introduced to Pisano's paramour and sat on the back seat cradling a Biretta and silencer in her lap. Despite an interruption to his night's pleasure Pisano was in a happy mood. A good meal, the best wine and cigars in Town and a scented vixen at his side, all added up to bliss in Augie's book and, as he drove along, he inharmoniously hummed an unrecognisable tune. As they crossed Manhattan Bridge and approached Flatbush Avenue he slowed down.

"Shall we take a left here, Carla?"

Carla was unsure and then saw a dilapidated notice board —'To Baseball Stadium.'

"Yes. Take a left Augie."

Within a minute they pulled up in a deserted parking lot. Little Augie laughed "We took a wrong 'un there, Carla. There ain't no other way outa this friggin place."

They had arrived at Ebbets Field, the ancestral home of the Brooklyn Dodgers. The Dodgers had moved their headquarters to Los Angeles in 1957 and their old stadium was now due for demolition. The car park was deserted. Pisano announced to no one in particular "I'll swing around here and make for Franklyn Avenue."

But Carla had reached the desired spot for her purposes. Mrs Drake was giggling and getting frisky and rested her head against Little Augie's right shoulder. He responded and buried his face in the bottle-blonde's beehive when, suddenly, he felt a cold pressure on the back of his neck and Carla's voice pronouncing the death sentence "This is for Cesare."

There was a muted thud inside the Cadillac and immediate oblivion for Little Augie. The front of his skull and portions of his brain were spattered over the windscreen and instrument panel. Mrs Drake screamed and clasped her head in her hands. Carla calmly grabbed the crown of her hair and released two shots into the back of her head producing a matching pattern of blood and brain on the passenger side of the shattered windscreen. Carla left the pair hunched close together, like cooing doves, and they were found exactly in this position by a roving police patrol car the following morning. Cursory investigations by law enforcement officers drew a blank and, as usual in gangland killings in the 50's, they were not too particular about finding the culprits who had perpetrated the killings. Carla walked away from the scene of the assassination without a backward glance. She had no qualms about putting Mrs Drake to sleep and, if the silly harlot enjoyed the company of gangsters, she should accept the fate which mobsters were exposed to day in and day out. On the slip road leading away from Ebbets Field car park Al Rizzi and Salvatore Falcone were waiting in an Oldsmobile.

"Hit good?" Al Rizzi asked.

"Yes, both hit good, Signore Rizzi" Carla replied and Al gave a nod of approval. They made their way sedately homewards to Long Island and, en route, dumped the murder weapon over Brooklyn Bridge into the depths of the Hudson River.

Carla had a week to wait before departing for Naples on the luxury liner Regina Italia. Dressed in all her finery she booked into the Waldorf Astoria three days after the hit on Augie Pisano and Mrs Drake. In Carla, Al Rizzi had a custom-built assassin to do a job for Lucky Luciano but she would need further motivation and he made up his mind the time was ripe to tell her about the existence of her long-lost son. They met in Carla's private suite at the Waldorf Astoria two days before she was due to sail for Europe. Al used a direct approach "When I was in Naples four years ago I met a twelve year old boy in the Big Boss' house. I think he was your son."

Carla felt faint and slumped heavily into a chair.

"Alfonzo is alive? No! No! Are you sure? Where is my boy?" and she burst into tears. Her thin frame shuddered and her wailing sobs reverberated around the room. Eventually she pulled herself together and Al continued "When Cesare came across to the States for the first time in 1950 he told me Franco Gicanetti was living in

Calabria and had two girls and a six year old boy."

Carla interrupted "But Franco and the fat boy Branco were killed by your soldiers outside Godrano in 1943."

"Apparently not. Franco got away and is now Naples' Capo. His boy, and your son Alfonzo, is living with Lucky Luciano. As you're returning to Italy you have every right to know."

Suddenly Carla was excited and paced up and down the floor.

"Will I meet my little Alfonzo in Naples?"

"Little Alfonzo is not so little. By now he's nearly sixteen years old and Lucky doesn't know you're his mother" Al replied.

"Then I'll tell him" said Carla aggressively.

"I don't think so, Carla. There's one obstacle in all this business and that's Franco Gicanetti. The Big Boss want's him put away. If you can hit him you could then lay claim to your son."

Al looked at her inquiringly. Carla's face was flushed but she spoke calmly and deliberately "Franco raped me when we ———— —-"and she blushed and stammered "I will do a hit on the swine."

Al Rizzi was satisfied with his night's work. He had managed to motivate Carla into performing a final assassination and to honour the Big Boss' long-overdue contract in Naples. He was also confident that Carla would carry out a professional execution and he was sending Luciano an expert terminator to do the job.

CHAPTER 19

Carla's revenge

SIGNORE FANTOCCIO, HOTEL TURISTICO'S MANAGER, had been in a flap all morning. By 11.30 am his prize patron had not turned up for coffee at his usual time of 10.15 am and he was a man of punctual habits. In an ancient green Oldsmobile coupe, Luciano regularly drove himself from his luxury lat at Vomero and called at a barber shop on his way to his 'office' at Hotel Turistico. Afterwards he went for an aperitif at Hotel Excelsiore on the waterfront and then, at around 12.30pm, on to Ristorante Giocomino for a spaghetti lunch. But on October 17th he was late and the absence of police shadows was sure evidence something was wrong. At 11.50 am the Big Boss appeared and Signore Fantocchio took a cup of cappuccino into his private 'office' at the rear of the dining room.

"Any mail today Signore Fantoccio?"

"Not this morning, Signore Luciano, but there's a Signora to see you in room 222."

Luciano was expecting a visiting hitman from New York and the lady could well be the mobster's mistress or wife. He drank his coffee and made his way upstairs. In response to a buzzer, Carla opened the door wide.

"Come in, Signore Luciano."

Luciano glanced at the diminutive woman and scanned the bedroom.

"You're a broad! I was expecting a wiseguy."

Her head held high, Carla proudly replied "I'm your hitman, Signore Luciano."

Charlie Lucky was momentarily stunned but quickly recovered.

"I trust Frankie Costello and Al Rizzi to make a good choice. I gotta be downstairs in a minute but I'll be here tomorrow at 10.30

to show you the sights" and, eyeing Carla up and down, he continued "Wear a plain dress. That outfit is too flashy and be ready at ten thirty prompt."

"I'll be in the foyer," Carla offered.

"No you won't! You gotta stay here for me" Luciano ordered and Carla knew better than to remonstrate with the Big Boss. Back in his office Lucky had a word with the manager "I was late today because I had to see a medico about some friggin chest pains. It's all baloney! Make sure there's some mail for me when I arrive tomorrow morning for coffee, Signore Fantoccio."

"Grazie, Signore Luciano" the fawning hotelier replied. Luciano had developed severe chest pains during the night and a physician diagnosed angina and prescribed GTN tablets. He was advised to take things easy but that was easier said than done. Charles 'Lucky' Luciano had a hectic lifestyle and did not know the meaning of relaxation.

Next day Luciano parked his Oldsmobile outside Hotel Turistico at 10-15am and the police surveillance agents took up their usual positions in the hotel's foyer. He made his way to his 'office' but diverted in an elevator to Carla's room on the second floor. With a 'opsided grin Luciano drawled "Follow me! I gotta half hour to show you Naples."

He led Carla down a fire escape to a courtyard and staff parking lot and they drove away in a battered old Fiat through Naples' backstreets. Lucky behaved like a truant schoolboy, excited at the thought he was evading the 'bum' police. Within ten minutes they were in the Quartieri Spagnola district where the streets were narrow and filthy and the people poorly-dressed and scruffy. Luciano pulled up outside a dilapidated house with a crumbling portico which, during Spanish occupation, had been the Commanding Officer's quarter. The only indication of its present use was a solitary red bulb over a weather-beaten wooden door. Lucky indicated with his thumb "Franco uses this brothel two or three times a week. I suggest you hit him when he's goin' in or comin' out. You do know Gicanetti?"

"Yes, I know him."

Carla spat out the words with venom and her body stiffened as if she was reliving her rape. On their way back to Turistico's staff car park Luciano outlined his plan.   " The hotel rooms may be bugged but it's safe to talk here. I wanna be away when you hit Gicanetti and I'm gonna Capri tomorrow. When you're ready to go collect a package from Signore Fantoccio. It will contain a loaded Biretta and a silencer. After the hit dump the gun and get back here and sit tight. I'll send someone to pick you up. Well, here we are at the hotel. Is all that okay?"

"Grazie Signore Luciano."

On her brief tour in the Fiat, Carla had seen the pensione she had shared with Cesare during their hit on Gicanetti senior in 1953. And, what was of greater import,the decrepit little hostel was only two blocks away from the seedy brothel in the Spanish Quarter.

Dressed in a shabby grey frock, and with her hair collected in an austere bun, Carla rang the bell of the brothel one evening later in the week. Announcing at the hotel she was off to Rome for a few days and wished her room reserved, she left via the fire escape and, carrying a few belongings and a pistol in a canvas bag, she had moved across to the rundown pensione in the Spanish Quarter. The brothel door was opened by a jewel-bedecked, fat woman in her mid-fifties dressed in a fluffy red blouse and a black skirt, so short it revealed her fishnet-stockinged thighs. Mutton dressed as lamb, the virago had a heavy-jowled, podgy face and held an ivory cigarette holder in her right hand. Her welcoming smile faded rapidly when she saw the thin figure of the bird-like woman standing on her doorstep.

"Yes, what is it?"

"I'm looking for work. I've just come off a Palermo ferry and a man on the boat said you might have a job for me."

The red-lipped harlot burst out laughing, revealing a row of jagged yellow teeth.

"The man had a sense of humour. No! I have no work for you. My House is full."

She began closing the door and, as an afterthought, added "I need a housemaid. It doesn't pay much but, if you're interested, you could start tonight."

"Yes, please, Madame. I need the money."

Carla followed the woman along a passageway into a large dimly-lit lounge with boarded windows facing the outside street. She sat on a plush leather armchair and the Madame took her seat behind an ornate mahogany desk. She fluffed the ruffles on her gaudy, red blouse and lit a fresh cigarette.

"My House is devoted to the pleasures of the flesh for the men of Naples. Do you understand? What is your name signorigna?"

"I'm called Carmelita. And, yes, I do understand what you told me."

"Good! Good! I am known as Madame Carmen which is the name of my House. I have ten girls working for me and we are open for business every night from dusk till dawn, excepting Sundays. We have twelve rooms upstairs and your job will be to tidy-up and change bed linen after each client. The motto of Carmen's House is cleanliness and my House has the best reputation in Naples. Clients are exposed to two diseases. One is prevented by the girls' three-monthly visit to Professore Magliocco's VD clinic and the other, bed bugs, is taken care of by changing sheets after each client has departed and that's where you come in. I don't pay a wage and the girls leave your tip in the bedroom. Part of your duties is to take used sheets to a laundry on your way home and bring them back, washed and ironed, in the evening. Do you still want the job?"

"Yes, please, Madame Carmen."

Barely larger than a generous-sized broom cupboard a stockroom was located in a cellar down some stone steps leading from the front hall and, on the lintel above the doorway, nine numbered electric bulbs were evident.

"When the bedrooms are vacated the number of the room ready for cleaning will come up on this panel. You will then go upstairs, tidy the room, change the sheets and bring any dirty linen down here to be packed for the laundry. That's all you have to do. Do you think you can manage it, Carmelita?"

"Yes, Madame Carmen. I'll start work tonight."

The blousy Madame had neither asked for Carla's surname nor her address. The brothel's employees were acting on the blind side of the Law and many of their clientele were businessmen, the judiciary and off-duty police officers in mufti.

On her first night at the brothel Carla learnt a lot more about Madame Carmen's establishment. The Madame sat behind a mahogany desk in the lounge and, when not entertaining clients, her string of prostitutes lounged around in various states of undress, smoking, drinking and chatting. To distinguish her from the working girls Madame issued Carla with a white apron and linen bonnet and, during non-business hours, these clothes were kept in a locker in the basement. On her second night at work Carla hid a loaded Biretta and silencer behind her locker. During a lull in business the lounge became a communal gossip parlour and the whores sat around discussing the merits, sexual deviations and copulatory prowess of their various clients and, on these occasions, Carla was all ears. On a quiet period on Thursday night in the second week she overheard a conversation between two whores.

"The Beast hasn't been in this week has he Maria?"

"Don't call him by that name Renata! He's really quite nice though he gets a bit rough at times. Anyway, he pays me well."

"A little rough!," Renata snorted, "I saw your backside last week after he'd finished with you. It was black and blue. I'm glad you're Franco's favourite. You can have him as far as I am concerned."

Maria sniggered "I'll have him all to myself tomorrow night. He pays me extra on Fridays."

Carla heard what she wanted to hear and scurried off to the basement to pick up a load of clean sheets. The light bulb from room 5 requesting a valet service was on and tomorrow night Maria would be entertaining Franco Gicanetti in one of the rooms. Carla hoped it would be No 9, her lucky number, and it might turn out to be an extremely unlucky number for the Beast of Naples.

Franco Gicanetti and three drunken mobsters came into the bordello at around 10.00 pm on the Friday. Three prostitutes were 'busy' upstairs and another four were draped seductively on chaise longues in the lounge. Carla hovered in the background near the cellar stairs and immediately recognised Franco as he strode up to Madame Carmen's desk and bellowed "Buonasera Signora Carmen! What have you for me tonight?"

"All the girls are available, Signore Gicanetti. Maria is free."

"She'll do me fine," Franco sneered. The Madame glanced at a printed list on her desk and called out "Maria! Take Signore Franco to room 9."

Dressed in a revealing negligee a black-haired harlot glided across the floor and held Franco's elbow, guiding him unsteadily upstairs. On the first floor they met a client and Victoria coming out of room 3. Franco leered at the embarrassed man "Did Victoria give you a good time Signore? She's nearly as good in bed as my little Maria" and he slapped a large, horny hand on Maria's right buttock. The whore giggled and they staggered along to room 9 at the far end of the third floor corridor. By this time Franco's bodyguards were chatting and mingling with the prostitutes in the reception lounge.

Carla waited ten minutes before emerging from the cellar carrying a dozen clean sheets and her loaded Biretta and silencer were sandwiched between two pillows. She tidied room 3 on the first floor, replaced the bedsheets and picked up a 10.000 lire note from the washstand. She then went to the third floor where two lighted green bulbs indicated the bedrooms were occupied and the noises from within left little doubt as to the nature of the activity inside. Madame Carmen's house rules were strict and no one could enter a bedroom when a green light was showing and, for the safety of her girls, clients were forbidden to lock bedroom doors. Listening to the increasing tempo of the sexual activity Carla lingered for half a minute outside room 9 and then, gun in one hand and pillow in the other, she silently opened the bedroom door and closed it noiselessly behind her. The bedroom was in near-total darkness and lit only by a low voltage table lamp which revealed two naked figures copulating wildly on the bed. Franco was at the climactic zenith of his sexual frenzy, grunting, groaning and bellowing in turn, while his servile partner lay under him, eyes tightly shut, simulating orgasms and urging Franco on to further excesses. In three quick strides Carla was at the bedside and, using the pillow as a baffle, she thrust the Biretta's silencer against the side of Franco's forehead and pulled the trigger. The grunting and bellowing stopped abruptly and, still coupled, Franco's jerking body lay slumped on top of his sexual partner. Carla's second shot was delivered to the back of Franco's head and ploughed through his skull to exit at his forehead and slam into Maria's left eye socket. The prostitute screamed and struggled to get her head clear from under Franco and, as she opened her mouth to scream again, Carla knew Maria would have to join Franco in eternity. She thrust the Biretta into the whore's open mouth, pushed the pillow over her face, and the bullet went through the roof of Maria's palate and shattered the base of her skull. The muffled thuds of the shots went unheard by occupants of bedrooms along the corridor. They were making enough noise of their own to deaden any unusual disturbances and Maria's piercing scream was put down to an overexuberant orgasm.

Without a second glance Carla left the bodies in their compromising position and hid her Biretta in the folds of a linen sheet. She calmly descended the stairs, walked across the reception area, and dumped the soiled laundry in the basement. In the stockroom she removed her apron and bonnet, thrust the pistol inside her underclothes, and let herself out of the brothel through the front door. Gicanetti's car was parked at the kerbside outside Madame Carmen's whorehouse and, wishing the driver 'buonanotte,' Carla strode briskly up the road into the heart of the labyrinthine Quartieri Spagnola. She discarded her Biretta in a drinking well and, half an hour later, she was luxuriating in a hot bath in her bedroom at Hotel Turistico. Carla had no qualms about murdering the unfortunate Maria, who would have been a key witness to Gicanetti's assassination. She had achieved a lifetime vendetta - to kill the man who raped her in 1943 and the same man who abducted her son in 1947 - and her only regret was not being able to taunt Gicanetti before dispatching him. As she stretched out in the hot water she felt surprisingly euphoric which proved the axiom 'revenge is sweet' to be true in every sense. Franco Gicanetti had been a thorn in their flesh for two years and his death came as a relief to the Neapolitan Carabinieri. Twice arrested for manslaughter, on each occasion, he walked away a free man thanks to Lucky Luciano's intervention and protection. When the assassination was committed, Luciano was under surveillance at his Anacapri villa and naturally denied all knowledge of the crime. Mafia mobsters were never missed by the Carabinieri who were none too thorough in their investigations into the double shooting in Madame Carmen's bordello. The unfortunate prostitute had no known relatives and Madame Carmen was anxious to protect the good name of her establishment as, in her opinion, it was the best whorehouse in Naples, if not in the whole of Italy.

Lucky Luciano came up to Naples for Franco Gicanetti's

funeral, a low-key affair only attended by members of Neapolitan crime families. Lucky was accompanied by a dark-haired, good-looking sixteen year old boy elegantly dressed in a dark suit. It rained heavily throughout the funeral service and Alfonzo shared an umbrella with his Uncle Charlie. The boy was present to offer his last respects to his departed father but felt no remorse, or sense of guilt, only gratitude that Luciano had taken him under his wing and now treated him as his own son. Carla watched the cortege drive slowly past on its way to the cemetery and, for the first time in twelve years, she saw her son sitting next to Luciano in a chauffer-driven car. She burst into tears as happy memories of their spartan days at St Giorgio's convent came flooding back. A curious woman bystander saw her grieving.

"I don't know why you're crying, Signora. That man in the coffin isn't worth two lire bits and we'll be better off without him."

But Carla kept sobbing uncontrollably, tears of relief and joy at seeing her handsome, grown-up son again. And now she wanted him back and was prepared to go to any length to achieve her goal. She did not have to go to this extreme and, unwittingly, Lucky Luciano played into her hands over lunch at Da Giocomino's Restaurant on the Saturday after Gicanetti's funeral. The Big Boss was in a jovial mood.

"I have two villas south of here, one on Capri and the other at the seaside about fifteen miles south of Sorrento. Gicanetti's sixteen year old boy lives in my Sorrento joint and I wanna housekeeper to look after him. At Villa Annunziata we gotta tutor five days a week. The job is yours if you want it, Miss Carla."

Luciano was playing right into her hands by inviting her to look after her own son. Carla did not hesitate in replying "Yes, Signore Luciano, I will keep house for you at Villa Annunziata."

Lucky Luciano smiled "Okay Carla. Signore Fantoccio will arrange a jalopy to take you down to Sorrento at the weekend. And please call me Charlie from now on."

But Carla could never bring herself to use his familiar name and he remained Signore Luciano for the rest of their time together.

At Franco Gicanetti's funeral, Lucky Luciano made a point of introducing Alfonzo to a few Neapolitan mobsters and, a fortnight later, he convened a meeting of top-ranking Neapolitan Families at Hotel Excelsiore to discuss Gicanetti's successor. Luciano's ambition was to promote Alfonzo to the position when he became of age and, for the intervening four years, he himself was prepared to re-assume the mantle of Boss in Naples. But his plan misfired miserably and the mourning mobsters were intent on arguing about the spoils left after Franco Gicanetti's execution. The bulk of their illicit income came from drug-trafficking to which Luciano was outwardly opposed. His stance led to bitter outbursts and his suggestion for Alfonzo's future placement was rejected out of hand. The mobsters decided to go their own separate ways and to fight their own corners. The meeting broke up in disarray and aggravated Family feuds and vendettas and, as drugs were the main bone of contention, the cancer spread to Sicily which was recognised as the drug-trading centre for Europe and North America. By 1960 Luciano had virtually lost control of the Italian and Sicilian F milies and, added to his bust-up with Meyer Lansky in the States, his power and sources of income as Boss of Bosses of the worldwide Mafia had almost completely dissolved into thin air. These worries and stresses contributed to a deterioration in his health and placed an extra strain on his already failing heart.

CHAPTER 20

Lucky Luciano's Waterloo

ON THE FIRST SUNDAY IN NOVEMBER 1959 Carla was driven to Luciano's seaside retreat south of Sorrento. Villa Annunziata was located on a peninsula jutting into the Tyrrhenian Sea and equidistant between Sorrento and the seaside township of Annunziata. There were two other secluded ,illas on the promontory and each had its own private pebble beach, reached by stone steps on the steep cliff face, and a boat house at the water's edge. A homely middle-aged Italian couple served as caretakers and Senora Franconi was also maid, cleaner and cook. The Franconi's made Carla welcome and she was allocated a bedroom in the villa and the simply-furnished room became her home for the next two years.

At teatime on the day of her arrival Carla was sitting on the sun terrace admiring the magnificent panoramic seascape when an old man, with an unkempt head of frizzly white hair and wearing unrimmed spectacles, casually approached and inclined his head "Buonasera! You must Alonzo's new governess. Let me introduce myself. I am Professore Enzio Tutti, Alonzo's tutor."

They shook hands formally and Carla immediately took to the grizzly-haired academician. The Professore poured himself a cup of lemon tea and sat down beside Carla.

"I'm thirsty after my bicycle ride from Sorrento. I return home on Fridays and get back here on Sunday evening. Alonzo has lessons each day between eight in the morning and three o'clock. Signore Luciano took me on in 1957 and, in two years, the boy has come on in leaps and bounds. At first he couldn't read properly, or write, and his language was typical of a backward giardini. But now he is a polished speaker and accomplished in the classics and mathematics. Signore Luciano wants Alonzo to join his family business in Naples but I insist he should go to University."

Fearing he had over-exceeded his remit, and the pale, stern-faced woman facing him might have other ideas about Alonzo's future, the over-enthusiastic Professore stuttered and stopped speaking. Even worse, she may have been appointed by Signore Luciano to countermand his influence over the boy's development. But Carla had no designs to guide her son into a life of crime and violence and calmed the Professor's fears "Thank you for all you've done for Alonzo, Professore Tutti. Together we'll get the boy into University."

From that moment onwards they became firm friends. Little did the Professore know about the relationship between the governess and his star pupil and he had no idea Carla had more than a vested interest in Alonzo's future career.

"And where is the boy, Professore Tutti?" Carla inquired.

"Every weekend is free time for Alonzo, no lessons and no homework. He spends two days with Signore Luciano at Anacapri, though they sometimes go up to Naples. He'll be brought back here before it gets dark."

The Professor sniffed the air "I can tell Signora Franconi is cooking a carbonara dish. Alonzo loves pasta or a home-made pizza."

A rueful smile crossed Carla's face as she remembered little Alonzo guzzling an ice-cream cornet, a rare treat at Saint Giorgio's convent in those far off days. And after twelve years she was about to come face to face with her son again. Would he recognise her? Her reverie was interrupted by the sound of a car pulling up in the courtyard and, in a matter of seconds, Alonzo came striding on to the terrace.

"Buonasera Professore Tutti."

The boy then turned to Carla.

"Buonasera Signora."

Weak at the knees, and quivering internally, Carla stood up and extended her right hand. Her first contact with her son after so many years sent a pleasant thrill through her body and, gazing into Alonzo's deep-brown eyes, she spoke softly "I am your new governess. Please call me Auntie Carla. Professore Tutti speaks highly of your work and we have agreed you must go to University."

The Professor nodded vigorously but the boy's face screwed up in a perplexed frown.

"I'll have to speak to Uncle Charlie first."

Carla smiled.

"You leave your Uncle Charlie to me and Professore Tutti. We'll work on Signore Luciano!"

At that moment Signora Franconi sounded the dinner gong and Alonzo spun on his heel and made a dash for the dining room. Carla laughed outright as she and the old-fashioned Professor linked arms and followed slowly behind. Carla remarked with a smile "Alonzo must be starving!"

Professore Tutti winked.

"He loves Signora Franconi's cooking and, for that matter, so do I."

The venerable old academician had three loves in his life- his books, his tutoring and traditional Italian cooking.

From Monday to Friday the governess and Professore Tutti had complete control over Alonzo's education and development. His weekend breaks were more liberal and exciting but Alonzo soon came to realise Luciano's lifestyle was a façade covering some dubious and underhand activities. He enjoyed the wining and dining but there were times, and they happened quite frequently, when he was ordered to make himself scarce to allow his Uncle to transact 'business' deals. He believed his Uncle Charlie had been a celebrity business man in America but wondered why the Carabinieri kept him under constant surveillance? And then there was a string of visitors, both male and female, who came to Luciano's apartment in Vomero. Lucky Luciano spent Christmas 1959 at Villa Annunziata and brought an attractive Italian showgirl with him. He had teamed up with Igea Lissoni in Rome in 1947 and intermittently kept her as his mistress in his penthouse apartment in Naples. Alonzo could not stomach the girlfriend and the childish, posturing actress and the youth both vied for Luciano's favours. By the spring of 1960 Alonzo was winning and Igea Lissoni moved out of Luciano's apartment and out of his life forever. Another of Luciano's regular visitors was a loud-mouthed, brash woman from New York called Virginia Hill who told Alonzo that Luciano had been boss of a large security company and was, in fact, a glorified super-policeman which accounted for the Italian police escorts. However he made his money, Uncle Charlie was a wealthy man. Generous to a fault, he threw his money around and restaurateurs and hangers-on were attracted to him like bees to a honey pot. And when the American fleet was in port, dozens of sailors plagued him for autographs and free drinks. On these occasions Charlie Lucky was indeed a celebrity and basked in the adulation showered upon him by his visitors.

Alonzo was not quite sure what to make of his Auntie Carla. Starchy, stiff and correct at first she soon mellowed and started mothering him. Nudging towards manhood, he found her fussy attention overpowering and, yet, a part of him craved for the motherly love he had never experienced. Auntie Carla was kind and considerate but overprotective to a fault and weekends with Uncle Charlie were a welcome break form the regimentation at Villa Annunziata. But by the summer of 1960 even these breaks were beginning to wane. Lucky Luciano was feeling the loss of his mistress and, together with curtailment of his American income by Meyer Lansky, he was driven into the doldrums. Added to all this his general health was causing concern and at Eastertime 1961 he consulted a medical specialist and took Carla with him in support. The specialist explained his diagnosis "The chest pains you suffer are a warning that blood isn't going freely to your heart muscle. I will prescribe a tablet for your pain. It will dissolve under your tongue and another tablet has to be taken once a day to improve your circulation. For severe chest pains you need a morphine injection which you must always carry with you and which must be administered by a nurse, or a doctor. Will the Signora be able to inject you when necessary?"

Lucky Luciano looked across at Carla who simply nodded.

"Yeah, Doctor, my governess will do that."

The specialist continued with his advice "The final answer to your problem lies with yourself. You will have to take things easy, lose weight, cut out cigars and alcohol and eat healthy food."

Luciano retorted "How canna I take it easy? The guys from Hollywood wanna me make a movie."

The exasperated specialist looked at the ceiling and rolled his eyes.

"Your life is in your own hands, Signore Luciano."

Following the consultation with the specialist Luciano became paranoid about his health and insisted Carla should be nearby at all times to supervise his medication. He started spending his weekends quietly, en famile, either at Anacapri or Villa Annunziata and Carla was impressed by the bond which existed between the big-time American gangster and her son. On Alonzo's seventeenth birthday in May Luciano was in one of his melancholic moods and concerned about his own mortality.

"When you get to be eighteen years old I wanna you change your surname. My family came from Lecara Friddi, a small village in Sicily, and I was born there. We'll go together to see it one day. My proper family name is Luciana."

"Yes, Uncle Charlie. That'll be okay! I promise to change my name to Luciana."

Luciano smiled at the boy's usage of American slang. Alonzo

had passed an entrance examination to Rome's Law Faculty in April and Luciano was reconciled to the fact that his 'adopted' son was going to University in October. He argued that a lawyer in the Family would not be a bad thing for his business and, together, he and Alonzo might make a triumphant return to the States in a few years time. In the meantime he had to concentrate on keeping alive to see his adopted son reach his goal. If only these blasted bouts of chest pains would go away! By now Carla was indispensable and he thanked his lucky stars she was totally trustworthy and a loyal, dependable companion.

Alonzo left Villa Annunziata for Rome to start his law degree course in October and Carla moved up to Luciano's Vomero apartment in Naples. Number 464 Via Tasso was a six-roomed apartment, austerely furnished, with marble floors throughout and a capacious sun terrace overlooking the Bay of Naples. She was not comfortable at Vomero and developed a strong dislike for an ox-like concierge and Bello, the German shepherd dog, both of whom jealously guarded the property and their master. She accompanied Luciano on his daily rounds to Naples' waterfront hotels and restaurants and reluctantly went along with him to weekly race meetings at Agnano Hippodrome. In a depressed state most of the time, Charlie Lucky came out of his shell at the racecourse and for tourists and service-men and presented a brave face to a steady stream of authors and newspapermen who flocked to Naples in the hope of getting an exclusive story from the most famous mobster in American gangland history. Visitors inflated his ego and, when they were around, Luciano was all smiles and benevolence and his diet and alcoholic restrictions were rapidly forgotten. But once they departed he descended into a gloomy pit of depression and depended utterly on Carla. She soon got to know his technique for dealing with reporters and newshounds. He would put on a bold front at first, boasting about his lifetime exploits during Prohibition and in the American underworld. He would then become conspirational which aroused the newshound's interest. Names would not be mentioned but promises of revelations at an unspecified future late would be freely bandied around. Secrets of the Honourable Society were never revealed. Omerta was not strictly obeyed but 'honorata' was observed in the truest definition of the word. Many authors and reporters returned to the States claiming an 'exclusive' with the Big Boss in Naples but, in print, there was no factual corroboration to their stories. The names involved in Luciano's enterprises in America and Italy never came form his lips and he reasoned that, in this way, the Cosa Nostra's honour was upheld.

American crime bosses were becoming alarmed that the exiled super-mobster in Naples might turn stoolpigeon and, by 1961, newspaper reports and articles inflamed their suspicions. One reporter claimed he had obtained verbal agreement from Luciano to publish his life story and another columnist alleged the Big Boss was on the verge of revealing all the Mob's underworld activities. But the Mafia bosses really became concerned in September when a Hollywood film mogul flew to Naples to meet Luciano and proposed a contract to shoot his life story and, what is more, offered him a leading role in the production. This development stunned the American underworld and brought matters to a head. A film about the most notorious mobster in living memory would inevitably expose many of their rackets and identities. Himself under pressure and under investigation by the FBI, Meyer Lansky reacted violently. He ordered a hit on the Big Boss in Naples and, via Frank Costello a contract was passed on to Alphonse Rizzi. Allegedly acting as a courier to take Luciano's skim to Naples, Al flew across the Atlantic in October. Costello implored him to warn off Charlie Lucky from proceeding down the path of offering his services to Hollywood. If Lucky Luciano did this, Costello argued, Meyer Lansky might feel disposed to call off the assassination contract. But if Al failed in his mission, he was ordered to pass on Lansky's contract to Carla Cecci.

A late summer scorcher had given way to a balmy, mimosa-scented evening as Lucky Luciano and Al Rizzi sat on the terrace of No. 464 Via Tasso in the Vomero district of Naples. It had been Al's second long-distance flight and he was jet-lagged and tired. Carla was busy indoors in the kitchen when Lucky cut a fresh cigar and eyed Al "I've cut down on these Cubans since I saw the specialist but I still get friggin chest pains."
Luciano then fussed over lighting his cigar.

"Its safe to talk outa here. My apartment may be bugged and we've had Carla with us all day. Now shoot the craps! What's happening with the Syndicate? How's Frankie Costello?"

"Frankie's fine and sends his blessing. He regrets the skim ain't a lot more."

"Yeah! I'm friggin disappointed too. And what's up with the Little Man in Miami?" Luciano asked.

"Lansky's in trouble with the Feds and the taxman. The heat's on and he's lying low. That's why he aint been contributing to your skim."

"Friggin baloney," Luciano exploded, "Meyer is too clever for them Feds. He knows a legit way to get money across to me if he tried. It's all baloney I tell you! The little weasel's dead against his old pal. Christ only knows why after all I did for the friggin little Jew in the old days."

Luciano jumped to his feet and strode across to the balustrade. Suddenly, he clutched his chest. After a minute the pain settled as he calmed down and resumed his seat next to Alphonse.

"The pay-off aint enough to keep me goin'. I've been selling bits and pieces of my story to the Press lately. Nuttin' serious, just general stuff about my bootlegging days and strictly no names. But now I'm into big bucks. A guy from Hollywood has offered to make a film about my life. He's coming across after Christmas to clinch the deal and he's giving me a leading part in the film. I fancy myself as a friggin movie star!"

Al grasped the opportunity to introduce the Mob's concern about his involvement with the Hollywood moguls.

"Frankie Costello advises you to lay off those Hollywood bums and the Mob feel the same."

For the second time in five minutes Luciano leapt to his feet and shouted at Al "The Mob don't friggin like it? Baloney! Tell the friggin Syndicate to mind its own business. They didn't do nuttin' to help Longy Zwillman. I'm their Big Boss and I can do what I like. Without me there wouldn't be a friggin Syndicate. Who the hell do they think they are? That little shit Lansky is behind all this. I've a good mind to shoot out a contract on him. Just wait and see what I'll friggin do."

At the end of his outburst Charlie Lucky's angina returned with a vengeance. He uttered a deep-throated groan, clutched his chest, and sat down abruptly. The blood drained from his face, his lips became blue, and a cold sweat broke out on his brow. Barely able to speak, he croaked "Get Carla quickly! This friggin pain's goin' down my arm and up my tongue. It's one hell of a friggin pain, Al."

Armed with an emergency medical kit Carla was at Lucky's side within a minute and placed two tablets under his tongue and, as the pain gradually eased, she made Luciano swallow his cardiac medicine. Together Al and Carla helped the Boss on to his bed where Carla administered a morphine injection. As Lucky Luciano sank into a painless and trouble-free sleep he managed a wry smile "Who needs a doctor with Carla about?"

Not for the first time Al noticed that Charlie Lucky avoided using swear words in Carla's presence and had been polite and courteous to the opposite sex all his life.

With Luciano soundly asleep, Carla joined Al on the terrace and they sat side by side on a wooden bench. By now Al was convinced Luciano meant to go ahead with the Hollywood project and it was time to bring Carla into the picture. He decided on a direct approach "The Big Boss is in big trouble with the Mob at home if he goes ahead with this Hollywood business. He must be stopped before he talks and you'll have to do it for us Carla."

Carla emitted a startled gasp "Signore Luciano has been good to Alonzo and me and I would find it impossible to kill him. I can't do it."

"You're the best placed person for the job and it'll be your final hit. It don't have to be a trigger job. You can fix his tablets to help him out or give him an injection to bump him off."

Despite his bombastic manner and posturing, Carla had grown fond of Charlie Lucky and, without his consent, Alonzo might have ended up as a Neapolitan hoodlum instead of a budding lawyer. She was, however, sensible enough to realise that if Luciano became a canary hundreds of Family members in Italy and America would be put to the sword. Lucky Luciano was such a vain person that all the persuasion in the world would not deviate him from his projected course and, technically, she was still Alphonse Rizzi's 'hitman.' She had little choice in the matter and reluctantly accepted Al's contract.

Alphonse Rizzi was literally on a flying visit and Lucky Luciano was well-enough to turn up and see him off at Naples' Airport.

"Give my regards to Frankie Costello and Tony Accardo. They're my only two buddies left in the Syndicate."

The Men of Honour embraced and kissed each other, not a deferential peck on the cheek accorded to Family members, but a full-blooded kiss on the lips. Such a kiss between bona-fide mafiosi usually indicated one, or the other, was ear-marked for execution. Luciano was oblivious to the significance of this kiss of death and bellowed his parting words "When my film gets out in Times Square be sure to go and see it Alphonse."

As he walked into the departure lounge Al Rizzi looked back at the tall man towering above Carla's diminutive figure. Little did Luciano realise that his erstwhile executioner wa. standing two feet away from him. Al hoped the end for Charlie Lucky would be quick and painless. The onetime supreme boss of the American Mafia deserved a swift execution and he relied on Carla to do the job professionally. Aboard the plane on the runway he crossed himself and settled back into his seat in preparation for the gruelling, nerve-wracking and tiresome flight to New York via London.

The 1961 Christmas holiday at Villa Annunziata was the happiest, and in some ways the saddest, time in Carla's life to date. Alonzo was home from University and Lucky Luciano was in a relaxed mood and his anginal bouts were few and far between. The bond between Charlie Lucky and Alonzo grew stronger by the day. Luciano now showed an interest in Alonzo's academic career and began mentally organizing his placement with the Neapolitan judiciary. He even threw out veiled hints of a possible legal career in the States. Throughout his exile, and to the very end, Luciano was convinced he would be allowed back to New York to resume his former position as Boss of the National Crime Syndicate and titular head of America's Crime Families. Meanwhile Carla stood aside and watched the friendship blossoming, knowing full-well that, at some stage soon, she would be instrumental in ending their filial relationship. On New Year's Day 1962, a cablegram arrived from America and Luciano was thrown into a state of excitement "Whaddya know, Carla? The Hollywood guy's are serious and it's not all baloney! A bum called Schwitzer is coming across to sign a contract. There's half a million bucks in it for me and more for acting in the film. They're talking about Sinatra playing a part."

Carla thought it was a good opportunity to attempt to dissuade Lucky from going ahead.

"Do you think you should get too excited about it Signore Luciano? The specialist told you to take it easy and you should listen to him."

"Goddamnit, Carla! It's a golden chance for me to become famous and make piles of legit dough."

The Big Boss was too dumb to realise that, by making the film, he was signing his own death warrant. Carla's contract was watertight. Charles Lucky Luciano was to be prevented, by any means in her power, from involving himself with the Hollywood pundits. A further cablegram from Los Angeles confirmed Arnold Schwitzer would be arriving on a Pan-Am flight on January 26th and, in anticipation, Luciano worked himself into a frenzy and suffered three major anginal attacks.

Accompanied by Carla, and with two Carabinieri in the background in attendance, Luciano turned up at Naples's airport to meet his visitor from Hollywood on 26th January 1962. The Pan-Am flight had been delayed in London due to adverse weather conditions and was two hours late. A stickler for punctuality Luciano could not abide hanging about and he began haranguing the airport officials. To calm him down they took him to a private VIP lounge where coffee and biscuits were provided and the plain clothes policemen took up position outside the lounge door. Being shut up in a room with no outlook did not help Lucky's composure and, despite Carla's exhortations to sit down, he kept crossing and re-crossing the small lounge all the while muttering to himself and blaspheming about the ineptitude of American airlines and incompetence of London's airport staff. The Pan-Am plane was still half an hour away from Naples when Luciano was struck by a massive, clamping pain in his chest which radiated up to the base of his tongue and down his left arm. He shouted in agony and, clutching his chest, sank to his knees. Slowly, and almost sedately, he slithered sideways and landed on his back on the plush, thick-piled carpet covering the VIP lounge's marble floor.

"My jab, Carla! Gimme my jab," Luciano croaked. Carla rushed to his side and felt for a pulse in his neck. Luciano's face was ashen-white and his drooping right eyelid was more pronounced than usual. He retched and suddenly vomited over his shirt front. Carla rummaged in her emergency medical bag and produced a phial of morphine and a syringe. She instinctively wanted to help Charlie Lucky but the opportunity to edge him over the brink was too good to miss. She emptied the morphine phial into the plush carpet and plunged the needle through Luciano's trousers into his right thigh. A faint smile appeared on Lucky's pain-distorted face and he whispered "Thanks Carla."

Carla pushed a GTN tablet into his mouth where it mixed with his spittle and vomitus and was immediately rejected. Breathing rapidly and shallowly, moaning and staring pleadingly at Carla, Luciano had been flat on the floor for fully a minute. This was the moment of truth. Carla had to act now or else her resolve would fail. Steeling herself she closed her eyes and, placing both hands around Lucky's windpipe, she squeezed hard and whispered "Sorry Signore Luciano! It's for your own good."

Luciano struggled for a few seconds and aimed a few ineffectual blows with flailing arms and then, as his lips became bluer and his face suffused with purplish blood, his attempts at breathing ceased and he lay perfectly still. Carla kept a pressure on his windpipe for a further minute and, when she released her grip, the corpse exhaled explosively, causing a gush of foul air to exude from its gaping mouth. Carla crossed herself.

"Goodbye, Signore Luciano. Alonzo and I will miss you."

She got slowly to her feet, crossed the lounge, and flung open the door. Lounging against a pillar and smoking cigarettes the Carabinieri sprang to attention. Carla pleaded in a distressed voice "Please help me in here. Signore Luciano has collapsed. Will someone call a doctor?"

One policeman rushed into the lounge and made attempts to

resuscitate the corpse while the other policeman found a doctor in the main lounge. The physician again attempted resuscitation but soon established that the man on the floor in the VIP lounge was dead. Acting stunned and stupefied, Carla hung about by the lounge entrance and broke out crying when an ambulance crew carried Charlie Lucky's body, wrapped in a blanket, out on a stretcher. She supplied Luciano's details and was informed the body was being taken to a mortuary at Ospedale Municipale. To add to the confusion Arnold Schwitzer came out of 'Arrivals' just as Lucky's body was being carted to the main exit.

"Who's that unfortunate stiff?"

"He's and Americani like you, Signore. He's lived in Naples for seventeen years. His name was Signore Luciano, but most people called him Charlie Lucky. It seems his luck has now run out!" a policeman replied. Schwitzer quickly realised his journey had been in vain and he had missed out on producing a film about the most notorious crime boss ever to emerge from gangsterism in the United States. He gave vent to his frustration "Damn and blast it! Why did the friggin punk choose to die before I got here? I've flown all this way for nuttin'."

The coro er at Ospedale Municipale confirmed Luciano died from natural causes, the result of a myocardial infarction. His brain was preserved by a prominent neurophysiologist in the misguided hope he could establish a cause for criminal behaviour. His body was embalmed and Al Rizzi came across to supervise arrangements for Lucky's final internment. A requiem mass was held at a Catholic church in Vomero attended by Al Rizzi, Carla, Virginia Hill, Alonzo and a few prominent Neapolitan dignitaries and, much to everyone's surprise, Joe Adonis turned up from Milan for the service. Though they had not spoken to each other for over five years, Adonis presented an enormous floral tribute to his late-lamented Boss with the inscription 'So long pal' on the wreath - a traditional final farewell from the Mob. Al Rizzi arranged for the casket to be transported across to New York and Luciano's body, minus his brain, was laid to rest at St Johns cemetery in a low key ceremony only attended by a few acquaintances. Meyer Lansky did not send a floral tribute and was conspicuous by his absence at the final interment.

Generous in his lifetime, Lucky remained generous in death and in his Will he left a thousand dollars each to Signore Fantoccio of Hotel Turistico, to the head waiters at La Terraza and Do Giocomino Restaurants, to his ox-like janitor at Vomero, to his housekeeper at Villa Annunziata and the gardener at Anacapri, to his favourite barber in Naples and, finally, five thousand dollars to Carla. Supervising Charlie Lucky's assets, Al Rizzi honoured the donations but the rest of his bank accounts and investments were frozen and cash transferred to the Syndicate's coffers in New York. Carla received a half-share in Villa Annunziata and the other half, and Luciano's main properties, were bequeathed to Alonzo who was now eighteen years old and, in accordance with Charlie Lucky's wishes, had adopted the surname Luciana.

CHAPTER 21

'Whatever Man sows that he will also reap'
(Galatians, Ch. 6, Vr. 7)

BY CHRISTMASTIME 1962 LUCKY LUCIANO'S affairs had been settled and Alfonzo Luciana spent the festive holiday at Villa Annunziata with his Auntie Carla. Over a glass of wine on Christmas Eve, Carla had a heart-to-heart talk with the young man. Unable to think of ways of breaking the news gently to her son, she plunged in feet first "What is the first thing you remember as a child, Alfonzo?"

"I remember the farmhouse in Calabria and chasing goats in the fields. I also remember going to sea in a boat with my father and two sailors. The sea was very rough but we caught some fish. I must have been about four years old at the time. Why do you ask Auntie Carla?"

"I have something very important to tell you, Alfonzo. I am not your Auntie. I am your real mother."

The young man gazed at Carla in disbelief. He always had niggling doubts about the woman who came into Uncle Charlie's household in 1960 but never in his wildest dreams did he imagine she could be his mother. Unable to grasp the reality he was stung into challenging his governess.

"How can this be Auntie? I know Signora Gicanetti was not my natural mother and my father told me she had died in an accident in 1948."

Carla felt aggrieved by the lie and immediately put Alfonzo straight "During the war your father, and another man called Branco, came to live and work on our farm at Godrano in Sicily and I became friendly with your father. The American army arrived in the summer of 1943 and Signore Rizzi was wounded at Godrano and was nursed in our farmhouse for nearly three weeks.

The American soldiers killed Salvatore Branco but your father escaped and went back to Calabria. You were born in May 1944 and we lived at St. Giorgio d' Genovese Convent in Palermo until you were four years old when you suddenly disappeared. Everyone thought you had drowned at sea but I now know you were taken away by your father. After a few years I got married and went to America. I next saw you sitting beside your Uncle Charlie in the back of a limousine at your father's funeral and I knew immediately you were my son."

The stress of relating her story was too much for Carla and she started sobbing and extended her arms towards the young man. He reacted instinctively and they clung to each other in a fierce embrace.

"Mamma! Mamma! I've never had a proper mother," Alfonzo cried, and the hugging and kissing went on for what seemed an eternity. Future plans were made that Christmas holiday at Villa Annunziata. Neither wished to live in Naples, nor Capri, and they agreed to sell the Vomero apartment and the Anacapri villa and to keep Villa Annunziata in their joint names. Carla had a hankering to return to Sicily and, with the proceeds from their property sales, they jointly bought a luxury harbourside apartment off Via Francesco Crispi in Palermo. By 1967 Carla was, at last, back in her country of birth and, at forty years of age, she looked forward to many years of peace and contented living. She had survived through a number of torrid experiences during her lifetime and now felt she deserved a quiet life and tranquillity. Signora Carla Ceserano's idyllic existence continued for seven years and only changed with her son's appointment to Palermo's justice department which drew the Mafia's attention to her own reappearance in Sicily.

At the age of 23 years Alfonzo Luciana graduated with honours from University and did his apprenticeship with a law firm in Rome specialising in criminal justice. His talent in his chosen field drew him into the complex minefield of criminal jurisprudence and inevitably led to clashes with Rome's Mafia fraternity. In 1969 he was appointed assistant prosecutor to the city of Naples and his confrontations with local Mafia mobsters escalated. His tenacity and relentless persecution of the criminal classes in Naples led to further promotion and, in 1974, he was made a judge to Palermo's Court of Justice and moved across to join his mother at her apartment. Judge Alfonzo Luciana's inflexible approach to underworld criminals enhanced his reputation and gained him fame in some quarters, and notoriety in others, and the latter led to veiled threats from unidentified sources. Though Alfonzo made light of the intimidation he was sensible enough to accept police protection at their apartment and when travelling to, and from, Palermo's Law Courts.

In 1975 Alfonzo Luciana was chief prosecutor in a trial on a Padrone from Corleone and an established Sicilian godfather. An illiterate peasant, Luciano Liggio had taken over the reins from Don Genco Russo and had killed and bribed his way to becoming Sicily's Capo di Tutti Capi. By now Sicily was a major centre for worldwide drugs and firearms distribution and the chief beneficiaries vere Luciano Liggio and his Corleonesi Family. Judge Luciana found Liggio guilty of drug-trafficking and tax evasion and sent him down for nine years. Instigated from gaol by Liggio, and planned to perfection by his Palermian mafiosi, an urgent vendetta against Alfonzo came into operation and was rapid and ruthless in its execution Alfonzo miscalculated and underestimated the power of the local Mafiosi when, on May 7th 1976, he was being escorted from his apartment to the Court House by two police cars and two armed Carabinieri motorcycle outriders. The motorcade became snarled up in a traffic jam orchestrated by Liggio's local mobsters. Consequently when he was dropped off at City Hall that morning he was very late for an important appointment and, without thinking, ran up a flight of steps ahead of his armed escorts. A group of four men were standing outside the court room and, without ceremony, a dozen bullets were fired in rapid succession into Luciana', body. He slid down the granite steps and his twitching body finally came to rest on the pavement. He expired almost instantly and his corpse lay at a grotesque angle amid a widening pool of congealing blood. The Carabinieri escorts fled and, to a man, they had been previously warned off by the Mafia. Alfonzo Luciana, the youngest Judge-Advocate in Italian legal history, was assassinated three days before his 32nd birthday. The Mafia 'hit' avenged Liggio's imprisonment and served as a warning to the judiciary, and the public at large, there might be other potential victims on their shortlist for execution.

Shortly after her arrival back in Palermo Carla, literally, bumped into Sister Carmelita from the Hostel for Fallen Women at St Giorgio d'Genovese Convent. She was hurrying down a busy side street outside Vucciria market when the Sister, accompanied by a novitiate, was out collecting alms. On recognising Carla, Sister Carmelita was dumbstruck.

"Signorigna Carla Cecci! I don't believe it! What are you doing here?"

Carla's first reaction was to ignore the Sister and then she considered feigning a case of mistaken identity. But the Sister of Mercy was one jump ahead and clasped Carla to her ample bosom in a fierce embrace. Realising the game was up Carla submitted to Carmelita's fierce hugging.

"It's good to see you again Sister. How are things at the Convent? I've been away for a few years but I'm back in Palermo now."

The well-built Sister released her strong grip and stood back, eyeing Carla from head to toe.

"You don't look any different to when you were with us at the

Hostel after the war. I see you are wearing a wedding ring. Any children?" and then she bit her tongue on realising she might be touching on a sensitive subject. Carla was on the point of breaking down but managed to suppress her emotions.

"I've been living in America for a few years. I came back to Italy after my husband died in 1959. I've only been in Palermo for a couple of weeks."

Carla deliberately concealed the fact that Alfonzo was alive and well and Sister Carmelita had the sense not to probe further and open up old wounds. The Sister smiled and readjusted her wimple "You must visit us at the Convent. I'm now next in line to our Mother Superior. You'll be made most welcome and do call to see us at any time."

Carla bowed her head in acquiescence and, as a parting shot, explained "My married name is Ceserano. I have an apartment nearby on the other side of Via Francesco Crispi."

The chance meeting with the Sister in charge of the hostel when Alfonzo was abducted had aroused a feeling of nostalgia and Carla was sorely tempted to take the plunge and visit the Convent. But, on balance, she felt it might rekindle bitter-sweet memories and do her more harm than good. For the following months, and years, she had frequent contact with the Sisters of Mercy but firmly declined their offer of hospitality and remained content to donate alms from time to time. And, when Alfonzo came to live with her in 1974, very little changed. He, naturally, was interested in his place of birth but refused to visit St Giorgio d'Genovese Convent. Though both of the Catholic faith, they rarely went to church and then only on religious celebration days. But all this changed after Alfonzo's assassination on May 7th 1976 and by the end of the year Carla Ceserano, now aged 49 years, was again alone and her world literally crashed around her. The old flame was dead and buried and she abandoned all thoughts of revenge for her son's murder. Never an outgoing person, she became a recluse and virtually confined herself to her apartment. In her hour of need she turned to religion and found some solace and support by visits from the Sisters of Mercy. Sister Carmelta became her soul mate and confidant and, in gratitude for her missionary services, Carla was persuaded to bequeath all her wealth and assets to St Giorgio d'Genovese Convent.

In the spring of 1978 Carla's health began deteriorating and, fussy and full of concern, Sister Carmelita arranged for her to see the Convent's visiting physician. In addition to his duties at the Convent, Professore Sylvano Battaglia also attended Palermo's County Prison and was chief pathologist to San' Pedro Private Clinic. In his spare time the squat, bald, bespectacled physician also dabbled in homeopathy and, unbeknown to the Sisters of Mercy, was a fully paid-up member of the Sicilian Mafia and one of their trusted lackey's. The inoffensive, mild-mannered Professor diagnosed a stomach ulcer and, for treatment, prescribed a bismuth elixir and herbal tea. His professional advice apart, he passed on Carla's details to Luciano Liggio in the County Prison. The Corleonesi Family became more than interested in her background and quickly made a connection between Carla and Judge Luciana. Carla's origins from Godrano, and her close relationship to the Cucinotta's of Portella Sant Agata, stimulated Liggio to resuscitate a thirty year old vendetta which had been in existence between his Family and the Godranesi since World War II. Mafia godfathers have long memories and Luciano Liggio, an Americanized version of the traditional old-fashioned Sicilian mafiosi, had no qualms about killing a female, particularly one that had caused his Family so much grief and anguish all those years ago. Added to this, Carla Cecci was the mother of Judge Alfonzo Luciana who had been a thorn in the flesh of Palermo's Cosa Nostra for two years. Liggio immediately contracted the homeopathic physician to undertake Carla's murder and Professore Battaglia devised a simple and foolproof method of eliminating his patient. Seemingly dissatisfied by Carla's response to the bismuth elixir he added stronger and stronger doses of arsenic to the medicine. Arsenic powder is tasteless and produces intense thirst followed by stomach cramps and vomiting. These were the very symptoms complained of by Carla from the beginning and her condition rapidly deteriorated. Just like her father at Godrano in 1943, the appearance of jaundice heralded the end and, during her last days, Professore Battaglia's morphine injections accelerated her demise.

Carla died at her Palermo apartment on May 7th 1979, three years to the day after her son's assassination by the Mafia. The Sisters of Mercy and the crooked physician were present at her death bed and Sister Carmelita supervised all arrangements for her burial at the Covent's cemetery. A cursory auto